Also by Sara Cate

SALACIOUS PLAYERS' CLUB
Praise
Eyes on Me
Give Me More
Mercy
Highest Bidder
Madame

SINFUL MANOR
Keep Me

THE GOODE BROTHERS
The Anti-hero
The Home-wrecker
The Heartbreaker
The Prodigal Son

BEAUTIFUL SERIES
Beautiful Monster
Beautiful Sinner

WILDE BOYS DUET
Gravity
Free Fall

BLACK HEART DUET
Four
Five

SPITFIRE
Burn for Me
Fire and Ash

WICKED HEARTS SERIES
Delicate
Dangerous
Defiant

Promise Me

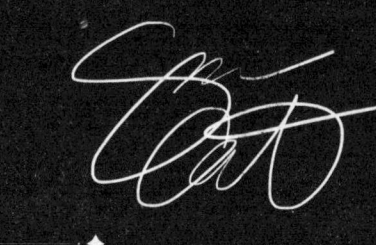

Promise Me

SARA CATE

For my friends.

Copyright © 2026 by Sara Cate
Cover and internal design © 2026 by Sourcebooks
Cover design by Stephanie Gafron/Sourcebooks
Cover images © Design Pics/Shutterstock, Olena Rudo/Shutterstock
Internal art by Chloe Friedlein

Sourcebooks and the colophon are registered trademarks of Sourcebooks.

All rights reserved. No part of this book may be reproduced in any form or by any electronic or mechanical means including information storage and retrieval systems—except in the case of brief quotations embodied in critical articles or reviews—without permission in writing from its publisher, Sourcebooks.

No part of this book may be used or reproduced in any manner for the purpose of training artificial intelligence technologies or systems.

The characters and events portrayed in this book are fictitious or are used fictitiously. Any similarity to real persons, living or dead, is purely coincidental and not intended by the author.

All brand names and product names used in this book are trademarks, registered trademarks, or trade names of their respective holders. Sourcebooks is not associated with any product or vendor in this book.

Published by Sourcebooks Casablanca, an imprint of Sourcebooks
1935 Brookdale RD, Naperville, IL 60563-2773
(630) 961-3900
sourcebooks.com

Cataloging-in-Publication Data is on file with the Library of Congress.

Printed and bound in the United States of America.
WOZ 10 9 8 7 6 5 4 3 2 1

Content Warning

Promise Me is a sexually explicit romance for adult readers. It includes scenes with kink and BDSM, meant for entertainment and not instruction. There are elements of grief, parental death, mental health struggles, depression, and anxiety.

Declan and Colin are about to take you on a long, sexy, and romantic journey that spans decades and continents, so buckle up.

Be safe. Read with caution. And enjoy.

Chapter One
Declan

"They are throwing rice all over the grass, Anna!"

Peering out the window, I watch in horror as the party of elegantly clad guests toss tiny granules of white rice all over the garden out back. There is a string quartet playing a blasphemous rendition of an old rock song, and there are tiny tuxedoed children stomping through the hydrangeas.

My sister scurries down the hall ahead of me, a chuckle under her breath. "It's a wedding, Declan," she replies with humor.

"A wedding at my bloody house!"

"You agreed to this, remember?" She stops at the end of the long hall before the door to the main section of the house flies open, and a flurry of servers and attendants hustles by, each carrying a floral centerpiece that towers over their heads.

Anna holds open the door for them as she turns her head toward me, giving me a look of impatience. "When Killian passed the house down to you, you said you didn't want it, remember? You said, *Anna, use it however you want.* Remember that?"

I groan out a disgruntled, incoherent response with a roll of my eyes, my sister quickly cutting me off.

"But then, you changed your mind. Yet you understood when

you moved back into Barclay Manor that we now host weddings and events. And *you* said that as long as you could use the third-floor studio to paint and sculpt as much as you wanted, you didn't care. Remember that, Declan?"

I roll my eyes even harder. "That was before I realized how much I *fucking* hate weddings."

"Declan, language," she scolds me, although she's only three years older than me, and I'm a thirty-two-year-old man.

"It's *my* house, Anna!"

"The third floor is," she bites back, getting her face close to me and clearly losing her patience. "So why don't you go back up there?"

"Like I could get an ounce of peace," I growl.

Leaving my sister at the door, I march back down the long hall toward the stairs that lead to my studio. The entire way, I grumble and groan to myself about how unfair this is. I rightfully inherited this house. It's *my* house, and I should be able to have the entire bloody thing—no matter what I said before.

Just because I didn't want to live here at first doesn't mean I don't care about the house. Watching these people come in to use and abuse it grates on my nerves, and it should grate on Anna's too.

Once upon a time, this manor used to be famous for its parties—wild, sex-crazed events my older brother held until our family name became synonymous in the county for debauchery. I far preferred that to these elegant soirees and haughty events.

But then he *never* left the house, and we had to send in a bold American woman to save him, and by some grace of God, it worked. The only problem is that now they're married, living life in domestic bliss. This former den of iniquity has since become covered in roses, its halls filled with classical music, the garden covered in rice, and the gazebo crowded with people. It all just makes me sick.

Rightfully, I could tell my sister to bugger off and have her weddings elsewhere, and I probably should. Maybe I will. She seems to love them so much, I'm sure she'd find another manor in the Scottish countryside to terrorize with these incessant ostentatious events.

As I reach the stairs, I nearly crash into a young woman dressed in black coming down. Long blond hair flies into my face, and after I brush it away, I'm staring straight into a pair of uncomfortable blue eyes.

"Blaire," I mutter under my breath, proud of myself for remembering her name.

"Declan, sir," she replies, correcting herself.

"Fuck, don't do that. Sorry for running into you."

"No, I'm sorry," she mumbles while looking at the floor.

God, I need to get out of here. The last time I rendezvoused with Blaire, I didn't exactly stick around for pillow talk. She hasn't been able to look into my eyes since. Now, she assists my sister with these weddings and is here nearly every weekend, so lucky fucking me.

"I have to go…" she stammers.

"Yes, of course," I grumble miserably. "Bye…Blaire."

With that, I turn and practically sprint up the stairs and away from that poor woman.

The sanctuary of my studio waits for me at the end of the hall. Once I reach it, I slam the door, closing myself inside. Immediately, I reach for my apron, tying it around my waist before slipping a pair of noise-canceling headphones over my ears.

The Smiths drown out the sounds of the wedding as I submerge myself in my work. An oil-painted delicate woman sprawled on a grassy knoll, naked as the day she was born, stares back at me.

It's the woman's hands that are giving me hell.

Nearly every artist on the planet would agree that hands are the worst to paint, draw, or sculpt. They never curve right. They're too long or too short. The subtle detail of wrinkles in the joints always comes across too harshly, making a woman's dainty fingers appear far too rough and weathered.

And this current woman on my canvas is about to be wearing gloves and nothing else because I have been working on her goddamn hands for two days now. As I focus on her fingers, I try to ignore the scene in my periphery.

Just outside the window to my left, I have a perfect view of the gazebo in the distance. Guests are gathered around the round structure in white folding chairs as the summer breeze tries to carry away the decorations.

Weddings must be the most ridiculous waste of time and money. This idea that someone would be willing to pledge their undying faith to another person is idiotic. Of course, they want to promise that *now*—they're happy now. What about when they're tired, miserable, cross? When they've found someone more suitable? When they grow tired of the way their partner chews or sings or drives?

No, marriage is the most foolish thing man has ever created.

It's far better to fuck for fun and collect a few friends along the way.

Or, in my case, just one.

The brush in my hand stills as the memory of my old mate comes to the forefront of my mind. I linger there for a moment, picturing his face as years of regret and guilt assault me into paralysis.

Pulling my hand from the canvas, I blame stiff joints as I flex my fingers and rub at my knuckles. It's some form of arthritis or carpal tunnel, and definitely not the fact that I haven't spoken to him in nearly seven years.

And even then, I don't know why it bothers me so much, because Colin Shelby was just my friend—nothing more, nothing less.

Chapter Two
Declan

When I venture out of my studio hours later, it's dark, and I hear familiar voices echoing through the halls. As I make my way into the kitchen, my older brother's voice booms loudly with laughter.

I step into the room with a grimace as I cross my arms over my chest. Killian is leaning against the kitchen counter, his petite wife pressed against him with his beefy arms wrapped around her.

My younger brother, Lachlan, is helping Anna tie bags of rubbish and carry them out the door to the back of the house.

The wedding is long since over, and only my siblings remain to either help clean up or drive me mad.

"What are you all doing in my house?" I scowl as I reach for the kettle to put some water on for tea. "Surely, we didn't all bother Killian as much as you all bother me."

They laugh. "That's exactly why we're here," Lachy replies. "You're a miserable grump. If we don't bother you, who will?"

"Exactly my point," I mutter.

"It's surprising that all these weddings don't bring you a little bit of joy," my sister-in-law, Sylvie, says with a smile. "I wasn't much for them either, but even I can admit, they are lovely."

My brow furrows as I turn the stove on to heat my water. "They are loud, obnoxious, and only make me more bitter."

"Says the man who hides away in his studio like some attic-dwelling ghost," Anna jokes.

"It's *my* house, and I have every right to haunt it," I reply, flicking water in her direction.

"Come now," Killian drawls. "Maybe if you came down occasionally and helped our sister with these events, you'd learn to love them."

I glower at my brother because I know he's full of shite. He was twice the miser I am, and he wouldn't have been caught dead hosting weddings in the manor when we lived here. He snickers to himself, clearly fancying my agony.

"Aren't you supposed to be returning to New York soon?" I ask, glancing between him and his wife. "What are you two doing here anyway?"

"We're on our honeymoon," she replies sweetly.

"You got married over a year ago," I say. "Twice, I might add. And Scotland is no place for a honeymoon when you've lived here for so long. Honeymoons are for places like Bali and Greece."

"I prefer rain and clouds," she replies before tipping her face up to her husband's. He leans down to kiss her on the lips, and I have to look away.

It's not the kissing that bothers me, but the brazen flaunting of marital bliss. Call it bitter jealousy, but I don't need to see just how happy and in love they are. I give it five years before they can't stand each other the way they did when they first got married.

Granted, that was because the family forced them into a sham marriage, but still…this period of passion will fade, and they'll despise each other again. It's inevitable.

While I wait for my water to boil, I cross my arms and look at my sister. She is the one who calls all the shots anyway. She's not technically in charge by rank or age, but she is the one the rest of us look to for guidance.

The last thing I want is to disappoint Anna and take away the one thing she loves, but I can't keep living like this, and she knows that. I did agree to come back to Barclay to spend a year or two on my art, and I did say she could continue to host events here, but after only a few months, it's clear this isn't working.

I deserve to have my house back.

And if I can't have that, I have to leave.

The fleeting expression of concern on her face shows that she senses it too.

"Wouldn't ye like a break, Anna?" I ask. "Hosting these events is so much work. And for what?"

"I enjoy it," she replies enthusiastically. "And I think you would too, if you'd give it a shot."

I scoff as my two brothers crack up in laughter. "Me? You think I would enjoy hosting these stupid, extravagant parties?"

"Yes! Sure, they're extravagant," she says with a roll of her eyes. "But they're also romantic. And it makes me happy to be around so many happy people. Instead of around a bunch of grumps like you."

"Come on," Lachy jokes. "Give it a shot, Dec. Maybe she's right."

"I'd love to see the miserable wedding you'd host," Killian adds with a haughty laugh.

"Thanks," I reply sardonically. "I think I'll stick to my studio in the attic. Haunting the visitors and being the ominous dark figure through the window that scares all the guests away." I add in a little ghostly sound for effect.

Everyone cracks up momentarily, but when the laughter eventually subsides, Anna is staring at me.

"But how much longer do you think you can do this, Declan?" she asks seriously.

I heave a sigh as I shrug my shoulders. "I don't know, Anna. Either I have to go, or the weddings do."

Truth be told, I don't want to leave the manor. I like living here in my family house where I was raised, where memories of my parents echo through the halls. Where my childhood still feels somewhat intact. Where I can pretend my family is still together and the happy lives we once lived still exist somehow.

Not to mention, it's beautiful here, even in the cold, bitter, depressing months. I find so much inspiration in the manor and on the grounds. There's something mystical and intriguing about it.

I haven't felt this inspired in a very long time. For the first time in ages, I feel compelled to paint something other than…him.

Anna's expression melts in disappointment, and I hate how I do that to her. Because no matter what I choose, she ends up disheartened. She'll either lose this thing that she loves, these weddings, or she'll lose me.

And for Anna, the only thing that matters is keeping this family happy somehow. Lord knows we don't make it easy on her.

"Oh, Dec," Killian says, noticing Anna's grimace. "You can put up with it for a little bit longer." None of us want to hurt her, not really.

"I can't," I reply with a groan as I rub my forehead.

Just then, the whistle on my teakettle pipes up, screaming through the kitchen and breaking the tension between us all. I rush over, grabbing a mitt to pick it up off the stovetop.

Call me old-fashioned, but there's something nostalgic about making tea on the stove the way our parents once did—with the kettle they once did. Without even asking, Anna pulls down five teacups from the cupboard, setting them on the counter while I rummage for the tea bags. For a moment, being here together with my siblings, preparing a late-night cup of tea like our mother always did, soothes my soul.

Judging by the comfortable silence among my brothers and sister, they feel the same.

As we stand around my kitchen quietly sipping our tea, it's Killian who seems to be scheming somehow. A look on his face says he's up to something. And after he sets his teacup down with a loud clang, nearly breaking it, he announces, "I suggest a wager."

Internally, I bristle. *I don't like the sound of that.*

"A wager?" I ask.

"Yes. You," he says, pointing at me, "need a shake-up."

Everybody snickers to themselves, eager to hear where this is going. Because, on one hand, I don't want to give Killian any power over me whatsoever. But at the same time, I do owe him.

At least in my mind, I do. I don't feel right after what happened with my brother. Our entire family tricked him into marrying a stranger while also deceiving him out of his house. And while it might have ended blissfully for him, he's still rightfully cross with the three of us for deceiving him at all. Then, on top of that, he passed down the manor to me free and clear.

The least I can do is hear him out.

"Aye, little brother, I think you don't give our sister enough credit for everything she does for this house."

"Sure," I reply with a shrug, uncertain where this is going. "But I also don't care."

Anna slaps me playfully on the arm.

Killian continues. "So I think in order for you to fully grasp just how much she does *and* accept what she'd be giving up if you made her quit, you have to take her job for one whole week."

"What?" I shriek in shock. "There's no way I could do that."

"Oh, it can't be that hard," Sylvie slips in. "By the time they show up, everything has already been planned. You just have to make sure it all goes smoothly."

"Excuse me," Anna snaps. "It is quite hard, actually. I have to coordinate decorations, flowers, the cake, the parking, the guests, the rehearsal, the food. I don't want Declan anywhere near these weddings. No poor fool deserves to have their nuptials ruined over some imbecilic dare of yours."

"Don't worry, Anna. We'll be here to oversee and make sure Declan has it under control," Killian says to calm our sister's nerves.

"Okay, wait," I say, putting my hands out toward them. "I'm not saying I'd agree to this, but what do I get if I can pull it off?"

"If you pull it off, it will be the last wedding held at Barclay Manor," Killian states flatly.

"No!" Anna shrieks.

I notice the way Killian shoots her a look as if to settle her worries.

"What, you think I can't do it?" I ask.

"Oh, I know you can't," he replies smugly. "But if you get through the week without screaming at anyone, and the wedding is beautiful, then you'll have the manor to yourself—everything you want. Anna, since we know how important it is to you to keep one of us living in the manor, you'll get to keep Declan here just like you want, and everybody will be happy."

"I won't be happy," she whines. "I like having the weddings."

"Then have them somewhere else," I say.

She huffs in frustration, crossing her arms over her chest.

"One wedding?" I ask Killian uneasily. I can't believe I'm even considering this.

"Just one," he replies, holding up a finger.

"Anna, when is the next reservation?" I ask.

She seems to calculate in her mind for a moment, and then her eyes pop open. "Oh, no, no, no. You can't have that one," she says.

"Why not?" I ask.

"It's a celebrity wedding. *I* don't even know who the couple is."

"Are you serious?"

"Yes. Some manager booked it and everything. I've only spoken to them over email. All I know is that it's two grooms, and they will be here next week."

"Okay, well, I obviously can't do that one," I say, holding my arms out toward my sister.

Killian thinks about it for a moment. "I think you can," he says.

"Not a chance," I reply. "I am not hosting a celebrity wedding."

"Now that I think of it..." Anna retorts, her mouth twisted in concentration. "Everything for this one is already done. They have their own wedding planner, and it's going to be quite simple. Not many guests. A very private affair."

"You can't be serious," I say.

With that, Anna turns around and picks up a brown leather-bound binder off the counter. Then she thrusts it against my chest with a smirk on her face. "Actually, I am serious, and I think you could do it."

"What the hell made you change your mind?" I ask.

She shrugs. "Killian has a point. This could be a good experience for you. It would let you see just how much goes into these events and how much the guests love them. Barclay brings people joy again, and *not* in the same way it did when Killian lived here."

He chuckles mischievously behind her.

"You really think this a good idea?" I ask. "You want me to deal with the guests and manage the entire event. You want *me* to be the face of Barclay Manor?" I ask, gesturing to my unkempt hair and shaggy beard. My sister tilts her head and ruffles my hair with a motherly gesture.

"The Declan I remember used to love to be the life of the party. The Declan I remember used to be happy. He used to smile. He might have even believed in true love. You might not remember that, so maybe this will jog your memory. Do we have a deal or not?"

My big sister stares up at me with her spine straight and her head held high, a look of fierce determination on her face. I mean, how can I say no to that?

"Fine," I mutter flatly as I take the binder from her. "Joke's on you." I laugh as I start to flip through it. "Because if I fuck this up, nobody will want to have their wedding here anyway."

Chapter Three
Declan

The sound of tires on gravel shakes me from my dreamless sleep. I force my eyes open, and as the light of the room cracks through my lids, I stare across the dusty studio at a blurry pile of green bottles strewn across the floor. With a groan, I roll to my back.

Just then, I remember that I stayed up far too late and drank far too much last night.

"I'm a daft idiot," I mutter to absolutely no one. I only binge drink when I'm under a lot of stress, and seeing as how I am about to host an entire bloody celebrity wedding at my house, I'd say the stress levels are pretty high.

The sound of a car door slamming outside jolts my eyes open wide.

Oh, fuck.

They're here.

My head wobbles and aches as I bolt off of the bed in my studio, climbing to my feet and waiting for the oxygen to reach the top of my head. Or wherever the fuck it belongs. In a mad dash, I tear off my clothes, replacing them with what I assume are clean ones, giving them a quick sniff before throwing them on. I kick over the green bottles as I rush to the door, padding quickly down the hall to the lavatory.

Another car door slams in the distance as I wash my face and quickly brush my teeth.

Fuck, fuck, fuck. I'm late.

Glancing down at my phone, I see that it's nearly one in the afternoon. I'm going to lose this bet before it even starts. My head is still pounding, and my stomach lurches as I rush out of my room, semi-presentable, and down the stairs toward the entrance of the house.

After Killian moved out and my sister renovated the manor for events, we sectioned off the eastern portion of the house so that I would have a place to live separate from where random strangers, guests, and employees would be meandering. When there are no events going on, I have the entire place to myself, save for a few of the staff who stick around most of the time.

Once I slip into the central part of the house, I hear voices outside of the wedding guests who have just arrived. It sounds like an American man and the familiar soft mumblings of what I assume is a British man.

After quickly fixing my hair, I pull open the main door of the manor and greet my new guests.

I can do this, I can do this, I can do this.

Nerves and anxiety lay claim to my insides, fueled by a terrible hangover and the fact that I haven't entertained or been the least bit social in a very, very long time.

I might be somewhat broody and grumpy in my mature age, but once upon a time, I was a charismatic, personable, outgoing man. Like Anna said, I used to be the life of the party at uni—the one with the stories, who made everyone laugh and never went home alone.

I can entertain a few celebrities for six days to win a bet. How hard can it be?

"Welcome to Barclay Manor," I announce from the exterior landing.

There's a Rolls-Royce parked on the gravel in front of the door. A tall man walks toward me from the car. Right away, I can tell he's an actor, probably in films. He is dashing and very familiar-looking—in a movie star sort of way. I have definitely seen his face somewhere before, although I can't quite place it. I'm not one for cinema, admittedly.

"Thank you," he announces as he puts out his hand. "Pierce Michael Hall."

The name rings a bell.

"Nice to meet you," I reply as I put my firm grip in his.

He's very tall, probably a few inches taller than me, with luxurious amber-brown hair that curls behind his ears. He might actually be the most handsome man I've ever seen. It almost hurts to look at him.

That is, until the other person pops out from behind the car. I would recognize his golden-blond hair anywhere, and it catches my attention first. Then I stare into the abyss of those cool ocean-blue eyes that I know far too well.

And not from screens or posters but from memory.

Colin Shelby.

He freezes on the other side of the car as he stares at me in shock, probably mirroring my own expression. "Declan?" he asks.

Hearing his voice again hits me harder than even the image of him standing in front of my house. It's like I'm transported back in time.

I don't respond as he rounds the car and walks toward me, his eyes never wavering from mine for a second. As he steps closer, I take in his appearance, the way he's aged in the seven years since I've seen him. There are new wrinkles forming around his eyes and lips, and it's somehow made him even more handsome.

He climbs the stone steps to where I'm standing until he's just two feet away from me. "Hi," he mutters lowly, as if confused.

"Hi," I reply in the same tone. Part of me wants to reach out and pull him against me for a hug. Seven years is a long time, and I've felt every single day, so now that he's standing here, I'm at a loss for how to react.

Before I can move, the tall, dashing man comes to stand next to Colin, placing a hand on his back as he asks, "Does anybody want to fill me in?"

Colin quickly shakes himself out of his stupor. "Honey, this is Declan Barclay. The one I told you about. We went to uni together."

"You're the famous Declan?" the man asks in astonishment. He uses the word *famous* ironically to describe me, and perhaps condescendingly, since he is the celebrity and I am not. Then he thrusts a hand out with a smug smile and takes mine, shaking it with vigor as he says, "Well, this is fantastic. I expected your sister to greet us, but this is a pleasant surprise. What a small world."

I feel as if I should smile at the American, but I'm finding it hard to tear my eyes away from Colin. His unexpected presence has me forgetting my manners…and how to function, apparently.

"When Pierce told me where we planned the wedding, I thought maybe… But I never imagined you'd be here," Colin says, stammering as a crease forms between his eyebrows.

I chuckle to myself. "Normally, I'm not. My sister usually handles these things, but I…" My voice trails, unable to remember how or why it's me standing here today and not her. Everything else just feels irrelevant now.

He laughs, creating dimples in his cheeks that I've never once forgotten about.

"God, it's good to see you," I mutter under my breath. Embarrassment floods my cheeks, and I quickly compose myself. *Was that an odd thing to say?*

Colin only reacts with a smile. "You too."

But it's his fiancé who shuffles his feet awkwardly for a moment. That's when I glance at the taller man, then back at Colin, putting two and two together. *Fiancé.*

Something cold and heavy expands in my chest. "You're getting married?" I ask, trying to remain casual.

"Uh, yeah," Colin replies, glancing over at the man to his right, who hugs him closer affectionately.

"We've had to keep things under wraps," the American man explains. "The media and paparazzi can create such a hinderance for these sorts of things. That's why this will be a private ceremony. Your sister said security would be tight, and we wouldn't have anything to worry about." He has a sense of arrogance I can spot right away, as if he expects the world to turn a certain way just for him.

"Of course," I say to please him, "and we have that all under control. Nothing to worry about."

"Good," the man replies.

Like a magnetic pull, I find myself looking back over at Colin. The more I stare at him, the more it feels as if my brain is broken. I forgot what I'm supposed to say or how to even say it. I still can't believe he's standing here on the front steps of my house about to get married…to someone else.

That's when I suddenly recall that not only has it been seven years since I saw Colin, but the last time I saw him was not on good terms. We fought and said some hurtful things to each other. I told him to leave. He said he never wanted to see me again.

And now I search his features for signs that that still rings true, but for now, he seems to be smiling, as happy and surprised to see me as I am to see him.

"Well," Pierce says, clapping his hands together, "how about a tour?"

"Yes, of course," I say, breaking myself out of the spell that Colin's blue eyes have put me under. Clutching my sister's brown leather planner against my chest, I turn away from the guests and focus on the task at hand. Regardless of *who* the wedding couple is, I still need to win this bet and get my house back to being just my house.

I tuck a messy curl of hair behind my ear and fix my wrinkled shirt as I lead the two of them away from the front steps.

"I will take you on your tour of the property and then show you to your room. A full staff will be on hand for you at all times over the next six days. And they've prepared a lunch for you today on the veranda behind the house. So once we finish our tour, I will leave you to it. Of course, I will be around, available for whatever you might need."

With that, I guide the two of them around the property, showing them the gazebo, where the ceremony will be held; the hall of the manor, where most of our parties are held; and the gardens, where we will hold their reception.

I feel Colin's presence behind me like a shadow the entire time. The memories come flooding back, but I shove them away, devoted to doing my job and winning this wager.

After the tour, I lead them to the table at the back, where our staff has already prepared their lunch. But as I move to step away from them, I feel a warm hand on my arm, sparking goose bumps across my skin. "You should have lunch with us," Colin says, looking me in the eye. Heat flushes to my cheeks. Then I glance at his fiancé.

"Of course! You're an old friend of Colin's," the man announces, pulling back the extra chair for me. "I absolutely have to hear what you two were like in college."

Instantly, Colin and I stare at each other with wide-eyed, surprised expressions on our faces.

And I'm sure he's thinking the same thing I am.

If he only knew...

Chapter Four
Colin

Fifteen years ago
Oxford

"I don't suppose it's acceptable to be seen with your mother on the first day of university."

"It's fine, Mum," I reply, walking down the residence hall toward my room at the end. She's not the only parent dropping off their child and getting them settled in their quarters. There are plenty of other parents escorting students around the campus.

She is, however, the only one in head-to-toe Armani, looking very out of place as her designer heels click against the dusty, weathered wood floors.

Clinging to my side with her handbag clutched tightly under her arm, she stays close as we pass a communal room with large threadbare sofas and a dinette set with mismatched chairs. A waft of bleach, cheap aftershave, and freshly brewed coffee drifts from the room and permeates the hall.

A moment later, a raucous group of teenage boys spills out and nearly barrels into my mother, laughing as their trainers squeak against the old floors.

Her eyes widen with surprise as one of them narrowly misses her. "Shit, sorry!" he calls before running after his mates down the hall.

When she turns toward me with alarm, I'm afraid she's about to call this whole thing off. After months of pushing me to stay in a flat near campus and hire a private tutor, as well as a personal driver, she finally relented and promised to give me what I want—a *real* uni experience.

My entire life, I've lived in comfort and luxury—complete with private school, chauffeurs, constant surveillance, and total containment—and it's been incredibly dull. I'm ready to *live*, and for me, that means getting to be an authentic, normal eighteen-year-old, although I'm afraid I have no saintly idea what that entails. I just know that I want to be unsupervised and uninhibited.

And one mob of rowdy boys has my mother shaking in her stilettos, threatening to ruin this for me. Little does she know, I ache to be one of them, in all of their wild and disorderly glory.

My poor mother is petrified for me, but I think I understand her fear. She's raised me in captivity and is now releasing me into the wild.

And she may never understand why I need this, but I do. Even I don't entirely understand why yet, but I can just feel it in my bones. I'll never figure out who I am while living in the warm, comfortable confines of my father's inheritance.

"This is it," I say as I reach the end of the hall. Room 212 has a battered brown door that is open just a crack. I gently press on it, and it squeaks as I peek my head inside.

It's minuscule, stuffy, and smells of the pine-scented cleaner they must use far too much of on all the old wood. To the left, there is a single oak-frame bed with a visibly thin bare mattress, an old six-drawer dresser, and a small plain desk.

My mother gasps from behind me.

Meanwhile, a smile of excitement creeps across my face.

I press the door open farther and freeze with a breath caught in my chest as my gaze lands on a dark-haired boy resting on the second bed on the right side of the room. He's reclining against the headboard with a sketch pad propped on his legs and dark-gray charcoal in his hand. His fingers are stained with the soot-colored dust all the way up to the middle knuckle.

"Oh, hey," he says with a hint of disappointment in his tone. "Was sort of hoping you wouldn't show up."

A chuckle escapes my lips as my mother gasps again—this time in indignation.

"This can't be right," she whispers.

"I'm Colin," I say, entering the quarters with my arm outstretched toward my new roommate. "Colin Shelby."

"Declan," he replies as he sits upright and takes my palm for a quick shake. "Declan Barclay."

I glance down at my hand, running my thumb curiously over the smudges of black now smeared across my palm.

"Scottish?" I ask, noting his accent.

"Aye."

My lips tug into a smirk as I fight to hide it. I can't explain why I find so much amusement in this. It's like entering society for the first time and feeling so enamored by every tiny mundane and ordinary detail.

Shoebox-sized living quarters among hundreds of unruly and vulgar teenage boys—perfect. A scraggly, strange Scottish artist for a roommate—even better.

The more appalled my mother appears, the more pleased I am. And just as she murmurs her discontent again, I'm reminded that she's standing there.

"Oh, this is my mother," I say, pointing to her behind me.

"You staying in here too?" he asks her before scooting over on the bed and patting the mattress by his side. "I'll make some room."

She scoffs, and I let out a clipped laugh.

"She was just leaving," I say, turning toward her with wide eyes.

"Lovely to meet you," Declan calls after her in a fake posh British accent. I delicately shove my mother toward the door and walk into the hallway with her.

"Are you really certain about this?" she asks again with worry and love in her eyes.

Holding her by the arms, I force her to look at me and not at the dust and dirt gathering in the corners of the floor.

"I'll be fine," I say with emphasis.

"But you don't have to do this," she argues. "Just come home, and we'll get you the best education in Great Britain."

"I know you would, Mum, but I need more than an education. I want…an experience. An *adventure*."

Her shoulders slump in defeat when she realizes that I'm not leaving with her after all. My mother just wants to protect me and keep me close; I know that. So it hurts me to bring her this pain, but it's for the best.

"If you change your mind—"

"I know, Mum. I'll call you."

"And you can come right home."

I nod. "I know."

"I love you *so* much," she says, holding my face in her hands. Leaning onto her toes, she presses her lips to my cheek. "And I'm so proud of you."

"Don't be proud yet," I say. "I haven't made it through my first term yet. Hell, I haven't even made it through my first day."

"You will," she says with a warm grin.

Just then, our driver appears with my luggage, and I wave my mother goodbye. She disappears down the hallway, and I take my suitcases under each arm.

Reentering the room and suddenly being alone with this new stranger is awkward for a moment.

"Fancy," Declan says as he watches me hoist my Louis Vuitton luggage onto the small bed.

"Uh, thanks," I mutter.

Chancing a glance back at the boy sitting on the bed, I notice that Declan is wearing loose dark jeans that are frayed at the edges, with ink stains around the pockets, much like the charcoal on his hand. His feet are bare, and his shirt is unbuttoned and hanging open, revealing a tight-fitting white tee underneath.

"I'm going outside for a smoke. Wanna join me?" he asks after standing with a loud breath.

"I don't smoke," I reply over my shoulder.

"It's never too late to start," he jokes, and I smile to myself as I unzip my first suitcase.

As my fingers linger over the perfectly packed clothes and toiletries, I consider turning him down again. But that's something the old Colin would do.

And I'm ready to be the *new* Colin.

"Fuck it," I say. "Let's go."

Declan has a wide, handsome smile as he claps a dirty hand on my back and leads me toward the door. He kicks it shut behind him but keeps the hand there as we walk down the hallway. He's nearly the same height as I am, and I'm the tallest person in my family. In fact, now that I'm glancing sideways at him, I realize he might actually be a bit taller.

Two minutes later, we're standing across from each other in the small outdoor space between buildings where the grass and weeds have sprouted between the cracks of the stones and pavement on the ground. And I'm coughing so hard it feels like my lungs might actually propel themselves from my body.

"Okay, maybe it *is* too late to start," Declan says with a laugh as he pats my back and takes the cigarette from my fingers.

My eyes are watering, and I can feel people looking at me. Seasoned, calm smokers who probably trained their lungs to handle the toxic smoke when they were young teens, not fully grown.

"Easy, Shelby," Declan says, rubbing my back. "Don't die on me. That's not how I want to start my term."

"I'm fine," I wheeze before coughing again.

When I can finally stand upright and get a good look at the man leaning against the brick building with a cigarette in his hand, I resist the urge to run away out of embarrassment.

"So what's your story, Shelby?" he asks as he takes a puff.

"It's Colin," I reply. I hate being called by my last name, mainly because it reminds me of my father.

"Sorry," he says, putting up his hands. "What's your story, Colin?"

"My story?"

"Yeah, what is a proper, rich young Brit like yourself doing in these halls and sharing a room with a commoner like me?"

His jet-black hair hangs messily forward before he uses his free hand to brush it out of his face. He carries himself with such confidence it makes my chest ache with longing. I'd kill to be half as assured.

"You're not a commoner," I say, shaking my head.

Declan's eyes pop open in surprise. "What is that supposed to mean?"

"I know that your family is wealthy," I reply.

"Mr. Shelby, have you been stalking me?" he asks with fake offense.

I can't help but smile but can't seem to manage a laugh without coughing again. "No, I haven't. But let's just say I know my parents. They always have a way of manipulating things in their favor."

Declan grins to himself as he pulls another drag through the cigarette.

I don't go into much detail, but judging by his lack of surprise, I'd say my suspicions were correct. My mother wouldn't let me board with just anyone. No, I would bet my life that they paid off the housing department and hand-selected my roommate, someone from a wealthy family, presumably. Someone without a dangerous background.

So, while Declan asked to know my story, I can already guess his.

"Wow," he says as he stubs the butt of the cigarette into a nearby ashtray. "I guess we're just two birds of a feather, aren't we?"

"Are you also running away to uni to escape your overbearing parents and try to live an authentic life instead of the charade of being rich?"

Declan's dark eyes are like an abyss as he stares at me, and it's almost too intense, as if his gaze is swallowing me whole.

"Close, Shelby," he says, crossing his arms over his chest. "The only difference is that my parents are dead. But everything else sounds right on the money."

My face falls. "Oh, blast," I mutter. "I'm sorry."

He laughs as he shoves my shoulder. "It's fine. I'm used to it by now. I do, however, have an overbearing sister and aunt that I'm here to escape, so I guess we do have a lot in common."

Heat flushes to my cheeks from the embarrassment. As difficult as my parents are, especially my father, I couldn't imagine not having any parents at all. How lonely that must be for him.

Desperate to change the subject and relieve myself from the torment of having my foot so far in my mouth, I ask, "So what are you studying?"

"Fine arts," he replies, kicking a pebble with his shoe.

That explains the charcoal.

"What about you, Shelby?" he replies, without expanding further on his topic of study.

I give a shrug. "Theatre studies."

He nods appreciatively before shoving his lighter into his pocket. "Theatre, huh? You want to be an actor or something?"

Wincing uncomfortably, I reply, "I don't know yet. Maybe."

"Well, you've got the face for it," he replies, and I freeze for a moment, letting the compliment wash over me. *Did he just call me handsome?*

It could have been some backhanded compliment, for all I

know. I'm not good at casual conversation. I don't always pick up on nuanced clues and jabs.

"Uh, thanks," I mutter in reply, making Declan laugh.

With that, he throws an arm around my shoulder and tugs me toward the door. "Come on, Shakespeare. Let's get some food."

The soft skin of his arm touches my neck as we make our way toward the cafeteria, and I turn my head toward him, absorbing the brief warmth of his smile like it's the sun hanging in the sky.

It might be a little too early to call it, but I think I've just made my first uni friend, and if my parents did have a hand in choosing my first roommate, I'm glad they chose Declan Barclay.

Chapter Five
Colin

I'm lying on the thin mattress in my room when Declan bursts in with nothing but a towel around his waist. The cold weight of something glass lands on my stomach, and I let out a grunt. The paperback I was holding falls from my hands as I pick up the brown glass bottle my roommate tossed at me.

"Thanks," I mutter as I inspect the cheap beer. "Where did you steal these from?"

Declan rips off the damp towel and throws it on the floor with the pile of dirty laundry. My gaze lands briefly on his bare ass as he tugs on a pair of tight black briefs. Forcing myself not to look at his naked parts, my eyes catch the rivulets of water dripping slowly down his back instead.

"That idiot at the end of the hall. They left their door unlocked," he jokes as he cracks open his beer and takes a swig.

"Malcolm?" I ask, fumbling to crack the cap off the beer with the corner of the bedpost.

"Yep," Declan replies.

"He's going to kick your ass," I say, still struggling and nearly splitting the wood off the bed.

"I'd like to see him try." Declan laughs as he takes my beer and swiftly pops the cap off with ease before handing it back to me.

"Have you seen that guy on the rugby pitch? He could fold you in half, Dec."

My friend only shrugs.

After living with Declan Barclay for the last three months, I've learned that he behaves as if he's invincible. And I get the itching suspicion that it's not something he acquired from being rich. I think he gets it from not having a care in the world. Declan isn't afraid of death or failure or injury.

I don't think he's afraid of anything.

It's just one of the many things I admire about him.

He doesn't bother getting dressed. Dropping onto his own mattress in just his underwear, he drinks his stolen beer without looking at me.

Living with another man my age for the first time in my life has been very enlightening. The level of comfort Declan has exhibited is new to me. He's not afraid to undress in my presence. He strolls around our small room with hardly anything on.

It's almost as if he acts like I'm not even here, and it's strange how much I like that. There's never anything uncomfortable or awkward between us.

"I'm bored, Shakespeare," he says with a groan as he reaches the end of the bottle.

I toss my book on the foot of the bed. "What do you have in mind?"

"I don't know about you, but I need a good shag. It's Friday night. Let's go out."

As he hops up from the bed and starts rifling around in his messy pile of clothes, my stomach clenches. The topic of sex and/or sexual partners hasn't exactly come up yet. From time to time, Declan has boasted about the girls he hooked up with in secondary school, but he never once asked me about my own experiences.

Which aren't many.

Or any...at all.

I sit up on the bed and do my best not to appear stiff. Taking a swig of my beer, I watch Declan throw on a wrinkled polo shirt and some loose black trousers that hug his hips and ass. Even with his unkempt appearance, I have no doubt my roommate will succeed in finding a bedroom partner for the evening. He has the good looks and charm to pull it off.

Me, on the other hand...

"You wearing that?" he asks, nodding his head toward my knitted cream-colored pullover.

I glance down at my attire in confusion. "Should I change?"

"You won't get your dick sucked in that," he quips as he takes my beer and pulls a swig from the bottle.

"I'll change," I say, standing from the bed. The truth is, I don't quite know what someone wears to get their dick sucked. It's never been the motivation behind my fashion choices, but maybe it should have been.

After looking through my wardrobe, I find a plain gray T-shirt and a nice pair of denim trousers. Declan lets his gaze rake over my body after I'm dressed before he shrugs and mumbles, "Good enough."

Then, we're out the door and on our way to...I don't even know where. Declan and I have never *been out* before. He sometimes stays out late alone, but in the three months we've known each other, even as close as we've become, he's never invited me. Truth be told, I always assumed he thought he was better off alone.

I follow Declan to a pub in town that is lively and crawling with uni students.

The energy is raucous and wild, and we have to squeeze our way through the crowd to reach the bar. It smells of beer and sweat, but with the music and conversation so loud, it overloads my senses.

If I'm going to last in here tonight, I need to get drunk, and fast.

Declan uses his dimples and flirty smile to score us each a pint of beer and a shot of whisky from the bartender. Then, we find a place near the edge of the bar to stand and get our bearings. Immediately, he spots two beautiful women who look around our age at a tall pub table. Even I notice the way they glance at us in the midst of their conversation.

The liquor burns its way down my throat as I take the shot. Then, Declan tugs me toward the women in a rush, as if they're about to be claimed by two other horny, drunk blokes.

"Hey!" he shouts over the music as we reach the pub table. "Can we buy you a drink?"

The woman on the left has long brown hair in perfectly placed waves. Her face is caked with makeup, and her eyelashes are unnaturally long and thick. The other woman has short strawberry blond coils that reach her shoulders. She doesn't have as much makeup on, but still, nothing particularly excites me about either of them.

They're both pretty—beautiful even, but there isn't even a spark of arousal or excitement in my body at the sight.

Of course, I knew this. I've always known this about myself. It might not be something I outwardly express or own up to, but it's plain as day in my own mind. I'm not attracted to women—not at all. I don't need to fondle their breasts or explore the space between their legs to know it.

As I stand behind Declan, who is charismatically flirting with the one with the makeup, I glance around at the other men filling the crowded space. They all seem so fiendish and feral for the opposite sex. With their puffed-up chests and lascivious mannerisms, they remind me of those exotic birds who prance and preen for a mate. And all I'd really like to do is take this beer home with my roommate and do literally anything other than this.

When Declan goes back to the bar to fetch two more beers for the ladies, I'm left to converse with them alone, and it's mind-numbingly painful. I try to make small talk about school, but it turns out both of them are American tourists backpacking around the UK during their gap year, whatever that is.

Thankfully, Declan doesn't take long with their drinks, and I rely on him to lead the rest of the social interaction. To my surprise, he's even more captivating when he's trying to get sex. His stories are funnier, and the way he talks with his hands is more mesmerizing. The women are totally falling for him—as am I. The three of us just watch him talk, laughing at all the right moments.

The beer keeps flowing, and the longer we stand there, the more comfortable I feel. I'm suddenly not so worried about the fact that I'm supposed to be flirting with one of these women and have no desire to. I'm out with Declan, and he keeps giving me that smile, and everything is great.

The details start to grow fuzzy. A song I love blares from the speakers, and I even start tapping my foot to the music, feeling light and carefree. I look away from Declan for one moment to scan the crowd with a sense of pride. This is what I came to uni for—a *real* experience. This noisy, smelly pub is a far cry from my sheltered life in London, and I'm ecstatic about it.

Declan is still talking, his flirtatious laugh piercing the din of voices around me. But when his laughter fades, I turn back to the group to find his lips tangled with the brunette's. Suddenly, the alcohol hits my system differently, making the room spin. I can't tear my eyes away from them, watching the way he strokes her jaw as his tongue presses into her mouth. She smiles against his lips, and my stomach drops like lead to the floor.

I'm abruptly aware of the curly-haired girl staring at me, but I can't bring myself to turn my drunk gaze to her face. I'm just watching Declan make out with that stranger, wishing I was sober enough to force myself to look away. The longer he kisses her, the more my stomach turns. It's no longer a lead heap on the floor. Now it's a roiling, rebellious thing, threatening to heave all over this table. Like a bolt of lightning, I stumble away from the group and rush through the crowd toward the loo.

I barely make it to the toilet before my stomach empties itself. Kneeling on the floor of a disgusting pub's bathroom stall, I continue to retch. This is definitely *not* the dream I had about coming to uni.

The vision of Declan kissing that woman replays over and over in my head. Jealousy and anger swirl in my now empty gut. He'd rather be with them than me. He'd rather kiss them, talk to them, fuck them.

What am I even saying? It's not like he would ever want that with me. Is that even what I want with him?

I'm too drunk.

The door opens and someone barrels in, bouncing off the stall doors clumsily. "Shakespeare!" a loud, slurring voice echoes in the cramped chamber of this lavatory. "Oh, mate," he says behind me, but the way his voice ricochets back and forth against the linoleum stalls, it sounds like he's everywhere.

Strong hands curl under my arms and hoist me off of the floor. I'm flooded with embarrassment as I try to hide my revolting, sweat-soaked, vomit-covered face from his perfect, handsome one.

He's drunk too, but he's *fun* drunk. I'm *regretful, sick, wretched* drunk.

With a laugh, he hauls me to the sink. When I see my reflection, I let out a groan. But Declan doesn't hesitate to clean my face with frigid water and his bare hand. It's humiliating and maybe a little comforting.

"I'm sorry," I mumble in shame.

"Ach, don't be sorry. She was a shite kisser anyway."

"I'll get a cab home alone. You go have fun," I stammer as I force my eyes to focus on one reflection in the mirror when it keeps trying to create two.

Declan laughs again. "I think not, Shelby. We'll be taking that cab together right after we have a little coffee to sober you up. I can't have you retching all over England. You're going to be famous someday, and famous guys don't puke."

As he slings an arm over my shoulder and leads me out the door, I lean into the comfort of his embrace. He smells familiar. Even his voice grounds me. After only three months, this stranger has somehow infiltrated my sense of home.

When we reach the crisp air of the night outside the pub, I suck it in and feel my head spin with how fresh and clean it is. Nothing like the stale, clammy air inside the building.

We stumble together like that, his arm around my shoulder and my face nearly pressed to his chest. I briefly wonder if this is normal. Would straight guys act this way? Who knows. I clearly have no frame of reference.

I'd like to think this is special. Declan doesn't act this way with anyone else. It's just another dangerous tendril of hope that's fallen out of place. But no matter how hard I try to tuck it back where it belongs, it doesn't stay.

The entire walk goes by in a blur. When we reach a small café open late for uni students, the quiet ambiance inside feels instantly more comfortable to me than the noisy atmosphere of the pub. I find a large velvet-upholstered couch and plop onto it while Declan goes to the counter and orders two cappuccinos.

When he delivers mine, I inhale the scent, and it smells divine. This is much more my speed.

Declan sits on the chaise next to me. His hip and arm are both pressed against mine.

I hate myself for how much I think about these little things now. I want to go back to the way I felt earlier today when he was just a friend, and I didn't relish every small moment for a brief sliver of hope that he might feel the same.

Of course he doesn't, you fool.

"You okay, Shakespeare?" he asks quietly, nudging my elbow.

"Yeah," I reply unconvincingly. "Why do you keep calling me that?"

"Do you want me to stop?" His voice is just above a whisper, and his head is turned in my direction, so I feel his breath on my ear. My stomach tightens, and my breathing stutters.

It's an innocent question.

But those words and the way he whispered them went straight to my groin.

Turning toward him, our eyes meet as I match his volume with a delicate whisper. "No."

The tense moment lingers, with our eyes boring into each other. With every passing second, my heart picks up speed and gathers more hope, like snowballing optimism.

Then, his mouth tugs into a bright smile. "Aye, good."

I swallow my discomfort and turn forward, pretending like nothing just happened. I take a sip of my cappuccino as he leans in and asks, "So you wanna tell me what happened back there? You didn't like the ginger?"

Managing a shrug, I reply, "She was fine. I just…drank too much."

"She wasn't your type." He says it so matter-of-factly I feel momentarily off-balance. I glance at him as he adds, "Neither of them were."

"I…" Closing my eyes in confusion, my brows furrow as I shake my head. My response slips from my mind before I have the chance to utter it. I don't want to hide or lie to him. He left the opportunity for sex behind at that pub to bring me home. Declan is more than a roommate at this point. He's my friend. And I don't want a friendship built on lies.

"It's all right, Shelby," he says as he puts an arm around my shoulder. It's playful and innocent. "I sort of figured it out."

My eyes pop open. "You did?"

"Aye. You never talk about lasses you've hooked up with in school. I figured maybe you were just shy."

I stiffen with discomfort. It's like he discovered a secret I wasn't even trying to keep.

The café is quiet, but the music playing overhead and the

gentle cacophony of hushed conversations disguise our voices. I don't respond as he continues.

"You can always tell me about the guys you've hooked up with. Doesn't bother me any."

A laugh slips through my lips.

"What's so funny?" he whispers.

"I don't have any blokes or lasses to tell you about."

I'm definitely still drunk if I'm letting this secret out, but my inhibitions are down the drain back at that pub.

"You don't mean…" he says with astonishment, turning toward me. His eyes are wide.

The couple at the table nearby glances our way as I shrink into the couch.

I nod with a tight smile. "Yep."

"A virgin, Shakespeare?"

"As virginal as they come," I reply.

"Well, virgins don't really come, though, do they?" he asks, and we both break out in drunk chuckles.

"Not with a partner, they don't," I wheeze through my laughter.

Someone hushes us from across the café. So when our laughter dies, Declan shoots back the rest of his cappuccino and then pops up from the couch.

"Let's get you home, virgin."

As he puts a hand out toward me, the dim light of the café illuminating him from behind, I know there's no hope trying to tame my heart now. The crush I'm forming on my new friend is too powerful. It's a hurricane that's decimated everything we were before this very moment.

"As long as you promise not to make that my new nickname," I say as he pulls me up.

"Just until it doesn't fit anymore," he replies with a wink.

With that, he turns and leaves me two steps behind him. For a guy who is royally fucked and bound to have his heart broken, I'm in a pretty good mood.

Chapter Six
Colin

The summer sun is scorching as I jog across campus toward the residence hall in my exam robes. My last exam of the year is done, which means I have nothing left to do for the next twenty-four hours but spend time with my best friend.

He leaves tomorrow on the train headed north, and my mother will be in Oxford bright and early to take me home for the summer holiday.

To be honest, I'm dreading it. I don't feel like the same man I was when she dropped me off. Save for the week I spent with her at Christmas, I've been here with Declan for nearly ten months.

For the first time in my life, I feel like I know myself. And I *like* myself.

I don't want to return to the meaningless existence I knew before.

Their son. Dutiful. Obedient. Proper. Quiet. Allegiant.

Declan doesn't have any classes today, so I know he should be in the room when I return. We can spend the rest of the day doing what we normally do. Get pissed somewhere in town and go home alone. We'll probably stay up far too late talking and listening to music.

For the most part, I've been able to shove aside this growing crush on my friend. At first, I was afraid it would get in the way of our friendship, but it's been fine. He spends all of his free time with me, so it's like I'm getting the best of both worlds.

There's a nagging part of me that worries about what Declan will do during the summer holiday. Will he have sex with someone? Fall in love? Get a girlfriend or a new best friend so he doesn't want to spend time with me anymore? What will I do then? Who will I be?

The hallway to our room is quiet today. So many of the students are still in their exams or have already left campus. Normally, there's more noise in the building just from people talking and music playing.

It's mostly due to this unique silence that my ears pick up a distinct sound as I approach the quarters I share with Declan. Our door is open a mere inch, and just as my hand touches the knob, I freeze.

I hear a moan.

It's not a sound I've heard Declan make before. It's low and breathless with a hint of a grunt.

At first, I don't think anything of it, but then he makes it again.

"Fuck," he rasps quietly, and heat swells in my groin. He's… getting himself off.

Is he alone? Did someone sneak into our room while I was gone?

But there are no other voices. Just his shallow groans and the distinct sound of quick movement of flesh on flesh.

My lips part, and my breathing grows heavy as I listen.

I should leave. My feet even shuffle for a moment as I prepare myself to run away and pretend this never happened. But then he does it again, this time with a hint of a whimper.

Instead of running, I let my eyes close and press my forehead to the wood of the doorframe, letting the sound of this gorgeous man pleasuring himself fill my ears and imagination. I can't see him, so I have to conjure up the image in my mind. I picture him naked on his bed, sweat dripping from the pale skin of his chest and abs. I can practically see his cock in my mind, strangled by his fist, as he pumps himself vigorously. His back is arched off the bed, and his head is thrown back in elation, his eyes closed and his bottom lip pinched between his teeth.

My own cock reacts to the filthy fantasy, growing thick with desire.

This is so wrong of me. I'm terrible for this. Invading my friend's privacy to lust after him without his knowledge or consent.

What is wrong with me?

His groans peak, stuttering as he reaches his climax. The sound is breathtaking. I've committed it to memory already, the sound and the fantasy.

It takes everything in me not to palm my own erection. Instead, I find myself leaning into the doorframe, subtly squeezing my cock between my body and the hardwood. The pain heightens the pleasure while also serving as a form of punishment for invading his privacy.

Once he's finished, the room grows quiet. I don't know what to do, and I don't want to be caught standing here, so I turn from the door and make my way quickly down the hallway toward the exit. I make it all the way to the door before I hear his call.

"Hey, Shakespeare!"

Spinning on my heels, I turn back toward Declan, feeling flush in the face and still sporting a thick erection in my pants, which I hide with one of my textbooks.

"You done with your exams already?" he asks.

I clear my throat and shuffle my feet like I don't know how to behave anymore. "Uh…yes, I am."

As he reaches me at the end of the hall, there's an unlit cigarette hanging between his lips and a charming grin on his face. There's no evidence that he just orgasmed moments ago, and he doesn't seem the least bit ashamed about it.

Me, on the other hand, I'm a wreck.

"Cheers, mate," he says, throwing an arm over my shoulder. "Let's get pissed then. It's our last night together before the holiday."

"Y-yeah," I stutter, following his lead.

Even as we stand in the brick courtyard alone and he puffs on the cigarette, I can't get the sound of his pleasure out of my head. As divine as it was, I'm so mad at myself for listening in. It's gotten into my head. Changed everything.

Hearing Declan stroke himself has altered the chemistry in my brain, and I'm afraid I'll never be able to right it again. I'm quite sure the lust is written all over my face.

"You won't have any chance to get away this summer?" he asks, leaning against the brick wall with one hand in his pocket. It takes everything in me to keep from staring at him longingly.

"Not likely," I reply, keeping my gaze down. "My mother likes to keep me close when I'm home from school."

"And what about your dad?" he asks.

I shrug, kicking a pebble across the cobblestones. "He doesn't come around much. Not anymore."

"But they're still married?"

"Yeah," I answer.

Even as much as Declan and I have spoken this term, I've never once explained to him how my father doesn't come around our family much and why. Truth be told, I'm a bit embarrassed by it, so I've kept the dirty details of it to myself.

"Well, it's just three months," he says, clapping his hand on my shoulder. I stiffen under his touch, remembering where that hand of his has just been and begging my cock not to react to that. He gives me a jovial shake as if trying to release me from my melancholy.

I think he can tell how downhearted I am about the long season away from school. Away from him. I feel pathetic for it.

Is he as sad as I am? Will he miss me? Or am I just another

uni mate to him? He's probably going home to a load of friends and a booming social life.

"Yeah," I murmur. "Just three months."

"But let's make a deal," he proposes. I perk my head up to listen. "Let's see each other at least once this summer if we can. Fuck it, I'll come to you if I have to."

My brows lift in surprise. "What? Really?"

"Aye, you're my best friend, Colin. I don't want to spend a whole three months without you."

"You called me Colin," I reply with a laugh.

"Because I'm serious, you daft prick. Do we have a deal or not?"

I can't help the smile that stretches across my face as he shakes me by the shoulder. For a bloke who's in love with his best friend, I really shouldn't be so enamored by hearing him call me his *best* friend, but I am. And not only that, but he wants to see me over the holiday. This whole time, I was afraid this friendship was one-sided, but it's not. He's going to miss me, and that sentiment is enough to get me through until we see each other again.

"Fine," I say, feeling a whole lot lighter than I did a moment ago. "Deal."

"Good." He stubs out his cigarette and throws it in the bin. "Then, we'll get drunk tonight, and after tomorrow, we only have to wait a month before we'll see each other again."

He flings an arm over my shoulder as we make our way out of the courtyard and down the road toward town. And suddenly, I'm not feeling quite as depressed as I was a moment ago. Declan Barclay made me a promise, and I know he would never let me down.

Chapter Seven
Declan

Six days until the wedding

THE COLD SCOTCH SMOLDERS MY TASTE BUDS BEFORE SLIDING down my throat, burning its way to my stomach. There's comfort in the heat, as if it could turn these feelings to ash. Exterminate this sickening jealousy in my bloodstream.

Across the table from me, Pierce Michael Hall, as he's referred to in his movie credits, sits with his arm around the back of Colin's chair, talking incessantly about anything he can. He hasn't shut up for the last fifteen minutes.

I hold up my glass to signal to one of the staff members that I need a refill. I probably shouldn't be getting drunk on the job, but I can't possibly get through this sober.

While Pierce, whatever his name is, drones on and on, I watch Colin. Is he really going to marry this guy? Does he love him? Does he act the same way with him that he did with me?

"How did you two meet?" I ask, interrupting the American. He doesn't seem bothered as he places a hand on Colin's leg and gives him a smarmy, insincere smile. Colin can't be serious about this guy.

"On set, of course," he replies, and it takes me a moment to realize that's where I know him from. Colin's WWII film last summer. I almost didn't recognize Pierce, because in the film, his hair was buzzed short and hidden beneath a Gestapo uniform. Colin's part was much more prominent and far better acted, if I say so myself.

"Oh yes, of course," I reply mockingly. Turning my attention to Colin, I watch his expression. He's tense and uncomfortable, although he wears a warm smile. His knuckles are white as he grips his glass, and his throat moves ever so slightly as he swallows.

"I pursued him," Pierce says softly as he gently strokes a strand of hair behind Colin's ear. "Wouldn't stop asking him out until he finally said yes."

"I said yes right away," Colin replies with his soft gaze on the half-eaten plate in front of him. "Who would say no to you?" He mumbles that last part, almost so quietly I don't hear it. Something about it puts me on edge.

Then, just as I'm about to respond, Pierce steals control of the conversation again.

"So tell me," he says. "What was Colin like in college?"

I stare across the table at the actor, noting the cool, deep, authoritative tone of his voice. His subtle arrogance. His calm pretentiousness.

He is definitely dominant with Colin. My molars grind at the thought.

My gaze drifts over to the blond man to his left. Colin stares back at me, and I wonder if he's reminiscing about the same memories I am. The ones I probably shouldn't include in my stories at this table.

"I had never met someone so innocent," I say with a smirk.

"Colin?" Pierce asks, like he doesn't believe me.

"Aye."

"My Colin, innocent in college?" Pierce says, smiling at his fiancé and kissing him on the cheek.

My jaw clicks as I grind my teeth together harder at the sound of him calling Colin his.

"I said he was innocent when I met him," I add, lifting my fresh glass to my lips. "I never said he stayed that way."

Colin's eyes narrow at me as the table grows tense with silence.

Eventually, he responds. "We did have fun in our younger days. And he was a *terrible* influence, but that's what I wanted… at the time. I was living a sheltered existence until I met Declan, and he cured me of it. We had our fun, but we were young. And those days are over."

"What a pity, Shakespeare," I reply over my glass.

"Don't call me that," he says without hesitation. His tone is still warm and playful, but I can sense something more beneath it, which means he's hiding his contempt. I suspect he's still cross with me for what happened last time we saw each other.

"Speaking of fun…" Pierce says as he waves down the waiter for another drink of his own. "This manor of yours has a bit of a reputation."

"Pierce!" Colin snaps, turning toward him.

The American only laughs as he rubs Colin's back. "What? I'm just curious."

Sitting up straight, I set my whisky on the table. "That was a long time ago," I say, wincing at the idea that my brother's infamous sex parties have made such a splash that people from as far as America have heard about them.

I don't say anything as Pierce commandeers the conversation, a bright, amused smile on his face. "Let's just say I've heard this manor used to be known for events very different from weddings."

"That was when my brother lived here," I mumble, my fingers squeezing the glass in my hands.

"That's enough," Colin says, growing more and more uncomfortable.

Then his gaze meets mine, and I have to bite back my smirk, because as humiliating as it is to hear some stranger talking about my family's dirty secrets as if they're nothing more than gossip, it is worth it to see that bashful expression on his face again.

As we stare at each other, I wonder if he's also remembering the year we came to Barclay. The year he nearly witnessed one of those parties himself. The year everything fell apart, and what happened between us that night.

For a moment, a hint of nostalgia-like pain lances my heart, and I wince as I take a drink of my whisky to dull the ache. Perhaps I missed Colin more than I thought.

He was my best friend for nearly a decade. Of course I missed him.

And sure, there was a time when we acted more like lovers than friends. But that's all it ever was. If I ever considered having romantic feelings for Colin Shelby, those days have passed. They were a mistake that would have ended badly.

So now, he's getting married, which is a good thing.

And I will make sure of it. I'll be here to ensure that every step of this wedding goes off without a hitch so that I can win this bet and finally have this house to myself the way I want.

I'm not about to let an old romantic entanglement mess that up now.

After lunch, I leave the couple to get settled in their room. They'll be staying for the week, and we have rooms for some of their wedding party as well once they arrive.

I'm thankful once again for the space between my quarters and theirs.

When I hear the familiar click of my sister's heels on the floor, growing closer to the library where I'm hiding, I say a silent prayer that she doesn't find me.

"There you are!" Anna says from the doorway when she spots me. She scurries closer, finding me slumped down in the large upholstered chair with my legs propped up on an old ottoman and a glass of whisky resting on my lap. "Are you hiding? What's wrong? How did it go this afternoon? Did you ruin it already?"

"Anna, for fuck's sake, calm down."

"What happened?" she asks, a bit more relaxed.

"Nothing happened," I reply with a slur, taking a sip of my drink. I've lost count of how many of these I've had today—at least three at lunch. "I gave them the bloody tour, and now they're getting settled in their room. Everything is under control."

"Thank God," she says with a sigh as she rests against the desk. "Are you drunk?"

There is judgment in her voice, and I sneer up at her before trying to focus my gaze. Changing the course of the conversation, I ask, "Don't you want me to mess this up? Then you win the bet and can go back to having these weddings to yourself."

"Of course I don't want you to fail, Declan. I want you to be happy."

"How benevolent of you. As a matter of fact, I want me to be happy too," I reply with a sloppy grin.

She rolls her eyes and steals the whisky from my hand. I catch her taking a sip before setting it on the desk out of my reach.

"So?" she asks.

"So what?"

"So…who is it?" She's wearing an excited smile, and it takes me a moment before I remember that Colin and Pierce are celebrities. And before today, no one knew who these mystery guests would be.

"Oh," I reply lazily. "Pierce Michael, something."

"Pierce Michael Hall?" my sister shrieks. She slaps her hand over her mouth with wide eyes while I grimace up at her like she's lost her goddamn mind.

"Yeah, he's not really that impressive," I mumble before reaching for my drink. She's so distracted by the celebrity at our house that she doesn't bother keeping it away from me anymore. Instead, she's scurrying over to the window to peek out in hopes of stealing a glimpse of the actor.

"Not that impressive?" she asks. "I don't believe you. He's so handsome. I had no idea he was even getting married!"

"I mean, honestly, Anna, who cares? You act like celebrities' lives are any of our bloody business."

She turns back toward me with a disgruntled expression. "What a miserable grump you are, Declan. I truly hope you are not rude to him or his groom just because they are celebrities. Oh, who is his groom? Is he an actor too?"

Biting her lip, she waits in anticipation. Meanwhile, I swallow down the rest of the amber liquid in my glass, relishing in the burn before I blow out a breath and quietly reply, "Colin Shelby."

My sister is frozen. If anything, her eyes widen just a hair as she stares at me in shock.

"No," she whispers.

"Yes," I reply.

"Declan," she says with a pleading, sympathetic tone.

"What a coincidence, right? My old mate from uni is getting married here this weekend."

With a groan, I peel myself off the chair and stumble toward the bottle near the fireplace. My sister rushes after me, grabbing me by the arm before I can reach it.

"Declan, I had no idea. How are you—I mean, what happened…? Are you okay?"

I respond to her, stammering with a laugh, "Relax, Anna. It was a surprise to see him, that's all. It was nice, actually. He's my best friend. Or at least…he was."

When I reach for the bottle, she puts herself between me and it. Then she takes my face in her hands and forces me to look in her eyes. "I think we both know it was more than that, Declan."

Scowling, I brush her off. "Don't be ridiculous. Of course it wasn't."

"Why don't we call this bet off?" she asks, trying to tame my wild hair.

"No!" I bellow. "Killian won't let me off that easily, and I am not going to roll over just because I happen to be friends with one of the grooms."

"I don't care what Killian says," she replies. "I'm worried about you, Declan."

"Well, stop it!" She flinches at the tone of my voice, and I turn away with a heavy sigh. Worrying is just what my sister does, but I can't stand being the focus of it. Especially since there is nothing to worry about here. She thinks I'm drunk because I'm heartbroken or upset over my old mate getting married, but I'm not. I'm just a drunk.

As I turn back toward her, I'm immediately assaulted by guilt when I see the tears forming in her eyes. "I'm sorry, sis. I just don't want you worrying about me."

Taking her shoulders in my hands, it's my turn to force her gaze to mine. Then, with as steady a voice as I can manage, I try to ease her concerns. "I promise you I do not have feelings for Colin, not anymore. That was a long time ago. If anything, I think this will make the wedding easier for me. I'm going to prove to you that I can do this. Then, maybe you'll leave me the hell alone."

When a tear slips over her lashes and down her cheek, I use the sleeve of my shirt to wipe it away. Then I gather her against my chest and hold her to ease her mind.

"I don't believe you, Declan," she softly whispers. "But I do trust you."

"Thank you," I reply.

After a moment, she wipes her eyes and pulls away. With a deep breath, she paints a smile on her face and claps her hands together excitedly.

"Okay, now introduce me to that hunky American."

Chapter Eight
Declan

I find peace in my studio, even this late at night and even after the day from hell I've had. The naked woman on the grass stares back at me as if she's waiting for me to find the inspiration, but there is none.

The allure in her eyes is gone.

All I see now is the look on Colin's face as he smiled at his new man.

I don't understand why I feel so crummy about this. I should be happy for my friend. Maybe part of me feels like shite because I've missed out on so much. He fell in love with someone, and I wasn't there to hear about it. He got engaged, and I had no idea.

I don't matter to him anymore.

God, I'm pathetic. I've been hanging on to this friendship when he clearly hasn't. He wasn't even going to invite me to his wedding.

There's a creak of a floorboard on the stairs followed by the quiet padding of feet as someone tiptoes down the hall toward my studio. Frozen on my stool, staring at the painting, I don't bother turning around because I know who it is.

"I don't like it," he mutters from the doorway.

I let out a huff of a laugh. Not because he hurt my feelings;

because with four words—an inside joke plucked from an old memory—he made it feel like us again. And I nearly forgot what that feels like.

"I don't like it either, Shakespeare," I say, staring at the painting.

"I told you not to call me that," he replies, walking into the room.

"Since when do I listen to you?"

As he comes to stand in front of the painting, his head tilts to the side like it always used to, and his eyes scrutinize every brushstroke. In my periphery, I take in the surreal sight of him standing in my studio.

"It's terrible," he whispers.

"You're just saying that," I say with a shake of my head.

"No, I'm serious," he replies, glancing toward me. "It's truly awful."

The corner of his mouth tugs with a smile, and warmth blossoms in the center of my chest.

"Thanks," I reply, knowing full well what he really means when he says how bad it is. It's an old game we used to play. Shelby knows how much I hate taking compliments, so he offers criticism instead. Like he could ever criticize me and mean it.

When he says he hates it, I know it means he loves it.

When he says it's awful, I know he means it's exquisite.

It's quiet again, and my traitor of a mind immediately goes to the last time Colin and I were alone in this room. Seven years ago, a night I will likely never forget.

Just before it all came to an end.

"So…" he says, turning toward me. "You're not really going through with this, are you?"

The question takes me by surprise. Rotating toward him with a furrow in my brow, I ask, "What are you talking about?"

"You can't host our wedding, Declan."

"Why not?" I ask, feeling blindsided.

His shoulders slump away from his ears, and his smile fades into a cold, flat expression. "You know why. Get Anna to do it."

It's cute when he tries to be bossy.

"Since when are *you* the one telling me what to do?" I quip back.

I have a choice here. Give in to his request and take the easy way out of this situation or make things difficult for everyone. And I've never been suited to make things easy on anyone.

"Don't," he mutters, turning his seething gaze from my face. I can't believe how quickly we've changed the tone in the room from playful old friends to bitter and resentful ex-friends. As if we left this fight lying on the floor and one of us just picked it back up again.

"Don't what, Shakespeare? You're the one who invited me to lunch today. You're the one who showed up at my house to marry your hot American boyfriend."

"I told you not to call me that!" he barks.

Seeing him fired up only gets me fired up. I've always loved Colin's antagonistic side. I never got to see it very often.

"Why? Because it reminds you that we were once friends? Until you left."

"Me?" he replies with outrage. "Do you not remember *why* I left?"

I stand from the stool and pass by him toward the table where my brushes and paints are stored. I'm purposefully not engaging with him. I don't want him to think he's getting under my skin or that I'm bothered at all by this situation.

"Honestly? No. I don't think about it much at all anymore."

"It is so typical of you to conveniently forget your own blame in any situation. You truly think of no one but yourself. You are such an arsehole, Declan," he says. The hint of pain in his words has me faltering as I reach for the black paint. It hurts Colin to be vexed with me. To call me names. To *hate* me.

"Don't act like this is news to you," I reply flatly.

"You're right. It's not. I always knew you were heartless," he says in a biting tone.

"Right, so you can go ahead and stop flirting with me or whatever this is. It's pathetic, Shakespeare."

"We are not flirting, Declan. We're not fucking either."

I let out a clipped laugh as I pry open the can of paint and sloppily stir it up, letting the thick black contents splash onto the table and my hands.

"You made that very clear when you brought your fiancé to my house," I reply with a chuckle.

"I'm not playing games here, Dec," he says with a serious tilt of his head.

"Och," I reply with a grunt. "That's exactly what you're doing, Colin. But don't worry. I can play games too."

"I'm not—" he argues, but something in me snaps. I put a paint-covered hand on his chest to stop him. Abruptly, I shove him back, and in typical Colin fashion, he relents, obeying my push.

"Yes, you are. You're the one who came up here, thinking you could tell me what I can and cannot do, but that's not how this works and you know it. You never could stand up for yourself, so why don't you go back to doing what everyone tells you to? Like the little pushover you are.

"And listen, I don't care that you think I'm a selfish, ignorant prick. I don't care that I hurt your feelings, so now, you want to hurt mine. And I don't care that you're getting married. I'm happy for you. I am, so why don't you stop trying to pick this fight just so you can feel something with me again, because it's not going to happen. We're done, remember? We ended things seven years ago, Colin. I feel *nothing* for you anymore. You're just someone I used to know. That's it.

"Now, if you don't mind, I have a wedding to host, and you have a man to marry. So why don't you just leave me the hell alone so we can both get what we want?"

He's breathing heavily, the sound of it audible in the now-silent room. And I'll admit, I love the vitriol in his eyes. After so many years of his eager compliance, I love seeing Colin show a little teeth.

It gives me something to tame. And tame him, I will.

My hand slides slowly from the center of his chest up to his throat. Carefully, my inky black fingers encircle it, feeling his pulse against my palm.

For a moment, we're frozen in this position. He's fuming, nostrils flared and chest pumping with rage. I notice a tremor in his bottom lip, and it brings back so many memories that singe my heart like poison. Memories of vulnerable nights and passionate reunions. It really doesn't matter how much I say I don't care about Colin anymore when I can still remember how that bottom lip feels against my tongue.

His gaze briefly drops to my mouth, and I wonder if he's currently reliving the same memories. But then, he roughly shoves me away until I stumble backward, releasing his throat.

"Fuck you, Declan. You are a miserable bastard. You're just jealous that I've found someone who actually cares about me, and you'll probably die alone."

"Good," I bark through gritted teeth.

"Honestly, that's what you deserve." There's a tremble in his voice, and it hurts more than the words themselves.

There is still black paint smeared across Colin's throat and the front of his blue satin pajamas as he rushes out of my studio. My heart is pounding in my chest as anger courses through my veins.

This is only the first day of this fucking bet, and already it's a disaster, but I don't care. I'm going to get through the next six days and finally have this place to myself.

Colin was right about one thing. I am going to die alone.

With no one to disappoint me. No one to abandon me. No one to break my fucking heart.

On that thought, I grab the can of black paint and splash the entirety of it over the painting of the woman on the grass. I watch as the last six months of work fades behind the darkness. It devours every inch of the image, and I try not to feel anything as she slowly disappears.

Chapter Nine
Colin

Twelve years ago
Oxford

THE PUB IS PACKED, AS IT ALWAYS IS DURING THE LAST WEEK OF the term. Declan has a table of eight enthralled with his story: two girls on either side of him, a few guys from our year, and then me. Although I've heard this story a hundred times already, it's his favorite to tell.

"So that fucker," he says with a drunk slur, pointing at me with an unlit cigarette, "decides to take off sprinting, piss drunk and stumbling all over the place."

The table erupts with laughter, and even the girls turn toward me with smiles, but I only shake my head at Declan.

Of course, he's embellishing the story a bit. He's telling them about the time we nicked a bottle of champagne at the Eiffel Tower from a couple of tourists making out on their picnic blanket. It was the summer between years two and three when we decided to ditch our families and spend a week in the City of Light.

I didn't take off sprinting, and the police didn't chase us. But I was piss drunk. That part was accurate.

It gives me something to tame. And tame him, I will.

My hand slides slowly from the center of his chest up to his throat. Carefully, my inky black fingers encircle it, feeling his pulse against my palm.

For a moment, we're frozen in this position. He's fuming, nostrils flared and chest pumping with rage. I notice a tremor in his bottom lip, and it brings back so many memories that singe my heart like poison. Memories of vulnerable nights and passionate reunions. It really doesn't matter how much I say I don't care about Colin anymore when I can still remember how that bottom lip feels against my tongue.

His gaze briefly drops to my mouth, and I wonder if he's currently reliving the same memories. But then, he roughly shoves me away until I stumble backward, releasing his throat.

"Fuck you, Declan. You are a miserable bastard. You're just jealous that I've found someone who actually cares about me, and you'll probably die alone."

"Good," I bark through gritted teeth.

"Honestly, that's what you deserve." There's a tremble in his voice, and it hurts more than the words themselves.

There is still black paint smeared across Colin's throat and the front of his blue satin pajamas as he rushes out of my studio. My heart is pounding in my chest as anger courses through my veins.

This is only the first day of this fucking bet, and already it's a disaster, but I don't care. I'm going to get through the next six days and finally have this place to myself.

Colin was right about one thing. I am going to die alone.

With no one to disappoint me. No one to abandon me. No one to break my fucking heart.

On that thought, I grab the can of black paint and splash the entirety of it over the painting of the woman on the grass. I watch as the last six months of work fades behind the darkness. It devours every inch of the image, and I try not to feel anything as she slowly disappears.

Chapter Nine
Colin

Twelve years ago
Oxford

THE PUB IS PACKED, AS IT ALWAYS IS DURING THE LAST WEEK OF the term. Declan has a table of eight enthralled with his story: two girls on either side of him, a few guys from our year, and then me. Although I've heard this story a hundred times already, it's his favorite to tell.

"So that fucker," he says with a drunk slur, pointing at me with an unlit cigarette, "decides to take off sprinting, piss drunk and stumbling all over the place."

The table erupts with laughter, and even the girls turn toward me with smiles, but I only shake my head at Declan.

Of course, he's embellishing the story a bit. He's telling them about the time we nicked a bottle of champagne at the Eiffel Tower from a couple of tourists making out on their picnic blanket. It was the summer between years two and three when we decided to ditch our families and spend a week in the City of Light.

I didn't take off sprinting, and the police didn't chase us. But I was piss drunk. That part was accurate.

"We got away with it," I say with a shrug.

"Aye, we did," he replies. "And we had a *very* romantic evening drinking bubbly while we watched the tower sparkle."

"*Très romantique*," one of the girls says with a bad French accent.

My eyes trail downward as I remember the rest of that night, and it actually wasn't romantic at all. We got wicked headaches from the cheap champagne, got sick, and passed out in our hotel room. Nothing that I desperately wanted to happen with Declan that night happened.

It hasn't been easy, but I've successfully managed to conceal my ever-growing feelings for Declan over the years. I'd rather have him as a friend than not have him at all. And I refuse to say or do anything that could jeopardize that.

For four years, I've suffocated this attraction. For four years, I've had to listen to his sexual escapades, all with women. Four years I've had the words on the tip of my tongue, wishing I could just tell him how I feel. Four years I've held off from pursuing others. And now, we're about to graduate. He promises we'll still meet up every summer, but what if that starts to fade?

He'll find love with someone else. New friends. New adventures. A new life.

What if this is it?

What if I spend the rest of my life regretting not telling him how I feel?

Declan gets into a private conversation with one of the girls while I'm staring at the messy, beer-stained table, lost in my thoughts of regret and fear.

"So did you?" a low voice to my left asks.

Glancing up, I stare into the eyes of a handsome, well-dressed British man I know from my literature class. I think his name is Niall.

"Did I what?" I reply.

"Did you two enjoy a very romantic evening alone in Paris?"

There's a hint of a smile on his face as he lifts his beer to his lips and takes a drink. I pause for a moment, trying to gauge what is happening. Is he being serious?

"Uh...no," I stutter with a shake of my head. "He's being daft. We're just friends."

"Pity," Maybe-Niall replies. "I mean...not that you're just friends, but that you didn't have a romantic..." He shakes his head with a wince of embarrassment. "You know what, ignore me. I'm drunk and I sound like an idiot."

Okay, I think he's flirting with me.

I glance up toward Declan, but his attention is focused on the woman. I'm not used to men flirting with me, and I need my friend for guidance or something.

"You don't sound like an idiot," I reply comfortingly.

When he laughs, I let my gaze rake over his features. He's very handsome, with deep, rich eyes and perfect white teeth. Could I see myself with someone like him? If he wanted to get me naked, would I let him?

"I'm Niall," he says casually.

So I was right.

"Colin," I reply putting out my hand for him to shake.

"I know who you are," Niall says, and it makes me pause.

"We're in the same lit class," he adds in a rush when he realizes his response sounded a touch clingy.

I laugh to ease his nerves. He's obviously uncomfortable.

My laughter catches the attention of Declan across the table, and I feel his scrutinizing gaze on my face. I like the idea of *keeping* his attention, so I continue to flirt with Niall just to see Dec's reaction.

"Any plans after graduation?" he asks.

"Going back to London," I reply. "Hopefully, working on the West End if I can."

"An actor?"

I nod. "Yes. Or at least, I hope so."

"You have a face for the screen," Niall replies, and I swear he's sitting a little closer than he was a moment ago. Our eyes lock, and I let his compliment wash over me.

Has a man ever called me handsome before? Other than Declan, who I assume is usually taking a jab. The exhilaration of this man's compliment seems new as warmth and arousal floods my bloodstream. I want *more*.

"Thank you," I whisper.

"Shakespeare, you need another shot." Declan's voice bellows across the table, stealing my focus from the man I'm speaking to.

"I'll get one for you," Niall says before placing a hand on my knee.

I glare playfully at Declan as I reply to Niall. "No, Declan is saying *he* needs another shot, and he wants me to get it for him."

Declan shoots me a wink, and I grit my teeth in annoyance—although the annoyance isn't real. I could never be truly mad at him.

As I climb up from my seat at the table, Niall follows. When we reach the bar, he stands next to me.

"Does your friend always boss you around like that?" he asks, sounding worried. I let out a laugh.

"Yes, but it's not like that." I wave down the bartender and gesture for two whiskey shots. She knows us well enough by now that I don't even have to say it out loud.

"Not like what?" he asks.

"It's not like he's *abusing* me," I say. Hearing how defensive I sound gives me pause. "I mean…he's my best mate. We take the piss out of each other sometimes. If anything, he hates how much of a pushover I can be. He's always on my ass, telling me to stick up for myself more. Or tell him to fuck off when he bosses me around."

The bartender delivers our shots, and I pick them up before turning back toward our table.

"Do you?" Niall asks. "Ever tell him to fuck off?"

I laugh. "All the time."

Do I ever mean it? No.

I pass both shots to Declan, but he nudges one back toward me with his signature wink. With an eye roll, I toss it back and grimace. Then, I shake my head and return to my new friend, waiting for me with a beer in his hand.

Instead of sitting back at the table, Niall and I inch our way over to a more secluded corner.

"So what about you?" I ask. "What are your plans after graduation?"

He lets out a disgruntled sigh. "Ugh, probably go work with my dad," he says. "Engineering."

"Oh," I reply, with a raise of my brow. "You're smart then."

This makes him laugh, and I like the sound of it. He has such a nice smile, I want to make him laugh again.

"In some circles, yes, I guess," he replies.

We carry on with some more small talk, but it's so loud in here that Niall has to continually inch toward me to hear what I'm saying. When he's nearly a breath away from my face, his eyes meet mine, and a chill runs down my spine.

"What do you say we get out of here?" he asks loudly.

The two beers and one shot I've had tonight help loosen the stiffness in my bones. Niall is so handsome. Hot, even. So why does the idea of going somewhere with him, kissing him, touching him, feeling his body against mine, make me so nervous?

I'm twenty-two bloody years old. I'm too old to be a virgin. It's humiliating. At this point, I don't even know what to do. Should I tell him this? Would he be understanding? Maybe he's a virgin too.

My gaze flits over to where Declan is still talking to the girls at the table. If I leave, I should tell him or he'll worry. Then again, it's not like he's never gone home with someone. Chances are he'll end up in the bed of one of these women.

There's an unspoken rule with Declan that we don't bring people home to our room, mostly because it's so small and our beds are far too close for anything to happen in the vicinity of the other.

But I've never been in this situation before. So what am I waiting for? It's not like I can save myself for Declan. And yet I still feel a hint of guilt as I nod to Niall.

"Yeah, let's get out of here."

With a smile, he takes my hand in his and tugs me through the crowd toward the door. I keep glancing back toward Declan to be sure he isn't watching. Why? I don't know.

"Does your boyfriend know you're leaving with another man?" A cruel, deep-toned, nasally voice says from in front of Niall. I look up to find Malcolm standing there laughing with his big ugly, pockmarked face.

Malcolm has been a constant source of torment since we started our first year at uni. He's disgusting, cruel, idiotic, and I suspect a bigot as well. He hates me and Declan.

"Fuck off, Malcolm," I say as I try to move around him.

"I'm telling," he teases, although he lets me pass.

When Niall and I reach the cool air outside the pub, I shove my hands into my pockets as we walk side by side. I let him lead the way because, again, there's no chance I'm going back to my room, and I'm pretty sure he lives alone in a flat downtown. Or so I've heard.

I should probably ask where we're headed, but I feel the need to tread lightly. I don't want to ruin a good thing.

"What's wrong with that guy?" he asks as we walk.

"He's a prick," I reply.

"And you and that guy back at the table…you're not boyfriends, right?" Niall asks.

"Declan?" I reply. "No. He's my roommate, and besides, Declan is straight," I say.

Niall's eyes are on me as we walk slowly side by side. "And you are…" His voice trails.

Glancing up and looking into his eyes, I give him a smirk. "Not."

This makes him smile even wider. I think it's the first time I've ever really said it out loud, at least to somebody other than Declan. My mother still has no idea. My father doesn't care. Who else would I have to tell?

Saying it out loud to a stranger, and possibly going home with that stranger, makes it feel more real to myself. Like it's not a secret anymore. Like it's just who I am.

We walk in silence for a few moments. As I let this sink in, it feels good. I like the way this liberation feels on me. Oddly enough, I think about Declan. About telling him this later, this minutiae of a moment where I came out to someone for the first time and how good it felt.

And just as I'm basking in this new self-confidence, Niall whispers my name from out of nowhere. Suddenly, I'm being tugged into a dark alley between buildings. My heart pounds in my chest as he shoves me against the wall. I glance up into his eyes just before his lips crash against mine.

It's not my first kiss. I kissed three girls in secondary school. And for the most part, they were enjoyable, but they just were what they were. Lips pressed against lips, tongues caressing. A unique form of intimacy.

But this is different. Niall groans against my mouth, his hands digging into my sides as he grinds against me. This is more than a kiss. This is sex without being sex. This is visceral and all-consuming and deliciously sensual.

I kiss him back, not quite sure what to do with my hands. They find their way to his sides, and I leave them there while his continue to explore my body.

"God, you're so hot," he murmurs against my mouth. This little bit of praise spurs me on and awakens something inside me.

For the first time tonight, I'm fairly confident that I can do this. I might not have been wildly attracted to Niall at first. He's good-looking, but there wasn't any chemistry. Now, as he touches my body and kisses his way into my mouth, my cock begins to harden in my slacks.

And I realize—*I want this.*

That is, until Niall mutters darkly, "Get on your knees."

In just a flash of a moment, everything changes inside of me.

Suddenly, the thing I was excited about a moment ago is slipping out of my control. My eyes widen. But it's too dark and he's too close, so he can't see my face.

His large hand presses over my growing erection, and I let out a yelp because it takes me by surprise. It's an invasive touch from someone I don't know. This is hot, but it's happening too fast.

And just like that, I'm uncomfortable. But I can't say that now. I've already let him kiss me. I've already let him pull me into this alley and get me hard. I've let him touch me.

"Wait," I mutter.

I just want it to slow down, I think in my head.

I want this. I just need a moment to think.

"Come on, Colin," he groans. "We're having fun."

I kiss him again, hoping it'll make him stop talking. Hoping it'll make him stop everything, but it doesn't. I hear the clang of his belt buckle as he undoes his pants.

"Wait," I say again, but it does nothing. He continues to massage my cock, but I swat his hand away as firmly as I can without making him angry. Then I kiss him again, in a futile attempt to gain some control in this scenario, but it still doesn't work. He's frenzied and excited. Not cruel. Not taking something that he shouldn't. But it's as if he's reading everything wrong, as if he thinks I want it this way.

What is wrong with me? Why am I not ready? I'm attracted to him. Why don't I just suck his dick? I can do that much. And then it'll be done. No harm.

"I'm so hard for you," he groans against my mouth. "Please get on your knees."

"Not here," I reply, using our location as an excuse.

"There's no one here that can see us. I'll be quick. Come on."

I thought this guy was nice. And he is nice, but he's not listening to me.

That's when I utter my first "No."

I don't want my first time to be like this. I don't want any of it to be like this. Why can't I just get my head in the game? Why can't I just enjoy this?

He puts a hand on my shoulder, his eyes meeting mine through the darkness for the first time since he pulled me back here. His expression is pleading as he tries to shove me down. "I thought you liked to be bossed around."

My stomach sours at his words. Not like *this*.

"No," I say again, a bit louder this time. "I-I'm sorry. I...really just..." I'm a stuttering mess.

Gently I try to push him away as he's still struggling to get me to my knees. Panic fills my gut as I realize I might not get out of this. I might not have a choice...

From out of nowhere, a familiar voice bellows, "He said no, arsehole."

Then Niall's body is yanked away from mine. I watch in shock as he's shoved against the opposite wall, a dark-haired man towering between us.

It takes my mind time to catch up before I realize the stranger wearing an expression of pure unadulterated rage is Declan. My jaw drops, and at that very moment, he rears back a fist and pummels it against Niall's cheek.

"Declan!" I shout, watching Niall fall to the ground.

"Let's go, Colin," he says, his voice growling in anger. Declan wraps a hand around my arm and drags me away from the alley. I glance back at Niall, who is holding his nose and glaring up at me angrily.

"I knew he was your fucking boyfriend," he mutters.

"He's not," I stutter, as Declan continues to yank me away.

He's walking briskly, and I'm still trying to catch up to what just happened.

"Are you hurt?" he asks without even turning back toward me.

I'm too busy shaking my head in astonishment. "What are you doing?" I ask dumbly as he continues to drag me away.

"What do you mean? That guy was an arsehole," he grunts. "I heard you say no *twice*."

"How long were you standing there?"

"Long enough."

I tear my arm from his grip. "What the fuck is wrong with you, Declan?" I argue, now fueled with anger and maybe some adrenaline.

He spins on me, meeting my gaze for the first time, and I'm swallowed up by the raw emotion in his eyes. "What's wrong with *me*? What's wrong with *you*?" he replies. "You let men treat you like that? Forcing you to your knees in a dark alley when you tell them you don't want to? And you were going to do it, weren't you?"

"It's none of your fucking business," I shout.

There is rage in his expression as he pokes me hard in the chest. "It is my fucking business, because you're my friend. You're my best bloody friend."

"Well, a best friend would have let me have sex," I snap, but I feel like a fool even uttering those words out loud.

"Oh, Colin, you weren't going to have sex with anyone. You were going to suck that guy's cock. And then you were going to come home." With that, he resumes walking.

"And what about you?" I shout. "Why aren't you off licking pussy or getting your dick sucked?"

This makes him laugh and shake his head, pulling a cigarette from the pack in his pocket. "I should be right now," he says with bitterness. "But I was too busy coming to save your arse."

"Oh, my arse didn't need saving," I argue back.

His arms are outstretched as he turns toward me. "All right, fine, Shakespeare. Have it your way. Go back there and suck that guy's cock in the dark alley on the ground. Although if you ask me, I think you deserve better."

"Well, nobody asked you," I reply, my anger dissipating.

"Go then," he shouts.

"Fine." I stop in my tracks as Declan continues walking. Absolutely no part of me wants to go back to that alley and do anything with Niall now, let alone suck his cock. And as infuriated as I am at Declan, I don't want to stand here all night either. So, after a few moments, I relent and continue following him home.

Chapter Ten
Colin

Declan and I are both silent when we reach the residence hall, but it's a tense, spiteful silence. He slams doors, and I throw pillows, but neither of us says a word to the other.

I'm not even sure why I'm cross with him. He did get me out of a bad situation, but maybe I'm mad that I was in it in the first place.

Maybe I'm mad that my one chance of actually being with someone turned out to be a nightmare.

Maybe I'm mad that everything is so fucking easy for Declan. He has no idea what it's like. He's handsome, charming, funny. Women flock to him. He hardly has to do anything. He doesn't have to worry about coming out or being bullied or threatened at all because of who he's attracted to.

He's naturally dominant. He doesn't ever have to worry that somebody is going to take advantage of him if he's too vulnerable.

After we've both crashed into our respective beds and turned out the lights, it's obvious neither of us is going to sleep. We both toss and turn, and I wonder if he's spiraling in his head as much as I am, fuming over these facts without doing anything to actually resolve them.

After nearly an hour of this, I'm dying to speak to him, but I don't know what to say. I'm too stubborn to apologize. I'm too proud to admit that I got myself into that situation, too arrogant to thank him for helping me.

This isn't how I want the end of our term to be. It's more than the end of the term. It's the end of our entire university life. After this week, he's going back to Scotland, and I'm going to London. And other than some weak promises to see each other every summer, Declan and I will no longer live together and will no longer see each other. This is it.

"Declan," I mutter darkly in the silent room.

"What?" he replies.

"I'm sorry," I murmur. It's a lame apology, but I need to do something.

"Sorry for what, Shelby?" he asks.

"For…" My voice trails as I mull over my response. "For not thanking you for helping me."

Declan sits up on his bed, leaning on his elbow, and even through the darkness, I can feel him scrutinizing me. "You think that's why I'm mad?" he asks. "Because you didn't fucking thank me?"

"I…guess so," I stammer with uncertainty.

"Jesus, Shelby, you think that's why I'm fucking mad? No, I'm fucking mad because you put yourself in these situations, and you let these arseholes walk all over you."

I want to clarify that there have not been *arseholes*, because there's never been an opportunity other than this once. Niall was the first man I had the prospect of actually being able to sleep with, but I don't say that out loud.

"I'm mad because you never fucking stand up for yourself. You're my best goddamn mate, but I'm not going to be around to punch the idiots in alleyways for you. You should have shoved his arse across that alley and pummeled his face like I did. You should have grabbed his cock and balls and ripped them clean off his body if he threatened to bring them near you again. But you didn't, Colin. You're too fucking passive."

I sit up in bed and stare at him in anger. "You think I want to be this way?" I ask. "You think I just want to do everything everybody tells me to all the time? You think I like this?"

"I don't know," he argues.

"And this is real rich coming from you, Declan," I argue. "You're the one who's been bossing me around for four years. I follow you everywhere."

"Because you can trust me," he says as he taps his chest. "That's the fucking difference, Shelby. We make a good team because I will always take the lead with you, but I will never let you get hurt."

My mouth hangs open as I let his words sink in. "But I can't live like this, Declan," I say. "I can't be a virgin for the rest of my life. I can't hide behind you. I can't let you take care of me. At some point, I want a relationship. I want to have sex. I want to do all the things you do. Or other men do. And yeah, someday I'm probably going to lose my virginity to some bastard who takes advantage of me, and that's just going to be the way it is. But oh fucking well, maybe I'll take advantage of him too."

"No one's going to be taking advantage of you," he argues. "You can't accept anything but the best because that's what you bloody deserve. You understand me?" he says.

A smile tugs at my lip as I realize that we're fighting about how much he cares about me.

"I'm sorry you didn't get to shag anyone tonight," I say softly across the dark room.

"Och," he murmurs. "I don't care about that. I just got worried when I didn't see you in the pub anymore. I was afraid you took off with that guy. I didn't know him, but I didn't trust him. And as it turns out, my intuition was right."

Suddenly, the memory of everything with Niall comes flooding back. Was he too persistent? Should I have seen the signs sooner? How on earth am I going to do this if I don't even know how to choose the right men?

"What's wrong with me, Declan?" I ask softly, like a whisper through the night.

Declan doesn't move for a second. He just stares at me. "There ain't a fucking thing wrong with you, understand me?" he asks. "You'll meet a good guy eventually. I know it. And he'll look out for you."

"As much as you do?" I ask.

"Nobody's going to fucking look out for you as much as I do," he replies. And I laugh.

"What kind of loser graduates from uni as a virgin?" I ask.

"You haven't graduated yet," he replies. "There's still time."

This makes me crack up. "We graduate in four days, Declan. I highly doubt I'm going to meet a good person and have sex in four days."

He reclines onto his bed, his hands folded behind his head as he smiles at the ceiling. "Fine, you stubborn fool. I'll make sweet, sweet love to you so you don't graduate a virgin. Is that what you want?"

My heart pitter-patters wildly in my chest as I stare at him. That is *exactly* what I want. But I can't say it. He's teasing me, making a joke. But it's not funny because it's true, and he has no idea.

As much as I wish that offer was real, I know it never, ever will be, because sleeping with someone like Declan would be perfect. Someone I trust. Someone who puts me first. Someone who genuinely cares about me. Who knows me.

In short, too good to be true.

When I don't respond or crack a smile, Declan turns toward me. And his smile drifts slowly off of his face. For a moment, we just stare at each other. It's loaded silence. The only sound in the room is the tick-tock of the clock on the wall and the steady cadence of our breaths. I let it get this way when I should have just laughed at his joke. But I couldn't.

And now, he knows that's what I truly want. He knows my secret.

Quickly, I force a chuckle. "Yeah, right," I say. "Thanks for offering." But even my voice sounds stale and uncomfortable. Like I'm not really laughing. And I'm not really cracking a joke.

He's still staring at me. The expression on his face says he's just learned something monumental.

Before he can say anything, I lie down on the bed and turn away from him. The last thing I want is Declan's pity, not when he knows what a pathetic, lovesick loser I am.

The next day is spent sleeping off a hangover and packing. My mother calls sometime around eleven, and I answer the phone as I'm walking through the hall toward the courtyard between the buildings.

"Hello," I say.

"Oh, darling, I just went and toured your flat down in London, and it is exquisite," she says excitedly.

With a grimace, I force a smile even though she can't see me. "That's great, Mum. Thank you," I reply.

"You're going to absolutely love it. And it's only a quick five-minute walk from home. So you can visit your father and me as much as you want."

"That's wonderful."

"Oh, my love, I'm so excited to have you living back home," she croons.

"Yeah, me too," I say stiffly.

"Rebecca Park with the Cambridge Theatre called yesterday afternoon. Of course, you know your father works with her eldest son."

"Yeah, Mum, I remember."

"Well, she said that there is an open position in their spring performance, and she would love to see you audition once you get back home. And your father has already agreed to make a hefty donation to their arts fund. So I think we've got this one in the bag."

Staring down at the cobblestone ground, I grimace to myself. "You don't have to do that, Mum. Really."

"Oh, Colin, don't be so humble. This is how the world works, darling. Do you think every part and every position in the world has been cast based on merit alone? You have all of the tools to succeed, Colin. And we are going to make sure that you do. Your father and I want nothing more than to see you achieve all of your dreams."

Yes, but I want to actually achieve them.

"I know," I reply. "And I appreciate you."

"I know you do, my love. Oh, I cannot wait to see you this weekend."

"Me too," I reply.

"And I'm sorry your father has to be out of town," she adds with regret in her tone.

I wish there was a part of me that felt a hint of disappointment at this news. But it's as if all of the emotions regarding my father have already dried up. Every moment of his time spent with his other family no longer burns the way it used to. And that's sad. Because it means a part of me has died.

My mother and I are left with awkward conversation where we don't bring up topics like the fact that he has another wife and two other children, one of whom I believe is graduating from primary school this weekend, hence why he won't be available to come to my university graduation.

They are the upgrade, after all. When it comes to families, we are last year's model—no longer new or valuable to him.

"All right, Mum, I really have to get back to packing," I say, desperate to escape this conversation.

"Yes, dear, I understand. I love you, and I will see you in just a few days."

"Love you too, Mum."

After the call ends, I turn around to find Declan standing against the wall, cigarette hanging from his fingers.

"Why the long face, Shakespeare?"

I let out a sigh as I shove my hands into my pockets. "I don't know. I don't want this to end, I think."

"Hey, we could always fail all of our exams and do another year if you want," he says, making me smile.

"No. We've got to move on. We've got to grow up," I say.

"Do we have to though?" he asks.

Declan's plans after uni are essentially to continue painting and making art. And he has that privilege. His family is incredibly wealthy. His parents left him a hefty inheritance. And he technically doesn't need to work another day in his life, which is great for an artist, but I can tell it is incredibly unfulfilling for Declan.

He's like me. He wants the blood, sweat, and tears that come with any struggle in life. He's tired of being handed things and denied the opportunity to have to actually *try* for anything. We are both missing the grit and labor that comes with a normal life. And I know it's pretentious of me to complain about being so wealthy, but no one else on earth will know how this feels except for him.

"My mother has promised me that she'll get me a role in some play in the West End," I say.

Declan's eyebrows shoot upward as he stares at me. "Wow, your mother really does love you," he says, making an obscene gesture.

"I meant with money," I reply, slugging him on the shoulder. "I meant they'll make a big donation and pull some strings because somebody knows somebody, and I'll get the part, and not because I'm a good actor. It doesn't seem fair."

"It's not fair," he replies, "but nothing ever is."

Isn't that the truth? I think to myself. *Like being hopelessly in love with my best friend for four years with absolutely no chance of him ever loving me back. There's certainly nothing fair about that.*

Suddenly, out of nowhere, I remember our conversation last night and the final words Declan said to me before we fell asleep. His little joke of an offer to sleep with me so I don't graduate a virgin. Deep down, I know I should be a little offended by this. Being treated like a pity fuck. Acting like just because he's a man, I would want to sleep with him at all.

Of course, I really do want to sleep with him, but he doesn't know that. I lay awake last night, wondering and replaying scenarios in my head. Like, what if that offer was real? What if I did take it? What would that be like? Would he enjoy it? Would he hate it? Would he do it just because he cares about me?

But what if he did? What if it was incredible? The best sex of my life? Setting the bar so high that no one could ever possibly even dream of reaching it?

What if it made me love him even more? What if it made this goodbye impossible? Would it be worth it?

One passion-filled, filthy, amazing, incredible night. Would it be worth a hundred years of heartache?

Yes. One thousand percent, yes.

Chapter Eleven
Colin

DECLAN AND I DECIDE TO PICK UP DINNER ON OUR SECOND TO last night on campus. We go to a pizza place we both love that's within walking distance of the university.

On the way back, we are caught up in reminiscing about our favorite memories from the last four years. And there are so many.

It's hard to believe I am the same person who showed up here four years ago. The old me was so naive and yet so ambitious. Since then, I've gotten drunk—a lot—discovered my sexuality, and, maybe most importantly, made a best friend. It's sad to think I never truly had a best friend before Declan. It's hard to remember my life before Declan was in it.

And he's right, we do go together so well. We just fit. With Declan, I understand myself better. With him, I don't feel so misshapen and different. With him, I'm not alone.

"Remember that girl I slept with a few times back in my second year?" he asks.

"The one who stole your socks?" I ask, making Declan laugh.

"She was such a wild bitch. I liked her."

"Yeah, I know you did. You slept with her three times," I

say. I'm not entirely fond of the memory of him sleeping with anybody, but I do like to see him laugh.

"Oh yeah, I wonder what happened to her," he says.

"And your socks."

We both break out in laughter as we approach our building. From afar, I can already see Malcolm standing out front with a group of his friends, and judging by the sound of their voices and the way they're talking, I can already tell that they are piss drunk. The hairs on my neck raise in suspense.

Maybe if Declan and I just keep our heads down, and talk to each other and not to them, they'll ignore us or won't notice us.

Of course, that's not what happens. As soon as we approach with no other way to enter the building but passing by them, Malcolm shouts at me from the side of his huddle of friends.

"Oh, it's the two lovebirds!" he calls. "Aren't you two so fucking cute together? What are you going to do without each other after this school year, eh? You two gonna live together?"

"Ignore him," I mutter under my breath. Naturally, Declan doesn't listen to me.

"You're just jealous, Malcolm! That you can't have a piece of this," Declan taunts, gesturing to his body.

I roll my eyes as I tug him toward the door. "I said ignore him."

"Oh fuck him, why do I have to ignore him? He's the ignorant bastard." He says it a little too loudly, and we're so close to the door when Malcolm shouts at my friend.

"What the fuck did you call me?" Malcolm bellows as he barrels toward us. He gives Declan a quick shove and something inside of me burns like I've never felt it burn before.

"He said you're an ignorant bastard," I bark back at him.

Malcolm stares down at me angrily. "You better watch it, you little bitch," he snarls. "I'll knock you out right here."

The only thing I have going for me right now is that he's drunk and I'm sober. I'm not taller than him, stronger than him, or tougher than him. I've never thrown a punch in my entire life, and I'm fairly certain it would only take one from him to completely knock me out forever.

But I'm fueled by hatred. I *hate* that he calls me names. I *hate* that he put his hands on Declan. I *hate* that he thinks he can do whatever he wants, and I'll just do what he says.

"Shelby, let's go," Declan mutters lowly from my side. Suddenly, it's him pulling me toward the door instead of the other way around.

"No. Fuck this guy," I say, staring up at Malcolm. "He's pushed us around long enough, Declan."

"Because you're a couple rich little bitches," Malcolm adds, shoving me in the chest. "What the fuck are you going to do about it?"

My hand balls into a fist and I don't think. I just swing.

I put everything I have into that punch. I just see him pushing Declan again. I see him calling me a sissy boy and other disgusting names I've heard him throw around in the hallways. I didn't need to tell him my secret. It was as if he already knew. He could see it on my face, and I hate him for that.

My fist connects with Malcolm's cheek, and I can tell immediately by the look on his face that I've taken him by surprise. So I don't give him a moment to react. I thrust my knee up into his gut and throw him toward the ground. He barely stumbles, and I hardly make it away.

Declan grabs my arm, and we take off in a quick sprint away from the group of guys. They are wild and howling with anger, chasing us as we run. Adrenaline courses through my veins, making everything blurry and terrifying.

My hand throbs. It hurts so bad I think I might have broken it, but I don't care. I like the pain. It's exhilarating, reminding me that I'm alive, that I'm not the same boy I was four years ago. That I don't have to be silent and acquiescent anymore. My heart is thudding in my chest as I gulp for each breath, running faster than I've ever run in my life.

Beside me, Declan's footsteps echo mine, and when I glance over to the side to see his face, instead of finding fear or surprise or shock, I see him smile at me.

There are not a lot of places to hide on the campus this late at night, when most of the buildings are closed and everything is pretty quiet, but I still hear the footsteps of the guys behind us, so we keep running. We have a good gap between us.

As we round the gymnasium, I'm confident that we're far enough away from Malcolm and his friends to stop running, so I pull Declan toward the door. By some miracle, it opens. The enormous room is still and silent, and in the center is a large empty pool. The lights beneath the surface are still on, reflecting the calm blue water on the walls with the smell of chlorine in the air.

Breathless, I stumble into the room and follow Declan as he scurries out of sight of the window. There is a thin sheen of sweat on my skin and pulsing adrenaline in my veins. Suddenly, Declan roughly fists the front of my shirt as he shoves me against the brick wall, the impact punching the air from my lungs.

He's standing so close, his face just inches from mine as I wait for him to shout and berate me for doing something so stupid. His eyes are wired and frantic as he stares at me, our chests heaving breathlessly in sync.

Then, a smile spreads across his face, taking me by surprise. "That was fucking incredible," Declan says with a laugh as he shakes me. "*You* are fucking incredible."

I laugh in return. That wasn't what I expected, but I'm not complaining. In fact, I'm loving how near he is to me right now. His breath is on my face. If I wanted to, I could just reach out and kiss him—and I do want to.

I'm too struck by this moment to care that there are men still chasing us or that my hand is probably broken. Because Declan is staring into my eyes with a feverish expression on his face.

Feeling bold, I grab his shirt and tug him closer, wondering if he even notices.

"I can't believe I just did that," I say.

"I swear to God, I could kiss you right now," he replies excitedly.

I know he means it as a joke, but still, my heart nearly explodes out of my chest. Hot, liquid arousal courses through my veins. Then he grabs me on either side of my face, and I respond only with a smile as he presses his lips chastely against mine.

It's a nothing kiss. A friendly kiss. The kind of kiss you give a family member.

But it's enough for me.

His lips are there for only a second before he pulls away. He doesn't move far.

I watch the shifting motion of his Adam's apple as he swallows, and we're still both panting, except now I'm panting from that kiss and his nearness. His hands are still on my face and my fingers are still wrapped around the soft fabric of his shirt.

Everything I want is in reach, and it feels reckless and dangerous. But after punching that rugby-playing bastard, I feel invincible. It has me thinking wild thoughts. Like...if Declan would just let himself kiss me for real, then maybe he would feel how good this is.

"Do that again," I whisper breathlessly. I hardly recognize my own voice. I'm not the kind of guy who demands what he wants.

But Declan doesn't hesitate. He crashes his lips against mine once more, but this time instead of a chaste, lifeless kiss, he holds his lips there before gently massaging mine with his. It's tentative at first.

It almost feels as if we're drunk, although we haven't had a drop to drink all night. He's my best friend and we've known each other for four years and now he's *kissing* me.

As amazing as this is for me, I'm dying to know what it's like for him. Does he want me to slip my tongue through his lips to taste his? Does he want me to grind against him, kiss his neck?

I will do it all.

I'll do anything.

After the long close-mouthed kiss, he rests his forehead against mine. Even though our run is long past over, we're still panting as one.

Finally, he whispers in a sexy plea, "Colin."

The sound of my name on his lips sparks a fire in my groin.

"What?" I whisper.

"What's happening?"

"I don't know," I say. "But you should kiss me again."

Declan's gaze finds mine as if he's searching for answers. His eyes trail down to my lips, and I swear I see desire in them.

But instead of kissing me, he just whispers, "You know, I was thinking," he says. "About what I said last night, about my offer, and it was a joke."

At his words, the heat inside of me withers and dies. He's letting me down. He's telling me that I should stop wanting this. That I should have never looked at him the way I did last night.

Then he continues. "But maybe it doesn't have to be a joke," he says. "Because I would. I will. I'll do that for you. I'm not afraid of—"

My mind is a mess, confused and turned on and hopeful, so I just do what I have to in order to get his mouth back on mine.

"Declan," I say, interrupting him. "Will you just kiss me again, please?"

He's still hesitant for a moment as his eyes trail back up to mine, and when they meet, he gives me a gentle smirk.

Then, instead of violently crashing his mouth against mine, he leans in and takes my lips in a delicate, passionate kiss. And it's more than the chaste pressing of skin together. He licks my bottom lip ever so gently with his tongue. My lips part, and the moment our tongues touch, sliding together in delicious delicate friction, I nearly melt to the floor.

I am assaulted by blazing-hot arousal. It strikes like lightning. The feel of his lips. The sight of his smirk. The reminder that *this is Declan*.

I let out a humiliating whimper, but it only seems to urge him on. He kisses me deeper and holds me tighter.

My grip on his shirt relaxes and my hands glide softly along his rib cage toward his back. Once I've met his shoulders, I move my fingers to the front, cascading over his chest, brushing against his nipples and then up to his neck. I wind my arms around him so I can pull him closer.

He deepens the kiss, nibbling on my lips, licking his way into my mouth, groaning as he does. His body is pressed against mine now and I try to memorize every rigid plane, every small detail, every ridge, the way his pulse feels, and the way his kiss tastes.

It's a dream I don't want to wake up from.

When something hard brushes against my hips, my body delights in excitement. He's hard. He's hard *for me*.

As Declan kisses me, I open my eyes, watching him as he devours my mouth, and I realize that he's not doing this for me. He's not kissing me because I asked him to. His eyes are closed, and he's lost in the passion of it. He's doing this because he *wants* to, because he feels what I feel.

I let out a groan as I pull him closer, wrapping my arms tighter around his neck and letting him devour every inch of my lips and my tongue and my face. I could stand here and let him kiss me for days—for *years*.

But all too soon, we hear the stomp of feet outside and we tense. No matter how dreamlike this kiss is, it won't protect us from the reality that waits for us outside those doors.

Declan pulls away, seemingly breathless and caught up in the moment as he glances toward the exit. He puts his body between me and the door, blocking me from the threat, and it makes my heart soar even more. We wait tensely, praying that no one follows us, that no one finds us here like this, that we can just be alone and be *us*. That's all I want.

But after a few moments, when it seems safe and like we truly are alone, Declan moves out of my reach. He turns away, staring at the pool and rubbing at the back of his neck—then shifting himself a little in his pants.

I'm still hanging on to that kiss as if I'm suspended over a cliff and it's all that's keeping me alive. I'm reeling in disbelief. That really just happened.

I want more. I want everything. I'd give him my body right now if he asked for it. He could do anything he wants to me. He has to know that.

He just offered, didn't he? He said that I could have his body if I wanted it. But did he mean it? Even after that kiss, I don't want to be a pity fuck to Declan. Does he want it, truly?

The only sound in the room is our heavy breaths as we wait for this moment to return to normal. To my utter shock, Declan reaches behind himself to grab his shirt and yanks it clean off of his body. My jaw drops.

"What are you doing?" I whisper.

"What do you think?" he replies.

I'm silently staring at him, waiting for anything to make sense, when he shucks off his pants and then his shoes. Then he's standing before me in nothing but his briefs, looking back at me with a coy smile.

"I think we need a little cooling off, don't you?" he asks. Then with a wink in my direction, he turns toward the pool and dives headfirst into it. When he pops back up, I laugh.

"You're out of your mind," I say.

"Aye. But we only have a few more days together, Shelby, so take your clothes off. Let's go swimming."

Smiling down at him, I do as he says, not hiding the fact that I am still sporting a pretty hard erection. But I don't want to hide it from him anymore. I want him to see it, even if he never touches it, even if we never go through with his little offer. I want him to see this, because *this is me*. I'm attracted to him, and I might be for the rest of my life.

And for the first time, I realize I'm okay with that.

Chapter Twelve
Colin

Water drips from Declan's brows, and I can't take my eyes off it. He's hoisted himself out of the pool and is sitting on the edge while I continue to float calmly in the deep end.

That kiss we shared has put me under some sort of spell. He's given me more than my imagination ever could. Now I know the taste of his lips and the feel of his tongue against mine. These memories will be locked in my mind forever, and I can access them whenever I'd like.

I don't think I've ever been more content.

He seems at ease too, not erratic and uncomfortable from unexpectedly making out with his male best friend. I don't know what that kiss meant for him, and I'm not sure I want to know. I'm blissfully unaware and would rather keep it that way than learn that he hated it or only did it for me.

"I can't ever go back to our room now," I say with a laugh, remembering those rugby oafs who chased us into this gymnasium.

He glances around at the large room before saying, "This looks cozy. We can just sleep here until we graduate."

I laugh as I use my arms to quietly paddle back toward where he's sitting. "I was worried about not doing a single sexual thing before I graduated. Now I'm afraid I won't do a single sexual thing before I *die*."

"Ach," Declan huffs. "I won't let him hurt you. You're not going to die."

"Easy for you to say," I reply as I reach the edge.

"All right, fine, Shakespeare," he says, splashing me with a kick of his foot. "What exactly would you like to do before you die?"

My fingers grip the edge of the pool as I stare up at him. "What do you mean?"

"If you're going to perish at the hands of an angry rugby player tonight, what would you like to do before you die?"

"You mean sex?" I ask, my throat feeling suddenly thick with nerves.

"Aye."

My eyes rake over his half naked form for a moment as I let that question settle. Is he being serious? If I say what I want, is he implying he'll give it to me?

"Well," I reply before clearing my throat. "I'd like to suck a dick at least once."

Declan leans back on his hands, nodding as he stares off into the distance. He looks as if he's contemplating something. Eventually, his eyes meet mine.

"All right."

My lips part as my brows pinch inward. "All right, what?"

"All right, you can…you know…" He glances down quickly at his own dick before looking back at me.

I let out a cackle that echoes in the near-silent confines of the empty gymnasium. "It's not a joke, Dec. I'm being serious."

"So am I," he argues. "And I'm not just saying this to get my dick sucked. You can trust me. I'll tell you exactly what to do so when you hook up with some guy after uni, you know you'll be good at it."

"I don't want my first time to be a pity fuck with a straight guy," I reply.

"Who said I was straight?" he asks, sounding offended.

I make a sound somewhere between a laugh and a gasp, assuming he's messing with me. But he's not wearing a smirk. He's just staring at me, the confusion on his face.

"But...you've only been with women," I say, trying to gauge if he's having a laugh or not.

"So?" He shrugs.

My mind is spiraling as I stare at him. Tonight feels as if it's flipped my life on its head, mixing up fantasy and reality. For four years, I kept my feelings for Declan a secret because I assumed he was straight, but I never bothered to even ask.

Is this real?

"Listen, Shelby," he says, using my last name, which is something he does if he's serious but not dire enough to call me Colin. "You don't have to do anything you don't want, but I'm offering. If you don't want to graduate from uni totally inexperienced, you don't have to."

"No, I..." My voice trails as I realize what I'm about to say. Am I really about to do this with him? My best friend. The man I've lusted after for four years. This might actually happen.

"I want to," I murmur.

His eyes darken as he stares down at me. Something like lust washes over his features. And I can barely breathe with how hard my heart is pounding in my chest.

"Then, come here," he commands.

A flash of blazing-hot arousal courses down my spine. I force myself to swallow before swimming toward him. His legs are dangling in the water as he sits on the edge of the pool, leaning back on his hands and staring down at me.

The water is shallow enough here that I can stand, so I move to my toes. I'm stationed between his knees, my head nearly reaching his chest. It's the perfect height so that I only have to glance down and see the outline of his cock inside his wet black briefs.

"Are you sure about this?" I ask without looking into his eyes.

His hand takes my face under my chin, and he forces it up so we're staring at each other. "If you want it, I want it."

"I want it," I whisper.

"Then take it," he replies. Releasing my chin, he leans back again.

My blood feels impossibly warm as I move my fingers to his body. With shaking hands, I ease the elastic band of his underwear down, revealing his half-hard cock resting against his lower stomach.

I nearly panic, swim away, and announce that I can't do this. But I want it. This isn't some random bloke from the pub in a dark alleyway. It's Declan. The person I trust most in this world. He's giving me something I want—I just have to have the nerve to take it.

For a moment, I just stare at his cock, taking in the sight. Like me, he's uncut. But he's thicker than I am, with a bulging head and prominent veins running down the shaft. And he's not even fully erect yet.

With my mouth watering, I lean down and hesitantly run the surface of my tongue along the length of him. On an exhale, I hear Declan moan.

"That was nice. Do it again," he mumbles.

So I do. Slowly and more assertively this time, I rub my taste buds delicately against his cock, feeling it harden under my tongue. When I reach the tip, I close my lips over the head before pulling away again.

He lets out a little grunt, and I'm ravenous for more sounds of pleasure like that.

Finally feeling bold enough, I wrap my hand around his cock and delight in the feel of it in my grasp. Like mine, it's smooth and warm to the touch. And since I know what I like, I slide the hood down and squeeze my fist around the head of his cock, twisting on the upstroke.

Declan hisses through his teeth as his legs writhe around me. "Aye, that feels good."

Nervously, I glance up at him, and the moment our eyes meet, it's electric. He's into this, and it gives me the courage to keep going.

Opening my mouth, I ease his cock along my tongue. Once he's reached the back of my throat, I close my lips around him and suck. Declan groans loudly, and I glance up to see him hanging his head back in pleasure.

"Like that, Shelby," he murmurs raspily.

I really have no idea what I'm doing, so his praise and guidance are exactly what I need. Not to mention, the sight of him in the throes of pleasure because of me turns me on more than anything ever has before.

I just try to think about what I would like, so I wrap my hand around the base of his shaft and bob my head up and down, sucking harder on each stroke.

"Fuck," he groans, drawing the word out in a gravelly, gasping sound.

My movements become more intense with each groan, grunt, and whimper that leaves his mouth. His pleasure is my goal, and I can't believe how good it feels for *me* to make him feel good. My cock is throbbing under the water, and I can't stop the way it thrusts subtly against the wall.

"Shelby, slow down," he mutters with a pained expression.

I do as he says, letting my lips linger at the head of his cock. And when I feel a drop of his salty precum hit my tongue, I nearly come in my briefs.

"Give me a little teeth," he requests, looking down at me with his pupils blown wide.

Confused, I gently scrape my teeth along the length of his shaft. Out of the corner of my eye, I see his legs break out in goose bumps, and he sucks an agonized breath through his teeth.

"Fuck, that hurts," he groans, so I quickly pop my head off and gaze up at him in shock.

"I'm s-sorry," I stammer.

With a sexy smile, he buries a hand in my hair and leads my mouth back to his cock. "No, I liked it. Do it again."

Unsure, I lean back down and take him back into my mouth,

letting him feel a hint of pain from my teeth again. He moans louder than ever and thrusts his hips up into my mouth.

"Fuck yes, Shelby. Now, make me come."

Lost to the sound of his pleasure, I stroke his cock with my tongue and lips, picking up speed, eager to hear more of his praise.

I'm so close to the edge myself as Declan fists my hair, writhing and thrusting. My cheeks hollow out as I move, sucking harder and harder. All I want is to feel his release on my tongue. This power over him is intoxicating.

My hips continue thrusting, searching for friction. With one husky grunt from him, I lose control. My body erupts with euphoria, my cock pulsing as I hum around him. The warmth of my own release fills my briefs, and I shudder with a hint of embarrassment.

"Did you just come?" he asks breathlessly.

Without pulling my mouth from his shaft or stopping my movement, I nod with a wince.

"Goddamn, that's hot," he replies.

The hand in my hair moves to the back of my neck, and he grips me affectionately as he guides my head down on his cock so he's fucking my throat. With a thunderous, fatal-sounding groan, he tenses.

His dick is impossibly hard as he releases. Warm, salty jets of his cum coat my tongue and throat. I don't want to take my mouth off of him, so I do my best to swallow, but it quickly starts to choke me.

I cough and spurt, his seed dripping into the pool water. My hand is still wrapped around his shaft, stroking him through his orgasm.

With his grip still on my neck, he melts onto the floor. Releasing his cock, I press my face to his bare thigh and try to force my heart to slow down.

"That was pretty incredible," he says breathlessly.

The praise makes me smile against his leg. There's not a sensible thought in my head. I'm just swimming in euphoria, literally. I just gave my first blow job to my best friend and came without even touching myself. Is this what heaven feels like?

Declan seems to be caught in the same postorgasm haze. After a few moments, he sits up. I lift my face from his lap and dare to look into his eyes. To my relief, it's not uncomfortable or weird. There's a part of me that fears everything between us will be different now, but judging by the look in his eyes, we're still us.

"So…?" he asks.

"What are you looking at me for?" I reply. "I should be asking you…how did I do?"

"Bloody good for your first time, Shakespeare." Casually, he tucks his softening cock back into his briefs.

I grin proudly to myself.

"But don't do the teeth thing to other guys," he adds with a furrowed brow.

My face falls as I stare up at him in shock. "What? Why?"

"Because most guys *hate* that."

I splash him with an armful of water. "What the hell, Dec?" I shout. "You were supposed to teach me how to give a *good* blow job!"

He laughs as he kicks water back in my direction. "Sorry, but I'm a sick fuck, and that's just what *I* like." With a shrug, he climbs from the floor and walks over to where our clothes lie discarded.

"Ugh," I groan, rolling my eyes.

"But if you ever suck my dick again, now you know," he says, slipping his shirt over his head. "I like a little pain."

Shaking my head, I climb out and grab my pants from the floor. "What is wrong with you?"

He laughs. "Hey, you should be thanking me. Now, you won't graduate completely inexperienced."

I shove him on the shoulder. "Oh yes, thank you for letting me bite your dick."

He's laughing loudly now. "You're welcome."

There's no use fighting my smile as I put on the rest of my clothes. The blow job was amazing, but I'm mostly just content to see that nothing between us has changed. I haven't lost my best friend, and that's what really matters most.

Chapter Thirteen
Colin

"Smile, my love!" my mum says excitedly as she snaps a picture of me holding my diploma in front of our university. There's a crowd around us of parents and their graduates. I lost track of Declan somewhere in the chaos of walking across the stage and then out to the common area to meet our families.

I think his sister is here—at least, I hope she is. I hate to think about him being alone.

My mother wraps an arm around my waist and reaches onto her tiptoes to kiss me on the side of the head. "I'm so proud of you," she murmurs.

"Thanks, Mum."

"Our driver has already picked up your things at the residence hall, so if you're ready, darling, let's get you home where you belong." She loops her arm through mine and tugs me toward the car park.

I glance around, seeking Declan. I can't leave without at least saying goodbye. "Mum, I need to find a friend. Can I meet you at the car?"

"Of course," she replies sweetly. As she releases my arm, she walks toward the lot, and I take off in search of my best friend.

Everything between Declan and me has been so normal and comfortable since the night at the pool—or as I'm referring to it, the greatest night of my life. I still can't believe that happened, and our friendship has only improved because of it. Now, the idea of being without him for months on end has me feeling melancholy and nostalgic. If I could start these four years over again, I would.

When Declan is nowhere in the crowd, I decide to go looking for him in our room. My side of the room is empty when I get there, but his is still packed in boxes on the floor by his bed.

And he's lying on it, still wearing his graduation robe and sketching in his book with the familiar black charcoal.

"Hey, Shakespeare," he says with a lopsided grin when he sees me enter. "I thought you left."

My mouth is set into a straight line, and a blank expression is on my face as I fight the emotion bubbling to the surface. Is that all he's going to give me? After all this time? Does he feel nothing?

"I wouldn't leave without saying goodbye to you," I mutter.

His eyes cast from the drawing to my face. "I don't care for goodbyes."

"I know you don't," I reply. "Did your sister show up?"

"Aye," he mumbles focusing back on his sketch.

He's shutting me out. I can tell, and I've known him long enough to know this is just how Declan reacts to tough moments like this.

Closing the door on the last four years is hard for me too.

Entering the room, I sit on my bed and watch him sketch for a moment. I just want to soak up the last moments of this time together before it's over.

"Every summer, Declan," I mumble softly.

"I know," he replies despondently.

"And maybe more if we have time. You know you're only a few hours away from me."

"Aye."

The longer he refuses to look at me or give me the attention I crave, the more tense I feel inside. I want to scream at him. I'd like to take that sketchbook and toss it across the room.

Instead, I act on impulse.

Lunging from my bed to his, I shove the book out of his hand and drape myself on his bed at his side. With his arm under my head, I wrap mine around his middle and hug him close.

"What the bloody hell are you doin'?" he asks, stunned by my erratic behavior. His body is stiff against mine.

"Stop ignoring me," I mutter into his chest.

"You are such a slut for attention," he growls, but after a moment he relaxes his body, wrapping me up into his arms and acting as if this is a normal thing for best friends to do.

We lie there for a moment as he holds me, and it doesn't feel sexually charged or strange at all. Maybe this isn't what other friends do, but I think Declan and I are just closer than any other friends are. Our relationship is special.

"Every summer," he says softly. The vibration of his voice hums against my ear.

"Every summer," I repeat.

"You'll be busy becoming a star in the West End, and I'll be... Well, I don't know what the fuck I'll be doing, but I'll keep myself occupied until we see each other again."

"You'll be making exceptional art and getting featured in galleries and museums," I say, staring at the wall as he looks up at the ceiling.

"You're just saying that," he replies.

"No, I'm not."

"Next time we see each other, you can tell me about all the stellar blow jobs you've been giving," he adds with a tight laugh. Something in me hardens at the sound.

I don't want to experience that with anyone else, but I can't tell him that. We are just friends after all.

Instead, I pick my head up to look at him. He turns his gaze toward me until we're staring at each other, only a few inches apart. Immediately, the mood between us changes.

I keep thinking about that kiss, wondering if I could kiss him again. Would it change anything? Would it ever make me more than his friend?

Time stills as we gaze into each other's eyes. Is he thinking the same thing I am? Does the memory of my lips haunt his dreams the way his do mine?

But if I kiss him now, then what? It can't go any further. Not here and not now. We will say our goodbyes and wait another two months before we see each other again, and only for a week.

If I learned anything from that night in the gymnasium, it's that Declan will always look at me like a friend. And I'd only be setting myself up for heartbreak to want anything more.

So, when I feel him lean in, I pull away.

"I'll see you in two months," I whisper. He looks stunned for a moment.

Then he quickly composes himself.

"Yeah, see you in two months," he replies, clearing his throat.

I climb from the bed and swallow down the emotion building in my throat.

When I take a step toward the door, Declan sits up in a rush. "Shakespeare, wait."

Turning around, I stare at him expectantly. He picks up his sketchbook and violently rips a page out. Then, with inky black fingers, he holds it out to me.

As I take the charcoal sketch, the pain in my throat gets worse. It stings relentlessly. And when I glance down at the drawing, I release the dam holding everything back.

A tear fills my lashes as I stare at the drawing on the page.

It's me.

I'm laughing, my eyes crinkled at the edges as I look off into the distance. It's so impressive and lifelike. I've never seen anything like it. It's not the proper and composed version of me, but the happy, relaxed version of me that matches how I feel inside. Somehow, Declan always seems to see the real me.

"This is incredible, Dec," I whisper, blinking a tear down my cheek.

I'm embarrassed for being so emotional. But I know he won't tease me for it.

"Please don't say that," he groans, clearly uncomfortable with the praise.

"Fine," I reply with a sad laugh. "It's terrible."

"Much better," he replies with a despondent smile.

"It's really, really awful," I add, smirking at him through my tears.

"Well, you've got a pretty face. Makes my job easy."

I soak up his compliment because I like the way it tastes. Hearing him call me pretty. Drawing me to look so handsome. I've never wanted anything more in my life.

Clutching the drawing to my chest, I wipe the moisture from my face. "Goodbye, Declan."

"Bye, Shakespeare," he replies softly.

His eyes don't lift from the empty page in his sketchbook as I back out of the room. He never glances up at me once as I go, which should make me sad, but to be honest, it gives me reassurance.

Declan doesn't want to say goodbye because I mean something to him, and I've never wanted to mean anything to anyone as much as I want to with him.

Chapter Fourteen
Declan

Five days until the wedding

"Where should we put these, Mr. Barclay?"

I spin around to find two young women each holding a box of crystal vases that I have never seen in my life.

"How the fuck should I know?" I reply, wincing as soon as I hear the words leave my mouth.

The girls stare at me wide-eyed and terrified, the boxes practically shaking, when a soft hand touches my arm and a warm voice says, "On the tables in the dining room should be fine."

I turn to find Blaire beaming politely at the trembling employees. As soon as they scurry off, I let out a sigh and rub my forehead.

"Thank you," I mutter with appreciation.

"It's fine," she says with a laugh. "They're just used to Anna, but I can handle you."

When she gives me a wink before going back to folding ivory tablecloths, I feel like the world's biggest dickhead.

"I'll be honest," I say, helping her fold another tablecloth. "I don't know what the fuck I'm doing."

"It shows," she replies with a smile.

"My sister gave me this bloody list of things to do, and I have no fucking clue how I'm supposed to do all of this in five days. Arrange the flowers. Finalize the menu. Pick the cake. Press the linens. This is ridiculous. All for a fucking wedding."

Blaire laughs to herself, and I glance over, momentarily admiring her sweet smile. I never should have skipped out on her after that night we hooked up. But I was drunk and an idiot.

And what am I even saying? What would be the point of prolonging things? The sex was good. We had fun. What else is there to do? No one wants me for a boyfriend.

Although if she'd like to rendezvous again...

"Can I be honest?" she says, turning toward me with the white fabric draped over her arms.

"Of course," I reply, expecting her to finally give me hell for the way I treated her.

"I hate weddings."

A laugh slips through my lips as I'm flooded with relief. "Trust me, I agree. They're the worst."

"Right?" she says. "So much work and hassle and this need for everything to be perfect."

Suddenly, my attraction to this woman just multiplied.

"I'm forced to live here because this is my family, but why on earth do you work here if you hate weddings so much?" I ask.

She walks the tablecloths over to a table and drops them with the rest. "I need this job," she says, "and I love working with Anna, but I could never tell her how awful this is for me. She and I have gotten close, and I consider her a good friend. And she *loves* this stuff."

Crossing my arms over my chest, I lean against a table, appreciating Blaire for the first time. "I thought you were going to tell me what a royal arsehole I was for skipping out on you that night."

She throws her head back and laughs. "Are ye kidding? I wasn't mad at all. I just didn't want your sister to find out."

"Oh God, me neither," I reply with a sigh of relief.

"Listen, I'm no romantic. That night was fun, but I probably should be more careful not to shag the boss's brother in the future." She keeps her voice low and makes an adorable face that makes me smile.

"I think I love you," I say with sarcasm in my tone that has her chuckling and smacking me playfully on the arm. "No, seriously, I think you are the female version of me."

This has us both laughing when I feel a pair of eyes on me from the doorway. Blaire notices them first, cutting her laughter short as her eyes dash over to the man watching us.

Turning, I find Colin standing there with a serious expression on his face. I give Blaire a nod before spinning to face him.

"Mr. Shelby, can I help you with something?"

Last night's argument is still fresh in my mind. I slept with the image of his vicious expression right at the forefront all night. The black paint smeared across his skin. The fiery red blush of anger on his cheeks.

Today, he appears calmer but no less hateful.

"Pierce has put me in charge of picking the cake flavor," he says as he shoves his hands into his pockets.

"Well, aren't you so obedient," I reply with a coy smirk.

His jaw clenches shut as he rolls his eyes. "Never mind," he mutters as he turns away. "I'll find someone else."

I let out a huff. "Follow me, Shakespeare," I say with an authoritative tone as I lead the way to the kitchen. According to the binder, the cake samples were dropped off this morning and are ready for tasting.

I don't need to turn around to know Colin is following behind me. He's never been able to resist following my orders.

And when I reach the large kitchen—not my smaller, more private one—there is a team prepping food for today. I pull open the fridge to find a box from the bakery with an assortment of cake samples arranged on an ornate silver tray.

I pull the tray out and drop it onto the table near the window.

"Here you go. Just let me know which one you pick when you're done."

With that, I turn my back on Colin and make my way toward the door. I'd much rather continue my conversation with Blaire than be in here with someone who hates me.

But I don't even make it to the door. The sight of Colin holding that fork alone with an array of beautifully decorated mini cakes pulls at heartstrings I haven't felt in a long time.

He's wearing a miserable expression as he sticks his fork in the first tiny cake.

"Shouldn't your fiancé be here to do this with you?" I ask with a sigh.

"Pierce is on a strict diet for a role. He won't be eating any cake," he replies coldly.

"He won't eat any cake at his own wedding?" I ask, but Colin doesn't respond. He just takes another bite of the red and white sponge.

Seeing him sitting alone feels unnatural to me. All through uni, it was my job to protect him. To make sure that no one ever treated him poorly and that he never had to feel like shit.

That's not my job anymore—he made sure of that.

And yet...I can't just leave him to do this alone.

I drop the leather binder on the table with a loud *thunk*. Then, I pick up the second fork and take a seat across from him.

His light brows pinch inward as he glares at me. "What are you doing?"

"I'm doing my job," I reply flatly. Then, I dig my fork into the yellow cake with the tiny lemon on top. Colin watches me skeptically as I chew, but when the tangy lemon zest hits my tongue, I practically melt into the seat.

"Jesus fucking Christ, that's good," I mumble around the cake in my mouth.

The corner of his lip lifts before he quickly forces it away. Then, he tries the lemon cake for himself. Once the flavor explodes on his tongue, he has the same reaction. The anger dissipates as he hums with pleasure.

"That is good," he murmurs.

"How was the red velvet?" I ask.

He gives a casual shrug. "Nothing special."

"We need something to cleanse our palates," I say as I rise from the table and find a bottle of whisky and two glasses in the cupboard. Colin's head tilts in scrutiny when he sees it.

"What?" I ask as I pour the amber liquid into each glass.

"I think water would have worked fine," he replies.

"What's water?"

He shakes his head but doesn't protest as he takes a slow small sip.

After the lemon cake, we both try the chocolate, and agree that it's good but doesn't blow us away.

"What about this one?" he asks, poking the light-purple icing.

"That's..." I say, finding the flavor on the chart they provided. "Oh, that's lavender honey. You hate lavender."

He sneers at the cake before pushing the piece away. "I do hate lavender."

Instead, he takes a bite of the vanilla, and I try the raspberry. Things grow quiet between us for a moment as we eat the stupid tiny cakes. I feel him watching me with a scrutinizing gaze.

"You remember that?" he asks.

I shrug. "You'd be surprised how much I remember."

Taking another bite, he doesn't say anything, obviously in contemplation.

So I add, "You're not as inconsequential to me as I was to you."

He drops his fork. "That's not fair."

"Nothing ever is," I reply without looking at him.

"You act like I didn't try, Declan. Like I didn't *beg you*."

"You're right," I argue. "You asked for something I couldn't give you, and to punish me for that, you did the one thing that would hurt me the most. You left. Forever."

His mouth sets in a thin line as he shakes his head. "I asked for what I deserved."

We're in the middle of a cold stare-down when approaching footsteps pull us out of it. "What's going on in here?" Pierce asks as he enters the room, where Colin and I are sitting across from each other.

Each of the little cakes on the tray has been picked at, and two forks lie among the mess. The only thing thicker than that frosting is the tension between us.

Pierce massages Colin's shoulders, forcing him to smile up at his fiancé. I glare down at the half-eaten desserts and try to swallow down the ire rising in my throat.

"So?" Pierce asks. "Which one won?"

"I think...the lemon," Colin replies with forced cheer.

Lifting my head, I smile up at him and then up at Pierce. "Definitely. The lemon was sublime. Very good choice."

Then I scribble *lemon* down on the notepad in the leather binder.

"Sounds great," Pierce says excitedly.

With that, I stand from the table. "I have a meeting with the florist," I say. "But if you need anything from me..." I level my gaze on Colin as I add, "Anything at all, please let me know."

He looks away as I hurry from the room, leaving the two men alone with their ridiculous fucking cakes.

I don't know what got into me back there or why I was so intent on arguing with Colin, but I really need to get my head in the game. There's no point in making this wedding any harder than it already is.

I don't care that he's my old friend. And I don't care that we crossed a line seven years ago. I won't let this wedding be ruined by deeply buried resentment. I refuse to lose this bet because of some hard feelings.

Colin doesn't matter to me anymore. The only thing that does matter to me is my future, my life, my peace. It's all I have to protect now, at all costs.

Chapter Fifteen
Declan

The cake-tasting incident with Colin stays with me all afternoon. He and Pierce have gone into the city for the rest of the day to do some shopping for the wedding, and I'm too worked up and irritated to relax.

I've crossed off everything I can on that stupid fucking list of Anna's, so now I want to let off some steam.

I head up into my studio, my hands moving erratically as I select a playlist from my phone and connect it to the Bluetooth player. Classical music is blaring so loud I can't hear myself think, which is exactly what I want.

All day, I feel like I've been plagued with memories. Remembering moments from uni or one of our summer trips afterward. Tender moments. Sexy moments. Funny moments. All of them are like a virus, only making me feel like shit. I'm mourning the loss all over again, and it vexes the hell out of me.

Why does it have to hurt so much when a friendship ends? Until Colin, I had no idea what it felt like. Does this one hurt more because of those lines we crossed? It was nothing more than some benefits of our friendship, no strings. Or at least I thought.

Maybe if we had never made things physical, we'd still be

friends. The memories wouldn't likely have been half as good, but he'd be more than a memory. And I wouldn't be so fucking mad.

Trying to distract my mind, I put on my apron and slice a large chunk of clay from the mass on the table, covering the rest with thick plastic once I'm done. I take so much satisfaction in slamming the clay on the wheel that I do it twice.

If Colin were here, instead of with his fucking fiancé, he would say that I only spin pottery when I'm angry. Just the same as how he's pointed out that I paint when I'm sad, I sketch when I'm content, and I sculpt when I'm horny.

It makes me even more irate to think about him pointing that out—like I need that sort of self-awareness. I was just fine before I knew that.

I douse the clay with water and start forming it into shape without any plan in mind. It topples in my hands more than once, and not because I'm clumsy when I'm mad, but because I like it when it breaks. I take some strange enjoyment in seeing how perfect I can form this vase or bowl or cup or whatever the fuck it is, just to break it down to a clump of wet clay again.

Is this what Colin did with me? He built me up year after year after year, only to break me down again.

Or is that what I did to him?

"Declan!" a deep voice hollers at me through the music. I don't have to turn to see my brother standing in the doorway to know he's there.

"Fuck off," I grumble to myself, focusing only on the clay on the wheel.

Killian smacks me across the back of the head before punching the off switch on the speaker so the room goes instantly silent save for the sound of the pottery wheel spinning.

"What the hell has gotten into you?" he asks, crossing his arms over his chest.

"I'm not allowed to be in a bad mood in my own bloody house?" I reply, chucking a piece of wet, muddy clay at his face.

He dodges it, and it instead splatters against the ruined black canvas.

"How's the wedding going?" Killian asks, ignoring my tantrum.

"Piece of cake," I reply.

"Anna told me who it was."

"Of course she did," I mutter to myself.

My brother's features harden for a moment, but he doesn't reply. Instead, he meanders around my studio, and I struggle with the desire to toss him out and tell him to fuck off again.

If anyone would understand the need to brood alone, it's Killian. He spent nearly a decade in this house without ever leaving. He buried his problems in sex and alcohol until an American woman came along and gave him a reason to give a shite.

"So what was that like?" he asks. "Seeing your old mate again."

I shrug. "It was fine. We're not friends anymore, though."

"Right," he mutters as he rubs a hand over his beard. I hear the concern in his voice, but I don't look up from the wheel as I form another vase, only to shove it down into a messy heap.

"What?" I growl.

"Let's call off the bet for this wedding," he says, stepping closer.

"*What?*" I reply with shock.

He grabs a stool from the other side of the room and drags it close to me. As he places it on the floor and drops his ass on the seat, I slam the hunk of clay against the wheel again.

"Killian, stop looking at me like that," I bark. I despise his pity, and I refuse to accept his concern. I am fine. Nothing is wrong with me other than a sour mood and a bloody bad week.

"Listen, if you don't want to talk to me, that's fine. But I've been a stubborn arse too, and I nearly lost the love of my life because I was too proud to admit when I needed help."

I wipe my clay-covered hands on the front of my apron. I'd rather eat this clay before having this conversation with my brother.

"There's nothing to talk about," I say, trying to force my voice to stay light. "One of the grooms just happens to be someone I knew from uni. That's all. We don't get along great now, sure, but I can still manage this wedding, and I am not going to just forfeit this deal."

"The deal is off."

My foot releases the pedal of the wheel, and I stare up at my brother with vitriol. "No, it's not."

"Why are you being so bloody stubborn about this?" he asks.

"Because if I let you call this deal off, then you'll be making something out of nothing, and this thing between me and Colin really is *nothing*. The sooner I prove to you and Anna that I can do this, the sooner I have this house to myself."

Killian nods, listening to my tirade before replying. "You know what…"

I let out a sound of frustration. "What?"

"I think you should do this wedding. The wager is back on."

My teeth grind as I glare at my brother. He's being condescending, but right now, I couldn't give a shite. As long as he gives me what I want, I don't care how he talks to me.

Crossing his arms, he tilts his head back and stares at me as if he's so bloody wise. Makes me want to punch him in his ugly face. "You sound like me."

"Ugh," I groan as I bury my clay-covered fingers in my hair. Ignoring me, he continues.

"I thought I knew what I needed too. So I put up a wall between me and my wife. I wouldn't let her in. Then, when I did love her, I was too fucking stubborn to tell her. And I nearly lost her."

"You're an expert on love and marriage now, is that right?"

He shrugs. "I consider myself a bit of an expert now, yes."

"I promise you that's not what's happening here."

"Okay," he replies nonchalantly, and it boils my blood.

Instead of arguing, I roll my eyes and get back to work on the wheel. Killian stays quiet for a while as I work. This time, I'm molding and forming the mass into something without letting it break.

"You used to make art out of whatever you could when you were a kid. I remember you painting on the dinner table with your food when you were a wee babe. And whenever I'd pick on you, you'd get so cross with me, you'd lock yourself in your room and draw for hours."

"What's your point?" I mumble under my breath.

"You had an outlet when Mum and Dad died—a healthy one. You were only a kid, and you painted every second you were awake. For weeks on end, that's all you did. You painted animals and landscapes and food and whatever you could think of. Anna had to start throwing the paintings in the bin because she didn't know what else to do with them."

"What is your *point*, Killian?"

He leans forward, his elbows on his knees as he speaks sternly. "My point is, Declan, that connecting with other people has *never* been your strong suit. It's okay; it was never mine either. We're both charmers, charismatic for a moment when it suits us best, but the walls would go up as soon as anyone dared get too close."

The wheel slows, and the vase built between my fingers stays upright, but I don't take my eyes off it.

"The difference is that I put real walls up, and I closed myself in this house for six years because I was so afraid of feeling anything for anyone ever again. But you, *you* went out into the world, and you met the *one* bloody person who made you feel safe, and you held on to him for eight years."

"He was just my friend, Killian."

"I believe you," he replies. "I'm just afraid that you're lying to yourself, and you lost the only person you ever let love you. And it hurts a lot fucking more than you're willing to admit."

It feels like the wind is knocked out of me. Suddenly, I want to tell Killian to fuck off and get out of my house even more. I don't need him and his cruel observations.

So I don't let people get close to me. It's no wonder after everyone in my life has either died or abandoned me.

Our parents died in a crash. Killian retreated from the entire family. Lachy ran off to the States as soon as he could. Anna was the only one who truly stuck around, and even that filled me with guilt for what she sacrificed.

Colin truly was the only person I let in, and look how that turned out.

"Even more reason for me to do this wedding," I mumble angrily. "To prove that I'm fine. That I've moved on, and I'm *happy* for him."

Killian leans back as he puts his hands up in surrender. "If you say so, Declan."

"Go back to your wife, Killian," I say.

"I'm going," he replies, standing from the stool and walking to the door. "I'm just glad you're fine. Bye, Dec."

I listen to his steps retreating down the stairs while I sit in silence and stare at the vase on the wheel. It turned out perfect. All I need to do is grab the wire and cut it loose from the base.

But I don't. I step on the pedal and watch as the motion forces the vase back into a shapeless clump of nothing.

Chapter Sixteen
Colin

Eleven years ago
Dublin

"But I don't give a shite about rugby!" Declan shouts over the din of cheers and applause around us.

"I know!" I reply with a laugh. I'm on my feet and cheering anyway, my shoes sticking to the beer-soaked floor of the arena. Declan takes a sip of his ale with a grimace as he watches the players on the field. He looks disgusted and miserable, and if I wasn't so happy to see him, I would feel bad for dragging him here.

"Then why are we here?" he complains.

The cheers die down, so Declan and I take our seats with the rest of the people in the stands. Turning toward him, I look into his eyes, soaking up the warm familiarity of those rich brown irises.

It's our second summer meeting since uni. Last summer was shortly after graduation, and it was short and uneventful. He had a few days in London with his sister, and we spent it together, feeling chaperoned and awkward.

Apparently, his family is going through a lot with his older brother, and it wasn't the best time for him to go away for too long, which I understand. So I didn't press it.

But this year, for ten whole days, he's all mine.

"Because," I say while the players on the pitch run to the sidelines for a quick break. "We're in Ireland, and their team is in the finals, so how could we not come?"

There's more cheering as the players return to the scrum, but I can feel Declan shaking his head beside me. "And you couldn't afford box seats or something?" he asks. "I could have if you had just asked."

Chuckling, I turn toward him and nudge his shoulder. "That's not our style. I wanted to sit down with the people and experience a *real* match. Besides…these tickets were a hefty price as it is."

"I'm sure," he groans.

"Just get drunk and have some fun, Declan!"

For a while, we get into the game, and I don't think I've ever been so happy. Ironically, Declan has never looked more disgruntled. He's hating every moment of this, and soon, I should really put him out of his misery.

When Ireland takes a healthy lead over Belgium, I nod toward the exit, and Declan says a prayer of thanks. We squeeze our way out, and I feel the beer buzz hit me before we've even left the stadium.

While we're walking next to each other back to our rental flat, Declan glances up and stares at me for a moment.

"You've changed," he says.

The grin on my face tugs a little wider. "Have I?"

"Yeah. Something about you is different. You got a boyfriend or something?" he asks stiffly.

A laugh bursts through my lips. "God, no."

"Then, what is it?"

Spinning around, I walk backward on the uneven cobblestones

as I stare at Declan with glee. Stretching my arms out, I say, "I don't know, Dec. Maybe I'm just happy."

"Then, you do like it in London?" he asks with a furrowed brow.

"No," I groan. "I mean happy here with you. I'm with my best friend again, and everything is right in the world."

For the first time tonight, he cracks a smile.

"I'm sorry I'm being a dick. I had fun at the match," he says after a moment.

"No, you didn't," I laugh as I grab his arm and walk by his side. "But the night is still young. Let's find a pub to get drunk in."

"Now, that sounds like a plan," he replies with enthusiasm, throwing his arm over my shoulder.

Declan and I find a pub with a lively band playing and a free table in the corner. Within the first hour, we're both two shots and two pints in, and I'm rightfully pissed.

I don't normally drink, mostly because I don't feel comfortable around people the way I do with Declan. With him, I can be as drunk and sloppy and silly as I want, and he doesn't judge me for it.

Declan has a higher alcohol tolerance than I do, so he stays mostly right-minded while I can feel just how belligerent I've become.

"Slow down there, Shakespeare," he says as I wave the bartender down for another round.

"What do you mean *slow down*?" I ask with a slur in my voice. "We're celebrating!"

"You'll be celebrating with your head in the loo again," he replies with a snigger. "And you're gonna have a massive hangover tomorrow."

"I don't care," I mutter.

What I don't say—because I have a thread of inhibition left—is that I'm also drinking tonight because I can't stop thinking about how we left things last year.

That kiss.

That *blow job*.

I can't bring it up if I'm sober, but I'm dying to know what exactly this makes us. Can we pick up where we left off? Is his offer still on the table? Are there more things he's willing to help me check off my list? Does he even want that?

The sober part of me knows that nothing has really changed for Declan. It was purely physical, and he did it because he was my best friend. He'll never look at me as anything more, but that hopeful part of my brain is clinging on for dear life.

"All right, out with it," Declan says as the bartender drops another round of drinks in front of us.

"Out with what?" I ask.

"I want to know if you've been putting those new skills of yours to any use since I saw you last," he says before lifting the beer to his lips.

"I don't know what you're talking about," I reply smugly with a smirk on my face.

"Horse shite. You can't fool me, Colin Shelby," he says.

"I'm not fooling you," I reply with a laugh.

"Are you telling me that mouth of yours has gone completely unused in the last year?"

My cheeks heat as blood rushes to the surface.

That mouth, he said.

My mouth.

He speaks about it so intimately. So filthily. God, I'd do anything to let him use it again.

"I beg your pardon," I reply flirtatiously. "As a matter of fact, this mouth has gone completely unused since I saw you last."

"Well, that's a fucking waste," he says before taking another shot.

I bite my bottom lip, watching as his throat moves with the swallow of the alcohol. This entire conversation is so incredibly sexy and enticing, but I'm still not entirely sure that it's not just all in my head.

"And why would that be a waste?" I ask.

"You know damn well why," he replies, staring me in the eye.

"So you're saying I was pretty good then?" I ask.

"Aye, you know fucking damn well you were good," he says with a smirk. "You might have ruined all future blow jobs for me," he adds. "I got one a few months ago that paled in comparison."

I'm caught somewhere between a flutter of excitement and a souring of jealousy hearing that someone else has put their mouth where mine has been. It stings to hear that, but mine was better, and that comment goes straight to my dick.

Feeling bold, I let out a sigh and shrug. "Fine, Declan, I'll suck your dick again."

He nearly chokes on his drink when he hears me. "Colin Shelby," he says with a gasp. "What a dirty little slut you've turned into."

A cackle escapes my lips as I throw my head back with a laugh.

"Hardly," I reply. "But for you, I will be."

Declan laughs over the top of his pint glass but quickly averts his eyes. I'm engulfed in embarrassment as I realize what I just said. We're not there. I just took things too far because I'm drunk.

"I didn't mean that," I stutter.

"Don't worry about it. You're drunk, Shakespeare," he replies casually. "And I brought it up."

It's like I've been doused with cold water, turning my excitement into dread. Quickly, I grab the shot waiting for me on the table and toss back the burning whisky.

Within minutes, my vision doubles, and my head starts to spin as I stare straight ahead at the crowd of people filling the pub.

"You all right, Shakespeare?" Declan asks, but it sounds like he's far away.

"No, I'm still a bloody virgin," I stammer drunkenly. "And the only person I've ever had the guts to even touch is my best friend. How pathetic."

He rests a hand on my shoulder, but I can barely feel it. "You are not pathetic, Colin." His tone is serious and scolding, as if I've suddenly pissed him off by talking bad about myself.

"What is wrong with me?" I mumble.

"Nothing is wrong with you."

Declan stands from the table and slides his hands under my arms. "What are you doing?" I ask.

"It's time to go home, Shakespeare."

"I don't want to go home," I argue.

"Too bad, lover boy."

Once he gets me to my feet, he wraps an arm around my shoulders to maneuver me through the crowd toward the door. I plant my feet and pull myself out from under his arm.

"Stop calling me names," I say, but the words are difficult to manage—each one feels like a wad of chewing gum in my mouth that I have to speak around.

"Okay, I'll stop," he says, putting his hands up in surrender.

I'm growing irritable with the way he's talking to me and trying to force me out of the bar.

"I'm not a child," I argue when I feel the brisk night air hit my lungs. I shove him angrily and try to storm away, but my foot catches the cobblestones, and I tumble into the brick wall of the pub.

Declan is there in an instant, hauling me back to my feet. I expect him to wrap a hand around my shoulders and guide me. What I don't expect is his warm hand circled around my throat and his body forcing me against the wall. Suddenly, his face is inches from mine, and the tone of his voice drops an octave as something between us changes.

"You listen to me," he mutters assertively. "I know you're not a child, but you're acting like one right now. I am trying to help you, so you are going to do what I say. Understand?"

I can't explain the way his words affect me. I don't know if it's arousal or the alcohol, but something about the way he's talking to me right now with his grip on my neck has me nearly melting into the cobblestones. I'd do anything he asked. I turn into a passive, obedient pile of flesh for him with one word.

"Yes," I reply in a whisper.

He doesn't let go and only leans in closer. "You are my best bloody friend, so stop talking about yourself like that and just let me take care of you."

My head tilts, and although I see two of him, I stare into his eyes—both sets—and let his words sink in. I am his best friend. And he will always take care of me.

And if I push this with him and try to make him love me in a different way than he does now, I could ruin it.

Wordlessly, I nod.

"Good," he mutters before releasing my throat. My skin misses his touch immediately.

I cling to his arm, looping mine around his as he leads me back to the flat. And as much as I try to make sense of what just happened, I can't. I just know I've never felt so at peace as I did when he had me under that spell, when he had me under his control, when I was fully surrendered to him.

I don't know if it was all in my head or if Declan did that on purpose, but now that I know what it feels like to have his power over me, I don't know if I'll ever be able to let it go.

Chapter Seventeen
Colin

The thin ray of light bleeding through the curtain on the window is enough to make my head scream in pain as I peel my eyes open. Immediately, my mind starts to replay the events of last night.

Oh God, what did I say?

What did I do?

I remember being at the pub with Declan. I remember a very arousing and slightly embarrassing conversation about the skills of my mouth. I remember leaving and him having to practically carry me. I remember a very strange moment after we left when Declan seemed so cruel and yet so…controlled.

But after that, I'm drawing a blank.

God, how do I not even remember coming back to the flat we rented?

Slowly and carefully rolling onto my back, I wait as my head stops throbbing from the movement. It takes a moment for the room to stop spinning. My stomach clenches with nausea.

I lift the blanket over me and glance down to see my nearly naked body under the covers. The only thing I'm wearing is a tight pair of boxer briefs, and they're not mine.

I scan my memory again, hoping for something to come up regarding last night. Did Declan and I...

I turn my head to the left, surprised to see another body in the bed with me. Declan's dark-brown mop peeks out from under the blankets. I peel them back to see him sleeping peacefully at my side, regardless of the fact that there's another bed in the flat he could have slept in.

How on earth did I end up in his boxers?

Did we have sex, and I don't even remember it?

I lift the blankets a little more to find that Declan is wearing a tight white T-shirt and a pair of his own boxer briefs.

"How you feeling, Shakespeare?" he mumbles sleepily when he notices I'm awake. His eyes are still closed, and his voice is groggy.

"Like shite," I reply.

He chuckles into his pillow. "I tried to tell you."

Why did I drink so much? It's so not like me. Was it that I was just so excited to be around him again? Was it because I truly wanted my inhibitions gone in hopes that we could recreate a moment from last year?

"Are you not hungover?" I ask. "We drank the same amount."

Declan rolls onto his back and stretches his arms over his head. "Aye, we did, but I'm a bit more used to it than you are."

"God, what is wrong with me?" I mutter.

He chuckles in response. "There's nothing wrong with you. You just had a little fun."

I tense beside him, glancing down at his T-shirt. He seems to pick up on my discomfort immediately because he chuckles to himself as he adds, "Don't worry, we didn't do anything."

I don't know if I should be relieved or not, but I am. If I'm going to lose my virginity to my best friend, I'd like to remember it.

"Then where are my clothes?" I ask.

"You don't remember streaking naked through the streets last night?"

My eyes widen in terror as blood rushes to my cheeks. "What?" I shriek. "Are you serious?"

Declan breaks out in laughter. "I'm joking, Shelby. I gave you a glass of water to take your aspirin with, and you spilled it all over yourself, that's all."

Flooded with relief, I let out a sigh and cover my face with my hands. "So you changed my clothes?"

"I couldn't let you go to sleep with wet briefs. And your suitcase is organized quite meticulously. I didn't want to mess anything up, so I just gave you a pair of mine."

I rest an arm over my eyes to block the light as I beg my stomach to settle down. My head is throbbing, and I can't escape the urge to throw up. I don't want to spend my day with Declan hungover.

Then it's as if he reads my mind like he always does. "I think we should just be lazy in the flat today," he says. "Watch some telly. Maybe even catch another one of the championship rugby games you like so much. We can just order in."

"You're the best friend a guy could have," I say with a moan, making him smile.

"I am."

After a long, grueling shower in which I just stand under the stream without moving for thirty minutes straight, Declan meets me in the kitchen after he's made a trip to the local bakery and returned with croissants and coffee.

Then, we do exactly as he had planned. I stay in my pajamas all day and manage to stave off the sickness as we watch movies and television and sports games we don't care about, most of the time carrying on conversations over the sounds of the television. It feels like life in the dormitory again. It feels like home.

Although Declan and I do talk nearly every day while we're apart, I still love these moments when we can catch up as if no time has passed since we last were together. He tells me about the wild escapades of his older brother, the less-wild escapades of his younger brother, his pain-in-the-arse sister, and how he sold two paintings on commission.

I tell him about the play I was in, disappointing my mother for turning down the role she had secured for me on the West End and opting instead for a smaller production on the other side of the city.

"And you really haven't shagged anyone all year?" he says.

"Really," I reply.

"Why not?" he asks. "You're just not interested in anyone?"

I respond with a shrug. "I don't know. To be honest, intimacy kind of scares me."

"It scares you?" he asks. "What the hell scares you about it?"

I twist my mouth in concentration as I think about my response to this question. Picking at the cotton of my flannel joggers, I carefully assemble a response that feels closest to the truth.

"You know, it's like that night in the gymnasium by the pool. How you said I could do things with you because I can trust you, because some people would take advantage of me. Just the idea of giving so much power and a part of myself over to a complete stranger terrifies me. And it's not that I'm afraid they're going to hurt me. It's that I'm afraid…" My voice trails as I reconsider what I'm about to admit. But then I remember this is Declan, and I never have to worry with him. "I'm afraid they'll reject me."

I watch as Declan's brows furrow, and his head tilts to the side. "Are you daft?" he demands. "Reject you? Why would anyone reject you?"

A chuckle slips through my lips. "I don't know. Lots of reasons, I guess. What if I'm too passive or too soft, or I'm not good in bed, or I'm not a good kisser, or I'm not funny enough or smart enough or good-looking enough?"

"All right, stop, stop," Declan urges, waving his hands in front of him. "You are being ridiculous. You hear yourself, right?"

"Yes, I hear myself," I reply. "I'm not being ridiculous. It's just insecurities, Declan."

"But that's the thing, Shelby," he says. "Sex is fifty-fifty. If you're passive, you find somebody who's more dominant. If you're too soft, you find somebody who's a bit rougher. You don't have to be the best at sex. You're not the only person doing it, and it shouldn't all be on you. You put too much pressure on yourself. You act like it's all up to you to please the other person, but is that other person pleasing you?

"Sex is supposed to be fun," he continues. "It doesn't need to be so much pressure. And if anyone, *anyone*, rejects you, then they must have their head so far up their own arse they can't see."

My lips tug into a tight smile as I stare across the couch at him. "You're just saying that because you're my best friend," I say with a blush on my cheeks.

"I don't think this is the kind of thing best friends say to each other, Colin." His tone is suddenly serious, and he's staring straight into my eyes, making my own smile fade. There's heat drawing around my belly.

We both turn our attention back to the TV, staring at it numbly, but I can't stop his words replaying in my head. Declan seems uneasy. I can tell how uncomfortable he is. And I start to worry that it was something I said.

"Are you hungry?" I say to kill the tension.

"Not yet," he replies, going back to biting his bottom lip.

"Everything okay?" I ask.

"Aye," he replies with a nod of his head. But I can tell he's still pondering something in his mind.

I fall asleep on the couch after a little while and wake up a few hours later to the smell of Chinese food filling the flat. Declan is in the kitchen, and I rise slowly from the couch to greet him.

We eat in comfortable silence and then make our way back to the couch, where he puts on another movie. It grows dark through the window in the living room, and I start to feel restless, knowing that something is still bothering my friend—possibly something I said.

When the credits on the movie roll, I stand from the couch with a yawn and announce that I'm going to bed.

Declan only nods absentmindedly as he watches me go. But even as I get into bed, I am tossing and turning, bothered by the conversation we had this afternoon. And just when I'm about to climb out of bed to go out and speak with him, I notice him standing in the doorway.

"Hey," I deadpan, sitting up.

He seems nervous, eyes wide, hands shoved into his pockets. He shuffles into the room as he responds, "Hey."

"Everything okay?" I ask, growing anxious that he's decided he doesn't want to be my friend anymore or doesn't want to keep up these summer meetups.

"Last year, before we graduated, I offered to have sex with you, so you didn't have to graduate a virgin," he says, cool and confident.

My cheeks start to blush, and arousal tightens in my groin. I clear my throat. "Uh-huh."

"And I let you…" His voice trails, clearly uncomfortable with saying out loud exactly what went down last year.

"Declan, it's okay," I say to ease his nerves. "I'm not holding you to that."

Ignoring me, he continues, "What we did was fun, but it was wrong of me to take and not return," he says.

My jaw drops. "I never expected you to."

"I know, but I should have."

"It's…it's okay," I stammer.

"No, it's not," he says in a scolding, serious tone. "I don't want people taking advantage of you. You shouldn't feel as if you have to please others without getting something in return."

"Declan, seriously," I say, growing agitated. "You don't have to beat yourself up about it. I really didn't—"

And then he interrupts me, stepping farther into the room. "I want to do it now," he declares.

I'm frozen for a beat, staring at his silhouette and wondering if I'm hearing him correctly.

"What?" I croak.

"If you'll let me. If you still want me to."

Oh, my God.

Then, to my utter surprise, he begins to climb onto my bed. "I need to hear you say it," he whispers.

Is he really offering what I think he's offering right now? He's telling me that he wants to put his mouth on me. Why would I ever say no to that? My mind is spinning.

But does he really *want* to, or is he just saying this out of guilt because I did this for him last year? He did just say he wanted to, so I should take his word for it, right?

He crawls closer, resting a hand on my leg, and my mind instantly goes blank. It's incredible the way he can silence every thought in my mind with just one touch.

"Colin, your words."

"Yes," I blurt out, although I don't know how I can speak when I can hardly breathe. "I want you to. God, Declan, I've always…"

I cut myself off before I admit to something I will regret. He crawls closer as my heart nearly hammers its way out of my chest.

"Have you ever done this before?" I whisper. He looks into my eyes as he shakes his head.

Then, with a gentle shove on my chest, he pushes me until I'm lying down on my bed.

As he crawls over me, I swear I stop breathing. I've never felt my cock harden so fast in my life.

"If you want me to stop, just say it," he whispers.

Declan slides his fingers under the elastic waistband of my joggers, and I shudder from the sensitive sensation. He doesn't even need to put his mouth on me. He could just do that, and I'd be happy.

"Wait," I say with a gasp as I move up to my elbows. He jerks his hand away from my body as if he's burned me. I take a moment to compose myself before I ask, "Could you just…?"

God, I feel like an idiot for asking this.

"Could you…maybe…kiss me first?" I squeeze my eyes closed and pray that I didn't just make this weird somehow. But I don't *just* want his mouth on my dick. I need more than that.

Without responding, he crawls up my body until he's hovering over me. Then, he smirks at me for a moment before running a hand along my jaw and pulling my mouth upward toward his.

Just before our lips touch, he murmurs, "Whatever you want, Shakespeare."

I think I've died. When his mouth grazes mine, it's like last year in the gymnasium all over again. Hesitant at first and then ravenous.

At the exact moment his tongue brushes mine, he lowers his body until he's lying on me, and we both groan at the same time. I clench his T-shirt in my fists as he kisses me, constantly changing direction and going from nibbling to licking to sucking. Our mouths dance in perfect harmony, anticipating each other's every move.

When he grinds himself against me, I let out a mortifying whimper. We're getting carried away, and I'm elated about that. I can feel him losing control, and for a moment, it feels like power. Then Declan remembers what he was supposed to be doing. So he lifts away from the kiss and licks his lips before moving downward again.

I've never felt so hot or aroused in my life. I keep staring at the ceiling, trying to figure out if I'm dreaming or dead. Because there is no way this is real.

Gathering the top of my briefs, he tugs them down with my joggers, and I feel the cool air of the room breeze against my cock.

This is happening. This is really bloody happening.

His breath releases in a shudder as he stares down at my hard, hooded length. I glance downward to see him and notice the expression of hesitation on his face.

I can feel the moisture from the precum at the tip of my cock, and I'm embarrassed for a moment. How could I help it? The way he was kissing me and grinding on me, he's lucky I didn't come already.

But maybe the precum is freaking him out or something, because he's not moving.

"You really don't have to," I start, but my words are quickly cut off as he leans down and runs the flat surface of his tongue from the base of my cock to the head. Then I feel the tip of his tongue slip under the foreskin, and instead of words, I release a strangled moan as if the air has been punched out of my lungs and my body is clamped tight in a vise grip.

"Dec," I gasp. He wraps his hand around my cock, easing down the hood as he glances up at my face.

Our eyes connect before he lowers himself over me and engulfs me in the warm, wet heat of his mouth.

Another shameless sound escapes my lips. I've never felt anything like this in my life. It's like experiencing everything and nothing all at once. It's like flying and falling, like heaven and hell. I expected his blow job to be awkward and apprehensive, but Declan is devouring me as if he can't get enough. He's moaning wildly, slurping on my shaft, moving his mouth up and down in quick, hungry succession. His lips are curled under his teeth, and I pray that he won't use those on me the way he asked me to use mine on him. I'm not one for pain.

Then he fully closes his mouth around me and sucks, and I swear I am levitating off the bed. My groans are like shouts. Breathing is downright impossible, and I don't care if this is how I die. This is a good way to go.

It feels like heaven, but the struggle of keeping myself from coming too soon is almost torture. I'd be humiliated to come so fast, but with the way his mouth is working me over, I don't know if I have a choice.

Up until this point, my hands have been clutching the sheets on either side of my body. But as he begins to suck, they fly by instinct to his hair, gripping him at the scalp to hold him in place.

"Fuck, fuck, fuck," I groan. Does he have any idea what he's doing to me? Does he even know how good this feels? Was I this good to him?

"Declan, wait. I'm gonna come," I moan. His mouth slows, and the sucking relaxes, which is a relief and a disappointment. It gives me a moment to catch my breath, so I don't suffocate on this bed.

But I don't release his hair. Instead, I gently stroke the dark-brown locks. His mouth is moving slowly now, running his lips and his tongue along every inch of my cock. I melt into the mattress, savoring the slow, pleasant sensation.

"Goddamn, that feels good," I whisper. He moans in response as if he's replying to me. With his free hand, he softly grips my testicles, massaging them gently as he moves his mouth up and down on my shaft.

My head is hung back, my neck extended long as I groan. "You are so fucking good at this," I mumble. I feel him smile around me. Glancing down, I see his lips—those perfect, full pink lips—wrapped around my cock. I see myself fucking them. My best friend, the man I have loved for four years, is letting me use his mouth. I am more and more convinced that I've died and gone to heaven.

No one will ever compare to Declan. And maybe it is because he's my friend. Maybe it is because I trust him more than anyone. But no one will get this much of me, ever.

"Tell me I'm yours," I groan without thinking. His mouth stills around my cock, and I grow instantly terrified that I've just ruined this. That I made it too personal, too intimate. He's just my friend. He's just doing this to return a favor.

But then he pops his mouth off from my cock and grins slyly up at me. With my balls still in his hand, he says, "Is that what you want, Shelby? You want me to tell you that you belong to me?"

That feeling from last night returns. A calm settles over me as if I'm crawling into the sound of his voice, making myself at home there. His raspy, warm tone tells me that he's into this. That he's just as aroused by the idea of ownership as I am.

"Yes," I reply with a whimper.

"Do you think you're mine?" he asks.

"Yes," I say breathlessly as he strokes my cock with his free hand.

"Good," he replies with satisfaction that I can hear. Then his hand squeezes my cock on the upstroke. "Because you are mine. All fucking mine. My little fuck toy. This cock is mine, isn't it?"

"Yes," I breathe.

"And these balls are mine."

"Yes," I reply. Then he presses my knees open and slides a finger between the cheeks of my arse as he delicately rims my back entrance. Chills erupt all over my skin, and I nearly come on the spot. His touching me there makes me feel both exposed and eager.

"And this hole is mine, isn't it?"

My body ignites with heat and desire. "Yes," I scream.

"You want me to tell you you're allowed to come now?" he adds.

I bite my bottom lip, nodding my head as I give him an affirmative sound. "Mm-hmm."

"That's good," he mumbles before kissing the tip of my dick. "My good boy."

I'm going to commit every moment of this to my memory forever. I'll remember every little thing that was said, the way he feels, the way he sounds, the way the room smells. It is forever mine in my memory.

"You've been so good," he mumbles against my cock. "So good and all fucking mine. So be a good boy and come down my throat," he adds.

I nearly stop breathing again with a loud groan. He wraps his lips around my cock, sucking once more and making my back arch off the bed. He doesn't hold back this time, and he's not playing anymore. He's sending me coursing straight for my own orgasm. Every inch of my body is tingling with pleasure.

And when I do finally come, I'm practically shouting, sweat dripping, heart pounding, and body shaking. It feels like the first time I've ever come, and it won't stop.

Pleasure radiates in pulsing waves over and over and over until it feels like I'll never recover. My ears are ringing, but in the distance, I hear him moaning as he continues sucking, swallowing down every drop.

I must pass out because the next time I open my eyes, it's like I've woken up in a different room, at a different time, and I'm a different person. I blink my eyes open to find Declan lying on the pillow next to me. He's staring up at the ceiling with a lazy smile.

"Welcome back to the land of the living, Shakespeare," he says, resting his hands behind his head.

"Did I pass out?" I ask.

"Possibly," he replies. "You took a long time to catch your breath."

My skin is still tingling. "Jesus, Dec. Have you ever done that before?"

"No. I take it I did well?"

I break out into laughter and cover my face in embarrassment. Declan only chuckles at my side, a gleaming smile of pride on his face.

And just like that, we're us again. It's casual and comfortable, and I don't have to worry about being rejected, used, or hurt. Because Declan is my best friend, and he always will be.

Chapter Eighteen
Declan

Four days until the wedding

THE FRONT OF MY HOUSE HAS TURNED INTO A CAR PARK. WHY IN God's name anyone would have an engagement party four days before a wedding, I'll never understand. I swear these people will look for any excuse to party.

I'm hiding out back, enjoying a smoke, when I hear my sister scurrying around the side of the house to find me. I roll my eyes when she comes barreling around the corner.

"I thought you quit!" she snaps, stealing the half-smoked cig from my fingers and throwing it into the gravel. As she stomps it with her shoe, I glower at her impatiently.

"And here I thought I was a fully grown man."

Waving me off, she asks, "How are things going?"

"Well, let's see. The blood sacrifice is at four, orgy is at six, and then at eight, we're driving all of the cars into the loch. So you're just in time."

"I'm being serious, Declan," she says with a head tilt.

"What, Anna? What could possibly go wrong? It's a wedding.

The two most important people are alive and accounted for. I mean, what else does this event really need?"

"Did you order the flowers? Pick the cake? What about their tuxes? Did you send them in to be pressed? We have a steamer in the back if you need it because it might be too late—"

"For Christ's sake, Anna. Will you relax? Everything is fine. And you can't be meddling. I'm supposed to be doing this by myself," I say with a sigh.

"Aye, but you're not over there. You're out here."

"Och, fine!" With a huff, I stomp toward the party behind the house. It's an intimate affair, mostly with friends who are almost all high-maintenance celebrities.

There's an entire waitstaff handling the food and drinks, so I don't know what she wants me to do. Anna and I stop in the periphery of the party and watch to be sure everything is going smoothly.

Immediately, my eyes catch on Colin at Pierce's side. The American has his hand on Colin's back as if he's holding him in place, and I feel something in me tighten.

Anna turns to look at me. "Are you sure you're okay?" she murmurs.

"I'm fine," I mutter as I turn away and walk toward the house.

"Yo, Barclay!"

I freeze in my tracks as the party goes silent, all eyes on my back, I'm sure. The American actor's voice carries across the garden, and after a deep breath, I turn to face him.

"Yes, Mr. Hall. How can I help you?"

Anna stiffens by my side.

"Oh, don't be so formal. Come have a drink with us!"

Turning toward my sister, I force a fake expression of enthusiasm on my face. "See? I'm doing great. Now relax."

But she doesn't. If anything, she seems even more tense. Leaving her behind, I close the distance between myself and the party. As I reach the couple, I take a flute of champagne from the server's tray.

"Of course, Mr. Hall," I say politely as I raise my glass. "To the lovely couple."

I'm an impostor, pretending to be posh and congratulatory, although I'm neither. I'm slobbish, disorderly, obnoxious, and unruly. And I'm not happy for this *lovely couple*, but I will be happy when this wedding is over and I get what I want. Until then, I can fake it.

Everyone raises their glass before we all take a drink in unison. Colin's watching me with a guarded expression, and it's as if he's the only person here who can see past the facade. He knows I'm faking it.

When Pierce's glass lowers from his lips, he smiles at me. "My friends here were noting the beautiful art in the main hall of the house. Is it true you painted those?"

"Not all of them," I reply with a polite nod.

"The portrait of the family, though?" a beautiful woman asks.

I clear my throat as I feel my sister's presence next to me.

"Yes," she says sweetly. "That was Declan's work. He painted that from memory, eight years after our parents had passed. Isn't that so impressive?"

"Quite," Pierce says as if he's sizing me up. I gulp down the rest of my champagne and immediately reach for another.

"He's so talented," my sister says, grinning up at me. "He also sculpts and sketches as well, but his portraits really are his masterpieces."

"Anna," I mutter before taking another drink. "Please stop."

"What?" she asks innocently.

"I think it's awful," Colin mutters and there's a collective gasp around the party. The corner of my mouth lifts in a smirk as I stare at him with gratitude in my eyes.

"Thank you," I mumble to him while his fiancé and my sister stare at him in horror.

"What? It was a joke," he says with an uneasy smile. "He doesn't like compliments."

Pierce looks away with stone-cold judgment on his face as he picks up his drink.

"Oh, he never did," my sister says with a giggle. "I'm afraid our brother used to torment him about it."

"This is an engagement party, and yet we're talking about me," I complain.

"How long does it take you to do a portrait?" Pierce asks, obviously ignoring my protest.

"Depends," I reply with a shake of my head. "A day for a sketch. A couple weeks for the paint if it's small."

I don't think anything of his question or my reply until Pierce looks at Colin adoringly. With his arm still around his shoulder, he squeezes him tighter and leans in to press his lips to Colin's. I force myself to look away.

"I know you're so busy with the wedding, but I would love a painting of my soon-to-be husband."

"Oh, no. Absolutely not," Colin says, immediately shutting down the idea.

"Why not?" Pierce implores.

"Because he's busy, and I don't want to sit for a painting."

"I'll pay him, of course. But how special would that be, Colin? The artist who owns the place where we got married could do a portrait of you as a gift for me." There is something in the way he enunciates each word that spears the haze of my champagne buzz. He's showing off. Or rather…he's rubbing it in my face. *His* soon-to-be-husband. *His* painting. This is a show of ownership and intimidation because he thinks I care.

Pierce is enthusiastic and quite compelling, but I'm standing across from them both, frozen in place and oddly hopeful he actually talks Colin into this. Why? I don't know. I can see this overinflated, chauvinistic pissing contest for what it is, but at the same time, I accept his challenge.

Not that I want to be alone with someone who clearly can't stand me. But I'll take the work and the money.

"Then why don't we both get our portraits done? Together," Colin argues.

"Because I don't want to be in it," Pierce replies. "But I might want to watch," he adds with a mischievous wink.

My cheeks grow hot as I silently watch them argue. I have to admit, Pierce does seem enraptured by Colin. He's always admiring him, touching him, smiling at him as if he's thinking of devious and filthy things he'd like to do to him.

For some reason, it makes me despise Pierce even more. He's arrogant and obnoxious. There was a time when I was myself both arrogant and obnoxious. But things have changed.

"What do you say, Barclay?" he asks, and by the look on his face, I can tell he would never expect me to deny him.

"Of course," I say without expression. "I could make it work. Perhaps tonight…after the party."

I watch the movement in Colin's throat as he swallows.

Then, I spot a hint of mischief in Pierce's expression that has my eyes narrowing and my spine stiffening. Something about him has my suspicions raised, but I can't quite put my finger on it yet.

"We should really get back inside to check on the caterers," my sister says, tugging gently on my arm.

"Yes, of course," Pierce says with a charismatic smile. "Thank you for everything you both have done."

Colin doesn't say anything as Anna and I move away from the party, but I feel his eyes following me. We're barely out of earshot when my sister starts.

"I don't feel right about this," she mumbles under her breath. "There's something strange about him."

I shrug it off as I pick up the pace. I agree with her, but I won't voice it. I won't let Pierce's peculiar behavior get in the way of this wedding and my future.

Besides, their relationship is none of my business. No matter how uncomfortable it makes me.

It turns out running a wedding is bloody exhausting. Sometime after working out table assignments and making flower arrangements, I pass out on the chaise lounge in my studio. I skipped dinner altogether, so when I hear someone calling my name and wake up to see the windows are now dark, it takes me a moment to figure out if it's very early or very late.

Then I recognize the blond figure standing over me with his arms crossed over his chest.

"Oh hey, Shakespeare," I say groggily as I force myself to sit up.

"I'm going to tell him you're too busy to do this," he says in a flat tone.

"Too busy for what?" I ask.

"The painting, Declan."

"Oh shit… Yeah, I forgot about that."

"We're not doing it," he says coldly. "I'll make up an excuse."

I stand from the couch and run a hand through my long messy hair. "What are you talking about?" I ask. "You're here. I said I'd do it, so I'll do it."

I keep a coffee press in the corner, so while I prepare myself a caffeine pick-me-up, I feel Colin standing like a statue behind me.

"Have a seat," I say over my shoulder.

He doesn't listen, which isn't like him. I watch him skeptically from the corner of my eye as he starts to wander around my studio. When I notice him approaching the large chest in the corner, I tense, ready to pounce if he tries to open it.

My studio is a mess, still half in boxes and packaged-up old paintings. It has been my studio for as long as I can remember. Although it was never my bedroom growing up, I slept in here more often than not. I have a memory of my mother making my dad carry up an old mattress because she was tired of finding me sleeping on the dusty floor. It's not the same one that's up here now, but it's in the same place.

It's an incredibly large room, so there's space for the couch, a few tables, and heaps of boxes. I think it was once meant to be a nursery for children—ironically, it now belongs to a very immature grown man.

After I put the electric kettle on to boil, I follow Colin to where he's snooping around.

"You remember this room, right?" I ask, slamming closed the closet he's moving toward.

He glares at me for a moment before muttering, "Of course."

"We're keeping our clothes on this time," I joke, knowing full well it's only going to set him off.

With a scoff, he turns away and marches toward the door. "We're not doing this, Declan."

"Okay, okay, relax. It was a joke, Shelby. Just sit down."

He pauses by the sofa and turns back to stare at me with a heavy sigh. To my surprise, he actually listens this time. Sitting on the chaise, his posture is stiff, and his face is flat and guarded. Nothing like the living, breathing man I once knew. The one who harbored so much curiosity and excitement for the world. Something has extinguished that since I saw him last.

My kettle beeps when it's done boiling and I finish preparing the coffee in silence. I offer him a cup and he accepts it, so I prepare his like I know he once took it—with milk and lots of sugar. He seems touched that I remembered when I take it over to him.

Then I set mine on the table next to the easel where a fresh canvas waits. I hate to sketch on the easel, so I grab a charcoal and prop the canvas on my propped-up legs. Then, I rub my eyes and take in Colin's position on the chaise.

"Sit back," I say, slipping on an assertive tone with him that brings back a lot of memories.

He scoots to the back of the sofa without looking any more at ease.

"Relax, Colin." I can tell that he tries, but he's physically unable to. His shoulders slump unnaturally and his back rounds.

"Jesus, you're an actor," I tease.

"Yeah, well…this is different," he says, looking painfully uncomfortable. And for the first time, I try to see things from his point of view. He was supposed to have a beautiful, uneventful wedding this week. Instead, he's up in his ex–best friend's attic, where we once had a very passionate lovemaking session followed by the fight of the century. None of this must be easy on him.

So I decide to take some pity and stand from my chair. I walk over to him and gently nudge him until he's reclining against the arm. Then I put his elbow up on the side and lift his leg just a touch until he's sitting in a more natural position.

When I delicately brush the hair from his forehead, I catch him staring up at me. My thumb leaves a trace of charcoal behind, so I rub at it gently. His warm gaze stays on my face. Being this close, I inhale the aroma of his aftershave and the familiar scent of *him*. It makes my mouth water and my heart pick up speed.

My attraction to Colin was always something I couldn't quite explain. His body and his beauty have always drawn me to him, but it's his personality and his character that were far more arousing to me. I knew from a young age that my attraction wasn't restricted by gender, but with Colin, it was so much more than that.

It was the essence of being so close to him and knowing him better than anyone else. Watching him mature, *corrupting* him, feeling his trust and his knowledge that no one would ever know my heart the way he did. These were the parts that truly brought out my sexual longing for him.

If I was the moon, he was the tides—in sync beyond reason. Connected in ways neither of us understood. He altered the chemistry of my brain, and no one would ever be as attractive to me after him.

His posture is much better now, but I stick around, making

small adjustments just for the excuse to be able to touch him. When I move his shoulder just a tad back, I feel him lean into my hand, and I wonder briefly if it's all in my head.

"Perfect," I whisper before standing upright and forcing myself to go back to my seat. Picking up the canvas and charcoal, I shake away the dirty thoughts in my head. I can't go back down that road with him, so I might as well forget it.

The room is thick with tension as I start sketching. I keep waiting for us to start fighting or for him to call me a selfish bastard or remind me of what I did wrong seven years ago, but we don't. In fact, it grows perfectly comfortable after a while.

Colin melts into the chaise lounge and we lose track of time. Before I know it, it's past two in the morning, and he rests his head on the couch once while I take a sip of my cold coffee, but his eyes close and he never picks it up again.

Instead of waking him, I set the canvas and pencil down on the table and walk over to where he's sleeping. I grab a blanket from the end of the sofa and drape it over his body. For too long I stand there and stare down at him.

It's stupid of me, but I let myself miss him. I reminisce on the good days and even the excellent days. The way he'd smile and the way it felt to know I was the one who made him do it.

Mostly, I miss loving Colin. Because when I let myself love him, my heart was in use. That dusty, nearly broken, battered old organ of mine actually beat when Colin was in my life.

And even I know deep down, he was always more than a friend.

Not to say he was my lover or my boyfriend. More than that. What we were was special. What we had was bigger than life itself.

I lost track of who ruined it. Was it him for meddling with a good thing? Or was it me for not having more to give? I'm not sure. But it feels cruel to have him here now, a merciless reminder of how perfect I once had it.

Now he's tainted the idea of being alone. He's filled my head with memories of how wonderful it could be to love someone.

It's careless of me to think this way. There's not a damn thing I can do to change it. So I have two choices—live alone or live in the past.

With that, I click off the tall lamp and walk over to the bed in the corner. As I crawl onto the mattress, pulling the thick blanket over my legs, I close my eyes and choose the latter.

Chapter Nineteen
Colin

Ten years ago
Los Angeles

"Curtain call!" a voice whisper-shouts in the dark hallway backstage. I'm sprinting along with the rest of the cast. I died fifteen minutes ago in the third act, so while my fictional widow has been sobbing onstage and, I'm sure, drawing tears from the crowd, I've been peeking from the wings to see if I can spot Declan in the audience.

I never did find him.

But the moment I walk out onstage for my solo bow, I hear him. He's somewhere near the front of the audience, hollering and hooting so loud I nearly die onstage for the second time tonight. This time from embarrassment.

I can barely make him out through the stage lights, but I squint down at where I think he is and give him a wide-eyed expression. It doesn't stop him. He just keeps whistling and shouting.

After the curtain closes, my castmates crack up and poke fun at me for my very *enthusiastic* friend.

"Your *not-boyfriend* is very excited to see you," Maeve says as she wraps an arm around my waist and hugs me closer.

"How do you think it went tonight? It was so weird knowing he was out there," I say as we go to the dressing room together to change and take off this makeup.

"Are you kidding? You were brilliant and moved all of LA to tears," she says, shoving me on the arm.

"Thanks," I say with a tight smile. "So were you."

"I know," she replies with a quirky head tilt.

Maeve has been one of my best friends since she and I met in a production in London last fall. We hit it off immediately. She talked me into moving to the States, and with how overbearing my mother has been, it wasn't hard to convince me. I've been living in her flat and got a part in the play almost immediately after moving here—on my own.

She's hooking me up with her agent, and we're even going to auditions together nearly every day we have off. It feels like my life is finally starting.

"What are your big plans with your *not-boyfriend*?" Maeve asks as she wipes the thick stage makeup from her face with a white cloth.

"I rented a place by the beach, and I think I just want to spend the week in the water, getting drunk with him," I say.

"Mm-hmm," she replies with a knowing smirk.

I've told Maeve everything about Declan, from the blow job in the pool to what happened last year in Dublin. She knows how much I've been anticipating this trip of his out here to visit me in hopes that we finally take things to the next level. I can open up to Maeve without shame or embarrassment. With anyone else, I think I'd be humiliated to admit that I'm still a virgin at twenty-four and that I've been holding out for someone who I only see once a year and isn't even my boyfriend.

Maeve thinks it's romantic and not at all pathetic.

Once we're all cleaned up, we make our way out of the stage door. There's a horde of fans waiting, and flashes go off as she and

I wave to those hovering around us. We sign a few playbooks and take some selfies before I notice the dark-haired man holding the obnoxiously large bouquet of flowers.

Maeve gives a little squeak of appreciation before disappearing into her Uber. "Have fun," she calls out before the door closes.

"Wow," I say to Declan as I take the flowers from him. "Thank you."

"You were bloody incredible," he bellows, his thick Scottish accent sounding so much thicker and more prominent since I've been living in America for the last six months. Just the sound of it makes me feel instantly nostalgic and happy.

He looks so good too. A bit out of place, but good. With his shaggy brown hair and slightly baggy clothes, he is exactly as I remember him. But missing him for these past eleven months just makes his presence now shine brighter. He is more Declan to me now than he ever was before.

I let the flowers hang as I pull him into a tight hug, lingering there for longer than appropriate.

"God, I missed you," I say into his neck, and I feel him tighten his grip even more.

"I missed you too," he mumbles.

I already dread the day he leaves.

"I'm so glad you came," I say feeling oddly emotional.

He grabs the back of my neck and pulls me toward him until our foreheads are touching. "I wouldn't miss this for the world, Shakespeare."

I have to swallow down the stinging emotion building in my throat, quickly sniffling away any tears as he releases me.

"Let's go get drunk," I say with a smile, which has him cheering with excitement.

"That's what I'm bloody talking about!"

Declan and I decide to skip the bars tonight and drink at the place I rented instead. It's a condo right on the beach, so we take a six-pack of beer and a bottle of whiskey down on the sand and get drunk with our feet in the water.

He's wearing nothing but a tight pair of black shorts, and I can't stop staring at his abs and chest. Declan has always had a fit body, but his twenties have treated him very nice. I feel like I have to work my ass off in the gym and keep a strict diet to maintain my physique, which isn't all that impressive to begin with.

"I can't believe you live in LA," he says as he lies on his back and stares up at the stars.

The beach is quiet tonight, so it's just us, and we're mostly hidden by the jetty of rocks and plants from the houses on the shore.

I feel restless. I'm tired of waiting. I want to know this week if things between us are going to progress. I still want Declan to be my first, but if he doesn't want that, I need to know now. I can't be a virgin forever.

"I can't believe you came to visit me," I say as I shove his bare shoulder.

"What? You think I'd miss this?" he replies. "Shakespeare, there isn't a place on this earth you could go that I wouldn't come to."

Everything gets quiet after he says that. I pick at the sand with nothing but the waves crashing to fill the void. I honestly wonder if he means what it feels like he means when he says stuff like that.

After a few tense moments, he turns toward me. "You're my best friend, and I made a promise. *We* made a promise."

"No one's ever kept their promise to me before," I mumble quietly. It's a vulnerable thing to say, but this is Declan. I don't have to worry with him. Nothing I say is a risk like it is with others.

"Yeah, me neither," he replies under his breath.

It gets quiet again, and I feel like I'm crawling out of my skin. Just as I'm about to say something or bring up this topic that seems to be hovering awkwardly around us, he starts first.

"So you got an American boyfriend yet?"

My head snaps in his direction. "No," I blurt out. "I don't have any boyfriend."

"Oh, come on," he says. "You must have hot guys crawling all over you here."

I scoff. "I don't."

"Nothing?" he asks.

Biting my lip, I look away. His gaze bores into me as I avoid his eye contact.

"I can see it on your face!" he shouts with a laugh. "Who was it?"

I shrug casually. "I hooked up a couple of times. That's all."

"Hooked up?" he asks, teasing me about my American slang. "What kind of *hooking up*?"

I turn toward him and try to bite back my smile. "I got a hand job at a New Year's party."

"Shelby!" he yells with a grin. "You slut."

"I am not!" I argue.

"What else?"

Trying to remain casual, I add, "And I swapped BJs with a guy in my cast. It was nothing."

"It doesn't sound like nothing," he replies.

His laughter turns tense and his smile starts to falter. Or maybe I'm seeing things.

So I add, "But that's all. They weren't that great, and I'm still a virgin, in the traditional sense."

The waves continue to fill the silence as Declan cracks open another beer and takes a long drink. He appears contemplative, a look I've seen before. I wonder if he's thinking about me with those other guys. I wonder if he's jealous. Call it wishful thinking.

Then, from seemingly out of nowhere, he asks, "Do you remember that night in Ireland?"

I assume he's talking about the night he crawled into my bed and sucked my dick, and to be honest, I'm surprised he's bringing it up. Here I thought I'd have to be the one to start the conversation. "Yes, of course."

"Did you like that?" he asks. "When I..."

"Uh...yeah," I stammer with confusion.

"I'm not talking about sucking your cock, Shelby. Of course you liked that," he says as he rolls his eyes. "No, I mean when I called you mine? I treated you like a thing that belonged to me. Did you...like that?" He won't look at me as he speaks. He just stares out at the ocean with a beer in his hand. My cock twitches in my shorts at the mere mention of being his *property*.

"Did *you*?" I ask.

Finally, he glances my way. Staring into my eyes, he replies, "Yes."

I can practically feel my pulse as the blood courses through my veins. After forcing myself to swallow, I answer his question. "So did I. I liked it a lot."

"What the fuck does it mean?" he asks like we're trying to figure out something mundane and ordinary instead of understanding a deeply rooted kink we both discovered with each other.

"I think it means..." My voice trails. "That I would do whatever you tell me to."

"Anything?"

I shrug. "Within reason. Unless I really don't want to."

"And you'd like that?" he asks.

I'm shaking deep within my bones, a tremble of excitement and anticipation under my skin. We've never really spoken like this before. For so long we've danced around the topics of sex together and treated it like swapping favors. Like it's just a normal thing friends do.

But now...we're discussing something deeper. Something far too erotic to discuss so casually. If we go down this road, there is no going back.

"Yes," I reply without having to even think about it.

He pauses for a moment; then he sticks his beer bottle in the sand and moves to stand. "Get up," he says assertively, and I move quickly, eager to obey. Once I'm toe-to-toe with him, he doesn't do anything for a while. He just stares at me as if he's appreciating me. His eyes rake over my face and down my neck and chest.

There is an all-consuming desire within me to please him. To be what he wants. To be what he *needs*.

When he rests his fingers on my chest, I nearly gasp in surprise. And I don't move as he slowly traces my pec up to my clavicle and over to my shoulder, then down my arm. Chills break out in the wake of his touch.

"I don't like thinking about you with other guys," he says quietly as he stares at my chest.

"Why not?"

"Because I do feel like you're mine. And I don't know if they're treating you right or hurting you or taking advantage of you."

I feel like I can't breathe. This moment is too delicate. One wrong move will shatter it into a million pieces.

"I feel like I'm yours too," I whisper.

His gaze lifts to my face and we stare at each other in the tense silence for so long, I forget what we were even talking about.

Then, out of nowhere, he lifts my arm and drives his shoulder into my stomach, hoisting me off the ground so I'm dangling over his shoulders.

"Declan!" I shout as I cling to his body. I might be a bit slimmer than him, but I'm easily as tall and probably weigh close to as much as him. And yet, he holds me as if I weigh nothing.

Laughing, he carries me to the water. I keep waiting for him to topple over with me on his shoulders, but he makes it all the way into the waves until they're crashing up to his waist.

The water is cold when we both go tumbling in together, a mixture of howls and shrieks of laughter. The tide comes in just as I'm popping out of the water, and it barrels over me again.

Declan's hands grip my waist, pulling me against him as we both stand up out of the water together.

"You prick!" I shout with salt water cascading over my face. Declan is laughing so hard it's infectious, so then I'm laughing too. He flips his head back to get his wet hair out of his face. And we stand in a spot where we can touch without being barreled over every time a wave comes in.

"I couldn't help it," he says.

His hands are still on my waist, although I can easily stand on my own now. He's just holding me to hold me. I can sense his hesitance. He doesn't know how to proceed now, and honestly neither do I. He's touching me like he wants me, but he's not sure what move comes next. There's no rule book for best friends who want to get off with each other.

"What is wrong with you?" I ask, putting my hands on his shoulders.

"I don't like serious conversations. I'm sorry," he replies with a smile. The only light in the sky is from the moon, and it's so dark I can barely make out Declan's face just inches from mine.

"It wasn't that serious," I say. "Now, I'm bloody freezing!"

"Come here," he replies, tugging me toward him. Our bodies are flush against each other, putting our mouths just inches apart.

He slides a hand down my back and over my ass, sending shivers in his wake, until he's lifting one of my thighs. I let out a small gasp, but I don't hold back. Resting my arms on his shoulders, I wrap my legs around his waist, and he holds me as close as physically possible.

If he was trying to warm me up, it works. I'm not cold anymore. In fact, I'm burning up.

"Go ahead," he mutters lowly as his gaze drops to my lips. "Do it."

"Do what?" I whisper.

"Kiss me, Shelby."

As it turns out, my favorite thing to do is obey him. Without hesitation, my fingers slide into his wet hair as I bring his mouth to mine, kissing him hungrily. I nibble on his lips and slide my tongue against his, tasting the salt water between us. There is no restraint in me tonight. I want him and I want it all.

Chapter Twenty
Colin

Declan and I kiss for a few moments before it becomes clear that we both want more. He carries me awkwardly into the shallow water, and then I'm forced to drop my feet as we move onto the shore. But his mouth never leaves mine.

Not when a wave hits us and not when I fall onto the sand. He just drapes his body over mine on the wet shore and continues kissing me until it feels like I could die of happiness.

My legs part, and he settles between them. Our wet shorts don't hide how much we both want this. His cock feels like steel as he presses it fiercely to mine.

"Declan," I whimper as he ruts himself against me.

"What?" he replies as he moves his mouth down to my throat.

"Please…" I can't make the rest of the words come out. I chicken out at the last second.

"What does my needy boy want?" he asks before sucking hard on my neck. My eyes roll back as I try to maintain some composure.

"I want you…" I murmur.

"Want me to what, Colin? Use your words and tell me what you want."

The use of my name and the tone of his voice send chills

down my spine. I have never been filled with more desire in all of my life. So why can't I just say it?

"I want you to…"

"Say it, baby," he mumbles. "Let me hear you say it."

"I want you to fuck me."

"That's my boy," he growls against my skin. I'm a whimpering, moaning, breathless mess as he grinds himself against me, turning me into something I don't even recognize. At this point, I'm hardly human. I'm only lust and desire.

"God, I want to fuck you so bad," he mumbles as his mouth moves downward over my chest. When his teeth close around my nipple, I make a sound I've never heard before. It's a carnal, rasping sound fueled only by the arousal currently keeping me alive.

I'm useless, lying on the wet sand as he sucks and bites the tight bud of my nipple. At this point, I've leaked so much precum I think I might have already come entirely.

"I want to get you off first," he hums against my skin. "Right here, I want you to be a good boy and come for me."

"Declan," I call in a needy plea. It's all too much. My back arches, and my body tightens. It won't take much to get me off at this point. And as much as I want to come, I don't want this torturous euphoria to end. It's the greatest thing I've ever felt, and we haven't even gotten to the sex yet.

But if this is what it feels like to be free with Declan, I want more. And I want it forever.

He continues to suck on the sensitive bud as his hand reaches into my shorts and wraps around my cock. He slips his finger under the hood and teases the sensitive head, and I suck in a breath through my teeth.

"Fuck," I cry out, writhing on the cold, wet ground.

He's desperate and eager, and he barely gets my shorts down before quickly bending over to take me into his mouth. He sucks hard and fiercely, sending me careening toward a quick and intense orgasm. It takes only a few pumps of his mouth on my cock before I'm forced to surrender to it.

"Oh God, I'm coming," I shriek. I lose all control of my own body as the climax takes hold. I'm shuddering and shaking as the pleasure pulses through me violently.

When I'm finally coming down from the euphoria, my body tingles like it's coming back to life. I barely have a chance to recover before Declan pulls me to my feet. Then he's dragging me up to the house, stopping every few moments to kiss me. I taste myself on his tongue, and it turns me on more than I ever thought it would.

At one point, he grabs my hand and slams it against his rock-hard length, and I squeeze it eagerly, desperate to hear his pleasured cries. He whimpers into my mouth as I stroke him over his shorts.

My back is covered in sand when we reach the house. But I couldn't possibly care at the moment. He yanks open the sliding glass door and tugs me inside. We are clawing at each other, riding this tsunami wave of desire.

"My bag," he mutters against my lips when we reach the kitchen. Then, he leaves our kiss for a moment to dig into his duffel bag on the floor. When he comes back, he's holding a strip of condoms and a clear bottle of lube.

The sight of them sets my heart ablaze. He planned for this. This is happening. This is *finally* fucking happening, and he *planned* for it. Goose bumps spread all over my skin as the anticipation floods through me.

I'm standing in the kitchen; the dim glow from the single lamp in the living room is enough to illuminate his face as he approaches me. His pupils are blown wide, and his face has never looked more sexy to me.

His hand goes to my throat, and I tilt my head back for him, giving him more access. Giving him more of me.

"Get on your knees for me," he commands, and I lower myself without hesitation. "Now open your mouth."

I do exactly as he says. Obeying orders has never felt so good.

Declan releases my throat and slides his shorts down to his ankles. Then he takes hold of his cock and slaps the head of it against my tongue with a wet *thwack*.

He looks so turned on as he stares down at me with his cock between my lips. He looks like he wants to defile me, use me, ruin me. God, I want that too. Right now, he can do whatever he wants.

"You look so good with my cock in your mouth. Such a pretty boy. Such a pretty little slut," he mutters, licking his lips. "Stand up, Colin."

I quickly do as he says, backing up until my ass hits the kitchen counter. Then, to my surprise, he kneels in front of me, gently tearing my shorts down and kissing his way across my abdomen as he does. My lips part, and my cock throbs, already hard again.

Once my bottoms are on the floor, Declan taps my hip. "Get up on the counter."

I quickly climb up, and he settles between my knees, kissing me ravenously again. My hands roam his body, eager to feel him now that I have the liberty to. The curves and ridges of his shoulders and chest.

While I'm touching him, he reaches for the bottle of lube on the counter, and I hear the bottle click. Something in me tenses.

What if I can't do this? What if it hurts, or I hate it?

Declan gently kisses my lips as he stares into my eyes as if he's reading the anxiety on my face. "You can trust me," he whispers.

As he backs up, I spread my legs wider, scooting myself to the edge of the counter. He loops one arm under my leg and holds me open for him when I feel the slick pad of his finger at the tight rim of my ass.

Immediately, I tense again.

He kisses my clavicle.

"Let me in, baby."

His soothing words wash over me, and I let out an exhale as something inside me loosens. His finger continues to massage the entrance, but when he applies pressure to enter me, our eyes lock, and I just focus on him.

This is Declan. The one person I can trust. The closest person to my own self. He is me, and I am him, and there is nothing between us anymore.

Right as his finger slips past the ring of muscle, I let out a gasp. It's like nothing and then everything all at once. He's inside me, and it might be nothing compared to the thick length of his dick, but this small moment feels monumental.

"That's it," he whispers. "Are you okay?" he asks.

Silently, I nod.

So he starts pumping his finger in and out, stretching me open as he moves. And from there, it's as if my body listens to him more than it listens to me. Before long, he's able to slip in a second finger and then a third. He curls them and finds places inside of me I didn't know existed. He teases me with sensations like fireworks that make me want to explore so much more.

He moans with every thrust of his hand, and I'm too struck by the feel of him owning my body that I can't make a single sound. My cock leaks with precum again, and it makes me feel filthy and sexy and all his.

"Are you ready for me?" he asks with a raspy voice. "I can't wait any longer."

"I'm ready," I groan.

Declan quickly slips his hand from between my legs and reaches for the condoms. I kiss his lips and down his jawline as he works the rubber over his cock. I never want this to end, and it hasn't even started yet.

Once he has the condom on, he douses it with lube and rubs a little more on me for good measure. Then, he's dragging me farther, so I'm practically hanging off the edge. I hold my cock in my hand against my belly, but I don't stroke, as tempting as it is.

His eyes cast downward as he watches himself line up with my hole. I'm gasping for each breath, gazing at him like he's my anchor, when I feel the warm blunt head of his cock pressing against my rim.

He presses against me for a moment, and I nearly panic that

it won't work, or he won't fit, and this was all for nothing. Then he slips past the ring of muscle, and I let out the loudest, raspiest sound I've made all night.

Declan's gaze pierces mine as he inches his way inside of me. I feel him everywhere. The sensation of being so full is foreign and new. He's filling me, so I become more him than me. It's painful and overwhelming but also amazing and consuming. The sting of pain is drowned out by the need for more.

He looks back down to watch my ass swallow his cock, and the rapture on his face is enough for me. My body brings him pleasure.

When I feel his hips against me, I know he's as far as he can go, and I let out a sigh of relief. He's really inside me. This is actually happening.

"Are you okay?" he whispers.

I nod enthusiastically. "Yeah, I'm okay."

"Does it hurt?"

"Yeah," I reply.

He winces at my answer, so I grab his hip and hold him in place. "But it's a good hurt."

While he's buried to the hilt, he pulls me closer, kissing my mouth with tender passion.

"Does it feel good?" I ask when the kiss comes to an end.

Declan squeezes his eyes closed and rests his forehead against my shoulder. "Like you wouldn't believe," he says with a groan.

A smile spreads across my face as my fingers dig into his hair, holding him closer and wishing I could preserve this moment forever.

"Can I move now?" he whispers.

I nod. "Yeah."

As he eases away, he hooks an arm under my leg again. Then he pulls out to the tip and slides slowly back in. The expression on his face is pained as he moves. Then he starts to pick up speed as if he can't help himself.

The faster he moves, the better it feels. My entire body starts to buzz, and when Declan latches a fist around my cock, I let out a grunt of pleasure.

"Fuck, you feel so good," he mutters. "Your arse is strangling my cock, Shakespeare. I won't be able to fuck anyone else ever again after this."

"I'm yours, remember? This arse is yours," I say between panting breaths.

"Yes, it is," he replies as he slams into me harder. "All fucking mine."

As he picks up speed, I am lost to the current of this passion. Then he pushes me backward until I'm reclining on my elbows. And with one minor change in the direction of his thrusts, Declan hits a spot inside of me that has me whimpering again.

"Oh God," I moan as I melt into the granite countertop. He's stroking my cock to the rhythm of his thrusts, and the faster he moves, the more intense my pleasure becomes.

"I can't take it anymore," I shout. "Fuck, Declan. I'm gonna..."

I never finish my sentence. My orgasm hits me like a storm, stealing the words straight from my chest. Warm, wet drops of my own cum land against my chest.

Declan practically roars as his release hits him. He thrusts hard two more times before stilling inside of me. I feel his cock pulse and twitch as he unloads into the condom.

Then, we're both useless heaps of flesh. He drapes himself over me, and I lie flat as the dead on the counter. My cheeks hurt from where Declan was driving them into the counter, but up until this point, I couldn't feel a bloody thing. My legs ache. My body is cold and sticky from the ocean water and sand.

But none of that matters. Because I just got everything I ever wanted. I'm not a virgin anymore. I just had sex with my best friend and quite possibly the love of my life.

Nothing could hurt me now.

Chapter Twenty-One
Colin

"Hold still," he mutters from behind the easel.

"How much longer? This is so boring," I groan from the couch.

"You got somewhere better to be, Shakespeare?"

"I've been lying here for three hours, Declan. Can't you just use a photo?" I ask.

"A photo isn't the same," he replies. "The light and angles don't look the same in a photo. I'm almost done. Just be patient."

His brow furrows as he scribbles fiercely with charcoal on the easel. The corner of my mouth tugs into a smile as I notice Declan's tongue peek out of his mouth. He always does that when he's really concentrating.

Then his eyes cast over to me, and I quickly hide my smile.

"What?" he asks, catching me.

"Nothing," I reply, trying to keep my expression neutral.

With as much as Declan and I have done together physically, we're not in a place romantically for me to tell him how cute he is when he's painting. His shaggy brown hair hangs over his forehead, in desperate need of a cut. His long eyelashes flutter as he works, blinking heavily as he sketches on the canvas. The way he concentrates creates wrinkles in his forehead and between his eyes, which are so handsome and endearing.

This week has flown by too fast, so I'm stuck in a constant state of bliss and dread. Since we had sex that first night, we haven't been able to keep our hands off each other. When I'm not at the theatre, or we're not on the beach, we are getting each other off in some manner.

I never thought of myself as a sexual person, but with Declan, I feel as if I'm learning so much about what I like. The sex is amazing. But it's so much more than that. The way he is with me, dominating me, making me feel so good, I can't imagine sex with anyone else would ever compare.

There's just a small hint of hesitancy from him, and I can sense it. Not physically. He's not afraid to touch me. Every morning this week, I've awoken to the feel of his lips on me *somewhere*. He's affectionate and tender and says things that steal the breath from my lungs.

But I'm not yet Declan's lover. And I'll never be his boyfriend.

He loves me as his best friend. And I'm afraid that it could go on like this forever.

The sound of the charcoal on the canvas quiets for a moment, and I look up to where he's sitting on the chair, admiring me with a smirk on his face.

"What?" I ask.

"I'm thinking about taking a break," he says before he bites his lips. His eyes aren't on my face, but they are glued to the spot between my legs. I'm splayed out naked on the couch for him. In fact, after we had sex this morning, I never got dressed. I haven't worn a stitch of clothing all day.

"Another break?" I ask with a smirk.

"I mean…I don't have to suck your dick if you have other plans," he says as he moves to all fours and crawls across the floor toward me.

"Oh, by all means," I reply. "I have no plans."

"Good," he mutters as he reaches the couch. His lips start on the top of my right foot and move slowly upward, along my leg and over my knee. "Can I be honest?" he asks before licking a line along the inside of my thigh.

I shift on the couch as my dick twitches from the sensation. "Yes, please. Tell me." I'm practically holding my breath, waiting for him to say exactly what I want to hear. Anything would work, really. He could say how he never expected to fall for his college roommate. Or how he had secretly hoped this would happen this week. Or how he wants to stay in LA and never leave.

All responses would be perfect.

Instead, I'm blindsided.

He climbs between my legs on the sofa and kisses my stomach as he says, "It's such a relief to have someone to just have sex with without any strings or obligations. I feel so comfortable with you, Shakespeare. We can fuck and get each other off. And no matter what, we will always be friends."

Immediately, I tense, feeling a chill rush over me from his words.

"Yeah," I mutter without inflection. "But we're more than that…" I say.

His mouth teases the area around my cock, and as thrown off as I am by his words, my body still wants him.

"Of course we are," he mutters before kissing his way up the length of my dick.

"I'm yours," I say breathlessly as he closes his lips around the head and sucks tenderly.

Then he pops off, teasing me as he says, "You are mine."

"That, uh…" I stammer, trying to form meaningful sentences and enjoy what's happening to my body at the same time. "That sounds like strings and obligations to me."

He chuckles against my shaft. Then he lifts up and smiles at me. "That's not what I meant, Shelby."

"Then what did you mean?" I ask, feeling more vulnerable than I want to at the moment.

"I just meant…" He rests his arms on my legs and stares up at me. The smile has faded, and the laughter is gone. All that's left is sober honesty. "Fuck, I don't know what I meant, Colin. I suck at relationships, and most people I sleep with want to try and make me promise something to them that I can't promise. But with you…"

His voice trails as he leans away from me, his back against the couch. I don't want to just lie here naked with a raging hard-on while we have this conversation, so I snatch the blanket from the back of the couch and drape it over my lap as I lean forward.

"What about me?" I ask.

"It's easy with you."

It's easy with me. It's easy with me because I don't demand anything. I let him have as much as he wants, and I don't ask for anything in return. It's easy with me because I will be whatever he wants me to be. His friend. His fuck toy. Anything.

I see what Declan wants—the ease of a friendship with all the benefits of a lover.

But why argue? Because it's true. I would be any of those things for him. If he wants me for a day, he can have me for a day. If he wants me for a hundred years, I'm his until I die.

So what's the point of arguing for more? I'll just give in anyway.

"It's easy with you too," I say.

When he turns to look into my eyes, his gaze stays locked on mine for a moment.

Maybe neither of us are good at this. We don't know how to navigate relationships well because we were never taught them.

But he's right about one thing: I am his. And that's all that matters anyway.

"Now, where was I?" he asks, turning back toward me and snatching the blanket from my lap.

On Declan's last night in LA, we take a drive. This week has been such a dream, and I can't help but feel like it's never going to be this good again. He's going to go home to Scotland, and I'm going to focus on my career, and even if we do meet up after this, it won't be the same.

I take him to a pull-off on the top of some mountain I don't know the name of, and I park the car so we can admire the lights of the city and the Hollywood sign.

He holds my hand as I drive, and it just makes everything worse.

I think I've come to accept that whether or not I'm more than a friend to Declan doesn't really matter, because he won't be able to express it anyway. And maybe this is just the role I'm meant to play for him.

He'll love me more like this than like a boyfriend.

It's depressing, but it's true.

After putting the car in park, I rest my head on his shoulder. He presses his lips to my hair, and we sit in silence for a while. I don't bother fighting the tears. He won't tease me for it. He knows I'm crying because I hate goodbyes, but I hate this one even more than most because this week was more special than all the rest.

So I just let them fall, wiping them away as they slide down my cheeks.

"I wish I could see how the painting turns out," I say with a sniffle.

"You will," he replies. "I'll post it online for the world to admire you naked as a wee babe, stretched out on that chaise."

"Oh God," I reply, laughing through my tears. "You're kidding, right?"

"Of course," he says. "You know I don't like to share my art. Besides, that one is for my private collection."

"I'd prefer that, thanks."

He kisses the top of my head again.

Friends don't do this. They don't cuddle and kiss and fuck and say things like Declan and I say to each other.

But maybe we're more like passing stars in the night sky. Never intersecting at the right time. Never landing in the same place.

If I could, I'd tell him right now that I love him. I'd do anything to hear him say it back. But it's not a risk I'm willing to take, so he'll say it in my imagination instead.

"You're not a virgin anymore, Shakespeare," he says, and I clench my eyes shut because I hate where this is going.

"I don't care about that."

"I'm glad I could make your first time so good, and that's always what this was about. I'm just trying to protect you."

"I don't need you to protect me," I say through a sob.

"I know you don't. So I don't want…" He pauses as his voice grows tight, and I swear he's bottling up the emotions he should let out. I wish he'd just say that this fucking sucks. It's terrible. We clearly love each other, but he won't stay. He won't be what I want. So he's going to tell me to give my heart to someone else instead, and it hurts worse than anything I've ever felt.

"I don't want you waiting for me, Colin."

"But I'm yours," I reply. I've given up on not sounding pathetic. I am pathetic. I'm a sobbing, heartbroken mess.

"You're goddamn right you are, but you should get touched and kissed more than one time a year."

"I don't give a fuck about that," I cry.

He takes my face and holds me by the chin, forcing me to look at him. Then he wipes my cheeks with his thumbs and kisses each one. He doesn't speak, but at this point, I don't want him to. Every word out of his mouth hurts, no matter how true I know they are.

I can't wait for Declan.

I can't fabricate something out of nothing.

I have to live my life, and put myself out there and experience what other relationships feel like. That was the point of moving into that residence hall in the first place. I wanted to experience real life, but I hid under his wing instead.

Now, I need to move on. Make mistakes. Fuck up. Fall in love. Have my heart broken.

Declan holds me while I cry, letting me bury my face in his neck as I do. His grip is so tight and so comforting because, at the end of the day, he is my friend, and this is what friends do.

That night, after we get home from the drive, Declan takes his time with me. He strips off my clothes and kisses every square inch of my body before fucking me slowly. We're lying on our sides, his arms wrapped around my waist from behind so he can hold me as close as physically possible as he drives himself inside me.

After we've both climaxed, he removes the condom and cleans me up before taking me back in his arms and holding me as I start to drift off to sleep.

"I'll see you next summer, won't I?" I ask.

"Every summer, Colin. That's a promise. Every bloody summer."

It's enough to ease my worries, because Declan doesn't break his promises. And with that, I finally let the dreams take me, and I fall asleep.

Chapter Twenty-Two
Declan

Three days until the wedding

I wake to the sound of rain on the window. The moment my eyes open, I look over at the chaise lounge to find it empty. I shouldn't be disappointed by that. Did I expect him to stick around? Have breakfast with me?

He'll be back in that seat tonight, so I can paint him some more. Is it so wrong that I've missed him? He's my friend. At one point, he was more.

With a groan, I rub my forehead. *God, I need to get out of my head.*

My phone buzzes relentlessly from the floor next to my bed, where it must have fallen last night. When I pick it up, it's riddled with notifications.

Anna warned me about today. Apparently, up until three days before the wedding, everything goes smoothly and seems like it will be fine, but it's the three-day mark at which everything seems to crumble. It takes me fifteen minutes to go through all the messages on my phone.

Due to a sudden summer deluge, there seems to be a rose

shortage. The baker in charge of the wedding cake suddenly came down with the summer flu, and Pierce's best man's suit came back from the dry cleaners missing a pair of pants.

I have my work cut out for me today.

I take a quick shower, get dressed, and prepare for all the fires that need to be put out to make this goddamn wedding go off without a hitch. The wedding I'm not sure should happen in the first place. But oh well. That part is not up to me.

When I reach the main part of the house, I find it abustle with frantic energy. The staff is running around in a mad rush, and Blaire finds me in the hallway with a bucket of sopping-wet drapery in her arms.

"Freak storm. Came out nowhere," she says with a roll of her eyes.

"It's Scotland," I reply with a laugh.

Ignoring my joke, she doesn't even stop as she hollers at me in her quick pace toward the laundry to have the wet linens cleaned. "Lunch will be served inside today."

"Fuck, sorry," I call after her, although I'm not exactly Mother Nature. Or a weatherman.

On my way to the kitchen, I pass the dining room, where I hear more familiar voices in conversation. So I stop and take a peek.

It's Pierce's booming voice first, that loud American accent, that grabs my attention. From around the corner, I can see them sitting at the large table together. Pierce is leaning back in his broad chair, steepling his fingers over his chest as he smiles at Colin, whose elbow is sitting on the table, and he's gazing lovingly at the other man.

Something inside me clenches, and I pause for a moment, searching Colin's expression for a sign that he truly loves this man. Is he the same way with him that he was with me? Does Pierce treat him like he deserves to be treated?

Colin has always had a way of falling for the wrong guys.

He loves attention, and he'll reward anyone who gives it to him. It used to drive me mad. But now we're in our thirties, and he's getting married. It would be futile for me to even bother worrying about this.

Pierce mumbles something I can't hear, and Colin smiles, almost blushing at the table, as he turns away, and I can't take my eyes off of them. Then I hear Pierce say, "Come here," and a protective part of me bristles.

Don't listen to him, I think.

But Colin rises from the chair anyway and walks over to his fiancé, sitting on his lap and looking down at him with love in his eyes. I should be happy for him. Colin has found love. He's able to be in a relationship, and that must be what I'm so jealous of. Despite everything, he was able to move on. Not only that, he was able to commit to somebody. Be vulnerable. Give his heart away. Trust that it won't be stomped on.

He was able to do what I never could.

Colin leans down and presses his lips to Pierce's, and my jaw clenches in response. Why am I watching this? It's too painful.

Then Pierce whispers something, and I notice the way Colin's spine straightens and the smile fades from his face.

"I don't know, Pierce," he says with uncertainty.

"Why not?" Pierce replies, rubbing his hand up and down Colin's spine.

"Because I told you that's not what I want to do. I don't feel comfortable doing that here."

"You've got to be kidding me," Pierce responds. "Do you know how special this is?"

Colin responds by standing from his lap, turning his back, and walking away from the man. A moment ago, I didn't want to watch, and now my attention is rapt as I try to piece together what they're fighting about.

"Will you please just listen to me this one time?" Colin pleads.

I couldn't look away if I tried. I'm an interloper, watching another couple's argument, and I know I shouldn't, but I can't help it. When Colin's eyes drift toward the doorway where I'm standing, I step backward, hiding myself behind the wall.

"Baby, I need you to trust me," Pierce replies. I hear the chair move as he stands.

"I do trust you," Colin replies. I know this tone in his voice. I've heard it before. This pleading, apologetic tone when he knows that he's not pleasing the person he's talking to. And I know how hard that is for him.

From the day I met him, Colin has been a people pleaser to a fault, a habit I've tried hard to break him of, although if I'm honest, there were plenty of times I've benefited from it too.

"You don't sound like you trust me," Pierce says. "You sound like you're ashamed of me. Baby, this is how I am. If you don't like it, then I should know now," Pierce argues.

"Don't say that," Colin replies with desperation. "I don't want you to feel ashamed. I'm just telling you how I feel."

"Yeah, and you're telling me that you don't like the same things I like. And you're bringing this up *now*? Is this going to be a problem?"

One of them crosses the room. I can hear the sound of his heels clicking against the floor. I only notice now that my fists are clenched, and I'm holding my breath.

"Of course not," Colin replies softly. "I don't want any problems. Can we just have the ceremony and get married? It can be a romantic day. We don't have to do any of this here. Another time, please?"

There's a pause of silence. And then, "Is that really what you want?" Pierce asks. The tone of his voice makes it sound as if he's questioning what Colin is outright saying. It takes everything in me not to storm into the room right now and tell this twit off.

And it's even worse when Colin lets out a sigh of surrender. "I don't know," he mumbles.

No! Fuck him, Colin. Tell him no. Whatever this thing is, stand your ground. Please, baby, stand your ground.

When I peek around the corner, I see Pierce wrap his arms around Colin, pulling him into his chest. I hear the sound of his hands running over the fabric of Colin's shirt.

"Just trust me, sweetheart, okay? All of our friends will be here. It's going to be so much fun, and it's going to be so fucking hot."

"What if he doesn't say yes?" Colin replies.

"He'll say yes. Trust me. This place was famous for these parties."

Fuck, is he seriously thinking about this?

"Fine," Colin says, his voice sounding despondent.

"What time will your parents be here today?" Pierce asks, changing the subject.

"I think around noon," Colin responds.

The reminder that his parents are coming to see the house today makes me instantly uncomfortable. I've only met his mother in passing a couple of times, and I've never met his father, but I don't have to meet him to know that I hate that son of a bitch. He treated Colin like second-best his entire life. How anyone could discard their own flesh and blood like that man did baffles me. But knowing he hurt my best friend, I've never hated someone so much in my life.

"Wonderful," Pierce replies. "We'll have a perfect day, and then the rehearsal in two days, and party that night... It's all coming together beautifully, my sexy little Brit."

The sound of that cocky American getting what he wants makes me sick. With a gnawing uneasy feeling in my stomach, I back away from the doorway and head into the kitchen quietly so the couple doesn't hear me.

What the fuck did Colin agree to? I know I shouldn't care. What he does is none of my business. But he's been here with his fiancé for the past four days, and I can tell something about him is off. He might smile and pretend like everything is great, but I know the *real* Colin. The affection Pierce shows him doesn't sit right with me, and I can't explain why. This wedding is making me uneasy, but I just have to keep reminding myself to go through with it, do the job, get the house, and move on. That's all that matters.

Colin is not my responsibility anymore. What he does with his life is up to him, and trying to live in the past isn't going to do me any good.

Two hours later, the impending doom of Colin's parents' arrival at the house is signaled by the sound of tires on gravel. It's been one fucking hell of a morning, and I'm really not in the mood to deal with pompous arseholes today. Nothing has been managed, and if I don't get the cake and the tux and the flowers figured out soon, there might not be a wedding after all.

But as Colin used to say when he was in theatre, the fucking show must go on.

Because of the rain, the staff meets Mr. and Mrs. Shelby with umbrellas by their car, ushering them inside where it is dry.

I stand off to the side as they enter, letting them greet Colin and Pierce first. Blaire is by my side, knocking my shoulder playfully with her arm and rolling her eyes to try and make me smile. It works for a moment.

"Please, for the love of God, win that bet," she whispers under her breath.

I give her a lopsided smile. What a mess this has turned into. A fucking bet. I nearly forgot that's what this was all about. The stakes seem higher for some reason now. Perhaps I'm just in over my head.

The Shelbys make a big fuss in the entryway, greeting Colin and then Pierce. Seeing Colin's father for the first time is a bit surreal after all the shit I've heard about him.

Colin resembles him far more than he resembles his mother. The man is tall and quite handsome, with fair skin, light hair, and piercing blue eyes. But that's where the resemblance ends because Colin's father carries himself with an arrogance that Colin never does.

Colin's mother affectionately hugs him, kissing his cheek and ruffling his hair in the same way I've seen her do it before. It's how I can tell she loves him very much. He smiles back at her adoringly as she touches his cheek.

Meanwhile, his father shakes Pierce's hand proudly, and Pierce is eating it all right up. With a big smile and an overdramatic show of excitement, Pierce proves to be quite the actor. Naturally, Colin's father approves of the attention.

Colin doesn't get half the enthusiasm when his father greets him. There is no pride. There is no joy. There is no love. It's almost robotic, the way he acknowledges Colin, clapping him on the shoulder, shaking his hand, and turning away as quickly as he can.

I watch the way this affects Colin, the subtle sadness in his eyes. It shatters something inside of me. I want to drag him away or put myself between him and them. That's my job. I'm his best friend—the person supposed to look out for him. I'm not supposed to let him feel shite like this.

These must be old feelings preserved from years ago when that's quite often what I had to do—when he needed me. But he doesn't need me anymore.

While the four of them make small talk in the entryway, Colin's eyes drift over to me. They stay locked with mine for a moment, and I wonder if he notices that I've witnessed his pain, as if maybe I was the only one who could see it. His fiancé is too busy laughing with his father, trying to impress him with his good looks, his money, or his charm.

"Mum, you remember Declan Barclay, don't you?" Colin asks as he guides his mother over to where I'm standing.

"Of course," she says excitedly as she reaches out her hands to pull me in for a hug. It takes me by surprise, so I awkwardly tap her back as she hugs me.

"It's very nice to see you again," I say.

"You too," she replies. "How fitting is it that Colin will be getting married in *your* house? You two really go back so far, old university mates."

I clear my throat and avert my gaze to the floor. "Yes, ma'am, it is quite a coincidence," I say. "I hope you enjoy the house while you are visiting today. The staff has prepared a lunch for you in the dining room. And I'm sure if the rain lets up, Colin and Pierce would love to show you the gazebo in the back where the ceremony will be."

"Oh yes, I would love that," she replies emphatically. That enthusiasm does not transfer to Colin. He appears guarded and uncomfortable as he stands there watching the both of us. I wish I knew what he was thinking. I wish I knew what that fight was this morning with his fiancé. I wish I knew for sure if this wedding is really what he wants.

Chapter Twenty-Three
Declan

The Shelby family is seated in the dining room while I hide in the kitchen, trying to focus on the things that need to be done. But I'm still within earshot of them, and I can't help but eavesdrop.

Throughout the entire meal, it's mostly Pierce talking. Well, Pierce and Colin's dad. There is a lot of bragging. Some criticizing of Colin, which I hate.

Whenever Colin's mother tries to speak up, she's immediately spoken over by her husband. And I can't help but notice the way she makes subtle jabs at him. She ever so subtly brings up the events he's missed or the times he's been away, with a sweet, high-pitched tone to her voice. Because everybody at the table knows those were the times when he was with his other family. It's the secret that's not really a secret at all.

It's infuriating the things this family lets him get away with without consequence. The fact that he can have another family, and yet, this one will just accept it.

But then they bring up Colin's career. My spine straightens, and I nearly drop the phone in my hand as I begin to dial the number of yet another bakery.

His father mentions a part in a movie Colin accepted, and

Pierce chimes in with a whole lot of "I tried to tell him not to," and not a word from the entire table is encouraging of Colin except from his mother, but no one listens to her anyway.

When I can't take another second, I snap.

"Where are you going?" Blaire asks as I march from the kitchen into the dining room. I don't answer her. I just waltz right into the room to find that their food is eaten, and they are just sitting back and talking lazily.

Everyone glances up at me expectantly as I enter. "I'm so sorry to interrupt, but could I please borrow Colin for a moment? I have a decision that needs to be made about the cakes, and I would like his input."

Colin's brow furrows and Pierce absentmindedly waves him away. "Of course, yes, go ahead."

I give Colin a look that silently tells him to stand up, before turning away and waiting for him to follow. Except I don't go into the kitchen.

I lead him down the hallway, through the house, to the back door. The rain has stopped, and I figure we could both use a breath of fresh air.

As soon as we're on the gravel out back, he practically shouts, "What on earth are you doing?"

"I'm saving you," I respond as we walk. I'm ahead of him, but I hear his steps on the ground behind me.

"Saving me? From what?"

"From your father. From all of that. I couldn't listen to one more fucking second of it," I reply.

I turn back to see Colin smirking for a moment before picking up his pace behind me. "I don't need saving, Declan," he mumbles before quietly adding, "but thank you."

"You're welcome," I reply. "We'll call it a cake emergency."

"Of course," he says. "A cake emergency. Out in the garden."

I smile to myself as we stroll through the grass toward the edge of the property.

For some reason, it feels as if we're heading toward the gazebo in the distance, where the wedding will take place. My brother was married there only two years ago.

"I mean, honestly, though, I don't know if you're going to have a wedding cake," I add.

"What?" he replies in shock. "What are you talking about?"

"Oh, the baker came down with the flu. I'm supposed to be finding a new one."

"We need a wedding cake in three days, and you're going to go for a walk with me instead?"

I shrug, fighting a smile. "Yeah, I guess I am."

With a scoff, he laughs and shakes his head. Then, he drops his hands against his side. "I don't bloody care about the cake, if we're honest," he says.

I pause. I suddenly want to ask if he cares about any of it. Is this wedding really that important to him?

"I do," I reply casually. "That lemon cake was fucking orgasmic."

"Orgasmic?" he asks with a laugh.

"It was," I reply, as a light sprinkle douses my head. I pay it no mind as we continue our stroll.

"I don't know if it was *that* good," he replies.

Suddenly, we're both smiling. We're alone, not fighting, comfortable, and that all feels like it means something.

And then, from out of nowhere, the sky opens up, and rain pours down in sheets.

"Oh shite!" I bellow, looking back at Colin, who is standing with his arms wide, stunned and getting visibly drenched.

For a moment, we stand frozen in place as if we're both trying to decide where we should run for shelter.

"The gazebo," I shout, because it seems closer. Then, I grab his arm and drag him toward the small shelter at the perimeter of the garden. We both take off in a run, laughter cracking through the sound of rain.

"I'm getting soaked!" he cries, and I turn back to look, and he is drenched from head to toe already. His wavy blond hair is matted against his head in wet locks. His skin is glistening from the moisture as it drips over his full pink lips and down the straight, perfect line of his jaw.

I'm so distracted by how stunning he is, on top of how slick the grass is, that my foot moves from underneath me, and I slam down to my ass.

Colin continues running while laughing at me, but a moment later, his right foot slips out awkwardly to the side, and he falls too. But his fall is worse.

Over the sound of the rain and our laughter, we can both make out the unmistakable sound of his trousers ripping at the back. Neither of us even bother trying to stand. I'm on my back, rain pummeling my face as I howl with laughter.

What a pair we are.

Colin has mud streaked across his arm and back. His tight gray slacks are split down the middle in the back, revealing his briefs underneath. He's also laughing so hard that his face is red. He's lying on his stomach, and he hides his face against the grass as he giggles.

For a moment, I'm transported back in time. It's no longer today, three days before his wedding. We're no longer in our thirties. For just a few moments, we are twenty-one again. We're in Los Angeles, Dublin, or Amsterdam, living without consequence, enjoying life for the moment, reckless and untouchable.

When our eyes meet, I think he feels it too. I nearly forgot what it felt like to have a friend. To laugh so hard it hurts. To be with someone who truly makes me feel carefree.

Our laughter eventually dies down enough for me to climb up to my feet, but I notice Colin struggling.

"Blast," he says through his laughter. "I think I really hurt my ankle."

Taking his arm in mine, I help him to his feet, and it's obvious right away that he cannot put weight on it.

"Ouch, ouch, ouch," he mutters. It is still pouring, and we're still getting drenched down to the bone. The gazebo is only a few more feet away.

"Come on, Shakespeare," I say as I put his arm over my shoulder. He hobbles a few steps, but it's too slow, so I slide my arm under his legs and lift him off the ground.

"What on earth are you doing?" he asks, but he clings to my neck anyway. I take each step more carefully than the last as I deliver him to the shelter.

There's nowhere to sit, so I set Colin on his good foot and gently lower him to the floor. He's wearing a white button-down that is drenched and sticking to his skin. I can't tear my eyes away from the translucent fabric and the muscles of his chest showing through.

Colin's always been a bit on the slender side. Try as he might to bulk up more to my figure, he's never had the meat on his bones that I do. And as much as he used to berate himself, I would reprimand him for it because he's perfect. He always has been.

"I can't believe my trousers ripped," he says, rubbing his forehead. "How am I gonna go back to the house like this?"

"How are you gonna go back to the house at all?" I reply, looking at his ankle. "You can't walk."

"Blast," he says, trying to flex it. "I hope I didn't break it."

"Let's take a look," I say, kneeling on the floor in front of him.

I take his right foot in my hand and rest it on my lap. "Tell me if I hurt you."

Then, I carefully peel off his shoe and then his sock. The laughter is gone, and suddenly, it's silent between us. The only sound is the pitter-patter of the rain on the roof of the gazebo. It's a delicate, quiet moment as I hold his bare ankle in my hand, inspecting it for anything blue or swollen.

"Does this hurt?" I ask quietly as I squeeze the joint.

He shakes his head. Then his eyes lift to my face, and we're staring at each other, me holding his foot, softly running my thumb across his ankle. As I slowly massage his leg, he winces in pain, and I stop.

"I'm sorry."

"It's all right," he replies. "I think it's just sprained."

"Let me carry you back to the house," I say as the rain starts to lighten up.

"No, you can't do that," he replies.

"Yes, I can."

"Do you really want to?" he asks.

"I don't want you to be in pain," I say.

His eyes linger on mine before he responds. "I'm not ready to go back with them yet. I think I'd rather stay here for a little while longer."

With that, and for no good reason at all, my heart lurches with hope.

"Okay, Shakespeare," I reply, sitting comfortably on the ground in front of him, his foot still resting in my lap. "We'll stay here for a while."

The rain won't stop. Even as it lightens to a drizzle, it never fully stops. Colin is sitting across from me on the cold, wet ground. Our clothes are still soaked, and his foot is still resting on my lap to keep it elevated.

"I really can't stand him," he mutters coldly while staring out into the rain.

"Your father?"

He nods. "You know, the only reason he's even here is because he's impressed by my movie star fiancé."

I tilt my head and furrow my brow. "That can't be true."

"It is," he replies solemnly. "He never came to a performance of mine. Or my graduation or any awards ceremony. Apparently, his *other* wife is pregnant again, and they take priority."

Hanging my head back, I let out a disgruntled sigh. "Do you

hear yourself? His *other wife*? Why do you and your mum put up with him? It's ludicrous."

"Why do you think, Declan?" His expression is deadpan.

"Money," I reply sadly.

Again, he nods. "I have his inheritance, but my mum has nothing. If they divorce, she'll be left penniless. And deep down, I think she's holding on to a fantasy. I don't know… Maybe he is too, and that's why he hasn't divorced her."

We return to silence, listening only to the rain. I can't help but look up at him, watching the solemn sadness wash over his features. He always was a hopeless romantic, clinging to the idea of love in a way that was never quite realistic.

Or maybe I'm just the cynic.

"You know, for what it's worth," I say. "I loved that historical biopic you did."

"You saw that?" he asks, looking up with surprise.

"Of course," I reply nonchalantly. "I've seen everything you've done."

His eyes linger on my face for a moment before he turns toward the garden. "Pierce doesn't like it when I say yes to the low-budget films. It makes sense. I don't make as much money off of those. They don't really further my career much."

"Aye, but you enjoyed it. I could tell."

"I did," he mumbles as if lost in a memory.

"Besides, it's your decision," I reply. "Who cares what he thinks?"

At that, Colin laughs, a bone-dry laugh. "He's about to be my husband. Of course I care what he thinks."

"Well, I'm not your husband, but I'm far more interested in what *you* think, and he should be too."

Colin heaves a sigh. "Stop it, Declan," he says before rubbing his forehead. He looks irritated with me, but I'm not sure what I did.

"Stop what?" I ask.

"Stop comparing yourself to him. Stop trying to be a hero. Stop thinking you're so much better for me than he is."

With a chuff, I shake my head. *Unbelievable.* "I never said any of that," I argue.

"Yeah, well, I can hear it in your tone."

"I'm not comparing myself to him, but if I was, I'd prove to be far better."

"There it is," he replies with a laugh. "So arrogant, Declan. And all talk."

"You think *I'm* arrogant?" My tone is dripping with sarcasm. "Compared to *him*?"

"You both are," he snaps. "The only difference is that he is my fiancé."

"Well, you've got me there, Shakespeare. I'm not your fiancé. I'm not your boyfriend, and I'm not your husband. I'm your *friend*. And as your friend, I'm always going to have your back. Can you say the same thing about him?"

I can see his jaw clicking from here as he grinds his molars with frustration. "You always were such a good *friend*," he mutters under his breath.

I don't argue. I can read the subtext, and I can hear the acrimony in his voice. I was never more than his friend, even when he wanted me to be. There's nothing untrue in that argument, so I keep quiet.

As if on cue, the rain pours even harder, like the sky is commiserating.

"So what about you, huh?" he asks as he turns toward me with a tired-sounding sigh. "How come you're not engaged, or married, or dating anybody?"

"When have I ever?" I reply.

"I figured you'd grow out of it eventually," he says.

"Grow out of it?"

"Yeah, it's a little depressing, don't you think? This idea that you have to be alone forever."

"Yeah, I do," I sigh. "But it's just who I am, Colin."

"I recall," he says with a hint of sadness in his voice. "So no one's caught your fancy and made you want to change your mind?"

You have. But I don't say it out loud.

"No one," I reply flatly.

"So what are you going to do now?" he asks. "You're just going to live in this big old house by yourself? Paint and waste away for the next fifty years?"

"It doesn't sound half bad," I reply.

"Sounds miserable and lonely," he quips with a downhearted expression.

It *is* miserable and lonely. I want to tell him that, but I've always tried to protect Colin from the darker, more depressing things.

"Hey," he says, looking up at me with a bit more enthusiasm. "You remember that asshole Malcolm from uni, the rugby player?"

The sudden change of topic takes me by surprise.

"Aye," I reply, my brow furrowing as I try to recall the memory.

"Did you know that he went pro?" he asks.

"I honestly haven't given him a second thought since we graduated," I reply.

"Well, he did," Colin says with a hint of a smirk on his face. "In fact, he married an actress, and *she* was in my last film."

"Really?" I ask, suddenly intrigued. "Did you see him?"

"I did. At our wrap party."

"Did you punch him again?" I inquire with a laugh.

He shakes his head as his smile pierces his cheeks with dimples. "No, but he asked about you."

My jaw drops. "About me? Why?"

"He thought that we were together, and he figured we were still friends."

"Huh," I say. "And what did you tell him?"

Colin takes a moment as he contemplates his response. "I told him that we had lost touch," he replies sadly.

I let my eyes drift downward, away from his face, as regret pummels my insides. "That was a nice way of putting it."

He nods back at me, and neither of us says anything for a moment. This lingering reminder that Colin and I used to be something amazing, even if there was no name to the thing that we were, stings.

We were friends. We were lovers. We were in love, and yet, never together, never in the right place at the right time.

Out of nowhere, I mumble, "Do you love him?"

Colin stiffens, his throat moving as he swallows. "Declan, don't do this."

"Just tell me you love him, and I'll stop worrying."

"You don't need to worry about me anymore," he replies, shifting against the cold floor.

"Does he protect you?" I persist. "Does he listen to you? I know you give him control, Colin. I can tell. But do you trust him?"

His eyes widen as he stares at me. I'm picking open an old wound. Bringing up Colin's submissive side is a low blow, and I know it, but I need to be sure.

"Of course, I trust him," he whispers. There's an unsteadiness to his voice that triggers my concern even more.

"Like you trusted me?" I ask, and moisture grows around Colin's eyes. When he doesn't answer, I grow eager and restless. Scooting closer to him, I reach for his hand, but he pulls it away. "I'm speaking as your friend, Shelby. You are too kind, too forgiving, too pleasing to guys like him. Don't give yourself away to someone who doesn't deserve it. Don't let him—"

"There you are." An American voice calls from across the garden. Colin and I quickly shift away from each other. I hadn't seen Pierce approach or even noticed that the rain has lightened to a drizzle. He's carrying an umbrella and walking toward us with concern on his face.

My heart is hammering in my chest as I try to look natural.

My gaze keeps skipping to where Colin is sitting uncomfortably against the cold wall of the gazebo.

"Baby, what happened?" Pierce asks at seeing Colin's ankle.

"I slipped in the grass," he stutters nervously.

"Oh no, are you okay?" Pierce crouches in front of Colin.

"I'm fine. I think I just need to rest it for the afternoon."

"Of course. And this is where the cake decision needed to be made?" Pierce asks with a haughty laugh.

"No," Colin replies, glancing toward me. "I just needed a break before going back in to face my father," he says.

"Oh, he's not that bad," Pierce replies, rubbing his shoulder. "Don't give him such a hard time."

Colin doesn't respond; he just seems to retreat in on himself a little.

"Come on," Pierce says. "Let me carry you back."

"All right," Colin replies.

My chest tightens with annoyance. I offered to carry him back. It should have been me.

I've never felt so helpless in all my life. And so out of place. What am I doing here? Why do I feel as if their relationship has anything to do with me? I don't belong here.

"I should get back to work," I say, rising from the floor and brushing the dirt from my pants.

Before I can leave, Pierce claps a hand on my shoulder. "Thanks for taking care of him," he says. "But I've got it from here."

I don't respond. I just glance down at Colin briefly before nodding at Pierce. Then I turn my back on them both and march out into the rain.

Chapter Twenty-Four
Colin

Nine years ago
Amsterdam

"I've never had sex on a houseboat before." Declan drops his bag on the floor of the rental, and we both look up at the same time, smiling at each other from across the living room. We haven't seen each other in a year, and *that's* what he starts with? The word *sex* from his lips has my heart pounding excitedly. The taxi just dropped us off, and those were Declan's first words when we stepped foot inside. I wasn't quite sure if we were going to pick up where we left off, but I was planning to follow Declan's lead.

So this is a very pleasant surprise.

"Um...I thought we could go on a canal tour or go take a peek at the Red Light District," I reply coyly, taking a step toward him.

"Sure," he says with a nod of his head, taking a matching step toward me. "Or..."

I smile widely before biting my lip and looking down to hide the blush on my cheeks. We both just flew into Amsterdam this morning. I came all the way from Los Angeles, and he came from Edinburgh, where he's living with his younger brother.

On our past summer trips, we've always danced around the line a little before jumping right into it. Last summer was different though. Los Angeles set a new precedent, and I'm not upset about it at all.

"Or…" I say, coming closer and letting my voice trail.

He reaches a hand out toward me and grabs me by my collar, tugging me closer until I'm standing flush against him. There's a jolt in my belly from excitement and arousal.

"Or this," he murmurs before dipping his head down and kissing my neck. It's instant heaven. My cock twitches in my pants, growing thick as my hips reach for him.

I hum with pleasure as I latch onto him, letting my head hang to offer him more of me. He can have it all. "I wasn't sure if we were going to just…" My voice trails with hesitation.

He moves his ravenous lips from one side of my neck to the other, traveling up to my earlobe to take a gentle bite that makes me whimper.

"Just what?" he asks.

"You know. Just jump back into this," I answer.

He pulls away and stares at me with his head tilted to the side. "Is this a problem?"

In a panic, I grab his neck and haul him toward me. "Fuck no."

Then his lips are on mine, and he's kissing me with ferocity.

It's almost embarrassing how much I'm grinding against him, but he's encouraging it. Grabbing my ass, he drags me against him, using me to find friction for his own dick.

We're tearing at each other's clothes as he backs up toward the bedroom. When his legs hit the bed, he falls backward, and I quickly climb on top of him, straddling his hips and kissing him hungrily.

I love the feel of his hands on my hips. The size of his body beneath me. The softness of his chest hair against my fingers.

I'm grinding against him when he starts fumbling with the zipper and button on my pants.

"Get these off," he says. "*Now.*"

I love his commands. God, I've missed them. No one could do it the way he does. And I've tried. This was the year I finally did what Declan told me to, and I tried dating other guys. I looked for more dominant men in hopes that I'd find someone who made me feel half as good as Declan does. No such luck.

My pants are off in a split second, but when I hesitate with my briefs, I glance up to see what he does. He tears everything of his off until he's naked, and I smile to myself, pulling every stitch of clothing from my body. Before I climb back onto the bed, he moves to his knees to face me.

"Come here," he commands.

I rush onto the bed to face him, and he pulls me in for another kiss. His hands move to my hips again, and he guides my movements, making my body grind against him. How is something so subtle so damn hot?

"God, I missed you," he mumbles against my mouth. His hand traces up my back and then down to my ass, squeezing the round globe tightly in his fingers.

"I missed you too," I reply with a whimper.

"Can I tell you something?" he asks, and I tense for a moment. There is absolutely no telling what he's about to say, and I find myself feeling more hopeful than I probably should.

Tell me you don't want this summer to end.
Tell me you don't want to say goodbye.
Tell me you love me.

"What?" I reply.

"I haven't been with anyone since last summer."

I freeze, pulling back with my lips parted. "Really?"

He nods. "I don't know if it was because last summer was so fucking good or because we've just had so much going on with my family, but I haven't done a single thing with anyone since you."

I'm frozen. What does this mean? What is he trying to say?

"That's why I didn't want to do any sightseeing first. I needed this, Shakespeare. It's just so easy with you."

"Right," I mutter in response. I'm not disappointed, or so I tell myself. I should be flattered. I'm the person Declan is most comfortable with. The one to scratch that itch.

"What about you?" he asks, and I stiffen.

His hands are still on my hips, our stiff lengths lying flat between our bodies. I'm working on a way to formulate a response when he wraps his hand around my shaft, and my eyes roll back in my head.

"Come on," he urges me. "Be honest."

I can't think straight when he does that. "Um…"

Then he releases my cock and says, "Spit."

I open my eyes to find his hand open under my chin, so I do as he said, and when he returns his wet palm to my cock, it feels even better. With a whimper, I answer him. "There have been…a couple…people."

"A couple?" he asks, and I force my eyes open to gauge his reaction. The idea of him being mad at me is debilitating, but he's wearing a playful smirk, so I take that to mean he's glad I've slept around this year.

Not sure how I feel about that.

"Yeah…just three."

"Good for you, Shakespeare," he says, but this time, the smirk fades, and I feel a bit uneasy.

Then he lines our shafts up together and wraps a hand around them, stroking them together, and I feel my hips thrust into his grasp. I couldn't stop if I tried.

It feels so good.

And the last thing I want to do is talk, but Declan is insistent. "Were they good to you?" he asks.

I nod, a pained expression on my face.

"Did you use protection?"

"Yes."

"Good boy," he says, squeezing harder, and I whimper again.

My hand is gripping his arm as he holds me upright. I want to fall into his arms, but the hold on my cock is divine, and I can't move from this position. His warm, soft shaft feels like heaven against mine. Every familiar inch of him puts me in a trance. Those tight pecs. His thick thighs. The tuft of hair at the base of his cock. It's all so *Declan*, and it's all I want.

"None of them were you, though," I mumble breathlessly. It doesn't register that this might be too intimate or the wrong thing to say.

"You're fucking right they weren't," he replies with a growl.

The next thing I know, he releases our cocks. I glance down to see him pressing the tip of his cock to the tip of mine and my brows pinch together in confusion.

"What are you doing?" I whisper.

"I want to try something," he replies.

Still slick with saliva, he slides the foreskin of his cock over the head of mine, and I let out a gasp.

"Declan," I call, like I'm trying to stop him from hurting himself. He sucks a breath in through his teeth.

"Just hold still." His face is practically feral with a sneer, and his pupils are dilated. Then he starts stroking, creating a tight sleeve that suddenly takes my breath away.

I clutch tighter to his arm as tingles travel down my spine and goose bumps erupt over my skin.

The sensation is heavenly. Like being wrapped up in him. Like getting to be inside him while he's also inside me.

My mind is spinning and my body buzzing. I never want this moment to end. And it's not just the incredible sensation of tight skin and precum around the sensitive head of my dick. It's that Declan wanted to try this with *me*. He must have thought about this when we weren't together. That thought alone nearly sends me over the edge.

He's stroking rapidly, our chests heaving in sync when I'm just about to come. My head is thrown back, my eyes closed, and cries of pleasure escape my lips when he says, "Look at me, Shelby."

I turn my gaze to his face and stare at him, watching him as he slowly comes undone. It's so vulnerable and intimate, and I'm shocked that he wants me to watch it. His lips are parted, and he's breathing harshly, swept away by his own orgasm.

The groan he emits is loud and raspy a moment before I feel the warm jets of his cum as they leak from his fingers. I'm so distracted by his pleasure that I let my own slip from my grasp. When Declan nearly collapses against me, my cock is still hard between us, but I'm not disappointed. Watching him lose himself and knowing he *let me* watch was better than anything I could have felt myself.

After a moment, with his chest still gasping for breaths, Declan lifts his head up and notices I'm still hard and throbbing, my shaft covered with his release.

When he slides his body downward, I grab his arm to stop him. "No, Declan. You don't have to—"

He swats my hand away. Then he gazes into my eyes with a deadly serious expression. "I take care of you, don't I?"

I'm stunned for a moment before nodding. "Yes."

To my shock, he uses his thumb to spread his release across the length of my cock and then eases it into his mouth. My mouth is hanging open as I watch him suck me into the back of his throat, unbothered by the mess or the taste of himself.

"Declan," I murmur, reaching my fingers into his hair.

Once again, my mind echoes—*This isn't what friends do.*

This is so much more, and he won't admit it. He's gazing longingly into my eyes as he brings me so much pleasure it feels as if I could drown in it. It's not depraved or dirty or wrong. He just wants to make me feel good, and he does. God, more than anyone, he does.

I'm being swept away on a warm summer breeze, and I feel it in every inch of my body. It's not just a soul-shattering orgasm that racks through me—it's him.

His mouth never leaves me as I come, taking every drop from my body to his as if we are one. And finally, I collapse onto the mattress, staring at the ceiling. He disappears for a moment, coming back with something to wipe me clean. And then he's lying next to me. Our naked bodies are pressed together as he pulls me into his arms as if it's the most natural, normal thing in the world.

I guess, in some ways, it is.

Chapter Twenty-Five
Colin

Declan and I walk side by side down the street in Amsterdam. I'm eating a chocolate-covered waffle, and he has his arm around my shoulder, mostly to keep me from wandering into the bike lane and nearly being killed.

"An advert, huh?" he asks before taking a puff off of his cigarette.

"Not just any advert. A *cologne* advert. They usually give those to, like, models and A-list celebrities," I reply before taking a bite.

"They chose you though, so they must know what they're doing then," he replies.

I smile to myself. There's something about his compliments that just feel better than anyone else's.

"This could be a huge break for me," I say.

"I have no doubt, Shakespeare. It's only a matter of time before the world discovers what a star you are."

"You're just saying that," I reply, turning toward him with a soft grin on my face.

"I would never lie to you." Then, he shoots me one of his signature winks and leans forward to steal the last bite of my waffle. He ends up with chocolate all over his face, so we both stop, and I wipe it clean. We're chuckling in the middle of a warm summer street in Amsterdam, and it feels like heaven.

We feel like a couple.

It's the only thing that gives me the confidence to bring up what I want to bring up. "So…" I say before tossing the paper and napkin into a nearby bin. "I've been learning some things."

His brows shoot upward. "Oh yeah? What kinds of things?"

We continue our walk along the canal, and while we're supposed to be admiring the architecture and city, I'm too distracted by him.

"Things for us," I say, starting simple.

His head turns as he stares at me quizzically. After discarding his cigarette butt, he puts his hands in his pockets casually. "Okay," he mutters quietly.

"You know…" I stammer. "Things you could tell me to do. Or things you could do to me…"

"I'm listening." He's watching me from the corner of his eye as he walks.

"It's not quite the conversation to have in public, Declan," I reply as I glance at the other pedestrians around us.

"We're in Amsterdam, Shakespeare. Whatever it is, they've heard it."

I laugh out loud as I spot a pub to our left. With a grin and a shake of my head, I grab his arm and drag him inside. We find a corner table and order two Heinekens while I work up the nerve to have this conversation.

"All right," he says, placing his hand on my bouncing knee. "Tell me everything."

The pub around us is noisy, but the corner we're in feels quiet and intimate. He's leaning toward me over the warm glow of a lit candle inside a small green jar. Suddenly, all of my nerves dissipate as I realize this is Declan. I can tell him anything. I can trust him with my life. He won't laugh at me or judge me.

I rest my hand on the table, and he instantly sets his on top of it as a show of comfort.

"So when I say that you can do whatever you want to me, I mean it. And I want you to. You could…" I gulp down my nerves. "You could tie me up. You could…punish me. Make me your slave or turn me into furniture for all I care. I just…like the idea of being…used by you."

Declan doesn't tear his eyes away from me for a moment as I'm speaking. And even after I'm done, he's staring across the small space as if I've just stunned him into a trance. When he finally blinks and turns his gaze away, he has to clear his throat before speaking.

"We would need a safe word," he says.

"Sure," I reply with a shrug. "But that's something you'd like?"

"Of course," he says breathlessly.

Then, I lean forward until we're just a breath away from each other. "I don't just want you to take control, Declan. I want to feel your power. I want you to use it on me."

He makes a noise somewhere between a growl and a whimper.

"Anything I want?" he asks.

"Yes, sir," I reply, testing the title on him, and he responds by biting his bottom lip.

I wish we were alone right now, and I think he does too. Under the table, he squeezes my knee to the point of pain.

"Pick a safe word," he says.

In my head, I know I'll never use it. But he wants me to choose one, so I will.

"Amsterdam," I reply.

"Fine," he says. "Now, let's get the fuck out of here."

We ditch our half-full beers on the table and practically bolt out of the pub. We don't say a word as we rush back to the houseboat. I stay just behind him as we go, loving the way this submission feels already.

I meant every word I said to Declan, but I wonder if he realizes just how far I'm willing to go for him. It feels as if our physical relationship is at a precipice, and it's up to us to take it to the next level.

When we reach the houseboat, he unlocks the door, and we rush inside. "Get on your knees," he barks immediately, not wasting one second.

I'm filled with excitement as I drop to the floor. My heart feels like it could beat its way right out of my chest.

He undoes his belt and walks toward me, looking sexier and more dominant than I've ever seen him. My cock is throbbing in my pants already.

"Listen to me, Shelby," he says, and I notice the way he uses my last name in sexy scenarios. My first name is only for very cross, serious moments. And Shakespeare for everything else.

I gaze up at him obediently, ready to be the best fucking sub for him.

"I want to hear you promise me right now that you'll use that safe word if you need to."

There's a flinch in my expression. That's not what I expected to hear. "Of course, but I won't need to," I reply, trying to show him just how much I trust him.

"We need limits, Shelby."

"I don't want limits," I argue.

He takes my chin in his grip. "I'm fucking serious, Colin. Tell me right now that you'll use it."

I hesitate for a moment. This isn't going how I planned at all, and we haven't even started yet. Is he expecting me to stop him? I don't want to do what *I* want. I want to do what *he* wants.

"I don't understand. I trust you. You know I do," I reply softly.

His shoulders melt away from his ears, and I see the disappointment wash over his features. Feeling the need to correct this situation, I add, "Declan, I *want* you to hurt me."

He releases my chin and steps away. With a withered sigh, he drops onto the bed and rests his arms on his knees.

"What did I do?" I ask.

"Come here," he says in a soft command.

I move to all fours and crawl toward him. When I reach his

knees, I settle myself between them. Resting his hands on my face, he pulls me up until I'm nearly kissing him.

"I know you trust me, Shelby. But I need to trust you. I don't want to *really* hurt you. I want to know that when I've found your limit, you'll tell me. But I can't."

"Yes, you can," I plead. "I'll tell you."

But he shakes his head. "No, you won't."

Deep down, I know he's right. I won't. There's no scenario where I'd be willing to stop him. No chance that I'd ever speak up or make him stop, because even that takes courage I'm afraid I don't have.

Emotion boils inside of me. It's anger and embarrassment and sadness. I feel my cheeks heating as tears fill my eyes. Humiliated, I try to pull away, but he stops me.

"I said come here," he says, holding me closer. And when he pulls me into an embrace, I try to get away, but he doesn't let me. Instead, I press my face to his chest and let out an angry sigh.

"What is wrong with me?" I ask.

"Why do you always ask that? There is *nothing* wrong with you," he whispers. "There's nothing wrong with wanting to be dominated, Shelby. But it's my job to protect you."

Trembling in his arms, I realize he doesn't mean his job as my friend, but his job as my Dom, and that shakes me to my core.

"Then, why can't I do this? Why can't I speak up for myself?"

"I don't know, baby," he replies. Every time he lets that pet name slip, it makes my heart stop. I hate how good it feels. "We can work on it, though," he says. "I think we just got excited, and we almost jumped into something that takes time and preparation. We can do little things until we get there."

"We?" I ask, knowing that there are only eight days this summer and then twelve whole months until we're together again.

"Yes, *we*," he says. "Because I'll be damned if I'm going to send you back to LA like this and let someone else who doesn't care about you step all over you. Not on my fucking watch."

I laugh into his chest as he holds me. Then I say something I haven't said in a very long time.

"You're my best friend, Declan."

He squeezes me tighter. "Aye. And I always will be."

Part of me thinks he says that because he knows I want more, and he wants to let me down gently. He knows that it will always be just sex to him and never beyond that.

But I also think that we are more. We might not live together or be romantic in ways other people understand, but we're both so messed up that this is enough for us. We don't make sense to others, but we make sense to each other, and that's all that matters.

"Let's get drunk," he says.

So we both stand up. He grabs two beers from the fridge, and we take them to the roof of the boat, where there's a small balcony and a beautiful view of the city. It's not what we had planned for tonight, but seeing as how that was an immediate disaster, this might actually be better.

Neither of us speak for a while, but finally, I find the nerve to say something first. "I came out to my parents."

Declan gapes at me in surprise. "Why the fuck didn't you tell me?"

I shrug. "Because it was nothing."

"Horse shite. It wasn't nothing."

"They treated it like it was nothing. They weren't offended or surprised or happy. They both just nodded their heads, and it was really uncomfortable until my father brought up something else."

"You've got to be joking," he says.

"Maybe that's why I'm such a people pleaser," I say with a laugh. "My parents raised me to never make a sound. Not a single peep."

"Fuck that," he mutters, taking a pull from the bottle. "We're going out to celebrate, because it most certainly is *not* nothing."

As I lift my beer to my lips, I feel a smile tug at the corners because I realize that Declan has been teaching me to cause waves and make noise since I met him six years ago. He's been slowly healing me this entire time.

Chapter Twenty-Six
Colin

"This list is quite extensive," I say, scrolling through the website on my phone that Declan sent me this morning.

"Extensive is good," he replies.

It's our last day in Amsterdam, and while the week has been filled with all of the sex and time with Declan that I have wanted, we've decided to slow things down on the kinky exploration.

At first, I was disappointed—no, devastated. But he's right. I'm not ready. Not if he can't trust me.

So it was his idea to find one of these lists online, things that a couple could do in the bedroom, and I would fill it out for him, or I guess for anyone. That way, boundaries are set in place beforehand, and it would potentially prevent anything harmful from happening.

"I mean, how do I know if I don't want…" My voice trails off before glancing around to be sure nobody can hear us on our walk. "Fisting," I whisper, "until I've tried it?"

Declan laughs. "That is where safe words come in handy, Shakespeare," he replies. "Because you don't want to be in the middle of that and decide you don't like it without a way of expressing it."

I heave a sigh. "True. Best strike it through for now."

I scroll through the rest of the list, feeling a bit bittersweet about it. As exciting as some of this is, I realize that a lot of it would require something Declan and I don't have—time.

"I wish you could come to California," I say, knowing how reckless it is.

"I would," he replies, which takes me by surprise.

"You would?"

"It's just that my family's going through a lot right now, with my brother and the house. We're still struggling," he replies. "I think we still need to be near each other, and I don't want to leave them."

"I understand." Even though I hate it. I hate that grief has caused more than pain. That it's maimed his entire life and future. "Maybe I could make it back to London more," I say in a hopeful tone.

"No. Your career is about to take off, Shakespeare. That should be your priority, not time with me."

I know he's right, but it still hurts.

"Now finish that form, because I want to show you something before I take you back to the houseboat. We still have one last night together."

I've never felt more motivated to fill out a form in my life, so I do as he says. We're walking slowly down a quiet side street as I scroll through the list, being a bit more conservative as I click the items that I feel quite confident I wouldn't say no to.

As usual, he holds me by his side, keeping me from walking into traffic. Just as I finish the list, he stops at a doorway down a quiet street.

"What's this?" I ask.

"I want to show you something," he replies, "but I don't want you to make a big deal out of it." His expression is stern, which makes me laugh.

"What are you talking about?"

"I have never brought anyone here, and I haven't even told anyone about it, okay? So it's just you."

He seems almost nervous, which is strange for Declan. He's always so confident and relaxed around me, but it's almost like he's looking at me for comfort.

"Just me? What on earth is this?" Then I read the inscription on the door. "An art gallery?" I ask.

"Come on," he says with a sigh. Then he opens the door and ushers me inside. There's a prickle of excitement under my skin.

A handsome man with curly hair and a sharp suit greets us at the door. With his hands behind his back, he nods toward Declan as he says, "Afternoon, Mr. Barclay."

"Afternoon, Karl," he responds.

"What is going on?" I ask in confusion.

"Please have a look around," the man says, "and let me know if you need anything."

"Thanks, Karl," Declan replies as he rests a hand on the small of my back. Then he leads me gently through a door of the gallery, and I scan the room, confused. We've been to a fair share of museums this weekend. We saw the Van Gogh Museum and the Rijksmuseum, so I'm a bit perplexed as to why we're at this small gallery with artists I've never heard of before.

"Like I said," he mumbles, "don't make a big deal out of it."

"Make a big deal out of what?" I ask, but then we turn a corner, and there it is. Or should I say, there *I* am?

"Just be glad I didn't use the naked one on the couch," he whispers in my ear, but I don't respond. I can't. I'm speechless.

To anyone else, they might not recognize that the man in the painting is me, but I know because I recognize the moment. It was a midnight coffee shop with intimate lighting. I'm slumped on a green velvet sofa, a drunken smile on my face as I hold my hands over my eyes, laughing behind my fingers.

Declan's paintings have such unique qualities. The way he captures light and emotion, the way I can feel what he's feeling as he paints his subjects. And yet, I've never seen this painting before. He must have done it from memory of that night. The one where I got too drunk, and he sacrificed whatever meaningless hookup would have awaited him to take care of me.

The night we shared cappuccinos and secrets.

The night he became my best friend.

It was always significant to me. I had no idea it was so significant to him.

"Declan," I whisper. "How? Why?"

"The guy who owns this place," he says, "is a friend of a friend, and he asked for a piece of mine to feature, so I gave him this one. It was hard to part with."

"How come you never showed me this?" I ask.

"I don't know," he says. "I was embarrassed, I guess. I didn't want you to think it was weird of me to paint you that night, but I just remember it so vividly that it was easy."

I take a step forward and read the inscription next to the painting: *A beautiful man in warm light.* A smile stretches across my face.

"You think I'm beautiful?" I ask, turning toward him with a coy smirk. Normally, I'm the one blushing, but this time, I notice a rosy tint on Declan's cheeks as he grins and shakes his head.

"Of course I do," he replies, trying to remain casual. "I wouldn't enjoy fucking you so much if I didn't."

I think he means it to be a sort of cool and macho answer, but I see right through it. Because the fact that Declan and I have sex with each other is about a lot more than him thinking I'm beautiful. He knows it, and I know it.

"Wait, is this your first artwork in a gallery?" I ask.

He presses his lips together tightly before nodding. "Aye," he mutters.

"And you showed me?"

"Who else would I show?" he asks as if to say no one is more important to him.

Reaching over, I interlace my fingers with his as I press my lips to his cheek. "Thank you," I say.

"Don't make a big deal out of it," he mutters. "But you're welcome."

I'm lying naked between Declan's legs, my face resting on his stomach as he brushes his fingers through my hair. It must be three in the morning, but I can't sleep. Even after nearly two hours of sex, I'm wide-awake.

And clearly, so is he.

I think we're both just trying to prolong the inevitable and soak up every last second that we can.

"Can I ask you a personal question?" I whisper.

"You've got your mouth just inches from my cock, Shakespeare. I think we're past having to ask that."

With a quiet snicker, I continue. "That day in the pool, you said you weren't straight. So what are you?"

"What am I?" he replies with a tilt of his head. "A drunk. An idiot. A horny Scotsman."

I laugh before twisting a patch of his chest hair. He howls as I add, "You know what I mean."

"Okay, okay," he chuckles. "To be honest, Shelby, I don't know. I've never found my attraction as something easy to define, but I've always wanted you. You, the person. You, the man. Do I need a label for that?"

A smile splits across my face as I softly spin my fingers across his chest. "No, you don't."

We're silent for a moment before I add, "Does your family know? I mean…would they have a problem with you and another man?"

His jaw clenches for a moment. "No. They just want me to be happy. We all do."

"And your parents?" I ask, uneasy about bringing them up since I know it sometimes sends Declan into a dark place.

"They would have loved you."

My chest warms as I stare up at him. As I rest my face back on his stomach, I think about how unfair it is that Declan was blessed with such a happy family only to have them taken so tragically. And yet, my father abuses his with deception and lies.

More than ever, I want to be someone significant to Declan. I want to patch the hole their deaths left behind.

And I think about the painting he showed me today. How clear that moment was for him. How perfectly he recreated it.

"Why is it that you can paint some things from memory so vividly?" I ask.

"Some moments just stay in mind, I guess," he murmurs.

"Like that night at the coffee shop?"

"Aye, Shakespeare. And that night in the pool. And that night in your room in Dublin. And the beach in California."

I rest my chin on my hands and stare up at him through the dim light through the windows. "So just me then?" I ask coyly.

He smiles. "You, yes. But not just you."

"Oh? Is there someone else?" It's a playful question with a hint of worry hiding underneath. Does Declan ever care about anyone as much as he cares about me?

"I remember my parents vividly," he says in a melancholy tone.

"How old were you when they died?" I ask.

"Thirteen."

"It's quite impressive that you remember them so well," I reply, gently running my thumb along the soft skin of his stomach. "Will you tell me about them?"

It's not that I've never asked or wondered in all of these years, but Declan has never been so open. It feels as if the doors to an estate with treasures inside have been briefly opened. Any small piece of Declan is like gold to me.

"My mother was very funny," he says with a crooked smile. "She had wild hair like Killian, but it was warm like Anna's. She was such a good mother, and she loved us all very much. That manor was our whole world, and she never wanted to leave it. She would say that she had everything she could ever need there."

I squeeze him tighter, noticing the hint of moisture in his eyes as he stares absently into the darkness of our room.

"Will you take me there?" I ask.

"I wish I could," he replies.

"Why can't you?"

He strokes my hair as he stares into my eyes. "Because I'm afraid if I take you there, I'll never want to leave."

"That's okay," I whisper. "I'd stay. I'd stay with you anywhere."

He heaves a sigh as he replies. "I know, Shakespeare. That's what I'm afraid of."

I swallow the emotion building in my throat. "Tell me about your dad."

"My da was a very serious and strict man. But he had a soft side. He loved animals, and he was always gentle with us. He loved my mother more than anything, though. I think she understood him like no one else could."

"They sound lovely," I murmur. "You must miss them very much."

"I miss…" His voice trails, and he freezes for a moment, swept up in his own emotions. Paralyzed by them. "I miss the way things used to be. When life felt normal. When the sun would shine, and the future felt bright."

"The future can still be bright, Declan," I say, reaching for his hand. "This doesn't need to hang over you forever. You can still be happy."

"How?" he asks. "I can look happy. I can pretend. But I can't feel it anymore, Colin."

Tears prick my eyes as I crawl up and lie closer to him. Bringing his face to mine, I kiss his lips gently. "It breaks my heart to hear you say that. I just want you to be happy."

"These summers with you make me happy," he replies.

"Then, let's spend all year together, Declan," I say.

Hope, like a flood, courses through me as I stare into his eyes. And when he doesn't immediately shut down the idea, I nearly get swept away by it.

"I'll come to London. I can work from there," I say, touching his face. "And you can live in London. It's close enough to your family, right?"

"Shelby…"

"Just listen," I beg. "Let me help you. There are therapists who deal with these things. You don't have to live this way. I'll be your sunshine."

When he blinks, a tear slips down his cheek, and I lean forward to kiss the track it leaves behind. Then I kiss his lips. And when I pull away, I wait for him to tell me how this plan won't work. How we can't be together all year.

Instead, he whispers, "Okay."

"Okay?" I ask excitedly.

"Aye." He nods. "But only if you're certain you can still work from London."

"I'll figure it out."

Then I kiss him hungrily. This feels like everything I've ever wanted is finally within my grasp. Not only will I have all of Declan all year long, but I can finally help him get the care he needs. I can be there for him the way he's always been there for me.

"It'll be like old times again," he mumbles against my lips.

I smile for a moment before the words sink in, and I feel my smile fade. *Old times.*

I don't want it to be like old times. Is that what he thinks this will be? Roommates? Friends again?

Pulling back, I stare into his eyes, searching for a sign that maybe I'm wrong. I misheard him. That's not what he means.

But I don't dare question it. Because this moment is too delicate, and if I ask for too much, I could lose it all.

Chapter Twenty-Seven
Declan

Two days until the wedding

THE RAIN WON'T STOP. THE FORECAST IS CALLING FOR A MAJOR storm this weekend. Not just rain, but gale-force winds and possibly even hail, in July.

On top of that, Colin's ankle is sprained. He's been instructed by the doctor to stay off of it all day. He and Pierce were supposed to have their photos taken today, but with the roads too dangerous, the photographer canceled. Which means everyone is just stuck in the house together.

Colin's parents are staying at a resort in the city, so thank God for that.

"I heard rain was good luck for a wedding," Blaire says to Colin as she serves him tea in the parlor. With nothing to do, he and Pierce are bored to tears. Pierce seems to be keeping busy with work on his computer and apparently practicing his lines.

And I keep finding reasons to go into the room they're in.

"Thank you," Colin says to Blaire with a warm smile. "I hope that's true."

"Don't you have an indoor gym or something?" Pierce complains. "We can't just sit stationary all day like this."

"Colin is supposed to be stationary today," I reply flatly, earning me a glare from the American.

"Fine," he says, closing his computer. "We can just use this time to plan our bachelor party tomorrow night."

"Pierce," Colin says in a warning.

"What? We obviously need a bachelor party, and we decided we were going to have one together."

The hairs on the back of my neck rise as I glance back and forth between the two of them. I have a feeling this has to do with the argument I heard them have yesterday. I was hoping I just heard it wrong, or they would let it blow over without bringing it up.

"Pierce," Colin says again, this time sitting up on the couch as if he's going to stand.

"Okay, okay, relax," he says, putting his hands out toward Colin.

Since there's not much reason for me to be in the room, I turn to leave, but Pierce immediately calls me back. "Please, for the love of God, don't leave."

"What can I do for ye?" I ask.

"Why don't you tell me some more stories about my Colin when he was younger? I'm bored to fucking tears, and I need something. Apparently, he can't fuck with that sprained ankle either, so I'm begging you. Entertain me."

My eyes narrow with my back to the man. I don't like that I find comfort in the fact that Colin told him no to sex and blamed it on the ankle.

"Okay," I reply as I go to the bar in the corner and pull out three glasses. Then I pour whiskey into each and deliver them to the two men, keeping one for myself. "What would you like to hear?"

I drop into the chair opposite Pierce and watch him over the top of my glass as I take a sip.

"We're all adults here. Let's not beat around the bush," he says with a mischievous grin. "How long did you two fuck?"

"Pierce!" Colin nearly flies out of the armchair he's sitting in. His bad foot is resting on the ottoman, but he lets out a wince of pain as he tries to move it. I put my hand up to stop him.

"Sit down," I say to Colin. Then I turn toward Pierce. "This is a conversation for you and your partner."

"He's already told me you've slept together. I just thought it would be fun to hear the dirty details. He won't tell me those," Pierce says with a wink.

"Then neither will I." My tone is dry, and my expression is flat. Everything about this guy rubs me the wrong way. He seems to think he is at the center of the universe, and Colin and I are mere satellites in his orbit.

I can't wait until this weekend is over and I never have to see him again.

"Oh, come on!" Pierce begs, taking his entire glass of whisky in one shot. "Don't be ridiculous. I'm not a jealous man. In fact, I think it's incredibly hot, and I just want to hear what you two were like."

"Don't you see how personal that is?" Colin asks as he rubs his forehead.

"Personal?" Pierce asks, sounding offended. He looks at me and then back at his fiancé. "You told me it was just sex."

My gaze snaps over to Colin as I wait for his response. He looks up sadly as he says, "It was."

That really should not hurt as much as it does. Being served a dose of my own medicine. Isn't that what I once told him? It was just sex.

It was *never* just sex.

I wish I could scream that at him right now. But he's using those words against me, and I know it. I can't argue with him, not here and not in front of Pierce, but if he wants to know how it was never just sex, I'll tell him. Let his bloody fiancé hear how *just sex* it was.

"Oh, come on, Shakespeare," I say. "Did you tell him how I was your first?"

Colin shoots me a surprised expression.

"Here we go," Pierce says with an excited smile.

"Yes, I did," Colin replies softly.

With a crooked grin, I continue. "Did you tell him about that night in the gymnasium when we were running from those rugby pricks?" I ask, never taking my eyes off Colin. His eyes are warm as he waits for me to continue.

"The night you put your mouth on me for the first time. I never would have believed you were inexperienced. Or the night in Dublin when you let me crawl into your bed. How you begged me to call you mine. Do you remember that night?"

"Of course I do," he mumbles. His tongue darts out to lick his bottom lip before tugging it between his teeth.

"How many times did we have *just sex* in Amsterdam?" I ask to make a point. Colin tries to bite back a smile, but I see it fighting to come through. "Twice a day, was it? No, maybe more."

"Definitely more," he says with a blush to his cheeks.

"We were both quite inexperienced, weren't we? But we learned together."

"Yes, we did," he says. The connection between us is visceral, and I wonder if he can feel it too. "The houseboat wasn't the only thing docked that week."

A cackle flies out of my mouth, and he snickers to himself at his little pun.

This is dangerous. I don't know why I'm doing this, reliving old memories and bringing up how good we used to be together.

"I bet you two were hot," Pierce says, and it's like being doused in ice-cold water. Suddenly, I realize he's here, and it shakes me out of my reverie.

Standing up, I go back to the bar and pour myself another.

Neither Colin nor I speak for a moment because we both got caught up in our memories. And Pierce thought we were sharing those moments with him. I would never invite him into those memories.

"Sounds like us when we first met," Pierce says, and the saccharine-sweet tone of his voice makes me sick. "Fucking like rabbits all day. I had you collared so fast, didn't I?"

I nearly spit out my drink. "Collared?"

My Colin...collared?

"How fast?" I add, turning toward them with scrutiny. Pierce smiles proudly, but Colin looks like he's trying to fold in on himself.

"What was it, baby?" Pierce asks. "Two weeks?"

"Two weeks?" I repeat, this time glaring at Colin.

It's wrong of me to feel so surprised.

What the fuck did I think was going to happen? That Colin and I would share a moment, and Pierce would just fuck off? Obviously not. That's *his* fiancé. Not mine. I can't speak about another man's lover and expect it not to take a turn.

But this? To hear that he let someone else take such intimate, devoted control of him after only *two fucking weeks*? Colin can feel my disappointment, because he won't look at me. He's ashamed of letting someone else take his trust without earning it. I taught him better.

"Did you ever have him collared?" Pierce asks with arrogance, and I'd like to punch him. Collaring is intimate and significant, and he's treating Colin like a show dog who's changed owners. I could wring his fucking neck for the way he's looking at *my* Colin right now.

I don't bother answering his question because the next time I open my mouth, I will certainly spew brutal honesty at this insincere prick.

I can't stand to be in this room anymore. Frankly, I don't care if Pierce is bored or if I'm supposed to keep them entertained. I can't take another fucking minute of hearing about them together.

"If you'll excuse me," I say brashly. Turning on my heel, I walk briskly out the door, feeling Colin's eyes on me as I go.

I'm marching toward the kitchen when I hear the harsh click of Pierce's shoes behind me in the hall. I let out a groan when he calls my name.

"Barclay."

I stop in my tracks, letting out a disgruntled sigh before turning around to face him.

"Can I help you?" I ask with as much forced enthusiasm as I can muster, as if that last twenty minutes didn't happen. As if we didn't just openly discuss my sex life with his fiancé like it was nothing.

He smiles as he approaches me and wraps an arm around my shoulders, and I find it disgustingly annoying just how charming he is. Everything about him feels fake, like a viper luring me to my death.

"Hey, don't sweat it," he says cooly. "If you think I was bothered by that conversation, I promise you I was not."

"I'm relieved to hear that," I mutter through clenched teeth. In reality, I couldn't care less about his feelings. That has nothing to do with my sudden disgruntled mood.

"You do realize I'm not one of those uptight, jealous types, right? In fact…" He glances back toward the room where we both just left Colin. "Listen, can I be frank?" he asks as he pulls me to the end of the hall.

"Of course," I mutter with hesitance.

"Watching the two of you together is hot. I can see the history you have, and there's clearly some chemistry there. And he's assured me that it was always just physical between you too."

"What is your point?" I ask with a grunt.

"Well, you should know that Colin and I have a special relationship."

"Special?"

"How do I put this?" he says as he crosses his arms. "I love my fiancé very much. I think he's fantastic. He's sexy, smart, and beautiful. Everybody wants him."

My spine stiffens as I listen to him talk about Colin this way. *My* Colin.

"And I take great pride in the fact that he's mine," he says, his voice lower and more menacing. "It's sort of like having a nice car. Something really rare, maybe even a classic. And rather than keep it in your garage, you like to take it for drives and show it off a little bit."

What the fuck is he getting at? Every muscle in my body is stiff and uneasy.

"I like lending out my car too. I want to show off how nice it drives. You get me?"

My blood turns molten with rage. I don't respond as he leans in with a smarmy grin.

"Do you understand what I'm trying to say, Barclay?" he asks, and I tilt my head to the side, afraid that I know *exactly* what he's trying to say.

"I'm saying that I'd like you to drive my car."

Instantly, I feel sick. My molars grind. My eyes narrow. My fists clench. I want to punch him.

No, worse. I want to put him in the hospital. I want to make him bleed. Make him cry. I want to make him regret the day he ever walked into my house. No—the day he ever touched Colin.

I want to make him regret ever talking about him like this or even getting this sick idea in his head. Something violent and hateful courses through my veins as I stare at him, disbelieving that I'm actually hearing what he's saying to me right now.

He shakes my shoulder, and I quickly pull it away. "Relax, Barclay. You know this is all completely consensual. He likes it."

No, he doesn't. Not my Colin. He wouldn't.

"What are you talking about?" I mutter darkly.

"I think you know what I'm talking about," he replies with a smirk. "I've watched you two together this week. I see the way you watch him. The way you *want* him."

I struggle to move away, but he holds me tighter, keeping me at his side. This is all a show of strength. Of power.

"So you want me to…"

"Yes," he replies, watching me with a villainous stare. "I want you to fuck my fiancé while I watch."

"So you can reclaim him, right? You can prove you're more powerful than me. That he really belongs to you." My lip pulls into a sneer.

"Now, you're getting it," Pierce says, shaking my shoulders with a laugh. "Colin and I don't want a regular bachelor party. We want something special, and we were hoping tomorrow night we could have that here."

"Why the fuck would I agree to any of this?" I argue.

"Because you want him, don't you? You can try to deny it, but we all know the truth. And if you want our wedding here…well, then you'll be accommodating, won't you?"

Something inside of me snaps. My hands collide with Pierce's chest as I shove him away. I ball them into fists and somehow manage to hold myself back from pummeling them into his face.

"You don't want to do that," he says with confidence, glancing down at my fists. His casual, arrogant manner only heightens my rage. He seems to think this all means nothing. Like he didn't just try to blackmail me into having a fucking sex party for him.

"Come on," he says just above a whisper. "I was hoping you'd try to challenge me. Tell me you'll win him over or make him pick you or some shit. This is really disappointing."

"What the fuck is wrong with you?"

"Me? What's wrong with you? I expected you to be into this."

"He's not a prize. He's a person, and he doesn't deserve to be fought over like this. It's sick."

Pierce laughs quietly, glancing behind him toward where Colin is still alone in the room. "You know he likes it. He wants it."

"No, he doesn't," I mutter again.

"You think you know him, but you don't."

Something about that line has me feeling nauseous. Maybe he's right. Maybe I don't know Colin anymore.

I'd still like to punch him, but I don't. Instead, I turn and march away, furious and indignant.

"Think about it!" he calls after me.

I don't respond. I just march through the door to my wing of the house, outrage and anger coursing through my veins.

This can't be happening. Colin can't possibly let this happen. Not my Colin. He would *never* agree to be treated this way.

My stomach is rioting, clenching. My mind is whirling. I'm so furious. I feel as if I'm on the verge of tears.

I want to scream.

I want to break something.

If it wasn't pouring out, I'd light that fucking gazebo on fire right now, so there's no place to have a wedding in two days.

I march up the stairs to my studio, ready to tear the entire room to shreds. I pull a pack of cigarettes out of my back pocket and light one with shaking fingers. I'm a mess. I can't think straight.

I just keep replaying that entire conversation, trying to find the part where I'm confused, because this can't be real. Why is this happening? I'm being fucking tested, that's what this is.

I couldn't get a simple wedding to win a bet with. No, I had to get a wedding with the one man I've loved and his sleazy maniacal fucking arsehole of a fiancé, and I have to go through with this.

I have to make this wedding happen. I have to. That was my goal. That's what I wanted.

Do the wedding. Win the bet. Get the house. Live in peace.

Because if I don't do that, then what? Then I'm stuck forever facing the dark void of infinity alone for the rest of my life. Forever watching wedding after wedding in my own home, knowing that I'll never have that.

I'll never find love or companionship—the things everybody wants and searches for. It will never be in the cards for me. Any chances of that were stolen from me somewhere in my youth by an ever-evolving tempest of grief and trauma that went uncured and instead built a man incapable of attachment.

I can't face that.

I can't face anything.

The only place where it's easy is when I'm alone, or I have my art and my demons, and we have no one to answer to. Where life isn't cruel but quiet, and I'm not constantly reminded of the person I had and the love I threw away.

Rather than pick up any brushes or clay, I dig for the bottle of whisky that rolled under the table before this whole charade began. It's only half full, but that will be enough for tonight.

Trading puffs off the cigarettes for pulls from the bottle, I drown myself until I can't feel it anymore. Until the gnawing reminder that I've lost Colin forever doesn't feel like the weight of an elephant on my chest.

Because this was the nail in the coffin. He's not just marrying Pierce. He belongs to him—truly belongs to him.

The way he once belonged to me.

When the bottle is empty, and the liquor hits my bloodstream, the room grows fuzzy and dark. It muffles the pain and quiets the voices. When I crawl onto the mattress, all I know is that I can't feel anything—except for a warm pair of arms wrapped around me as I drift off to darkness.

Chapter Twenty-Eight
Colin

Eight years ago
Tuscany

I'm waiting for him on my knees. Exactly as we discussed on the phone. My hands are shaking, and I'm biting my lip when I hear the cab door close outside.

What if it's not Declan? What if it's the Italian rental homeowner who's just popping in to find a British actor naked on his floor?

I need to get out of my head. We discussed this.

This week would be different from all the rest, because this week, I would be his *for real*. Well, for real, in the kinky bedroom sense. Not for real in the romantic relationship sense.

I've given up on that ship—it sailed a long time ago.

No, this week, Declan and I made very specific plans to take our sexual relationship to the next level. The hardest part might actually be not running into his arms when I see him. Missing him during our year apart gets harder and harder every year. And it never makes a difference how many people I sleep with or what I do.

In fact, I actually found another friend with benefits this year. Except we don't have sex. He's just taken me under his wing to show me all the kinky, submissive things I want to know. He helps me to understand why I enjoy this so much. And how to set boundaries for myself without feeling like a people pleaser all the time. So I no longer feel so weird about the things I like.

The automatic lock to the front door sounds, and my spine straightens with excitement. He's here. This is happening.

I bite my bottom lip to keep from smiling as he walks in and drops his bag by the door.

"Oh fuckin' hell," he mutters with a sexy rasp to his voice. "This place comes with some fancy bloody amenities."

I chuckle under my breath. "You're not supposed to make me laugh."

"Shite. Sorry," he says before clearing his throat. Then he takes a few steps toward me, his brown leather shoes clicking against the tile floor. "This is one of those moments that's going to burn into my memory, Shakespeare. The sight of you on the floor waiting for me. I could get used to this."

"I'm all yours," I say, glancing up at him.

He reaches down on an exhale and runs his fingers over the short strands of my hair. It's much shorter than normal for a part. I landed a role in a popular franchise, and the character I played had a buzz cut. It was hard to part with my gold locks, but it was well worth it. This role was by far my highest-paying job yet.

As for Declan, he looks better than ever. His hair is actually longer than I've ever seen it, down to his shoulders. Tucked back behind his ears, it curls so nicely and looks so sexy. His facial hair is short, but it's the first time I've seen him with anything resembling a beard.

"Lucky me," he mumbles in response. "And what shall I do with ye?"

"Anything you'd like," I reply.

"Honestly, you look so fucking good right now. I think I'd just like to look at you."

Leaning back on my feet, I gaze up at him as I fight the urge to smile. "All right."

After a moment, he walks to the large armchair in the living room. Then, he pats his knee and says, "Come here."

I move to all fours and crawl toward him, eager to please. When I reach him, he pats his knee again and says, "Up here. Let me look at you."

So I climb onto his lap, and he settles into the chair, letting his eyes and hands take their time with me. He absorbs me slowly as if he's savoring me.

It's a far cry from the two young men who found themselves making out in a university gymnasium after hours. How far we've come in just four years.

"You are so beautiful," he whispers as he runs his hand up my leg. My cock is lying half hard on my thigh, waiting desperately to be touched. But he teases me, taking his time. Instead, he draws his fingers up my spine and down my neck.

He pulls me toward him, kissing me under my ear and on my shoulder.

I know what he's doing. He's warming me up. Making me die for his touch. Getting me so needy for him that I won't be able to function without him.

It's a cruel and salacious trick.

And it works like a charm.

The more he teases me, the more fired up he gets, until he's humming against my skin, nibbling the flesh of my chest and back as if he's trying to take small bites of me. It's a mixture of pain and ecstasy, and I need more.

"Get on the floor," he mutters in my ear.

I move to my knees between his legs and wait for the word. He starts unbuttoning his shirt as he says, "Take my cock out, Shelby."

My fingers are ravenous as I work open his trousers.

"Take them off," he says as he lifts his ass off the seat.

I'm tearing them down and then working on each of his shoes to get his trousers off completely. It takes a moment of work, but finally, I have him on the chair in nothing but his tight briefs, and it's everything I wanted.

I wish I could stop time. I wish I could build my entire life around this moment right here. I'm kneeling naked on the floor for the love of my life. And the best part is him finally knowing he can trust me. We have gotten to this place, and it feels like one step closer to the life of my dreams.

"Go ahead," he says, nodding down to his cock. I can see it thick and straining against his briefs.

As he reclines back in the chair, his arms resting on the sides, he reminds me of a god. And I get to pleasure him. I'm the one he chose.

I peel down the elastic waistband and ease his cock out. I hold it in my hand, and it's like being reacquainted with an old friend. I love the weight of it in my hand. The smooth, hard surface of it. The thick veins running from the base to the head.

"Open your mouth, Shelby. Let me see that tongue."

I do as he says, giving him my eager mouth. Instead of sliding his cock down my throat, he holds me by the back of the neck with one hand and eases the two middle fingers of the other deep into my mouth. Immediately, I gag, so he lets up.

I can see on his face how much this turns him on. His pupils grow larger, his lips part, and his nostrils flare.

So he does it again, seeing how far and how deep he can force his fingers before I lose it and start gagging. I'm determined to prove to him how good I can be.

My eyes start to water, and my stomach clenches, but I manage to show him how deep I can take it. Seemingly overcome with lust, he pulls his fingers from my throat and replaces them with his tongue.

He kisses me deep and passionately, the grip on my neck so tight it's punishing.

When he pulls his mouth away from the kiss, he keeps his face near mine as he says, "What are you doing to me, Shakespeare?"

Hearing him call me that at this moment feels special and somehow makes it all so much more real.

"Use me. I'm all yours."

His eyes meet mine, and it's obvious to me at that moment that it's *us*.

He smiles at me for just a moment before dragging my face to his cock. And he doesn't need to tell me what to do from here. I already know. I've only been thinking about it every day for the last twelve months.

I wrap my hand around the base of his cock and waste no time taking it down my throat. Rolling my lips over my teeth, I lather his length up with saliva, reaching as much as I can reach on each stroke of my mouth. When I feel him hit the back of my throat, I challenge myself not to gag right away.

He grunts and groans when he feels how deep I can take him. Each one gets louder and louder, and I revel in the sounds he's making. I have never felt such pride as I do when I make him feel good.

"That's it. Good boy," he murmurs as I suck him off. "Don't stop. Make me come down that pretty throat."

Because I know he likes it, I let him feel my teeth at the base of his cock. He hisses and nearly levitates off the chair, but he doesn't stop me. So I continue to tease him, biting and scraping just enough to edge him with the pain.

I feel his cock tighten and swell. With that and the roaring sounds he is making, I know he's about to come. When I feel the cum fill my mouth a moment later, I'm overwhelmed by it. I try to swallow it all, but it's more than I expected, and I begin to choke.

Declan grabs my jaw and pulls his cock from my mouth.

Strings of cum and saliva drip from the length of his shaft to my lips as he finishes on my face.

"What a dirty little mess you are," he growls at the sight of me. "God, I love seeing you covered in my cum. You love it, don't you?"

Gazing up at him, I nod.

I do love it.

Using the grip on my jaw, he guides me to my back on the floor of the living room. There's an expensive-looking rug underneath me, and I can already tell it's going to need cleaning.

Declan is on me like a hungry animal. Climbing to the floor between my legs, he seems more eager for my release than he was his own.

"My turn," he says with a wicked grin. He strokes my hard shaft, using the saliva in his hands. With the other hand, he folds my legs up to my chest before leaning down to suck my balls into his mouth.

I let out a moaning howl from the warm pleasure of his mouth. "That's it, my little slut. Let me hear you."

He licks and sucks each one before moving up to my cock to swallow me down. I feel as if I'm being torn apart, only to be pieced back together again. He drags me all the way to the edge of euphoria and then yanks me back again like it's some sick game.

He's enjoying this.

Torturing me, making me work for it, never giving it to me too easily.

I'm writhing on the floor with my knees to my chest as he moves to my sack again, but this time, his mouth moves even lower. Nearly pressing me in half, he drives his tongue around the muscled rim of my hole, and I stop breathing.

"Oh fuck, Dec!" I shout.

He pulls his mouth away. "Want me to stop?" he asks.

"God, no," I cry out. "Don't stop!"

When he licks the tight ring again, it feels so good I swear I could nearly come from that alone. I'm moaning and mewing on the floor of this rental like a damn cat in heat.

"Such a needy boy," he says with a smile I can feel. "I want to see my needy boy come now."

He just has to combine the stroking of my cock with his lips on my sack and one finger prodding at my entrance, and I'm a mess. I come so hard, I see stars.

I shoot my own load all over my chest, and I don't even care. By the time I'm done, I can't even feel it. I'm deadweight on the rug, covered in cum.

Declan cleans me up before hovering over me and kissing me on the mouth.

"I must have done something right," I murmur as I stare up at him. "To deserve that reward."

"Funny," he replies as he leans down and rests his head on my chest. "I was thinking the same thing."

Chapter Twenty-Nine
Colin

I rented a convertible for our week in Italy, although Declan insisted we should have no transportation and spend the week in our private rental house in the Tuscan countryside. And as nice as that sounds, I do love getting out with him.

For one whole week, I like to feel as if this is our life. We are a couple who travel together and take romantic drives through the hills of Italy.

We are spending the day in a quaint town where I don't feel strange holding his hand or standing close to him. We could do this in LA or London, but at this point, I'm starting to get recognized more and more. The boundaries of my private life are growing smaller by the second—a sharp double-edged sword to this career path.

We're perusing the shops when he finally brings up the one topic I was dreading.

"So how was New York?" he asks.

I force myself to swallow and try to stay casual.

"It was great. The shoot took longer than we expected. I've never worked such long hours in my life," I reply with a chuckle.

Last autumn, I took a role that was the biggest in my career. And it meant six months in New York. Which unfortunately coincided with the time when Declan and I were supposed to move in together in London.

He told me he wasn't upset. He encouraged me to take the role and said he would never forgive me if I passed on it.

But there has been a small part of me since that wonders if he was glad I took that part because it meant he got an easy out from having to live with me again.

He called it like *old times* when we were roommates. Is that really what I wanted to go back to? At least with these summer rendezvous, we don't get two different rooms. We sleep in the same bed, and it feels like we are more than friends, even if it is just for eight days.

"I'm so proud of you," he says, resting a hand on my lower back.

"Thanks," I mumble as I lean into him. "I'm sorry London didn't work out this year, but maybe we can plan for something…"

My voice trails with uncertainty.

"Maybe," he says flatly.

This conversation is starting to depress me, so I turn our attention toward the jewelry in the shop instead. There's a thick silver chain that catches my eye, and I drape it over my fingers. He stands behind me as he eyes the jewelry.

"Does my good boy want me to buy him something pretty?" he whispers in my ear. My mouth tugs into a crooked smirk.

"Yes, sir," I whisper. "I would."

Is it too soon to tell him that I wish this was a real collar? Probably. I don't think he's ready for that. Hell, I don't know if I'm ready for that. These roles of dominance and submission are new to us, and collars are serious. They represent commitment and loyalty.

Not that I need one with him. He knows I'll be his forever. Or at least I think he does.

Declan nods to the shop owner as he pulls out his wallet. When the woman starts to wrap up the necklace, he waves a hand to her. So she passes it over instead.

"Grazie," he says with a courteous smile.

Then he drapes it over my neck and fastens it at the nape. It's perfect. Masculine with a shimmer of silver that complements the blue in my eyes.

Pleased, I look at myself with it in the mirror. Just then, he steps up behind me, and I get a look at him and me together.

Suddenly, from out of nowhere, I get that familiar foreboding feeling in my gut. What are we doing? We look and act like a couple, but we're not.

Why do I just put up with this? Why don't I demand more? I should tell him what I want.

"What's wrong?" he asks, noticing my change in mood.

"Nothing," I mumble in reply as I turn and leave the store.

He follows behind, keeping a hand on my back the entire time.

"Colin," he says after we walk for a while. He uses my name, which means I must be showing my cards. He can tell I'm upset.

And I'm tired of feeling like this. When we reach the plaza at the center of the city, I stop and turn to face him.

"What are we doing, Declan?"

He looks surprised by my abrupt questioning. "What do you mean?"

"I mean *us*, Declan," I argue, keeping my voice down to avoid attention.

"We're doing what we do every single year, Colin," he replies. "I don't understand."

"Neither do I," I reply. "I don't understand what you want from me. I don't understand how you can treat me like your lover one moment and your friend the next. How much longer can we really do this?"

He steps toward me. "Are you telling me you want to stop? This whole thing was your idea."

"No, I don't want to stop," I say, growing louder and more worked up.

"Then what?"

"I want *more*, Declan," I reply, exasperated. "I don't want to be with you once a year. I want to be with you every bloody day of the year. I want to be yours, *really*. Not just during sex or when it suits you."

My hands are starting to shake, and I'm worked up. His expression turns concerned as he reaches for me.

And suddenly, a panic starts to set in. Why did I bring this up? Why did I start this? What if I've ruined everything?

"Okay, baby, just breathe for a moment. We can talk about this more when we get home, okay?"

"Yes, let's go," I shout.

I'm feeling too frantic as I turn away from him and start to march toward where we parked our car. He's quick on my tail, but I need space. I need to think.

I'm too distracted, and I just keep taking deep breaths to try and calm myself down. Where on earth did this attack come from? What is wrong with me? Why am I like this?

The questions swirl wildly in my head as I scurry to the car, emotion building like a storm inside me. I see the car down the road, and I walk between two parked trucks to cross the street toward it.

Then everything happens so fast. I feel the abrupt, painful slam of the motorbike as it collides with my body. I hear Declan's terror-filled scream as he calls my name. I surrender to the violent crash of the hot Italian cobblestones as they rise to meet my skull.

And then, it's dark.

The hospital smells like lemons, which is weird, and it's the first thing I notice when I open my eyes. My head is throbbing, and the lights are too bright. When I lift my fingers, I find gauze wrapped around my head, and I remember the traumatic events of the day.

I came to when they were loading me into the ambulance. It's a memory I couldn't wipe from my brain if I tried, because Declan was by my side, frantic and emotional when they had to peel him off of me.

I must have passed out again shortly after because I don't remember anything about the ride to the hospital or being put in this bed.

"Excuse me," I croak when I notice a nurse scurry by. This isn't a large American or English hospital with private rooms and million-dollar medical equipment. It's a small Italian hospital that probably doesn't handle much outside of concussions and common illnesses.

When the nurse scurries by again, I realize she is the only one.

"Mi scusi," I call. She rattles off something in Italian before she disappears into another room.

My head hurts so bad, and I realize my odds of getting prescribed the good stuff here are slim to none. There seem to be two other patients separated by thin curtains.

When the nurse returns, she comes to me first. She pulls a flashlight from her pocket and shines it in my eyes.

"Please," I say. "My friend. Is he here?"

"Italiano," she replies, and I let out a groan.

"I don't speak Italian," I say before collapsing on the bed.

Just then, I hear a commotion in another part of the building and what can only be described as an enraged Scotsman somewhere in the lobby.

"I don't bloody care!" he bellows as I hear him coming closer.

"Signore, per favore!" a young voice calls, but she is no match for the tall, furious man who barrels through the door a moment later.

"Oh bloody hell," he says when he sees me. He looks both relieved and horrified as he takes in my appearance.

"I'm fine," I say, but it doesn't stop him from rushing toward me and pulling me into his arms. The woman chasing him surrenders and leaves us, walking back up to the front while muttering something under her breath as she goes.

Declan is holding me so tightly I can feel his heart pounding through his chest. He's breathing hard, and there seems to be a tremor in his bones.

"Are you all right?" he asks as he pulls away to inspect my wounds. I have some bad scratches and bruising on my rib cage and knees, but the worst of it is definitely my head.

"I'm fine, I promise," I say, just trying to ease some of his worries.

"You gave me such a bloody fright, ya ken," he says. His eyes are wild, and he looks like he hasn't slept in days, although I've only been in here no more than a couple of hours.

"I'm sorry," I mumble.

He takes my face in his and pulls me close, pressing our lips together.

"Don't you apologize. I'm just relieved you're alive."

"Alive?" I ask with a scoff. "Declan, I was hit by a Vespa, not a truck."

"Aye, but…" The sentence dies on his lips as I notice something in his expression change. Like sadness spilled over his features, and he's trying to blink it away.

Then, realization dawns. *His parents.* They were killed in a tragic car crash.

Oh God, my poor Declan has been alone and terrified this whole time, thinking I suffered the same fate.

I reach for him and pull him into a tight embrace. "Oh, Declan, I'm so sorry. I didn't mean to scare you. I'm fine."

He doesn't respond. Just lets me hold him until I feel the unmistakable shudder of his stifled tears, which he tries to mask by clearing his throat or pulling away, but I feel them. He puts himself through hell just to keep from crying. Sometimes, I wish he'd just let it out.

"I'm glad, Shakespeare," he whispers into my neck. "I'm so glad."

Chapter Thirty
Colin

Declan hasn't been the same since the accident. I'm fine, healthwise. I suffered a concussion and likely some bruised ribs, but nothing life-threatening.

And yet, it's like he's come down with some emotional flu he hasn't been able to shake since.

I think that even though I am okay and I didn't die, he spent at least two or three hours imagining that I had. And the trauma from those hours doesn't just go away.

He's been sketching more than usual. Even after we have sex in the morning, he stays in bed most of the day and just draws in his book. It breaks my heart to see him like this.

Six days after the accident, I finally feel good enough to go for a drive, so he takes me to the nearest beach, after I spend hours begging him to, of course.

We're sitting on a large blanket under a massive blue and orange umbrella, watching couples and families frolic in the water. So I reach for him.

As he takes my hand, he offers me a sad smile.

"I'm sorry," I whisper with my cheek resting against my knees.

His brows fold inward. "Sorry for what?"

"For bringing all of that up that day. I shouldn't have started a fight with you while—"

"Shakespeare," he says, cutting me off. "Stop it. Stop thinking everything is your fault. Or that you're responsible for everyone's emotions, because you're not."

"I know, but…"

"No *buts*," he says, squeezing my hand. "You were right. I do treat you like a friend sometimes, but it's only because I don't know what else to do."

"What do you mean?" I ask, scooting closer to him.

"You have your life in California, and I have mine in Scotland, and I don't do well with relationships as it is, so how on earth could I be any good at a long-distance one? And what if it doesn't work? What if I'm a terrible boyfriend, and it ruins us? You're the most important person in my life, Colin Shelby. If I lose you…"

I loop a hand around his neck and drag his mouth toward mine. "You will never lose me."

When I press a kiss to his lips, he returns it, but with little life. As I pull away, he asks sadly, "Can you give me more time? Next year. I promise. I can give you more next year."

"Of course," I reply before kissing him again.

We lie on the blanket for a while, cuddling together and enjoying the sunshine. Eventually, I talk him into coming into the water with me.

So we walk hand in hand to the waves, but they are colder than I anticipated. He has to drag me in until they reach my waist, and then we're both full of laughter and smiles.

It's a bandage. A temporary fix on a more permanent problem, but for now, it's enough.

Back at the house, Declan gets into the shower first as I unpack the car. We both head home tomorrow, and another eventful week together comes to an end.

The months between these visits feels like just passing the time. Even when I'm chasing roles, memorizing lines, and working to further my career, it still feels like an interim in my own life. Just something to kill the time before I'm where I belong—with him.

When I walk into the bathroom, he watches me from behind the frosty glass doors of the shower. After pulling off my shirt, I stare at myself in the mirror. My bruises and scrapes have started to heal, and as soon as I get back home, I'll be back to my gym routine with my personal trainer to prepare for the next role.

Passing the time.

"Why don't you join me?" Declan asks from the shower.

Turning toward him with a coy smile, I reply, "I think I will."

Peeling off my swimsuit, I climb into the large stall alongside him. He gently tugs me under the warm spray of water, and I tilt my head back to allow it to run down my scalp.

Declan lathers his hands with soap and begins washing my short, cropped hair. It feels so nice. I let out a hum, and when he rinses it under the water, I reach behind to touch his hip. He's taking delicate care of me, washing my hair like I'm something fragile and breakable.

"You don't have to be so gentle with me anymore," I say.

His wet hand slides up to close around my throat, pulling me back against his body. Reaching farther behind me, I grasp his shaft in my hand, squeezing and stroking to make him hard.

His mouth is by my ear as he mutters, "Does my boy want it rough?"

"Yes, please," I cry.

I know there is a part of Declan that wants to pamper me because he almost lost me. In fact, in his mind, he *did* lose me. But I'm here, I'm alive, I'm with him, and I want him to treat me that way.

He fills his palm with more soap, using it to lather my body, starting at my chest and working down my abs. His fingers toy with the happy trail of hair leading from my belly button down to my cock. I let out a husky groan as he wraps his hand around me, stroking it to life.

But he doesn't stop there. His lathered hands explore every inch of my body, caressing my testicles and reaching even farther back to tease my taint. Then his hands move down my legs, covering me with soapy bubbles clear down to my feet.

He knows every inch of me. My body is more his than mine at this point, and I love that. I can't explain the comfort it gives me to be so adored, so treasured, and so *valued*.

Today, he said I was the most important person in his life. I will take that sentiment with me to get me through every moment we're apart.

"Hands against the wall," he mutters.

I press my palms to the tile and close my eyes in anticipation as he kneels behind me. He works the soapy lather up the back of my thighs and between the globes of my backside.

He loves to tease me. I think he likes to make me beg for it.

"Please," I say with a sigh.

"So needy," he replies. "Now let me hear you whimper."

Using even more soap, he works me open with two fingers, and he's not gentle about it, which is exactly what I want. His strokes are rough until I'm a trembling, whimpering mess of need.

I'm practically shoving my hips back toward him, waiting for him to fill me, needing him inside me as if I'm not completely whole without him. When he stands and presses the blunt head of his cock against my hole, I let out a soft sigh of pleasure.

Right now, I wish I could tell him I love him. Not as a friend but as a man. *His* man.

He pushes himself inside me, past the ring of muscle, and we groan in unison as if him being buried deep is a relief.

"You were made for me, Shelby," he mutters as he bottoms out, pressed in as far as he can go. "You know that? No one else will have you the way I do."

"No one," I reply breathlessly. He eases out to the tip slowly and back in even slower, like delicious torture.

"Please, Declan," I beg.

"What does my boy want?" he asks, his voice strained as he slowly pulls out again.

"Please fuck me," I ask.

"Like this?" he replies. With a harsh grip on my hips, he slams back inside me. And I let out a deafening, gravelly moan. My cock leaks at the tip as he grazes my prostate. But now that he's started, he can't stop thrusting relentlessly inside of me with heavy grunts.

Moments like this, I'm glad we decided to get tested before each of our visits so I can feel him inside of me with nothing between us. I will never tire of the feel of his cum filling me up, then dripping down my legs. It makes me feel as if I've been branded by him. Like he's marked me as his forever, his scent embedded into my skin like some sort of primal mating ritual.

He picks up speed as he fucks me, his hip bones bruising my ass as he pounds without mercy.

"Stroke yourself, Shelby," he says between grunts. "I want to feel you come when I'm inside you."

Completely bent over, my face is pressed against the wall as I use my right hand to stroke my aching cock. I try to match the rhythm of his thrusts, and it doesn't take long before my orgasm coalesces inside of me.

For a moment, it's like I cease to exist. I groan loudly as my own cum spills over my fingers and lands against the wall.

"Fuck yeah," Declan mutters as his grip tightens. "I can feel your ass tighten when you come," he says. "God, you feel so good. My good fucking boy. My good, dirty fucking boy."

His thrusts slow as he meets his release. I can feel his cock shudder as he comes inside me. And when he's done, I almost don't want him to pull out. I don't want his seed to leak from inside me.

And I don't want to wash it away, because I know it'll be another year before I get to feel it again.

When he's spent, he pulls out of me and gathers me into his arms, kissing the side of my head like I'm something he adores. Like I'm someone he loves.

"I'm sorry I don't say the things I'm supposed to say," he mumbles against my cheek. "I'm so bad at this, Shelby, but you should know you are the best thing in my life. I hope you know that. And I do want you as more, I do. It's just…I need you as my friend more than anything."

For a moment, it feels like I can't breathe. To hear him acknowledge this thing between us and the way we've been stuck as friends for so long feels like a big change from the man who used to just admit how easy sex with me was.

To hear him even say he wants more is enough for now.

Turning around, I stare into his eyes as I say, "I'll be whatever you need. And I mean it."

He smiles as he leans forward and takes my mouth in a tender kiss.

Chapter Thirty-One
Declan

One day until the wedding

I WAKE UP WITH WARM ARMS AROUND ME. PEELING MY EYES OPEN, I look down to see Colin's hand resting on my chest. It tugs at my heart to feel him so close. To know he was here, comforting me in the middle of the night.

What does this mean?

I run my hand along his arm and intertwine my fingers with his. Holding our clasped hands over my heart, I take a deep breath and imagine waking up like this every morning.

What have I been doing with my life that I let him out of my reach?

"Good morning," he whispers behind me.

"Morning," I reply.

Neither of us moves. Surely, it's highly inappropriate to be lying with one of the grooms in bed like this the day before the wedding, but he doesn't seem to mind.

"I came in to sit for the painting last night, but you were already asleep," he says.

"So you decided to lie down and cuddle with me instead?" I ask.

After a moment of hesitation, he says, "You were restless. Having a nightmare, and I couldn't leave you."

For reasons I don't understand, I squeeze his fingers. "Thank you."

As I climb from the bed, I let out a groan from the pounding in my head. "What time is it?" I ask.

He glances at his watch. "Just past seven in the morning."

Turning back, I stare at him in my bed, and it does something to me. The sight of him sprawled on my mattress, his golden-blond hair against my pillow. His warm, blushing skin in the early morning light.

Too many memories come flooding back. *Good* memories. *Exquisite memories.*

"I need to wash up," I mutter as I stand from the bed. But before I leave the room, I turn back to him. "Don't…go anywhere," I stammer.

He rises onto his elbows and stares at me. "I won't."

Heat blossoms in my groin. It's arousal that feels too much like hope.

As I disappear into my bathroom and stare into the mirror, I let the reality of this situation settle in.

My heart is betraying me. What I want is to get through this week and this wedding and prove my siblings wrong and finally be alone and at peace. *That is what I want.*

But right now, my heart is trying to convince me that I want to walk back to that room and pull him into my arms and tell him he can always trust me. It's trying to tell me that I should forfeit everything I want for him. To hell with this wedding and that fucking fiancé of his.

I should make Colin mine again.

As I'm rushing through my morning routine, I'm replaying the conversation with Pierce, and anger begins to boil inside me.

How can Colin be such a pure and kind soul and be willing to marry that selfish and arrogant prick?

When I make it back into the bedroom, Colin is still there, and I'm a bit surprised. I mean, I did tell him to stay, but I have to wonder…why is he here? Why did he sleep with his arms around me all night?

"What's wrong?" he asks, noticing my disposition.

I take a deep breath, and it feels like I'm breathing in rage. Why do I care about what Colin does?

But I do. I care a lot. Try as I might to not care about him, I do. More than anything.

"Declan, talk to me," he says as he stands and reaches for me.

"Why the fuck do you let guys treat you like trash?" I bark. My hands itch to grab him, shake him, hold him.

"What are you talking about?" he asks suspiciously.

"That…" I point to the door but hold myself back from calling Pierce some very harsh names. "Do you know what that fiancé of yours just asked me to do last night, Colin?"

His face falls and I watch him shrink into himself. "Yes, I do."

"What on earth is wrong with you?" I can't hold back this time. I step toward him, taking his face in my hands and backing him against the wall. "Is that what you want? To be treated like a piece of property? I mean *really*."

"So what if it is?" he replies defiantly.

"Is it?"

He pauses as he stares at me intensely. "It's not about what I want."

"What?" I ask with a gasp. "What are you saying?"

"You know what I like, Declan. You remember how I am. If it's what Pierce wants, then I'm going to give it to him."

"You're infuriating," I growl.

"If you don't want to do it, then just say no, Declan."

"Of course I'm going to say no, Colin."

"The thought of sleeping with me again repulses you so much," he mutters sadly.

My eyebrows leap upward. "Don't be daft," I argue. "You know that's not why."

"Then what is it?"

"You don't get it," I argue, squeezing him tighter until he winces. He leans into me, closing his eyes.

"No, *you* don't get it," he whispers. "Just because you don't like it doesn't make it wrong. So what if he likes to see other men appreciate what's his."

"What's *his*?" I growl. "That's not how you should be treated. Not unless it's what you truly want. If you are really his, Colin, he should protect you and listen you."

"If I'm going to do it with anyone, I want it to be with you," he argues, opening his eyes and staring into mine.

Fuck.

My thumb runs along his cheek as I let those words dismantle me one by one. A piece of my chest warms as if it's overflowing with heat and love. My sweet, beautiful, perfect Colin.

"It's nice to be someone's," he whispers.

"Does he truly appreciate you, Colin? Does he know what he has?"

I'm saying too much. Letting too much out.

"What does he have?" Colin whispers.

My mouth hangs open as all the words I wish I could utter hang on my lips unspoken. Instead, I draw him closer, pressing my forehead to his. I feel his breath on my face, the familiar scent of him. It's almost too much to resist.

I'd like to remind him that he was once mine.

Or that he still is.

He's clinging to my arms as if I'm holding him up.

"Colin," I mumble in a low rasp, but he cuts me off before I can continue.

"Don't call me that," he says. His gaze is pleading and hopeful as he stares at me.

"Shakespeare," I say and notice the way his mouth twitches with a hint of a smile.

We're standing too close, and this is far too intimate. Warning signs are going off in my head, but I don't pull away or stop myself.

"Say it, Declan," he whispers, staring into my eyes. "Please."

Like always, the words are tied up on my tongue. I know what he wants to hear, but do I have it in me to say it?

Instead, I tug him closer and hover my lips over his. "You don't need me to tell you that you deserve better. No one deserves you," I add.

His gaze flashes to my lips briefly and then back up to my eyes, and I think he's waiting for me to kiss him. And I want to. More than anything, I want to, but then what?

Then frustration flashes over his face as he shoves me away. "Nothing has changed. What is wrong with me?"

"What are you talking about?" I ask, grabbing his arm before he can leave.

"This!" he shouts, waving his arms. "You! It all feels a little familiar, Declan. You always want me within reach, available to *you*."

"What do you want?" I ask frantically.

"God, I can't believe we're having this fight again," he says with a laugh.

"We never had the fight, remember? You just left."

"What was the point, Declan? It was too late then, and it's way too late now."

"Don't say that," I mumble in defeat. "It's not too late."

He lets out an acrimonious huff. "It's not too late? So suddenly, after seven years, you've decided that you love me? That you're willing to give me more than eight days in the summer? That you'll be faithful and committed to me? Now, after all this time?"

He steps toward me, the morning sun catching hints of gold

in his warm blue eyes. And in this moment, right now, I realize that I will fight for him. I have to. I was a fool to ever think I could let him go after this week.

"Admit it, Declan," he says, softly touching my cheek. "What we had was fun, but I always loved you more. You haven't given me a single thought since I left this manor seven years ago, and that's okay. But I can't let myself get attached only to be heartbroken again."

For a moment, I can't move. I'm reeling as his words play over in head, because they don't make any sense. He thinks he loved me more? As delusional as it sounds, I could understand that.

But he thinks I haven't thought about him since he left?

Without a word, I walk away from where he's standing, and he watches me with a perplexed expression. There is a chest across the room covered with a dusty tarp and some paint supplies that I toss to the floor. They clatter noisily, but I don't care. After unlocking the chest, I hoist it open, and it creaks while papers spill out near my feet. I knew it was overfilled, but I didn't know it was this much.

Colin shuffles over. "Are those…me?"

But I don't answer. I just grab page after page and toss them toward him. Some are charcoal sketches. Some elaborate paintings. It sort of depended on my mood and the amount of emotion tied to the memory.

But every single one is him.

He picks up a piece of paper and stares at it. I'm suddenly reminded of the day in uni, moments after we graduated, when I handed him the sketch I had done of him. It wasn't close to being the first, but it was the first I had given him, and I watched his expression when he accepted it. The teardrop that fell, and how I was mortified because I thought it meant he knew my secret—that I was in love with him.

Only someone who drew portraits the way I did of him was surely in love. A classic tell.

"Declan…" he whispers. "What is all this?"

I continue tossing pages of him on the floor. "This was the last fifteen years. Most are from memory, but when I ran out of those, I used your movies."

His mouth is hanging open as he flips through drawing after drawing. They are of him up close and full body. Of his hands and his legs and his lips. This is how I held on to him when I had nothing else.

"Shakespeare, I'm sorry it was only eight days a year to you. It was never just eight days to me. You were with me every bloody day."

Colin is staring at me with his mouth hanging open, his eyes searching mine as if he's seeing me for the first time. Goose bumps erupt across my skin as I wait for his reaction.

Being vulnerable is hard. Will he think I'm out of my mind for this? Will he hate it? Have I revealed too much of myself?

But then he lunges. Crinkling the papers on the floor beneath us, he throws himself into my arms. Taking my face in his hands, he crashes his mouth against mine.

I wrap him up and delight in the taste and feel and scent of him. It's all the same. A memory wrapped in skin and bones.

His tongue slides against mine and his teeth take gentle nibbles of my lips. His passion and need are so intense, I let out a yelp just from the feel of him in my arms.

My hands eagerly roam his body, sliding up and down his back before easing down to his arse. The moment I squeeze the firm globe in my hand, he hums into my mouth, grinding himself against me the way he always did.

"Fuck, Shelby," I mumble as I back him up toward the table. There are pages everywhere, under our feet as I lift him onto the surface.

As I settle between his legs, he wraps them around me and pulls away from the kiss to stare into my eyes. We are breathless and turned on, like we've been swept up in a storm.

For a while, neither of us moves.

As much as I want to kiss him and make him truly mine again, Colin is still engaged to someone else, and I know his heart. He isn't the type to betray someone he cares about, even self-righteous dickheads.

Finally, he rests his head on my shoulder and just breathes as if he wants to stay frozen in this moment. As for me, I'm dying to know where his head is at.

I drift my fingers up and down his spine. And I wait.

Then we hear footsteps down the hall and we both pull apart in a rush. Staring at each other with wide eyes, we freeze and wait to see who is approaching.

When Blaire finally appears in my doorway, I breathe a sigh of relief.

"Sorry," she says, averting her eyes. "Mr. Hall is looking for Mr. Shelby. I'll tell him he's sitting for the painting then."

"Thank you, Blaire," I reply.

"Might want to come down soon though," she adds.

"I will," Colin replies in a rush.

As she disappears out of the room, I look at Colin with my brows raised and my mouth set in a thin line.

Now, I'm the one waiting for validation.

"I don't know what to do," he whispers.

"You don't have to do anything, ya ken," I reply.

He nods. Then, he appears flustered as he drives his hands in his hair. "Why couldn't you have just shown me all of this sooner?"

With a shake of my head, I shrug.

"Dammit, Declan," he mumbles before turning toward the chaise lounge and dropping into it as if in surrender.

Even with him on the other side of the room, it's like there is a string from him directly to my heart, and the farther he is, the more it hurts.

"I just…need to think," he says, sounding flustered.

I don't respond. I can't even move. I'm just standing in a sea of Colin, staring at the sketch on the easel and the living sight of him in the same frame.

They both belong to Pierce.

I'm too numb to move, wondering if that kiss was the last one I'll get. Will he still marry that man after everything? Have I messed things up so badly?

What is the point of wanting? It only brings pain.

Eventually, I do what I always do when it hurts. I reach for my apron, and I lift it over my head. In a drunken-like stupor, I begin preparing my paints, like I'm moving on autopilot. Somehow I can do these tasks while also replaying the events of this week from the moment Colin arrived to this one right now. How every single encounter was a minor tipping of the scales.

And I never saw this coming.

This longing. This doubt. This *love*.

Colin reclines on the couch in the same position he was in two nights ago. The kiss we just shared lingers between us and neither of us speak of it. We ignore the fact that there are things to do today and a wedding tomorrow. I get to work and he watches me as I do, and for one more precious hour, we exist as *us*.

When we are together like this, I live for him and him for me. As if we were designed to be together. Like I am the night sky, and he is the stars.

Chapter Thirty-Two
Declan

Regardless of the lovely morning spent painting and briefly kissing Colin, I still have a massive hangover and another shitstorm of things to deal with before this godforsaken wedding. If there even is one.

God, I hope there's not.

He can't possibly go through with this after feeling what we did this morning, can he? It's like we opened a book we can't just close now.

After my shower, I take enough aspirin to kill a horse and pound a cup of coffee to try and cure this hangover. When I come downstairs, the grooms are nowhere to be found, but the house is abustle with activity.

"You look like shite," a sweet voice says, finding me in the kitchen with my forehead pressed against the cool marble of the countertop.

"I feel like shite," I reply, not bothering to clarify that I mean physically *and* emotionally.

"I've got a good hangover cure," Blaire says as she opens the freezer and comes back a moment later with a cold bottle of something, placing it on the counter. When I lift my gaze and see the frosty glass of a vodka bottle, I nearly throw up.

"Get that godforsaken thing away from me," I bark.

"Relax," she says with a laugh. Then, she goes to the fridge and retrieves a pitcher of orange juice. She pours it into a glass and adds a dash of turmeric, some grated ginger, and a shot of vodka. "Drink it."

With a scowl, I take the glass. "Where is everyone?" I ask before taking a sip. It tastes foul, but I chug it anyway.

"Have you forgotten there's a wedding here tomorrow?"

"I wish I could," I mutter.

"They're all out back for the rehearsal," she replies casually. My stomach turns again, and I nearly lose the contents.

The rehearsal.

"Fuck," I bark.

"What?" she asks.

"And Colin's out there?" I ask with a wince.

She stares at me as if I've sprouted horns. "Of course. Where else would he be?"

I let out a sigh of frustration. Maybe he's still thinking about things. He's still confused and hasn't worked up the nerve to tell Pierce that the wedding is off.

"I need to be out there," I say in a rush.

"Why? You've done everything already. Stay in here."

"No, I should go," I mutter with a groan.

Dropping the half-drunk glass of screwdriver from hell onto the counter, I turn to rush out the back door. I hear the commotion of the crowd in the distance, and by some miracle, Mother Nature has actually given us a break from the rain long enough to hold a rehearsal.

Then, I look up.

Suddenly, I'm gazing across the yard at the two men stationed together, and it all hits me like violent storm.

I feel like I've been slapped. Sucker punched. Delivered a deadly blow.

Colin and Pierce are hand in hand as they stare each other. And Colin is…smiling.

For some reason, I can't move. I'm paralyzed by pain. Intense, visceral agony like someone is violently clawing my heart from my chest.

"Declan..."

My brow furrows as I turn toward Blaire.

"Are you okay?" she whispers.

"I'm fine," I snap.

"Declan." She repeats my name in a way that makes me pause, with sincerity and alarm. Then she gazes into my eyes as she says, "You're not fine. And it's okay if you're not."

Tears prick behind my eyes, and it feels as if a tree has sprouted roots in my chest, weighing me down and pinning me to the earth.

This entire week I've felt like I'm losing Colin all over again. But I'm not losing him—he's already gone.

All this time I've wasted thinking that I'd be better off alone. Thinking that he'd eventually come back. Thinking he truly belonged to me.

What a fool I am.

Turning away from Blaire, I march back up to the house. With a feeling of defeat, I disappear into the manor.

"Declan," she calls as she follows me through the kitchen. "Where are you going? What about the wedding?"

Grabbing Anna's leather notebook from the counter, I shove it at her. "I don't care about the wedding. Call Anna. The bet is off."

Blaire slams the notebook on the table. "What about you?"

"I need to get out of here," I growl.

"Where will you go?"

"I don't know," I reply as I dash out of the kitchen toward my room. She is on my heels, following me up the stairs.

"But aren't you going to stop him?" she asks frantically, and it almost makes me laugh. A woman I shared a drink with in a pub and ghosted the morning after has suddenly become my closest friend.

"Don't you see?" I reply. "I can't. I have to let Colin make up his own mind."

"Declan," she says from the doorway of my bedroom.

"What?" I ask, pulling my suitcase from under my bed.

"Talk to him."

"And say what?" I ask with a laugh. "Sorry about being an arsehole seven years ago but now that you have your own life, I was wondering if you would throw all of that away and give me another chance? Besides, Colin knows where I stand."

"That guy he's marrying is a prick, and you know it."

I do know it. "I have no right…"

"Yes, you do," Blaire argues. "You're his best friend, and correct me if I'm wrong, but the love of his *fucking* life."

"I *was* his best friend," I mumble despondently. "And I *was* the love of his life. But I fucked it up once, and I'd surely fuck it up again. Besides, I tried. I showed him everything this morning. I made it very clear…"

Didn't I? Was it clear enough?

Fuck, why am I so bad at this?

"Listen," she says, stepping into the room. "I have been watching you two the past six days. The love between you is still there. I can see it. You're just both bitter and chafed about something that happened a long time ago. Don't throw away your chance for true happiness because you're a stubborn arse."

"You don't understand," I say through the pain.

"Okay, try me." She crosses her arms and leans against the doorframe.

"I'd be a terrible boyfriend. I'm not good at being romantic or transparent. I have no business being in a relationship. Colin would be better off marrying that American arsehole."

Blaire tilts her head and glares at me. "You don't really mean that."

"Okay, you're right, I don't mean that, but he'd better off with someone else."

"Why? Because you don't know how to say romantic things and wouldn't buy him flowers? Do you hear yourself? Do you truly think someone else could love him more than you do?"

"No," I reply without hesitation.

"Then bloody tell him that. Fight for him, you idiot!"

"Fine!" I shout in return.

"Thank you! Tonight, at that bloody stag do, you're going to waltz in there and take your goddamn man back."

"All right!" I bellow.

"And you're going to stop it with all of this second-guessing bull shite!"

"Will you stop yelling at me?"

"Put the suitcase away first," she argues.

I throw it under my bed and toss my hands up in surrender.

"Much better." This time there's a smile on her face.

"I don't think I like you very much," I say with a glower.

"Good. Now, come on," she replies cheerfully as she loops her arm through mine. "Let's make you look so good for this party tonight he won't possibly be able to say no."

I glance up at her perplexed. "What's wrong with the way I look now?"

She just laughs, tugging me to the door.

Blaire sets me up on a chair in my bathroom and cuts inches off of my hair while my knee bounces nervously.

"Relax," she says. "What are you so afraid of? That man is no match for you. I've seen the way Colin looks at you."

"It's not that," I mutter as I glare at my reflection. The man looking back at me is a fool. He once had everything and threw it all away. Something I have never forgiven him for.

"Then what is it?" she asks, shaking the strands of my hair with her fingers.

"I've already fucked things up with him once."

"You don't think he'll give you another chance?" she asks.

"I don't think I deserve it," I mumble. "Not to mention... losing him last time nearly killed me. I never fully recovered from that. I can't do it again."

"How did you lose him? Whatever you did, you must have learned, right? Don't do it again."

I chuff, and she looks at me expectantly.

"You don't understand," I reply. "Colin and I were friends first. For four years, we were best friends. And then we became friends who fucked. But he wanted me to be his boyfriend. We were at a party like...this one tonight, and he wanted me to..."

"To what?" she snaps when I don't finish right away.

"It doesn't matter," I reply. "The point is I wouldn't give him the commitment he wanted, nor the freedom. I took Colin for granted for so long. It wasn't fair of me," I mutter, feeling like utter horse shite as the words leave my lips.

"At least you can acknowledge it now," she says, softly tapping my shoulder. "Show him that you've changed. Prove it to Colin so he knows he can have everything he wants—a man who loves him and who will give him the commitment he needs. If you do that, he won't possibly say no."

Blaire greases up some cologne-scented wax and runs it through my now-short locks.

"Where the bloody hell did you get that?" I ask.

She smiles mischievously. "I stole it from one of the groomsmen's rooms."

I shake my head at her.

"But I mean...look at how hot you are!"

She moves out of the way, revealing my new look in the mirror. I hardly recognize the man staring back. I look like a version of myself. My hair is pristine. My black-on-black shirt and trousers fit like a glove.

I can't help but wonder if this is the version of me Colin wants. The version whose life wasn't turned on its head. Who didn't wallow in self-pity for two decades. Who doesn't drink too much, and whose fingers aren't constantly covered in charcoal and clay.

"Do you like it?" Blaire asks timidly.

"Aye." My voice is just above a whisper.

"You don't look like you like it," she replies.

"It's just…"

My voice trails as I stare at the mirror, because I know that when I finish that sentence, it will break. But I'm tired of feeling tied up by own my feelings, hiding my emotions behind fake smiles and alcohol.

"I look like my father."

My throat burns as the pain of that realization claws its way out. Tears prick my eyes as the pressure builds, and it feels like my head might explode.

"Oh, honey, I'm sorry," she whispers as she hugs me tightly from behind. A small smile tugs at my lips as I stare at the ghost in the mirror.

"No, it's…good," I reply, a smile splitting across my face.

"Really?" she asks, and I notice her eyes are wet too.

"Aye. It's really good."

On the next blink, a tear spills over my lashes and down my cheek. She quickly wipes it away with her sleeve before hugging me again.

It's incredible how just a few tears release so much pressure. Just allowing myself to express how much I miss him—how much I miss them both—feels like a slab of stone has been lifted from my chest.

Because I do. I was barely a teenager when they died, transitioning from childhood to being a man, and their deaths created a chasm in my life. In a lot of ways, I think it stopped me from truly growing up.

Never facing responsibility.

Always running from my feelings.

Afraid of commitment.

Terrified of loving again.

Trauma literally stunted my growth, but falling in love with Colin healed so much of that. And I'm not ready to let him go now. If I don't fight for him, then what was it all for?

"I'm ready," I mutter as I fix the collar of my shirt.

"You're bloody right you are," Blaire replies, wiping the tears from her eyes. "The party is just starting, so get down there. Get your man back."

She shoves me toward the door, but I turn around quickly before she can truly boot me. I throw my arms around her and pull her into a tight hug.

"Thank you," I whisper against her head. "And I'm sorry for being such an idiot to you before. You didn't deserve that."

Looking almost bashful after our hug, she shoves me on the shoulder. "You're sweet, but no hard feelings. You're not quite my type anyway."

With a laugh, I kiss her on the forehead, and she pushes me in earnest this time. "Now, go!"

As I make my way down the stairs, the sounds of the party boom through the empty halls. Most of the staff is gone for the night, and I know that whatever is behind those doors is far more than a stag do. Even if it starts that way, I have a feeling it's going to get out of hand.

But none of that matters to me now. I only have one goal for the evening.

Pierce said he wanted to watch me with his fiancé, only to claim him when all is said and done. And he can watch all he wants, but he won't be claiming him at all. Because when I get to Colin Shelby, I intend to remind him who he belongs to.

And this time, I won't let him go.

Chapter Thirty-Three
Declan

I slip through the door and into the main hall of the house. The lights are low, and the bass of the music in the ballroom nearly rattles the walls. There is a couple entangled on the stairs as I pass, but it's a man and woman, so I walk on by without paying them any attention.

There's only one person I'm worried about finding. And hopefully, I'm not too late.

Turning the corner into the room, I scan it to find him. There are roughly two dozen people here, mingled in groups in the corners and on the furniture. In the center of the room is a makeshift dance floor where bodies writhe and move as one to the fast-paced music.

"Barclay!" a deep voice bellows over the music.

There in the center of the room is Pierce. And under his arm is Colin.

My eyes connect immediately with Colin's as I pace across the room toward them. He's watching me with a look of astonishment and awe. His lips are slightly parted, and his brows are pinched inward. My appearance takes him by surprise, which is good. It's supposed to.

"You made it!" Pierce calls as he claps me painfully on the shoulder.

I shrug away from his touch and stare at the man on his arm. A feeling of betrayal threatens to build inside of me, but I know better.

Colin might still be with Pierce. Hell, he might even plan to marry him tomorrow. But this is who Colin is. He doesn't stand up for himself enough. He doesn't fight against authority.

"Let's get you a drink," Pierce says haughtily. There's a man tending bar who definitely doesn't work for us. As he passes me a whisky, I eye them both skeptically. "Relax," Pierce says with a slur. He's clearly already drunk. "The party is just getting started."

I can't take my eyes off of Colin. The feeling that is currently coursing through my veins is half determination and half terror. What if I'm wrong? What if he does want Pierce more?

I'm just a memory to him now.

No. Like Blaire said, I'm the love of his fucking life.

"So," Pierce says, leaning toward me. "You're here, so I assume you've given some thought to last night's offer."

My molars clench as I stare into Colin's fierce blue eyes. He looks so innocent right now, although I know he's far from it.

"I need to hear him say this is what he wants," I mutter coldly, nodding my head toward Colin.

His eyes widen a fraction. He expected me to turn this down.

Pierce presses his lips to the side of Colin's head. "Go ahead, baby. Tell him."

"Don't encourage him," I say in an angry tone. "Let him speak on his own."

Pierce turns a bitter glare on me, but he doesn't say anything. And he won't. Not in front of Colin, who is currently standing still as a statue, watching me intensely. I think he's trying to read my mind. He wants to understand why I'm doing this.

And I understand his hesitation. He knows as well as I do that once he says yes to this, there is no going back. One touch. One kiss. One moment together, and he'll be mine again.

"Yes," he murmurs before swallowing and speaking louder. "Yes, I want to."

Pierce grins wickedly. "Wonderful. The night is still young. My love, why don't you go fetch me and Declan another drink?"

I glance down to see my glass is still full, which means he's sending Colin away to speak to me alone. After gazing at me suspiciously, Colin disappears back to the bar to get us another round, and I take the opportunity to throw mine back.

The moment Colin is out of earshot, Pierce steps up toward me. "What are you playing at?" he asks coldly, all charm and glamour gone.

"I think you know exactly what I'm playing at," I mutter in response.

This makes him laugh sarcastically. "You really think you have a chance because you got a little haircut and put on some clean clothes?"

"I know I have a chance because I'm a hundred times better for Colin than you are," I spit back.

I realize that by having this very argument with him, I could be ruining my chances of having Colin where I want him tonight, but I can't hold back. Pierce wanted a challenge, and I'm going to give him one.

"We'll see about that," he argues.

"Aye, we will," I say.

"When I found him, he was so broken," he mutters in my face. "I built him back up and trained him exactly how I want him. You won't take him away from me. Not after you were the one who broke him."

"He's not a fucking dog, you arrogant prick," I growl in return.

"Maybe not," he replies before leaning in and whispering next to my ear, "But I'm the one who makes him howl like one."

I shove him away as he laughs, and it takes everything in me not to punch him in the face. Colin walks up with two drinks in his hand, giving one to each of us.

"Is everything all right?" he asks.

"Yes, baby," Pierce replies, kissing him on the side of his head while staring at me. "Now, why don't you go dance with our host? I want to watch you two together."

Colin watches me skeptically before I turn sideways, gesturing to the small dance floor. I shoot back the fresh whiskey before dropping the glass on a nearby table. Colin looks nervous as he lets me lead him out to the crowd.

The music has a steady beat, and most of the people are writhing together, so I hold Colin around the waist and pull him against me. I'm not one for dancing, and you'd never catch me on any dance floor, but I'm making exceptions for him. I will always make exceptions for him.

Colin's arms wind around my neck as he sways his body along with mine.

"Why are you doing this?" he asks, concern etched into his features.

"Shakespeare, you know why," I mutter as I stare into his eyes.

"I think I need to hear you say it, Declan."

As we move, I tighten my grip on his body, tugging him closer. Then, I bring my mouth close to his ear as I prepare myself for what I need to say. When the words come, they feel right and long overdue.

"Tonight, I intend to remind you what it feels like to be mine. I'm doing this to prove to you that I've changed. I'm not afraid of fighting for you anymore. I'm not afraid of telling the world just how much I love you. And I'm not afraid of trusting you to do what *you* want. Shelby, when you leave him for me, it won't be because I told you to; it'll be because you want to."

He pulls away and stares into my eyes. "He wants you to challenge him."

"I don't give a shite what he wants," I reply. "I only care about what you want."

"And what if I choose him?" Colin asks timidly.

"If that's what you truly desire, then I'll let you go. I'll live the rest of my miserable life on the greatest memories anyone's ever been gifted."

"And we'd be friends?" he asks.

I squeeze him tighter again. "I don't want to be your fucking friend."

The corner of his mouth lifts in a subtle smirk, and I realize just how long he's been waiting to hear me say that. I just hope it's not too late.

There's a whistle from across the room, and we both turn to see Pierce watching us with a smug grin.

"I have to go," Colin says, but I don't release him.

"You do not have to go," I say. "Especially not when he fucking whistles."

He turns his gaze up to mine, and there's something apologetic in it. "Pierce gives me what I want, Declan. You might think it's bad to be treated like someone's property, but I like it. I *need* it."

"I'll give you what you need," I say with a growl as I hold him against me.

"Prove it," he replies, holding my gaze.

"I intend to."

With that, he pulls himself from my arms, but before he can escape my reach, I grab his arm and tug him closer. Putting my face in his, I mutter, "I'm not fucking you here with an audience. If they want a show, I'll give them one, but the next time I'm inside you, Colin Shelby, you'll be mine for good. After all of this, if you truly believe I've done enough to prove how serious I am about you, I want you upstairs in my studio. Understand?"

His mouth hangs open as he stares at me with uncertainty. Then, with a deep breath and a glimmer of hope in his eyes, he nods.

Chapter Thirty-Four
Declan

"Why don't we move this party somewhere more intimate?" Pierce says after about an hour of watching everyone drink and loosen up.

I notice the way Colin tenses, and it takes everything in me not to drag him away from all of this. But he wants me to prove that I respect his desires. That I listen to him. Trust him.

Love him.

And I will.

When we reach the parlor, Pierce reclines on the chaise and pats his lap for Colin to sit. The energy in here is suddenly different. The way people are touching each other, no longer dancing but still moving and grinding. The size of the party has diminished noticeably to only a few.

It has me feeling tense at first, so I drop into the seat opposite the couple. Then I lean forward, propping my elbows on my knees as I wait.

I'm ready to get my hands on him. I'm ready to feel his body, his mouth, his weight on my lap. And I'm saying it all with my eyes.

Pierce is glaring at me as he grabs Colin by the back of the neck and hauls him to his mouth for a bruising kiss. Based on Colin's body language, I can tell he's tense. I don't know if it's because the kiss is unwanted or because he knows I'm watching. Either way, I hate it. But I know that's exactly why Pierce is doing it.

When the kiss is done, Pierce nudges Colin and points my way. Slowly, Colin lowers to the floor and crawls toward me.

Goose bumps prick my skin as he stares up at me, and I have to remind myself that this is us. The same *us* from Ireland the first time he asked me to call him mine. The same *us* from Los Angeles when we acknowledged how much we both liked this. The same *us* in Italy when I walked in to find him waiting on his knees.

Colin and I were made for this—made for each other.

When he reaches me, stopping at my feet, I close my fists around the hair at the nape of his neck and bring my face close to his with a wicked grin.

"There's my dirty boy," I mumble against his ear, and I feel him smile. "It's about fucking time."

Tugging his head back, I force his face upward toward me and softly whisper, "Are you okay?"

His eyes soften, and he swallows before nodding.

"You should never enter into these things without going over the boundaries and limits. Your Dom should know better."

I glare at Pierce for a brief moment before turning my focus back to Colin.

"He's not my Dom right now," Colin says. "You are."

Those words send a coursing heat through my bloodstream and straight down to my cock. We've never really used the language, not like this. Maybe we were afraid or unsure. But to hear him call me that for the first time feels so right. Better than *lover* or *friend*.

I am his Dom, and I will always take care of him.

"You're goddamn right I am. I always was," I say with a growl. "Now give me your word again. You want this?"

"Yes, sir," he replies with a slight smirk.

"And you know the safe word color system?"

"*Red* for *stop*. *Yellow* for *slow down*," he says obediently.

"Good boy," I reply. "Now get up here. I need to feel you on my lap."

Colin climbs onto my legs, straddling my hips, and it's the first time I feel like I can breathe. I let out a sigh of relief, closing my eyes as I press my face to his chest. His fingers slide down my scalp, and his heart beats quickly against my cheek.

My hands climb up his back and down to his ass, remembering the shape of his body and every single vertebra of his spine.

His hands are resting on my back as if he's remembering what I feel like too. Once I reach the nape of his neck again, I tug his face toward mine, muttering a soft "Come here" before I taste the softness of his lips.

The way he melts into me gives me hope. He seems comfortable and at peace in my arms. I kiss him to make him remember and to make him never want to leave again.

When our lips break part, I mumble with a gravelly command, "Grind against me."

His hips start to move, and I let out a moan just to feel his eager motion.

So perfect. So beautiful.

"Remember this?" I murmur against his mouth. "Remember how good we feel together?"

"I never forgot," Colin replies breathlessly.

My lips travel down from his mouth to his neck. He hangs his head back, exposing himself to me as his blond waves fall down over his neck.

When I lift my eyes to see past Colin, I find Pierce watching us with keen interest. He's reclined on the sofa, his legs spread as a woman on his left and a man on his right kiss their way up his neck and roam their hands over his body.

He can have them. This man right here is mine.

"Get back on your knees, baby," I growl against Colin's neck.

Lust-drunk, he moves back down to the floor between my legs and gazes up at me as he waits for his next instructions. I lean back on the chaise, my heart pounding rapidly.

"Take my cock out, Shelby. I need to feel your hands on me."

I see him shudder before he reaches for my zipper, tugging it down slowly before looking up at me. We're staring intensely at each other as he works to open my trousers and pulls down the waistband of my briefs. Then, he wraps his warm, soft hand around my cock, and my eyes flutter closed.

It's heaven. Like the first time I've been touched in seven years.

I don't care that people are watching or that I'm at risk of losing him forever. All that matters right now is what exists between him and me.

"Spit on it," I say.

Colin hovers his mouth over my hard cock and spits, coating my length in his saliva. Then he wraps his hand around me again and starts to stroke.

"That's it, baby," I murmur as I slide my hand toward his throat. His eyes seem to shine with arousal as I squeeze my grip and drag him toward my cock.

Replacing his hand wrapped around my shaft with my own, I drag the head of my cock across his lips. He closes his eyes, looking euphoric as I tease his mouth with my dick.

"I miss this mouth," I say with a low growl. "Does this mouth miss my cock?"

He opens his eyes and nods with my hand still around his throat.

I glance up at Pierce to see that he's still watching us, and he licks his lips as he stares at Colin. The pair that was both kissing his neck a moment ago has since moved their lips to his cock. I wonder briefly if Colin knew this was part of the arrangement, that Pierce could fuck whoever he wants while watching Colin with someone else.

If Colin was mine, I'd never let another pair of lips touch me for the rest of my life. I wouldn't need to.

With that, I turn my attention back to Colin and drag his mouth toward my cock again, this time sliding into his mouth along the soft surface of his tongue. When I reach the back of his throat, he gags, and I pull him off.

It feels so good I have to breathe slowly to keep from coming.

"You want to be used, Shelby. You want me to treat you like my dirty little fuck toy? Then I will, because that's exactly what you are."

I fuck his mouth again, holding his head as I reach the back of his throat and hold myself there for a moment before pulling away again. He gulps in a breath of air, and I let out a roaring sound to fight off the urge to lose it already.

Three more times, I strangle him on my shaft, and he keeps his hands on my thighs so I can gauge how he's feeling. My balls are throbbing, and the sight of Colin red and drooling on my cock has me ready to blow.

"Give me a color, Shakespeare," I say, holding him by the sides of his head.

"Green," he says, panting.

"Good boy." Then, I move closer as I mutter, "Now suck my cock like you did that night in the gymnasium pool, but this time, you better fucking swallow."

With the haze of sex and desire in his eyes, he grins up at me. Then he settles himself between my legs and takes my cock in his hand. As he closes his lips around my length, I look up to stare at his fiancé. I'm softly stroking Colin's hair with a smug expression on my face as he sucks my cock, stroking his tongue and lips from the base to the head over and over.

Then he scrapes his teeth along the tip, and I let out a yelp of pleasure, closing a fist around his hair. I can feel him smiling as he continues—sucking, sucking, biting.

The pain-laced pleasure has my body tight and buzzing like a live electric wire. One more touch, and I'll detonate.

I can feel his humming around my shaft, and I hardly notice that I'm murmuring as I let him bring me to the brink of ecstasy.

"Good fucking boy. You are so good. So perfect. *And mine.*"

Reaching down, I grip his fingers, a show of true intimacy. I want him to know this isn't just about sex to me. This is about *us*.

When I finally come, the whole room seems to just melt away. It's just me and him again. The pleasure washes over me like a warm tide pulling me under.

Opening my eyes, I let my gaze absorb the sight of Colin swallowing, and I imagine my seed in his belly as if it's feeding him. Becoming a part of him. Making us one.

I reach for him, ready to pull him into my lap, when I hear that fucking whistle. Pierce is looking sated and relaxed across the room; his gaze focused on the man kneeling at my feet.

Colin's eyes widen as if he forgot Pierce even existed until this moment.

"Don't," I say as I reach for him.

"I have to," he replies.

"No, you bloody don't," I reply with a growl. My hands close around his arms, and I pull him to my lap.

There is raw emotion in his eyes. It's fear and confusion. It's everything I'm supposed to protect him from.

"End things with him," I say with determination. "If you felt what I felt, Shakespeare, I'm begging you. Call it off and come to my room."

"What?" he murmurs.

"Colin, we belong together."

He stares at me for a while as if he's trying to discern how serious I am. Then, with an expression of frustration, he wipes his hands over his face.

"I can't believe you're doing this to me. I really can't believe it."

"Don't say that," I reply, reaching for him. "Colin, I love you."

To my surprise, he lets out a frustrated, pained sound. "Declan, your love hurts."

Just then, the large clock against the wall chimes, and we look at it at the same time. *Midnight.*

"It's officially our wedding day, my love!" Pierce calls from across the room.

I can't take my eyes off Colin, letting his words and the pain etched in them hit me like lightning.

After a defeated sigh, he looks at me as he says, "I'll come to your room."

"I'll be there," I reply. "I'll be waiting."

Before he can leave, I stand and quickly zip my pants as I pull him into my arms one more time. "Please believe me. I'm sorry for the damage I've done. I will make it up to you."

He closes his eyes. "Declan, all you have to do is tell me that you want me for real, and I'll come."

"I do," I reply, holding his face and pulling him in for another kiss.

"That's quite enough," a cold voice growls as Colin is ripped from my arms.

With a snarl, I reach for him again, but Pierce places himself between us. With a puffed-up chest, he glares at me with vehemence. "You're too fucking late, Declan. And frankly, it's pathetic."

"Pierce, stop," Colin calls from behind him but is ignored.

Nostrils flaring and veins pumping with adrenaline, I step up to the American. I've never hated someone so much in my life. Not even the rugby-playing bigot we faced in uni, because this bully is different. This bully wants to take something away from me that I'm not willing to part with. Not again.

"I'll tell you what's pathetic," I snarl. "Preying on someone's vulnerability to make yourself feel bigger and stronger. You think Colin submits to you because he wants to? You don't even know him."

"I know him far better than you do," Pierce snaps in return.

"Both of you stop!" Colin pleads.

"No one knows him like I do," I growl. "Because if you did, then you'd know that he doesn't want to just be controlled, he wants to be adored. You couldn't possibly know that he lights up when he gets attention from someone he loves. You don't love him, not like I do."

Pierce laughs in my face, that smug, indignant, self-righteous snicker that I despise. If I never hear it again, it will be too soon.

"You think this is about love?" he says, like this is a performance.

My brow furrows. "Of course it's about love," I argue. "This is a bloody wedding."

Pierce presses his chest closer. "Love isn't enough for Colin, and you know it. He needs a *real* Dom, someone with enough balls to put him in his place, and you just have too much of a soft spot for him, Declan. You could never own him the way I do."

His words are laced with maliciousness, and it cuts me down to the core. My fists clench, and I resist the urge to knock his lights out right here in the middle of this party.

"God, you think you actually had a chance," Pierce laughs. "I hope you had your fun rekindling an old flame, but I'll be taking your friend with me when I go."

My control slips, and I throw my hands against his chest with a scowl. "Get the fuck out of my house. Take your fucking wedding and your ridiculous fucking friends and get out."

Pierce grins wickedly without obeying my commands. Tearing my gaze away from him, I look for Colin, who is standing off to the side. He's watching us both with a guarded, angry expression.

"Colin, come here," I say in my calm, commanding tone, but it has a shake to it. I'm too worked up. Too afraid that I've lost control.

He doesn't move.

"Baby," Pierce says with a forced softness to his voice, and I pray Colin can see through it. Pierce is charming when he needs to be, no doubt to appeal to Colin's sentimental side.

"Don't listen to him," I bark.

Colin is looking back and forth between us, and my heart starts to hammer with panic. This should be an easy choice. He should come straight to me. What is his hesitation?

His lip trembles, and the party of people around us is frozen, watching the scene unfold. I'm silently imploring Colin to just look at me. If he gives me one glance, then I know he'll remember how much we belong together.

But he won't meet my gaze. And maybe that's why.

Instead, he marches between us and rushes from the room. When Pierce moves to follow him, I grab his arm and grit my teeth. "Leave him alone," I growl.

He shrugs himself out of my grasp. "Fine," he mutters. "I'll just see him at the altar tomorrow."

"You don't love him. Is all of this really just a show of dominance to you?" I demand.

He leans in with cold, dead eyes as he deadpans, "Everything is a show of dominance."

With that, he turns away and reaches for his drink still sitting on the table. As he lifts it to his lips, I resist the urge to tackle him to the ground. "Besides," he adds. "If he was going to choose you, he would have done it by now."

I don't respond as he turns back to his party. They laugh, wide smiles on their faces as they pick up right where they left off, dancing and grinding on each other like nothing has happened.

His words burrow their way under my skin. As I take off in search of Colin, I can't stop thinking about what Pierce said. Do I have a soft spot for Colin? Could I ever truly be the Dom he needs if I'm not willing to control him?

When I don't find him in his room or mine, I collapse on the chaise lounge in my studio. Doubts swirl in my mind as I beg it not to go to that dark place where I've already lost everything and where nothing is worth fighting for anymore.

Because when Colin doesn't show, that is what it feels like.

While I wait, I wonder if I've done enough. Did I make him

believe how much I've changed? How much I love him? Did I give Colin the peace of mind he so desperately needs?

Every passing hour feels like a heavy wave crashing over me, pulling me deeper and deeper out to sea. Before long, the sun begins to fight its way through the thick clouds and heavy rain, and I realize that whatever I did, it wasn't enough.

Maybe if I had told him I loved him sooner, things would have worked out.

Maybe if I had been vulnerable when it mattered, he would have shown up to my room.

But then again, maybe if I had never messed it up in the first place, everything would be different.

Chapter Thirty-Five
Colin

Seven years ago
Barclay Manor

"Holy shit, Declan," I mumble as he leads me through yet another hallway in his giant manor of a house. "This place is amazing."

He laughs. "Doesn't your dad have like two mansions?"

I shrug. "Yeah, but they're not old and cool like this."

His chuckles feel forced as he keeps his back to me. Something is different about Declan this year. He seems more guarded, as if he's holding something in.

I hate that. I wish he'd just open up to me. Let me in.

"Show me your room," I say, wrapping my arms around him from behind. He links his fingers with mine.

"Oh really?" he asks, peering at me over his shoulder. "So you're done with the tour already?"

"I still want a tour," I reply. "I just want it to start with your room. Specifically, your bed."

He hooks his hands under my thighs and hoists me off the floor and onto his back. I laugh in his ear as he carries me to his room.

When we get there, everything is great, but everything is off at the same time. There are no *good boys* and talk of possession. He doesn't force me to my knees and make me feel like I belong to him.

The sex is good like it always is. We tear our clothes off in a frenzy, devouring each other like we've both been starved, but he doesn't look me in the eyes like he normally does. When he enters me, he buries his face in my neck and fucks me like he needs it—not like he needs *me*. His pleasure is laced with pain, and his fingers interlace with mine painfully as he drives me into the mattress.

It's heated and wonderful until we're both coming loudly and collapsing in a satisfied heap on the bed. But it's different, and that plants a seed of worry in my gut.

I'm lying on his chest, softly toying with the dark patch of hair, and I can't stop thinking about how we ended things last year. In fact, it's been gnawing at me all year. The way we both clearly expressed how we want different things.

Declan isn't interested in a relationship, and I understand.

But I'm afraid he thinks it's the relationship that's important to me. All I really want is him. And not only eight days a year. I need him in the fall and winter. Over the holidays and on my birthday in the spring. I want Declan involved in every big moment of my life and not just a text message or a phone call.

I guess that *is* a relationship, isn't it?

Round and round we go.

"What do you want to do this week?" I ask, lifting up to stare at him.

"This," he replies, running his fingers down my spine.

"I want to meet your family," I say. "I mean, your brothers."

Declan tenses. "Killian lives here, so you'll meet him."

There's something in his tone that sounds unsure or uncomfortable with that, but I'm afraid to press it. The idea to come to Barclay Manor was mine, but Declan didn't protest. I wanted him to feel at home. And I didn't want some travel destination to overshadow our time together.

"And Lachlan?" I ask.

"He's in New York."

"Oh," I reply flatly.

It's quiet between us for a few moments before he finally says, "Colin, listen…"

I bolt my head up, alarmed at the sound of my first name on his lips.

"There's something you need to know about my brother."

"What?"

"He has a tendency to drink too much, party too much, go a little off the rails. I just want you to be prepared. He can get rowdy and a little mean when the mood strikes."

I squeeze my arms around him. "I'm not afraid."

"I hoped that having me here for the summer would help…" he says somberly.

"It hasn't?" I ask.

He shakes his head, so I move from his chest and sit up on the bed. Declan lies on the pillow next to me, and I softly stroke his hair.

"I'm sorry," I whisper.

"You don't need to apologize," he replies.

"I know, but I'm still sorry that you're going through this."

"It's better when you're here," he says, and it tugs on my heart to hear him say that.

After a while, Declan's eyes close. With his arm looped around my thigh and my back to the headboard, he falls asleep, and I feel content just watching him.

All I keep thinking is that we just need to get through this week, and everything will be fine.

"You have a horse?" I ask as I approach the stall where a beautiful white mare stands. We decided to take a walk around the property after Declan woke up from his nap. I filled the time reading and rehearsing lines for a part I'm playing in a few weeks.

"Aye," he replies. "That's Moire, but don't ask me a thing about her. Killian is better with the horses and farm stuff than I am."

I laugh at that as I leave his side and approach the animal. She's gentle, letting me stroke her head and pet her mane.

"You like horses?" he asks as he comes behind me and touches my back.

"I was trained to ride when I was a kid, but I haven't done it in ages. We should take her out while I'm here."

"You'd like that?" he asks.

Turning toward him with a smile, I notice a sense of hesitation on his face. There's a storm brewing inside of Declan. I can tell. I just wish there was something I could do to help. I'm here. I'm giving him all the comfort and affection that I can, but I can't scale this wall by myself.

If he wants to be happy, he's going to have to let me in.

"I would," I reply softly.

Declan's hands rest on my hips as he kisses my neck, making me groan and pause my hand on the horse. This intimate affection always throws me for a loop. When did this happen? When did we go from friends to friends who have sex to lovers?

I wish I could pinpoint the moment. Does he still think me his best friend when he kisses me like this?

"You know..." I say as he turns me around and presses my back to the wood fence. Moire loses interest in us and slowly walks away. "I have a big premiere in October. I can bring a date."

He kisses my throat, licking a line from my collarbone to my chin. "You want me to go to a Hollywood premier, Shakespeare?"

"There's no one else I'd rather take," I reply with a whimper as he nibbles on my jaw.

"I'm not sure I'm cut out for that."

I consider dropping it, because that's what I always do. I don't press the issues or argue for more. Never rock the boat.

What has that ever got me?

"It'll be fun. There's nothing to worry about," I say as I hold his body against mine.

"We'll see, Shakespeare."

"Please," I whine.

With a huff of frustration, he pulls away, and it feels like I've killed the moment. As he runs his hands through his hair, he turns away from me. "I said we'll see."

His voice is tense and uncomfortable, and regret rolls through me. "I'm sorry," I say, reaching for him.

"What do you have to be sorry about?" he asks. He sounds livid, and I have to swallow down my guilt.

The sound of tires on gravel distracts us as we both turn to watch a pair of cars driving toward the manor. They are expensive-looking sports cars, and Declan lets out a grunt of frustration.

"Not again," he mutters under his breath.

"Who is that?" I ask.

"My brother's friends. Look like he's throwing another party tonight."

"Parties are fun," I say, carefully gauging his reaction.

"I don't want you at these parties," he replies sternly.

"Okay," I say, reaching for him. I wish he'd touch me again. I just want to silence all of the demons in his head, even the ones I don't understand. I'd use my body to do it if he let me.

When he finally looks at me, his features soften, and we just stare at each other for a moment. Then he reaches for my hand, and we intertwine them as we continue our walk. Dark clouds roll in from the east, cutting our walk short when the rain starts.

It's pouring by the time we make it back to the house. He ushers me in through the back, music and laughter spilling through the halls, but he won't let me anywhere near it. Instead, he tugs me up the stairs, and we take a quick shower together before getting ready for bed.

When we reach his studio upstairs, I go back to my book, and Declan works on a painting, but I find it hard to relax. I'm restless. And it's not just about going to the party. It's about Declan letting me see past this veil he's putting over my eyes.

It's like he doesn't want me to see the bad parts of his life, but that's not how love or friendship works.

When I can't take another moment, I climb from the bed and go to Declan, running my hands along his shoulders.

"Come to bed," I whisper. "It's late."

"Go ahead," he replies. "I took a nap. I'm fine."

"Declan," I mutter, kissing his neck. "I don't want you to come to bed for sleep."

He lets out a heavy sigh. "Let me finish this."

Swallowing down my frustration, I try to fight against the brewing anger in my gut. This need to push back swells inside of me like a storm.

"Fine," I say with a hint of indignation. "If you won't play with me, I'll find someone who will."

His hand pauses. "You will not."

"Why?" I ask, trying to remain playful, although this defiance feels more real than it should. "What will you do? Punish me?"

He turns his head to glare daggers at me. "You bloody know I will." The way he said that definitely was *not* playful.

I shrug my shoulders, although they feel stiff. "Fine by me. Maybe I want to get punished."

Dropping his brush, he turns toward me. "I'm not playing, Colin."

"Well, maybe that's the problem, Declan. You're being too serious. So what if it's a party? So what if there's alcohol and sex? What are you so worried about?"

"I'm not having this argument with you," he growls as he turns back toward his painting.

"Then why can't I go have a little fun?"

"Because you're mine!" he bellows, slamming his fist on the table. I jolt, heat flushing my cheeks as I stare at him. Tears begin to prick behind my eyes as I fight the urge to cry.

When he looks at me, the anger melts away, and it's like a switch has suddenly been flipped.

"Fuck, Shelby, I'm sorry," he says, reaching for me. And when he tugs me into his arms, I let him. Wrapping his arms around me, he kisses my cheek, but I don't relax against him. "I'm such a bloody arsehole," he murmurs into my ear. "I'm sorry."

"It's okay," I mumble before pulling away.

"Come on, let's go to bed," he says as he stands from the stool. But I quickly shake my head.

"It's fine. Finish your painting."

As I move back toward the bed and climb under the covers, it feels as if I bring a live wire of tension with me. He eventually turns back to his painting, but his movements are slow and melancholy. Nothing is the same as it was a moment ago. And nowhere near what it was years ago.

I let silent tears soak the pillow as I realize that he's right—I am his. But suddenly, it feels more like a prison than it did before.

Eight days a year was never enough and will never be enough. It can't bridge the gap we've created as we grow and change over time.

And worst of all, I realize that I only matter eight days a year to Declan. That's all I am to him.

How could I put up with this for so long? How much longer would I keep it up before finally demanding more? I don't want to waste all of my good years on a love that takes more than it gives.

I don't know how much time goes by before I sit up on the bed, placing my feet on the floor and facing him.

"Declan," I say as I place my hands on my knees.

When he doesn't even turn his head toward me, I feel as if I'm bracing myself for battle.

"Please look at me," I say.

"I can't," he replies sadly.

This sadness grows thick in my throat like a disease, but I can't keep shoving it down. So when I speak again, I let it all out. The sadness, the regret, the pain. It cracks and shatters my voice, but I don't care. He needs to hear it.

"I wish you'd tell me why you're so sad. I'm here to listen. Let me help."

"I can't," he mumbles quietly.

"When I needed you in uni, you were there. When I was in the hospital in Italy, you were there. Please, Colin, let me be there for you. Let me in."

"It's not that easy, Shelby," he mutters.

"Why not?"

He turns toward me with red-rimmed eyes, and still...no tears. "Because this isn't an arsehole in an alleyway we can punch and make go away. This isn't a wound that heals with medicine. Don't you understand? I'm *broken*."

"I don't believe that," I argue.

"Well, this is just the way I am, Colin. You can either accept it or..." His voice trails and something inside of me shatters.

"Well, I can't keep doing this," I say with a sob.

He hangs his head, and it only makes it hurt more. Moments pass by as I wait, but he gives me nothing.

"Declan, say something!" I cry.

"I don't have anything to say," he replies.

"Really?" I shout as I stand up. "After eight years, you have nothing to say?"

"Colin, if you want to leave, then you should leave."

My mouth drops open as I stare at him in shock. This is the man who broke another man's nose for hurting me. This is the man who called me his. Who told me I was the best thing in his life.

"Well, if you won't fight for me, then maybe I should."

The old Colin would have never left. The old Colin would

have never walked out that door, but the old Colin is the one who got me into this mess in the first place.

If Declan has taught me nothing else, he's taught me that I'm worth so much more than this.

So, in an angry huff, I slip my pants back on and throw a shirt over my head. Declan doesn't even move as I pull on my shoes.

But I see him flinch out of the corner of my eye when I tear open the door and march angrily out of the room.

Chapter Thirty-Six
Colin

I'M FUMING AS I MAKE MY WAY DOWN THE STAIRS, FOLLOWING THE sound of the music and laughter. It seems to be coming from the parlor, but before I reach the room, I drop onto the stairs of the house and put my head in my hands.

What am I doing? I can't go to that party. Not like this. Not without Declan.

But this need to be so defiant burns inside of me. I would rather make him angry just to get a rise out of him than be complacent and get nothing. I need to take a stand in order to have what I want—which is him, all or nothing.

So I stand from the stairs and march toward the sound of the music. I first notice that the lights are low and the music is loud, almost as if the people in the room are trying to hide what is happening there.

But as I turn the corner into the parlor, I realize that it's just a normal party. People are congregated in pairs and small groups. Everyone seems to be having a good time, drinking and dancing.

"Well, hello there," a beautiful woman says as she nods at me. I slowly meander my way into the room, not making eye contact with anyone but feeling them all stare at me like I'm fresh meat. I go straight for the bar, in desperate need of a drink.

There's no bartender, so I help myself to a glass of wine, guzzling it down far too fast. And then filling it again.

It's then that I look at the party again and start to notice something different—the way people are gathered, the way they are moving. This isn't a regular party at all. It's a sex party.

My eyes catch on a man, sitting on a lounge, watching the woman across from him as she writhes on another man's lap. But it's not her that interests me, it's him.

The way he looks at her. Like he owns her. Like he treasures her.

This whole time I've been trying to get Declan to fight for me, but I've made things so easy for him. I've handed my heart and my body to him on a platter. On his terms. For his pleasure.

Maybe this is what we need.

Maybe this is what I need.

"You must be Colin," a drunk voice says in a thick Scottish accent. I look up to find Killian watching me as he sways in his spot. I recognize him from photos, but I've yet to officially meet him until this moment.

"Umm…" I clear my throat. "Yes, I am. And you're Killian."

"Aye," he says before scanning the room with unfocused eyes. "Where's my brother?"

"Upstairs," I reply. "He didn't want to come."

"He never does." Killian takes a long drink from his glass, and I swallow down my discomfort. This doesn't feel right, talking about Declan with his brother. Being here without him. Doing something I know he doesn't want me to do.

"He used to love parties," I say, more to myself than to him.

"I know," Killian replies. "And you're the reason he's changed so much."

My eyes shoot wide. "Me?"

"Aye. You made him grow up. You made him boring like you."

Glaring at him through narrowed eyes, I mutter, "Declan warned me that you could be cruel."

He only laughs. "Good. I'm glad he warned you, but I wasn't being cruel. I was being honest. Before *you* came along," he says, jabbing me hard in the chest with his finger, "he had nothing. He was fun and wild. Then, he started carrying himself differently. Trying to be better than he was. Drinking less. Bettering himself."

"Those are good things and not at all boring," I argue.

"I didn't say they weren't good," he says, his voice slurred. "But I'll sure as fuck never fall in love. Sounds miserable."

"He doesn't love me," I mumble to myself.

"What the bloody hell are you talking about?" he bellows. "He loves you more than anyone. For fuck's sake, he wouldn't be here if he didn't."

"Huh?" I ask, looking at him quizzically.

Killian nods his head toward the door I just walked through, and Declan stands there watching me with an angry expression. For a moment, I feel intense relief. Any room he's in feels instantly more comfortable to me, but I won't let myself fall back into these old patterns. Not tonight.

Instead of going to Declan, I turn back to Killian. "Pour me another, please."

"You best get back. He looks quite cross."

"I don't care," I mutter through clenched teeth. "If he wants me, he can come and get me."

With eyebrows raised, Killian pours wine into my glass, and I quickly drink it, although it burns.

It only takes Declan a moment before he stomps toward me, latching his fingers around my arm. "Let's go, Shakespeare."

I pull my arm from his grip. "No. I'm having fun, and you don't own me."

"I'm serious, Colin."

Spinning toward him, I press my face toward his. "So am I. Upstairs, I asked you to give me something, Declan. Anything.

And you couldn't. Maybe someone down here can. In fact, maybe making you watch me with someone else will finally give you the pressure you need to fight for me."

I watch his molars clench. "What did I do to you?" he asks. "To make you want to break my heart?"

My jaw drops. "*Your* heart? How could I break your heart, Declan? We're just friends, remember? You can't have a relationship, remember? So please tell me, how could I break your heart? Why does it even matter what I do?"

I'm shouting, and suddenly, I realize there are tears in my eyes. And everyone in the room is staring at me. Humiliation burns through my veins, so I quickly bolt past Declan and out of the parlor. I don't stop when I reach the hall, and I can't bear the thought of going back up to that studio. So I run straight through the front door and into the pouring rain.

"Colin!" Declan shouts. "Get back in here!"

Spinning on him, I want to scream. Warm tears streak down my face with the sheets of rain. "No, Declan! I can't go back into that house. I can't go back into that room. I can't..." My voice trails.

He follows me into the rain. "So let's get out of here. We'll go somewhere else."

"For how long? A week? Until next year, when you'll let me love you for a brief moment? Declan, I meant what I said. I can't keep doing this."

"I already told you," he says before wiping the wet hair from his face. "I can't do relationships, Colin."

"Why?" I plead. My chest aches so painfully it feels like I could die from it. "All I'm asking you to do is love me," I cry.

He takes a few more angry steps toward me. "Don't you understand?" he shouts. "It's because I love you that I can't keep you. I don't want you to live in this hell with me. You see what a bloody mess I am. I refuse to drag you under. I refuse to dull your shine."

"But that's what love is, Declan! It's showing someone the worst parts of ourselves and trusting that they'll love us anyway. And if I haven't proven to you over the past eight years that I love every part of you, even the dark, messy, sad, angry parts, then what the fuck have we been doing?"

"It's not that bloody easy," he replies sadly, and I want to scream at how infuriating he is.

When I don't respond for a moment, letting the rain drench me from head to toe, he takes another step closer. And for the first time ever, I take a step away.

He notices.

With alarm in his voice, he begs, "Please come back inside, Colin."

But I don't move.

"Colin. Come back inside."

Even his command doesn't get a response from me.

"Colin, I'm begging you. Please."

The desperation in his voice is hard to hear. It's like I'm dying right in front of him, and he doesn't know what to do. Although I've told him. I've expressed it already. But I'm asking for more than he can give. And if giving me the bare minimum is too much to ask, then I know what I need to do.

I feel a sense of pride for what I'm about to say, but I'm a coward because I can't look him in the eye when I do it. "I love you, Declan, more than anything, but you're bad for me. Loving you…is bad for me."

I don't need to lift my gaze to his face to know that his eyes are bloodshot and sad. I don't need to look to know his jaw is clenched shut, and his face is expressionless and dead.

My heart is rotting in my chest. Decaying into a painful husk. And yet, I still manage to get the words out.

"I don't think we should do this anymore. I think…I need to just be free from you."

He doesn't speak, not at first, but I can practically feel the pain radiate. What I'm saying feels impossible and drastic, but it needs to be said.

"Then, you should go," he mumbles sadly, loud enough for me to hear through the rain. "Because I never want to hurt you. And if loving me..." Emotion steals the words from his lips, and he stops speaking. The silence that follows feels like knives stabbing my chest. This all hurts too much. Knowing that I could take it all back and go back up to his room again only makes it throb worse, because I *could* do that. But I shouldn't. And I can't.

"I'll call a car in the morning," I mutter with my eyes down.

Then, I walk past him and into the house. I don't know if he follows, and I can't bring myself to check. I find an empty guestroom to sleep in, although I don't get a moment's rest all night. It is by far the worst, most agonizing night of my life. It feels like dying. Like watching every good memory fade into oblivion.

The next morning, a black car pulls up to the front of the house, and Declan is nowhere to be seen. My eyes are puffy, and my head is pounding when I climb inside, and just the slamming of the door has me crying again.

The driver doesn't say a word as I quietly sob in the back seat. And it's not just that I miss Declan already, which I do, or that I regret what happened between us last night, which I also do.

It's that he forced my hand. He's the one who taught me to stand up for myself and make the choices that need to be made while also denying me the love and attention I deserve. He was the one who made me believe I deserved it in the first place.

I'm not just grieving the loss of Declan, but the loss of what we had. I'm mourning for what could have been and for the greatness that we were. Because even if it all fell apart, I know in my heart that what Declan and I had was the real thing—a love bigger than the both of us combined. If he was the moon, then I was the tide. Deep down, I know I will always be the tide.

But just because it ended doesn't mean it didn't matter.

Chapter Thirty-Seven
Declan

Day of the wedding

Surprisingly, I've learned a lot about love over the years of my life. I've learned that it can hurt as much as it can heal. I've learned that it's not enough to make someone happy. I've learned that it's more selfish than selfless.

And I've learned that I'm really bloody bad at it.

I didn't touch a drink all night. Instead, I listened to rain pummel our house as I picked up all of the messy memories scattered around the floor. Then I put them all back in the chest, and I closed it—for good.

I'm not angry at Colin for not showing. I could never be really cross with him. And how could I blame him for making his choice when that's what I've been urging him to do all these years? From that night in the alley to last night at the party. I had spent eight years trying to prove his own worth to him.

If nothing else, I could consider myself lucky for the sheer greatness of what we had when we had it—because it was great.

By some miracle, I manage to get ready. I think I'm numb at this point. Sleep-deprived.

Heartbroken.

Either way, I'm able to shower, brush my teeth, and don my white shirt, gray jacket, and kilt for my best friend's wedding. Every few steps, my feet falter, and I nearly lose what little composure I have left.

Nevertheless, I reach the main floor of the house to find it far quieter and eerier than I expected. The rain and wind pound on the windows of the house, which means any plans of a ceremony in the gazebo are out of the question now.

My feet halt, another small stumble and a moment of dizziness before I swallow down the pain and keep going.

The familiar click of my sister's heels against the hardwood draws my attention to the foyer. She's scurrying toward me with a look of concern on her face.

"Mum's heels," I mutter with a sad smile.

Her head tilts with confusion as she approaches me. "What are you talking about?"

"Whenever I hear you walking around here in those heels, it always reminds me of Mum."

Sadness morphs her features. "Oh, Declan," she says, reaching for me. As she wraps me up in her arms, I try to stay tough. I'm not a small boy. This is nothing like that day she broke the news to me, holding me while I proceeded to not shed a single tear.

This is nothing like that day.

Although it feels familiar.

I rest my cheek against my sister's shoulder as she rubs my back. "I won the bet," I mumble sadly.

"I don't care about the bet, Declan," she murmurs against the side of my head. "I care about you. The same way I care about Killian. And Lachlan. I just want my brothers to be happy, and it seems like you are all defiantly against that."

I laugh a little into her embrace. "We don't make it easy."

"No, you don't."

Pulling away from her hug, I let out a heavy sigh.

Then my sister makes a face as if she's realized something. "Wait, you didn't win the bet."

I pause with an expression of scrutiny. "What?"

"I thought you knew," she says. "The wedding is off."

"Because of the weather," I reply, glancing at the window.

Slowly, she shakes her head. "Because Colin called it off."

The vise around my chest is released, and I take a deep, life-giving breath. One I feel like I've been holding for twenty years.

"Where is he?" I ask.

"Dunno," she replies. "Blaire called me and said it was off. By the time I got here, everyone was gone."

"I have to find him," I mutter, passing my sister to run straight through the house toward the parlor, then the kitchen, and then up to the guest rooms. Each one of them is empty, and the staff is pulling sheets from the beds. I hear a car door slam outside, and panic builds inside of me as I sprint out toward the drive.

As I barrel out the front door, I stop in my tracks as Pierce stands at the back of his Rolls-Royce, his hands on the boot. With a placid expression on his face, he turns toward me. His eyes are half lidded, unimpressed as he shoves his hands in his front pockets. The rain has lightened to a typical Scottish drizzle, but it soaks the both of us in moments regardless.

"Where is he?" I mutter, gazing to the windows of the car in search of my Colin.

"How the hell should I know?" Pierce replies flatly.

My brows furrow as the American waltzes toward me with indignation in his eyes. My mind is swirling with questions I can't seem to form.

"I knew it was a risk bringing him here," Pierce says as he leans against his car. "Maybe that's why I did it. To test him. To see if I truly had his loyalty. Turns out I didn't, because he chose to stay here with you."

I glance back up at the manor behind me, hoping to find Colin staring out one of the windows in search of me, but they're all empty. When I don't respond, Pierce continues.

"You can't give him what he needs, you know?" he says, this time with less haughty confidence than he had last night.

I take a menacing step forward. "Yes, I bloody can, and I will."

"You're too soft on him. He craves control. That you could possibly pull off, but the degradation? Never. You love him too much."

"That's the most absurd thing I've ever heard," I growl.

He lets out a sardonic laugh. "The most absurd thing I've ever heard is you having him for nearly a decade and letting him go. If you love him so much."

"A mistake I won't make again." There's a tension headache brewing from how tightly I'm scowling at the man in front of my house. I don't know why I'm even bothering to argue with him. Maybe because he got in my head last night. He had me thinking I was wrong for Colin, which is ridiculous. I was made for Colin.

"I'll be waiting for him when you do."

Fueled by resentment, I take two fuming steps toward the man, grab him by the collar of his shirt, and shake him as I snarl in his face. "You will never touch Colin Shelby again, because he's *mine*. He has always been mine, and he always will be mine. And not because I fixed him or trained him or preyed on him in his weakest moments like you did. But because he chose me. Because I give him a voice and I encourage him to fucking use it. I will be everything that man needs and more, because we belong to each other. That's what love is for, and if you even dare to speak to him again, I will do whatever I have to in order to protect him, ya ken? Now get in your ugly car and get the fuck off my bloody property. *Now*."

Releasing him, I take a step back and let out the heavy breath I was holding. To my relief, he doesn't utter another word. With a huff of frustration and a shake of his head, he climbs into the driver's seat and takes off, kicking up gravel in his wake. As I watch his taillights disappear in the distance, a sense of contentment washes over me.

It's over.

Spinning around toward the house, I find my sister standing in the doorway, waiting for me. There are tears in her eyes and a tight, thin smile on her face.

"Anna, I'm sorry," I mumble with defeat as my shoulders slump.

She scurries toward me, wrapping her arms around my shoulders. "Don't apologize to me," she whispers in my ear. "I've never been prouder of you. That is the Declan I know and love."

"I just ruined the wedding and kicked out the groom," I argue. "Aren't ye mad?"

Pulling away, she holds my shoulders with a look of motherly affection. "Not a wee bit. Now, go upstairs and make things right. There's someone waiting for you."

My gaze shoots up to the third floor, and this time I find his blue eyes watching from the window. I take off in a mad dash, but first I hug my sister again. She kisses my cheek before I slip out of her grasp.

"I'm leaving," she hollers.

"Good," I reply, stopping at the door. "You should."

I hear her laughter before slamming the front door behind me and stomping through the house toward the stairs.

My mind is racing as I run down the hall toward my studio, and I make my plan. I'll move if I have to. I'll live in Hollywood or London or on the bloody moon if he needed me to. I'll be whatever and wherever he needs me, without question. I'll tell him I love him, and I'll even fucking marry him if that's what he wants. I'll prove to him over time that he can trust me, and I won't shut myself off like I did last time.

And when I reach the end of the hall and step into the studio, I come to a screeching halt as I find Colin Shelby standing by the window, looking down at a sketch he's holding. His golden waves shine even without the sun's rays, as pure and beautiful as the day I met him.

Every breath I drag into my chest shakes as I stare at him, trying to make time stop so I can soak in this moment.

Then, for some reason, and for the first time in a very, very long time, I feel tears begin to moisten my eyes. It stings the more I try to fight them off, but when I finally blink, they begin to spill over.

"You came," I mumble through the tears.

"Of course I did," he replies. "I'm sorry I'm late."

I let out a noise like a laugh and a sob. Then, I do what feels the most natural in the moment and I drop to my knees on the floor.

"You can be as late as you want, Shakespeare. I told you I'd be waiting."

He turns to face me, pausing for a moment when he finds me kneeling and sobbing for him.

"Oh, Declan," he says as his face morphs with empathy. "You're crying."

It's like a dam has been broken. A thunderous wave of emotion pours from my heart as I stare at him. Grief, gratitude, and love—so much love.

"You're here," I say, wiping my eyes.

"I told him I couldn't marry him. I'm sorry it took longer than I expected."

"I don't care," I reply with a slow shake of my head. "As long as you're here."

For a few moments, the only sound in the room is the rain on the windows, and it's so beautifully tender that I don't want to disturb it. I have so many questions, so many thoughts and apologies and promises, but right now I just want to look at him.

All I want is for Colin to cross this room and come to me, but I sense his hesitation. I don't blame him for it. I hurt him once, and it will take time before he trusts that I will never do it again.

Colin is the first one to start, breaking the silence.

"He said you would break my heart again, and I'll be honest, Declan. Part of me thinks that too, but I don't stand a chance of resisting you. I'd let you break my heart a million times in a lifetime."

This moment feels like now or never. All of the things I should have said that night as he cried in the rain, begging me to give him what I should have already given, no questions asked. I owe him that and so much more.

"I'm a fool," I mutter from the floor. "For ever breaking your heart at all, I'm the world's biggest fool. It was wrong of me to use you like I did and push you away, and I'm sorry, but I will *never, ever* break your heart again. Not as long as I live. I've got seven years of misery to learn from."

He takes a step toward me, and it fills me with hope as I continue.

"I was so afraid of losing you, I never let myself fully have you, and for eight years, I thought I was the only one suffering for that, Colin. I didn't see the pain I was putting you through. But if you give me another chance, I promise I will spend the rest of our lives making it up to you and proving to you just how much you mean to me. I love you with every cell in my body. Shakespeare, you are perfect, and I don't deserve you, but I promise that I will love you enough to make up for every moment in the last fifteen years when you doubted it."

When his throat moves as he swallows and his nostrils flare, I know he's about to cry. Before long, tears prick his eyes as his cheeks turn pink.

"Declan, I want you to get better, and I want to be here for you when you do. I don't want you to push me away again."

"I won't," I say with promise. "I'll go to therapy. I'll get out of the bloody house. I'll let my sister boss me around and make me take care of myself."

He's just out of reach, only a few feet away, and I wait patiently for him to come close enough to touch, but it has to be his move. He has to make this choice for himself.

"And what about me?" he asks with a hint of hesitation. "You can still give me what I need? I like this lifestyle, Declan. Can you promise me that?"

"I'll do my best to always give you everything you need, but at times, Shakespeare, I don't want you kneeling for me. I don't want you to *always* be my submissive. In our lives, I want you as my equal. I want to hear your voice."

He takes another step closer. "I want to get married someday, Declan. I want a life with the man I love, not one week a year."

"I'll give you every day of my life until I die, I promise."

He takes another step closer.

"Say it again," he mumbles through his tears. "Promise me."

"Colin Shelby, I promise. I promise you everything you want and everything you need," I say, staring into his eyes. "I'm yours if you want me."

He wipes the tear from his cheek before he takes the final step, and he's close enough to press my face against him. I let out a sigh of relief as he touches my head.

"Of course I want you, Declan. Every person in the world could be in this room, and I'd still pick you."

I squeeze my arms around his legs as I let my tears of relief soak his black trousers.

"Declan, for Christ's sake, please stand up and kiss me."

I nearly burst up to my feet, grabbing his face and bringing his lips to mine. He clutches my shirt as my mouth devours his. I'm moaning into our kiss, and he lets out a whimper when I tug his bottom lip between my teeth.

"Declan," he gasps as I continue kissing him hungrily.

"What?" I grunt.

"You're wearing a kilt," he says plainly.

I pause, glancing down at my tartan and back up at his face. "Aye, for your wedding, remember?"

He bites his bottom lip, glancing down at it again, then letting his eyes rake their way up my body. "I've just…never seen you in a kilt before."

My brows shoot upward as I notice the effect it has on him. Grabbing him by the ass, I tug him against me, grinding myself against him. "Shakespeare, are you thinking of all the dirty things you'd like to do to me in this kilt?"

"So what if I am?" he replies with an adorable smile through the fresh tears.

"Noted." Then I dive back in, desperate for his mouth, and I kiss the smile right off it.

Chapter Thirty-Eight
Declan

It's been seven years since I've had Colin Shelby in my bed. I intend to never let that much time go by again.

He tastes divine, and his lips are pillowy, soft, and warm. His body is exactly how I remember it. Eager, pliant, responsive. It's like we were made for this. Made for fucking and finding life's greatest pleasure in each other.

I groan into his mouth as he grinds his hips against me, and I feel the stiff cock straining behind his trousers. And as much as I'd like to prolong this, I've waited far too long for this moment, and I need him now.

Hooking my hands around the backs of Colin's thighs, I hoist him off the floor and carry him the few steps toward the bed, dropping him on the mattress with a bounce.

As he reaches for me, I grab the hem of his white cotton T-shirt and tug it over his head. Then, my fingers move toward the button of his trousers.

Meanwhile, his fingers are trailing up my thighs, seeking out my hard shaft, and when he finds it, he wraps his hand around it with a wicked grin. Pushing my hands away from his pants, he sits up and lifts the hem of my kilt.

"You really don't wear anything underneath," he says with a gasp.

"Not customarily," I reply as I stroke my fingers through his hair.

As he licks his lips with his gaze focused on my cock, I predict his next move with accuracy. Diving forward, he lets my kilt fall over his head as he takes my cock in his mouth, nearly to the hilt.

I let out a loud growling moan as I thrust my hips toward him. He's hidden under the tartan as he moans and bobs his head up and down. If I had known the sight of him sucking my cock under my kilt was so hot, I'd have done it a long, long time ago.

When he eventually pops his mouth off and emerges with a sloppy, wet mouth, I feel dizzy with arousal. My cock tents up my kilt, and Colin leans back and stares at it.

His expression is laced with lust as his eyes dilate and his lips part hungrily. "Good God, that's hot," he says with a sigh.

"If it makes you act like that, I'll wear it every bloody day."

"Promise?"

With a devious smile, I tug on the ankles of his trousers to pull them off. Once he's naked for me, my expression matches his, because this happens to be my favorite outfit of Colin's.

At the sight of his cock, the first time I've fully laid eyes on it in far too long, my mouth waters. It's hard and pink and leaking from the tip. Leaning down, I engulf the length in one motion, sucking eagerly and making Colin fall back on the mattress, arching his back with a throaty gasp of pleasure.

"Oh God, Declan!" he shouts.

It's almost vulgar how messily I'm sucking on his cock, but I can't seem to help myself. My fingers grip his balls, massaging them delicately as I suck, and with the way he's writhing and moaning so beautifully, I may never stop.

"Fuck, I missed you," I mumble to his cock after popping my mouth off. "And you," I add, leaning down to suck one side of his sack into my mouth. Colin has a fistful of my hair as I continue reacquainting my mouth with his body.

With a growl, I shove Colin's knees up toward his chest as I get a sight of his tight hole. "And you. I've really fucking missed you."

Diving in, I lick a sloppy, wet circle around the entrance. Colin begins to tremble, his sounds changing from husky groans to delicate whimpers. He melts into the bed, surrendering his body to me as I bring him to the brink of ecstasy.

Before long, I begin to grow painfully restless and can't take another moment before fucking him. Standing from the bed, I smile down at him where he's lying lust-drunk and breathless.

I quickly unbutton my shirt, slip out of my shoes and socks, and step out of the kilt as I stare at him. "I'm going to paint you like this," I say. "Then I'm going to hang it above our bed and recreate it every single night."

"I like the sound of that," he mumbles from the mattress.

Just those two words, *our bed*, have me feeling lighter than air. He's really here. He's really mine. Everything is right with the world. My future no longer looks bleak and lonely, but vibrant and beautiful.

As I turn away from him in search of the lube and condoms stashed away in my nightstand, I pass the table covered in an assortment of oil paints. On my way back, I get a wicked idea.

"Or what if I paint you now?"

He sits up on his elbows. "What? Now?"

"Lie down, Shakespeare."

With a look of trust and anticipation on his face, he lies on his back on the bed, watching me as I pick the colors. After I have all the ones I want, a feeling of pride and excitement washes over me.

I kneel between his legs as I open the first tube and squeeze the thick blue oil paint on his chest. He hisses from the cold temperature on his skin. Then I pick up the yellow and the white, adding a dollop of each before mixing it to the perfect shade with my finger, swirling it around his chest and over one of his nipples.

Content to watch me work, he laces his fingers behind his head with a smirk.

"This is the color of the pool in the gymnasium that night. Remember how blue that water was?"

"I remember," he replies.

"It's also the color of your eyes," I say.

He smiles at me before peeking down at his chest to see what I'm sketching with the paint.

Next, I reach for the green, the red, the black. Before long, I have his chest covered, different pools of color all over him. While I paint the slick mixture up his throat, loving the way it contrasts his light skin, my cock twitches.

"I'm tested regularly," he says, noticing the condoms in my hand. "And I don't want anything between us."

My body lights up with desire.

"I haven't been with anyone in ages," I reply. "And I'm always cautious."

"I trust you," he mumbles. Leaning down, I press a kiss to his lips. The paint smears onto my chest, but I love it.

"My hands are a mess, baby. You'll have to prep yourself, and I want to watch."

Leaning back on my heels, I pick up the lube and click open the cap, drizzling it onto his waiting fingers and down the length of my cock.

Then I watch with rapt attention as he pulls his knees up and circles his tight hole with his middle finger. The other hand reaches for my cock, spreading the lube from base to tip.

The sight of him fingering himself is enough to send me over the edge. I feel the precum leaking from my cock while I continue to cover his skin like a canvas with thick globs of paint.

"I'm ready," he says with a moan as he brings my cock to his hole. "Fuck me, Declan."

Eager to be inside him, I drape my body over his, feeling the sticky paint transfer from him to me.

Wiping my paint-covered fingers across his cheek and jaw, I kiss him. He slowly opens for me as I ease myself inside, one inch at a time.

"Remember what I said last night?" I ask.

He's tense and breathless as he shakes his head.

I work myself in more. "I told you that next time I'm inside you, you'll be mine. Remember that?"

With a whimper, he nods. So I shove myself another inch.

"I'm inside you, Shelby. What do you think that means?"

"I'm yours," he cries out with a whimper.

Pulling out to the head, I slam back inside as I mutter, "Say that again."

"I'm yours," he groans. "I'm yours, I'm yours, I'm yours."

Finding his hands with mine, our palms meet, and our fingers intertwine as I pound him into the mattress. Fucking him feels like home. Both familiar and like a distant memory. I was meant to be inside of him.

We were made for each other. It's why we fit so perfectly.

Our tongues tangle, breathing the same breath and feeling the same level of euphoria.

"I need to hear you say it again," I moan against his lips.

"I'm yours, Declan Barclay. I always was."

I whimper into his kiss as I fuck him faster—nearly to the point of release. But before I'm about to come, I pull out with a loud groan. Then I release his hands and move onto my knees.

"On your knees, baby," I say, helping Colin to his front. There is paint splattered all over his chest and mine.

And as he moves to his stomach, it covers the sheets of my bed, a mess I won't even try to get out. I'd like to keep this masterpiece forever.

With his chest on the mattress and his ass in the air, I can't help myself as I thrust back inside of him. I'm being swept away in this storm.

"Look at how perfect we fit together, Shakespeare."

His hands squeeze the bedsheets in tight fists as I thrust inside of him.

"I can feel how perfect we are," he replies in a moan.

Picking up my speed, I fuck him harder and faster, listening to the sounds he makes as I do. It's like magic, the effect he has on me. Everything about him turns me on and drives me wild.

It's a symphony. Like poetry. A fucking masterpiece.

He's stroking himself hard as I pound into him, and when his arsehole tightens around me, strangling my cock, I lose it. My spine curls, and my muscles seize as the climax takes control.

It feels like I come forever. Wave after wave after wave.

He is the tide, and he carries me out to sea.

And what must be minutes later, I pull out of Colin and fall onto the mattress next to him. I'm staring at the ceiling, waiting for my heart rate to slow to normal, when he climbs on my chest and kisses my lips.

"How did you get paint on your forehead?" he asks as he tries to wipe it away.

I laugh. "Shelby, it's everywhere."

"You should see these sheets," he replies with a sweet smile.

"I'm keeping them forever. Framing them. We'll put them in an art gallery and call it *Make-Up Sex: Oil Paint on Egyptian Cotton*."

Colin laughs. "Oil paint and cum."

I lift my head and grin at him. "Shakespeare, did you just say *cum?*"

With a blush, he hides his face in the crook of my neck. "Yes, why?"

"Say it again," I reply, holding him close.

"What? *Cum?*"

"Wow, I've really corrupted you, haven't I? When I found

you, you were a proper English gentleman; now you say things like *fuck me* and *cum*. What would your mother think?"

"She'd think I found myself a vulgar Scotsman who makes me happy, and she'd be right."

"Well, right now, this vulgar Scotsman needs to get you into the shower before this paint gives us both a nasty rash. Then, you are going to eat something and get some rest."

"So bossy," he mumbles before climbing from my chest.

"I'll show you bossy," I reply before smacking him on the ass and shoving him out the door.

Chapter Thirty-Nine
Declan

Colin and I have to scrub each other for over thirty minutes in the shower to get it all off, but there are worse ways to spend half an hour.

Once we're both as clean as we can get, I tug him into my arms and hold him under the stream. As glorious as this day has been so far, I have to remember that Colin had to do something extremely difficult, and I wouldn't blame him for having some conflicted feelings about that.

As much as I don't want to talk about Pierce Michael Hall ever again, I have to at least ask.

"How are you feeling?" I mumble against the side of his head.

"To be honest, I feel terrible," he replies sadly. "I think he did love me, deep down, and I don't like to hurt anyone."

"I know you don't," I reply, squeezing him tighter. "But I'm proud of you for making a tough decision and doing what you want."

He pulls away and stares into my eyes. "He's too cocky for his own good. This was all his idea. Thinking he could challenge you. And I didn't fight him on it."

"Shelby, I gotta know. Why did you agree to have the wedding *here*?"

He twists his mouth for a moment as he thinks. "I told myself that you wouldn't be here. I told myself it was a form of closure. But I think deep down, I knew..."

"Knew what?" I ask.

"That it would bring me back to you."

Taking his face in my hands, I hold him close, his forehead pressed against mine. And we just stay like that for a while. Then, I kiss him, hoping he trusts that I won't let him regret that decision.

Once we get out of the shower, we each get dressed, Colin borrowing clothes from my wardrobe since his are in a different part of the house.

There's something about seeing him swimming in my shirt and trousers. It's not just sexy. It's comforting. I want him to infiltrate every crevice of my life. My clothes, my home, my space. I want everything that belongs to me to belong to him too.

After we're dressed, I take Colin down to the kitchen, where it's eerily quiet compared to how it's been all week. I assume my sister has arranged for a lot of the staff to come back on Monday, but for now, we have the house to ourselves.

There is a three-tiered cake and enough food in our house to feed the town itself. I notice Colin eyeing it all with regret, so I usher him out to the parlor while I fix us some lunch.

When I return with two plates piled with food, I find him staring out the window in contemplation. I set the plates down on a nearby table and approach him slowly from behind.

When he feels me coming closer, he turns toward me with a sad smile. As he takes my hand, I draw him toward the chairs, where we both sit and eat.

As usual, he breaks the silence first. "What now?"

I shift in my seat, afraid of where this question might lead.

"Well, Shakespeare, that's a tough question. You have a career and a life, and all I have is this fucking house."

"Are you sure you don't want to just meet up next summer?" he asks with a coy smirk.

My expression flattens as I glare at him. "Is that supposed to be a joke?"

He chuckles to himself. "A bad one, yes."

After a tension-filled moment, I say, "Do you have room in your life for me?"

There's a wrinkle between his brows as he lifts his gaze to my face. "Of course." Then he shifts in his seat before taking my hand. "Declan, does my life scare you?"

"Scare me?"

"Yes, my private life is not private. My name will be all over the internet by tomorrow morning, and if you and I make things public, they will share your name and your picture. Are you ready for that?"

I'm frozen in place for a moment as I tug him toward me until he's on my lap. I take his face in my hands as I say, "Shakespeare, they could share my bare arse on the internet tomorrow, and I wouldn't give a shite."

He chuckles in my arms before growing serious. "You're not afraid of being seen publicly with me…a man?"

"Fuck no. I'd be proud."

His eyes soften as he leans toward me, pressing his lips to mine. "Then come stay with me in LA. Maybe until we figure something else out."

"Or forever," I reply. "As long as I have you, it doesn't matter. They have therapists and art galleries in LA, don't they?"

His blue eyes glisten as he smiles. "They do."

"Then, I'll come."

"Really?" he replies tearfully. "Just like that?"

"Just like that."

I pull him against me for a warm, hungry kiss. But I can practically feel the exhaustion in his bones, so I don't let it get too heated. Instead, I maneuver us to the couch in a lying position, him nestled between my body and the back cushions, his head on my shoulder.

He yawns a couple of times before I tell him to close his eyes, which he does.

As he drifts off, I'm content with just staring at him. Then, I try to remember what it felt like to fall in love with Colin. And it's strange that I can't quite pinpoint a moment. It was more like he filled a void in my life so seamlessly that I barely noticed.

He needed someone to care about him, and I needed someone to care about. Someone to hold my hand as I learned to love again. Someone who was patient and gentle. But also someone resilient and selfless.

If there was ever a universe or fate in which I didn't find Colin, I wouldn't want it. No matter how painful this road was, it brought us here. And I'd endure it again a thousand times over if I had to.

Stroking his pale blond hair, I notice streaks of sunlight across his face. Which can only mean one thing...

I turn my attention to the bright window to confirm—the rain has finally stopped.

It'll come back eventually. It always does. But lucky for me, I've found someone whose smile is bright enough to get me through. And I don't need to feel bad for basking in its warmth, because I'm the one who makes him smile in the first place.

And I'll never let him go again.

Chapter Forty
Colin

Present day
Barclay Manor

"I think that's everything," the tall Scottish brunette says as he drops one side of the large trunk on the gravel outside the house. Declan's other brother, Lachy, releases his side with a wince, holding his back.

"What in the bloody hell is in here?" he asks, looking down at the thing.

Declan comes up behind me and places a hand on my back. "Colin. Lots and lots of Colin."

Killian makes a face of disgust. "I don't want to know."

The moving company takes the trunk and loads it in the crate with all of Declan's other things, which isn't much. Mostly paintings and supplies that I know he wants although he tried to argue that he doesn't.

Declan's sister, Anna, comes around and barks orders at the movers, making me laugh to myself.

It's been a week since the wedding, or lack thereof, and I need to get back to LA to start shooting a film next week. I didn't want to leave without Declan, so when he refused to let me, I knew for sure this was it. He means it this time.

He promised, and when Declan Barclay makes a promise, I know that he'll keep it.

"So you officially lost your bet," Killian says with a smug grin. "Which means our sister gets to keep your house and have as many weddings here as she wants."

I laugh to myself, squeezing close to Declan's side. He told me about the wager he made with his brothers, and I found it quite funny in the end. Because it sort of didn't matter anyway. There was no way he was winning that bet once I showed up. With every passing day, it seems more and more clear to me that I was never walking out of here with Pierce. I'm not sure I ever really wanted to.

"I'll never forgive you for that," a sweet Scottish voice says from behind me, and I turn to find Blaire walking up to our group. She gives Declan a despondent look as she adds, "Or for leaving me."

"I'm sorry," I mumble to her, and she grins through her tears.

"It's my fault for making him look so irresistible that night."

Giving her a warm grin, I rest my head on Declan's shoulder. I don't like to think about that night much, no matter how things turned out. Having to tell Pierce that the wedding was off was nearly the hardest thing I've ever had to do—second only to the night I had to walk away from Declan.

Pierce fought back. Tried to manipulate. Even tried to *command* me to take it back, and it was a little humiliating for him. Because I said no, again and again.

He was never the right guy for me, and nothing he could ever say or do would have changed that.

When Anna rejoins our group, she looks flustered and tired. Whenever she glances toward Declan, I see the sentimental sadness in her eyes.

"Well," he says, squeezing my shoulders. "We should probably get going. We have a flight to catch."

"Do you have to go?" Anna cries, tears filling her eyes. "You're all leaving me here. Killian's married and gone. Now, you're leaving."

"I'm still here," Lachlan says as he holds up his hands. Everyone chuckles for a moment, and Killian reaches over to ruffle his hair.

"You have what you want, Anna," Declan says softly. "You have the manor for weddings now."

"Aye," Killian adds. "Maybe it's about time you think about moving in."

Anna's spine straightens as she glances at the enormous house. "Alone?"

"Well, I'll be here to keep you company," Blaire adds from beside me. I glance over at her and notice the way she's gazing softly at Anna, who doesn't even seem to notice.

"I guess," Anna stammers nervously. She's chewing on her bottom lip, and I realize that Anna has probably never had no one to take care of. She's been the parental figure for her brothers since her parents died, and now that two of them have officially flown the nest, in their *thirties*, Anna is finally free to live her own life.

"Again, I'm still here," Lachy says, as if no one even notices him standing there.

"But you're not a mess like we were," Declan adds, shoving his little brother on the arm. "Anna prefers to clean up messes."

"I'm a mess," Blaire adds quietly, but again…Anna doesn't seem to notice.

After a few more minutes of small talk with his family, Declan grows restless and starts pulling me toward the car. We take a few minutes to hug everyone goodbye. His sister sobs as she hugs him, like he's going off to war instead of a cozy beachfront estate in California.

Before he leaves her, he passes her a manila envelope from the side of his jacket. Quietly, I hear him say, "You're welcome." With that, he kisses her on the cheek and walks away.

As the two of us climb into the back seat of the car, with a hired driver in the front, I glance over at the man sitting next to me.

It dawns on me that this really isn't another eight-day summer spent with the man I love. This is real. Having him is my life now, and it's everything I've ever wanted.

Scooting across the back seat, I rest my head on his shoulder as we watch the manor disappear in the distance. "So you did what she said? You put the manor in Lachy's name?"

He nods. "Aye. It's his turn to step up. He's been the baby of the family long enough, and it's time he took on a little responsibility. Besides, maybe it'll have the same luck for him it did for me and Kill."

Turning toward him, I press my lips to his cheek. "I'm proud of you."

He kisses my forehead, and our eyes close at the same time. It may have taken us fifteen years to get here, but we got here in the end. What started as best friends turned into lovers, and now we are both of those wrapped into one. He is my soul mate. The person I want to build a life with.

And I want to start living it immediately.

Epilogue
Colin

One year later
Los Angeles

"Colin!"

"Colin, over here!"

"Colin, who are you wearing?"

Lights flash from the crowd as I stand in front of the banner plastered with the name of my latest release. Moving between poses, I hold the smirk on my face that photographs the best.

Both hands in my pockets. Left foot forward. Right foot forward. Now one hand in my pocket.

Away they snap.

In my periphery, I see him waiting, his eyes on me. And when I feel like the photographers have everything they need of me alone, I reach out for him.

His eyes narrow with an expression that tells me I will have to pay for this later, but I only smile as he joins my side.

He can try to complain about this, but he's too good at it for me to believe it. The broody expression he holds as the cameras snap makes him look like a seasoned pro. Not to mention how damn good he looks in this tux. His dark hair is slicked back, and I find myself grinning at him as he holds me against his side, the cameras snapping away.

That's going to be a good one.

"Enough," he says in his gruff Scottish brogue.

"All right, let's go," I say, tugging him down the red carpet. The photographers are immediately diverted to the bombshell blond walking behind us. Declan breathes a sigh of relief once we're out of the spotlight.

"You did so well," I say before kissing him on the cheek.

"I don't know why you do that. No one wants to see me," he says, fixing his tie.

"Yes, they do," I reply, dragging him toward the theatre. "You're hot and rich, their two favorite things."

Not to mention, a scandal. The public loves a scandal. So last year, when my wedding to an A-list celebrity was abruptly called off and I was seen only days later around LA with a rich Scottish man, the media ate it up.

As for Pierce, we've mended things as much as we can. He was never cut out for marriage anyway, and I think he's accepted that. At least for this phase of his life. Our paths still cross in the industry and we keep it friendly, but any love I had for him is gone.

The next hour at the premiere drags on. Declan is a trooper through it all, really, the mingling, the ass-kissing, the networking.

But when it's time to take our seats, I beg him to leave with me. I hate watching myself on the screen, but he loves it. And this one I'm especially uneasy about, because for one, it has the most sex scenes I've ever done in a film, and it's more low budget and artistic than any of my more popular films.

Halfway through the film, when my character is having a mental breakdown and I look downright horrific, red face, blotchy cheeks, and dark, sunken eyes, I glance over at Declan to gauge his reaction.

And I'm surprised to find tears in his eyes and a look of

adoration on his face. Then he turns toward me, bringing our linked hands to his lips and kissing the back of mine.

"You're incredible, Shakespeare."

For the rest of the movie, I try to relax. And when it's all over, my costars and I receive a standing ovation as we join the director at the front of the theatre.

And who is in the front row hollering and shouting louder than anyone else? Naturally, my husband.

The champagne goes down far too easily at the after-party, which is something I never used to do. Drinking at these things always felt like mixing work with pleasure, and I could never let my guard down enough to let loose.

But I swear, Declan was made for this. He's a natural, far more than I am. It reminds me of the Declan I met sixteen years ago. The young, charismatic life of the party.

He links his fingers with mine, a flute of champagne in his other hand as he regales the crowd around us with another one of his embellished stories, and they love him. I mean, how could they not?

"So we nicked a bottle of bubbly right off the blanket, and the couple was too busy staring at the Eiffel Tower to even notice. Then, this guy here took off in a sprint until the cops started chasing us."

The crowd around us laughs, and I roll my eyes. "There were no cops, and I did not sprint."

"That's not how I remember it," he replies with a laugh, taking a sip of his champagne and giving me a wink over the rim.

The energy tonight is amazing, and I can't help but indulge a little. The rest of the cast is as drunk as I am, but I'm the only one with a hunk of a Scotsman to lean on and take me home when it's time.

"You're pissed, Shakespeare," he whispers in my ear as I pick food off the hors d'oeuvre table.

"I'm so pissed," I mumble in return.

"That's disappointing," he replies, turning me around to face him. "I was planning on taking advantage of you later, and I don't feel right about that now."

I quickly straighten my spine and try to paste a sober face on…and quickly fail. I break out in laughter as I stumble toward him, and he chuckles darkly in my ear.

"What a mess you are."

"Take me home," I reply.

"I plan on it," he says, kissing my forehead. "Say your goodbyes, and I'll call a car."

The ride home is short. We purchased our place in Santa Monica this past winter, and it's quickly become my own slice of heaven on earth. Overlooking the ocean, steps away from the sandy beach. I know without a doubt that Declan and I belong near the water.

We've talked a bit about considering another home in the UK, but so far, nothing has compelled us enough to go back. I think his sister likes to see him living his life away from the manor. That is, after she gave us the cold shoulder for three months because we eloped in Fiji rather than have the big lavish wedding she was hoping for.

But now that she's over that, I think she's happy that he's happy.

When Declan and I get home, our small black cat greets us at the door, purring against my leg until I pick him up.

"I'm sorry, Romeo," I say, nuzzling his face with kisses. "We left you home alone all day."

"He likes being alone," Declan adds, petting the cat's head. "Don't you, boy?"

Setting the cat down, I nearly tumble over onto my head, and Declan quickly grabs my arm and hoists me to my feet.

"Easy, Shakespeare. Let's get you to bed."

"Naked?" I ask with a slur and a coy smile.

He only chuckles as he slides my jacket off my shoulders and drapes it over the back of one of our leather chairs in the front room. Then he kneels in front of me and unlaces my shoes before helping me out of them.

As he drags me up the stairs to our bedroom with floor-to-ceiling windows that overlook the ocean, I nearly pass out as he continues disrobing me. And once I'm down to my knickers, I collapse into our bed, face-first, and shut my eyes against the silk pillowcase.

A moment later, the bed dips as he climbs in on his side. For some reason, even though I'm pissed out of my mind, I don't fall asleep right away. Instead, I peel my eyes open to stare at him through the moonlit darkness.

Warmth radiates in my chest as I take in the sight of him. He's gazing up at the ceiling, and I wonder what's going through his mind—that beautiful, creative, stormy mind of his.

Does he still love this life?

Will he continue to love it after another year? Ten years? Twenty?

Is there any part of him that misses the freedom he felt when he was alone? When he didn't have to go to therapy every week, and reopen old wounds and face the demons taking up space in his mind?

Will he ever resent me for the change I've brought to his life?

"Declan," I whisper.

He turns his head toward me in response.

"I love you," I say.

Shifting to his side, he hooks an arm around my waist and tugs me closer, until our bodies are flush on the bed.

"I love you too," he replies.

"What were you thinking about?" I ask.

"How bloody good you were in that movie," he says. "You're a shoo-in for an Oscar nod, for sure. So then I started thinking about if I'd wear a kilt to the Oscars, because as you said, I do look really bloody good in it, but I don't want to steal any of your thunder, so perhaps I'd just stick with a black tux…" He pauses in his long ramble. "Why are you laughing?"

I can't help giggle into my pillow as I listen to him go on and on, and it just seems funny to me that while I've been stressing about the past, he's been planning our future.

"Nothing," I reply with a hiccup. "I just love you. And you should definitely wear the kilt. That way, even if I lose, I'll still be the guy who brought the handsome bloke in the kilt to the Oscars."

"Deal," he says before sealing our lips with a kiss.

"Good night, Declan," I whisper as I close my eyes.

I can practically hear him smile as he replies, "Night, Shakespeare."

Epilogue
Declan

Eight years later

Colin is beaming in the seat next to me, holding the glistening golden statue in his lap.

"I'm so bloody proud of you, Shakespeare," I mumble, pressing my lips to the side of his head.

There are tears in his eyes as he glances up at me. "How was my speech? Too cheesy? I didn't forget anyone, did I?"

"No, you didn't forget anyone. You were perfect."

You're always perfect.

"It's about damn time," he whispers to himself.

We've been here two times before, but tonight was finally his night, and I couldn't be prouder. I could relive that moment in my mind over and over again. The sound of his name being called. The look of surprise on his face. The way he turned to me first, pulling me in for a kiss while everyone cheered.

And then the way he found me in the crowd from the podium with tears in his eyes as he softly whispered into the microphone, "To the love of my life for giving me a voice and encouraging me to use it."

I'll definitely be sketching that scene so it lives on forever.

We come home to a quiet house and walk into our bedroom hand in hand. I watch as he places his new award on the dresser, admiring it with a blush on his cheeks.

I can't remember the last time I saw him so happy. On our wedding day. When Will was born. And now this. It's a collection of memories that make up a perfect life, and I can't bear to think about how I almost missed this.

Coming up behind him, I kiss his cheek and let my lips trail down to his neck. Sliding my fingers under the collar of his crisp white shirt, I spot the silver chain of a very different collar.

I hum with delight when I touch it. He lets his head fall to the side as I pepper his neck with kisses and slowly unbutton his shirt.

Reaching behind, he slides his hands up my kilt, and his fingers graze my cock.

"I think my boy deserves a reward tonight," I mumble into his ear.

"I've been so good," he replies, slipping easily into the role that he plays in the bedroom. Although he wears the collar nearly all the time, we've both established that this dynamic only exists here.

In our normal everyday lives, Colin is not my submissive or my boy. He is my equal. My husband. My partner in life.

"And what does my good boy want as his reward?" I ask as I slide his shirt from his shoulders, revealing his bare chest and silver collar.

"I want my sexy Scottish husband to fuck me in that kilt."

With an assertive grip on his collar, I growl into his ear. "I think I can oblige."

I love watching the way he melts under my dominance. He's wearing an expression of pure bliss as I take control, dragging him toward me.

Holding his hips, I grind my shaft against him, feeling a jolt of arousal course down my spine and directly to my cock. Even after all these years, this man still turns me on so much I can barely keep my hands off of him. I can still find ways to corrupt him and keep things interesting.

Colin and I don't even make it to the bed. Moments later, he's frantically tugging off his belt while I'm ripping off my shirt until the kilt is the only piece of fabric left on my body.

Reaching into the drawer, I fish out the lube as he bends over and white-knuckles the dresser.

This is a well-rehearsed dance we've done a million times before. And one I will never tire of.

For a while, I tease him, prepping his hole as I stroke his cock just to bring him to the brink and make him whimper and plead for his release. His trousers are pooled at his feet, so the reflection in the mirror shows only his bare chest and the silver chain around his neck.

"Fuck me, Dec," he whines as he thrusts his hips back toward me.

"My needy boy," I reply, bringing my cock to his hole. After drizzling more lube on my shaft, I slide easily inside of him.

He lets out a grunt as he looks up into the mirror, his eyes landing first on my face and then on my kilt.

I have to hold it up as I thrust inside of him, finding heaven in the way our bodies come together. Like they were made for each other. He is my home, and this is where I belong.

"God, yes," he cries out as I pound into him harder. When he reaches for his cock, I swat his hand away.

"Not yet."

Quickly, I pull out and spin him around. Wrapping my hands around his thighs, I hoist him onto the dresser, shoving his Oscar to the side. It's not often that I have him in this position, but when I do, I remember the first time.

His first time and mine.

Not the first time I had sex, but the first time I felt what true connection was. The first time I felt someone else's orgasm like it was my own. The first time I admitted to myself that Colin was it for me.

Dragging him to the edge, I plunge back inside him, this time staring into his eyes.

"Fuck, I love you," I growl as I pound into him. Everything on our dresser rattles and falls over, and Colin has to cling to my neck to keep from being rattled too.

His cock leaks with cum as he throws his head back. "Don't stop," he cries.

"Are you close, baby?" I ask.

"Yes."

"Do you think you've earned it?"

"Yes!"

"Then stroke yourself, Shelby. Let me see you come."

He wraps his hand around his cock, stroking himself as I pick up the speed of my thrusts. My hips begin to ache and a sheen of sweat covers my back, but I couldn't stop if I wanted to. Not when we're both this close.

As my climax barrels into me, I feel Colin's body tense and shudder, cum spilling all over his chest. We're both moaning wildly before nearly collapsing and taking a grueling amount of time to catch our breaths.

Getting older isn't easy.

When I pull out and stare at him, he's wearing a fucked-well smile and staring at me with adoration in his eyes.

"I love you," he whispers.

Leaning in, I take his mouth in a tender kiss. I whisper the sentiment back, but we both know those three words will never fully express how I feel about him.

Colin and I take a quick shower together, and it's like the exhaustion hits us both at the same time. These award ceremonies are like marathons. I swear they last longer each year.

Once we're both clean, we put on our briefs and climb into bed. Sleeping naked isn't a luxury we can afford anymore, especially not since Blaire will most likely be over bright and early.

When we climb into our bed, our cat, Romeo, nuzzles himself

between our feet, and I drift off with Colin resting peacefully in my arms.

The room is bright when I feel something hard and much heavier than a cat bounce onto our bed, waking me instantly. Colin is still sleeping next to me when I peel my eyes open and spot a beaming five-year-old kneeling at the foot of the bed.

"Morning, Papa."

I glance up to see Blaire tiptoeing into the room with her finger up to her lips—as if that would keep Will quiet.

"Congratulations again," she whisper-shouts. "I gotta run."

"Thanks again for watching him," I whisper back and wave to her as she leaves.

As soon as she's gone, I gesture for Will to come lie in the bed between Colin and me. He nods with a toothless smile as he cuddles in my arms. His messy blond curls drape over his forehead, matching Colin's on the other side of the pillow.

"Shh…" I whisper. "Daddy's still sleeping."

Will wraps his arms around my neck, and as much as I wish I could let sleep take me again, I know there's not a chance my son is going to let me have another moment of rest.

"Did you have fun at your aunties'?" I ask.

"Yeah," he replies. "We made chocolate chip pancakes for breakfast."

That explains why he can't sit still.

"Papa, can I watch TV?"

"Aye. Go on downstairs. I'll be out in a minute."

He dashes from the bed and scurries out to the living room. A moment later, I hear a mind-numbing kids show playing on the telly. Before I climb from the bed, in desperate need of some coffee, I roll over and press my lips to the side of Colin's head. He barely stirs, and I don't bother him anymore. I hope he sleeps in for a long while. He's earned it.

When I enter the living room, I stop and smile at Will on the couch with Romeo on his lap.

"You hungry, kid?"

"Nope," he replies, wiggling in his seat.

"You want some coffee?"

He only giggles in response.

"Just a wee cup?" I tease.

"No, Papa. Coffee is gross."

"How would you know?"

"Because I can smell it. Can I have some chocolate milk though?"

In the middle of my coffee making, I pause and shake my head. Our half-British, half-Scottish boy has the strongest American accent, and there's nothing we can do to stop it. With the exception of summers spent in England or Scotland, and sometimes Italy, he was born and raised in California.

Regardless, he still is the cutest fucking thing I've ever seen—with those freckles on tan skin, bouncy golden curls, and beautiful blue eyes.

When Colin first brought up wanting a child a few years after we were married, I thought he'd lost his damn mind. Me, a father?

I felt destined to fail. I had myself convinced it would be a disaster.

But Colin as a father? Something about that image in my head was enough to turn me on to the idea. And I'm glad it did.

We found an egg donor, with Blaire as our eager surrogate. Then suddenly, it was like everything happened so fast. We were lucky. Blessed beyond belief.

Nine months later, William was here.

And that fantasy I had of seeing Colin as a father was nothing compared to the reality of it. There's nothing to prepare you for the moment you see the man you love holding your child. Nothing.

Watching the way our love for each other multiplied, evolved, spread roots, and grew to include another tiny person was like a miracle.

If I am the moon, and Colin is the tide, Will is the whole world.

Ever since becoming a father, I think about mine almost every day. I know Colin does too. Whether good or bad, I think how our parents raised us makes its way into how we raise Will. My father was a strict and serious man, and although I have so many good memories, I wish that the time I had with him had been more at ease. He had no idea that the moments were so precious and finite. Something I never forget when I'm with Will.

Most days, I still think I'm screwing this up, and I'll probably never be as good at this as Colin is, but I'm trying. I'd give my life for these two. I'm their protector. And they are my heart.

After my coffee is ready, I take the cup over to the sofa and sit beside Will, handing him his chocolate milk. I don't give a damn about his show, so I open my phone and immediately see photos online of my Colin standing on the stage, accepting his award. The public appears to be as enamored by his win as I am.

"I smell coffee," he says as he walks into the living room and stretches his arms over his head.

After getting his cup, he takes a seat on the couch on the other side of our bouncy five-year-old. The two of them cuddle together, and Colin kisses the top of Will's head.

Staring at the pair of them, I lose interest in whatever was on my phone, so I toss it to the side. Colin's hand reaches across the back of the couch, and I clutch it firmly in mine.

He smiles at me, and everything feels right. There was a time in my life when I thought I would never get here, when I thought promise and hope died with my parents. But then I found someone who made life worth living again.

He gives me promise and hope. And while nothing is guaranteed and I'm aware that hard days could come again, I know that's what makes moments like these so much more precious.

Acknowledgments

Thank you so much for reading *Promise Me*. I know in a lot of ways this book was very different than anything else I've written before, but it was a story I felt so compelled to tell.

Declan and Colin seized my heart, and for two characters I adore so much, I feel a little bad that I made them wait so long and work so hard for their HEA. For that, I know they will have the happiest and longest ever after there ever was.

I could have never gotten through this book without an incredible team of people behind me.

First of all, I dedicated this book to my friends because there are just too many to narrow it down. Jill, Phil, Becca, Misty, Amanda, Adrian—you guys are my rocks. You give me encouragement, support, laughs, advice, distraction, and hugs. The loves of my life that you are…thank you.

My incredible agent, Savannah Greenwell, who always has my back.

The team at Sourcebooks Casablanca, for always championing my stories and listening to my wild ideas.

My assistant, Lori, for always keeping me organized and on track.

My incredible Scottish babes, Rebecca and Ashleigh. Thanks for making sure I don't somehow mess this up.

And lastly, to you, my readers. Thanks for always coming along for the ride, no matter what turns I take. Thanks for always seeing more than just the spice. Thanks for loving the wild things I cook up in my head and for loving the characters as much as I do.

Much love,
Sara

About the Author

Sara Cate is a *USA Today* bestselling romance author who weaves complex characters, heart-wrenching stories, and forbidden romance into every page of her spicy novels. Sara's writing is as hot as a desert summer, with twists and turns that will leave you breathless. Best known for the Salacious Players' Club series, Sara strives to take risks and provide her readers with an experience that is as arousing as it is empowering. When she's not penning steamy tales, she can be found soaking up the Arizona sun, jamming to Taylor Swift, and watching Marvel movies with her family.

Website: saracatebooks.com
Facebook: SaraCateBooks
Instagram: @saracatebooks
TikTok: @SaraCatebooks